I0583247

OUR BRIGHT WINDOW

BOOK II

JAMES CHANCE

Copyright © 2025 by James Chance.

All rights reserved. Published by Feral Chance Press.

No part of this publication may be reproduced, distributed, or transmitted in any form or by any means, including photocopying, recording, or other electronic or mechanical methods, without the prior written permission of the publisher, except as permitted by U.S. copyright law.

All names, characters, and incidents portrayed in this production are either the product of the author's imagination or are used fictitiously. No identification with actual persons (living or deceased), places, buildings, and products is intended or should be inferred.

Book cover and illustrations by James Chance.

First Edition

ISBN: 979-8-9990941-1-7

*For Sketch, whose intellect, kindness, and friendship
have illuminated my life.*

TABLE OF CONTENTS

OUR BRIGHT WINDOW

BOOK II

JAMES CHANCE

CHAPTER 1

LONE WOLVES

Vincent's dreams always began in the dark.

He was used to darkness. It lived–thrived inside him. It was his birthright, his destiny. He was comfortable in it. At least, that was what he told himself.

But these days, his dreams never stayed that way.

Suddenly, blinding light blazed down from high above. It seared through his senses, his very core, laying everything bare, turning him to a tiny, pitiful animal, no longer able to hide in that deep, black chasm.

Then, a single merciful shadow crossed the light. A hand reaching down from high above.

Every time, following some instinct he never fully understood, Vincent flung himself upward. Their fingers locked. The hand tugged him up, and light devoured his senses.

He felt fresh air–crisp and cool, filled with a thousand living scents and sounds. The rustle and clatter of leaves against the wind, the chittering of distant birds, the hum of hidden insects. He was curled on the forest floor, surrounded by the cushion of fallen leaves against his body. Autumn painted the trees a firestorm amidst bright bursts of stubborn green. Their shade shielded him from the worst of the sun's greeting glare, which now fell in bright shafts through the treetops, misting the very air with gold.

Most of it seemed to find the man who lay beside him, dappling his crown like sunlit jewels. He was so close now, only a hand's breadth away, resting on his side in their bed of leaves. Although the sky was hidden by the canopy, it lived in the man's eyes–bright, clear blue, incandescent with life and vigor, hiding nothing. They gazed at Vincent with no fear, no hesitation or shadow of doubt.

Lost in those boundless skies, he nearly forgot the chasm at his back. The one this man had pulled him from. But he could feel its gravity still, always, as if his heart was chained to something deep within that fought every moment to drag him back into darkness.

He nearly forgot as that hand, steady and pale and delicate as marble, reached out to brush his own once more. Its strength had pulled him from the depths of the earth; now its softness cradled him, soothed him. He nearly forgot.

"*Vincent,*" came his whisper, like a breath of wind returning an echo of summer to autumn's chill. The familiar scent of clove and jasmine sweetened the air. His lips parted, and Vincent could almost taste their warmth still. He basked in it, surrounded by it, the whole world suffused with sunlight.

This time, the dream changed. Now he was somewhere else entirely.

He was falling. His stomach surged into his throat. His limbs went numb. Rocky cliffs blurred past as the water below leaped up to meet him. A sharp crack–pressure struck his skull, a white-hot pulse of pain–and then nothing. Nothing but the black water–

He blinked, and he was floating face-up. Black treetops, black sky. Distant murmurs, more felt than heard. He was so cold. Every part of him was cold.

Someone leaned over him.

A shadow. The deepest black of them all, unseeable, unknowable.

It stared down at him, unmoving.

He woke up.

But the shadow was still there.

A chill shot through his spine. He jolted up–but he didn't. He couldn't. His body wouldn't move.

Panic surged through his nerves. He fought his own muscles, straining, crying out, all the while fixed on that shadow looming over him. Its invisible gaze bored directly into his face, trapping him where he lay.

He knew three things instantly, preternaturally: it was very much real; it knew who he was; and it hated him.

He had forgotten her. But she was still here.

As soon as the thought trickled into his head, a switch flipped. Breath filled his lungs, his nerves fired, his body sprung up, finally following orders.

Between blinks, the shadow had vanished.

Vincent looked around wildly. The door to the room remained closed. There was nowhere for an intruder to hide, or run. But the coldness remained. It seeped back into the hollow that fear left in Vincent's heart.

Thirsty for daylight, he went to the window, pushing back the curtains. He found no relief. It was late morning, but everything was gray. The woods outside were clear of snow and the trees and undergrowth were budding, but even their fresh green seemed strangely muted.

No birds sang. He couldn't even hear the usual thump of music from the garage downstairs. The silence was broken only by his roommate Casey's soft snores from the bed on the opposite wall. She was nested so deeply that he couldn't even see more than a lump in her bedsheets.

She hadn't seen a thing.

He was seized by the urge to wake her, to buffer that lingering, crawling feeling of being watched. He knew better.

He hopped down from his loft bed, leaving his blankets rumpled. He tied back his dark hair in a low ponytail that didn't even reach his neck, and pulled on his usual fare: dark skinny jeans, a wine-red shirt, his favorite leather jacket, and his signature loose tie. He didn't bother fastening the top two buttons on his shirt, which left exposed a glimpse of the huge, deep scars clawed across his chest.

There was a time when nothing would have convinced him to show those scars. But things had changed since winter's first bite.

He passed a few rooms as he made his way down the hall, picking up louder snores than Casey's behind closed doors. Only one of the rooms was empty, its door wide open. As he slunk downstairs the clink of dishware greeted his ears, softening some of the ice inside him. He wasn't alone.

He wandered into the kitchen to find it cluttered with the evidence of his greatest hopes: breakfast. Among the used dishes and utensils stood his hero, a short and slender black man with dreadlocks tending a pan over the stove. A plate sat beside it on the counter, piling higher with pancakes by the minute.

"Uh-oh, look who's skulkin'," said the chef, glancing over his shoulder with his usual easy grin. It did its best to banish the chill of Vincent's morning. He jerked his free hand towards the counter. "Get yourself a plate, bacon's in the oven."

"I think I love you, Dex," said Vincent. Not for the first time, he noted the difference in how the two of them spoke—the edge to his own words that forged an accent untraceable among mortal tongues.

"Hey hey hey, save some for the others," Dex chided as he noticed Vincent's damage to the pile of food as he filled his plate. "C'mere, I'll give you an extra pancake if you put some of that bacon back—it's the full moon, after all."

Vincent paused, a piece of bacon hanging out between his teeth. "Ah. Right." He grudgingly began returning a few other strips to the platter. "I feel like you always use that excuse," he grumbled.

"Y'know, funny thing about it is, it happens every month," Dex teased, flipping a pancake. He eased it onto Vincent's plate when he came over. "There, see, man? You even get a fresh one. Can't tell me that ain't worth it."

Their eyes met over the plate, and a shrewd shadow crossed Dex's expression.

"Everything alright, Vince? You look like you've seen a ghost."

Vincent hesitated a moment too long. "Stranger things have happened."

Dex bent his head closer. "Again?" he murmured.

Vincent grimaced.

Dex gave a nod that trailed off. His gaze grew distant, pensive. Troubled. Then he turned back to his pan.

Vincent slunk over to the kitchen table and sat across from Dex's roommate, Sloane, who was the only other person awake at the moment. As he started on his breakfast, he couldn't complain. There were plenty of eggs to make up for the amount of bacon he wished he could abuse, and the pancakes were fluffy and filling. He had never met a food he didn't like, anyway. It was almost enough to forget his unease.

"Mornin' Vincent," said Sloane, already tucking into her meal and perfectly unbothered by the exchange. She was too pretty for her own good, with narrow, dark eyes and skin such a rich shade of brown it was almost golden.

Vincent couldn't help but notice how much bacon *she* was afforded, and he glowered at her enviously. She flashed him a sly smile as she hand-fed herself another strip. "What's the matter, cat got your tongue?"

"Oh, shut it," he growled, busying himself with his eggs mutinously. She only laughed.

"We'll catch plenty to eat tonight. Hope you like venison," she said smoothly, using her clean hand to brush her waterfall of sleek, dark hair behind her shoulder. "Oh wait, that's right—you don't hunt!" She descended into a fit of giggling, still chewing her bacon.

"Don't choke, Sloane," Vincent muttered.

"Ah, don't prod the man—he's lucky he doesn't need to hunt," Dex said, pacing over from the kitchen with his own plate of mostly bacon. He sat next to Sloane and began to eat, using a fork and knife unlike his companion.

"You gonna be a good little house-sitter tonight while all the big boys go out and play? I know you are!" Sloane reached out to pinch Vincent's cheek, but he was well used to her antics. He ducked out of the way with time to spare, shooting her a glare.

"You're lucky you have me to keep an eye on things," he shot back.

"He's right, y'know. Can't be too careful these days," said Dex.

"Oh yeah, like tonight's the night they're gonna kick the door in." Sloane rolled her eyes, cramming another strip of bacon into her mouth. She continued talking around it. "If they haven't done it now, they never will. My last three patrols, I haven't seen hide nor tail of the pigs."

"Well, maybe we're just that good at hiding," said Vincent. "Maybe they're off our trail."

"*Or* they're finally clearing out."

"Wishful thinking," said Dex matter-of-factly, brandishing a strip of bacon at her. "They'll be swarmin' as long as things are still screwy around here. There's no chance they don't know that portal's to blame."

Vincent caught Dex's pointed glance in his direction, so swift he was sure Dex hadn't meant for him to see it. His heart gripped painfully as a wisp of his sunlit dream returned to his mind's eye, mingling with the shadows of reality.

"Fat lot of good that does 'em, huh?" Sloane mumbled around her mouthful. She finally swallowed. "They don't know shit about how to fix it."

"You've just got cabin fever, and you know it," Dex told her with a smile. "Maybe a hunt tonight'll do you good."

Sloane shrugged. "Can't deny it. This place sucks ass. How long can you even keep us all afloat with the chop shop closed up, anyway?"

That seemed to strike a nerve. Dex stopped mid-chew, his face falling.

"Let me worry about that."

"But if they aren't going away anytime soon–"

"I mean it." Dex's silverware clanked sharply against his plate. He trained his attention on her in a warning, and Vincent swore he caught a flicker of something more canine in his silhouette. The cozy kitchen suddenly felt cold.

Even Sloane halted in her tracks. She slumped back into her chair with a scowl.

"She's just worried. We all are," Vincent dared to say. "It's been months now, since before the first snow..."

"You could always open the shop again," a new voice said from the doorway. Everyone glanced up to see Casey plodding in, her chin-length black hair rumpled and her naturally narrow eyes screwed up into slits against the light in the kitchen.

"You wanna wake up before you offer opinions?" Dex said gruffly.

"I'm just saying. What's the harm in a few jobs a week?" Casey crossed the kitchen to join them, snagging a piece of bacon off Vincent's plate. He let her, but bared his teeth at her.

"You owe me another one. Dex is rationing me."

"See? Rationing bacon–come on." Casey tore a piece off with her teeth.

"It's a treat," Dex insisted. "We can always hunt."

"And what about rent? Utilities?"

"You cut off my TV, I cut you," said Sloane, brandishing her unused table knife at him.

Dex sighed, but it sounded more like a growl. "And what if one of the clients is a Shadowhand, and they catch a whiff of somethin'? *No.* It's not worth it."

"A Shadowhand with a chopper? Now *that* I gotta see," Sloane sneered.

"How long are you gonna wait, then?" Casey asked roughly.

"As long as it takes. I'm not lettin' anything happen to *my* pack."

For a long moment Casey and Dex stared each other in the eye, unmoving. Vincent could practically see the two wolves sizing each other up. He had noticed over the time he had been here that this happened more often closer to the full moon. But he didn't think it mattered now. Tensions were higher than ever after so long cooped up in the safe house.

Finally, Casey broke away. She snagged another piece of bacon from Vincent's plate and retreated to the couch moodily. He let out a soft growl, but decided against protesting. He didn't want to be her next target. Instead he went to the oven to grab replacement slices. Dex didn't stop him.

After a tense silence, footsteps began thudding down the stairs, followed by the arrival of their last two housemates, Rolf and Terry. Both boys were tall, but Rolf won the contest, with a gangly silhouette to match. Terry was wider everywhere, built to pack a punch, and was as dark as Rolf was pale. Rolf's hair was red and ruffled, while Terry kept his in a buzzcut.

"Bacon! Alright!" Terry crowed as they both thundered across the kitchen towards the oven. It was only once they had piled their plates with food that they seemed to notice the chill in the room.

"You sound like the dog in the Beggin' Strips commercials," Sloane said loudly.

"So...uh...how about that full moon, ah?" said Rolf, with an awkward grin.

"How about it?" Sloane wore a sly smile. "You boys excited?"

"Always," Terry answered for him. "I feel it in my boooones!" He started up a mock howl, and Rolf joined him gleefully. It was so ridiculous even Dex couldn't help but chuckle, shaking his head.

"C'mon, guys. We gotta keep a cool head tonight, much as we can," he said. "It's graduation day at the college. There'll be more people around than we want."

Vincent's heart panged painfully. *Graduation.*

"In the woods?" Sloane scoffed.

"Yeah. We'd go into the woods all the time when we went there," Casey piped up from the living room couch.

"She's right," said Vincent. "People wander out there. Especially around the Devil's Maw."

Even saying the name sent a shiver up his spine. Again his dream returned to him, but differently this time. Instead came the feeling of that abyss he crawled out of, always looming at his back. He fought the urge to tighten his tie around his neck, to let the pressure of it soothe him in some sick way.

No. No more.

"Well no one's gonna go there anymore!" Sloane said with a laugh.

"You never know. Drunk college kids get brave," Dex pointed out. "But we won't go anywhere near the Devil's Maw, so we should be okay. Let's just be sure to head as far into the trees as possible, yeah?"

He looked around expectantly and everyone nodded, even Casey.

"I'm puttin' you on wolf-wrangling duties, Sloane," he went on.

"Aw, what's the fun in that?" she sighed.

"You're my beta," Dex reminded her. "You gotta earn your keep sometime. You're too lazy." He kicked her chair lightly, with a playful grin.

Sloane grinned back at him, waving him off. "Alright, alright. You hear that, boys? Behave, or I'll bite you."

"Yes ma'am." Terry saluted her, and Rolf copied him with a snicker.

"Call me ma'am again, and I'll bite you anyway!"

Suddenly, the doorbell buzzed. Everyone's heads snapped up, startled. They all looked at each other.

"Are we expecting anyone?" Sloane asked.

"Not that I know of." Dex frowned. "I'll get it. Someone wanna back me up?"

Casey jumped off the couch before anyone else could move. Dex looked surprised, but gave her a grateful nod. The two of them went to the door that opened into the shop at the front of the building, disappearing through it.

The wait was excruciating. Even Vincent's sharp ears couldn't pick up any voices through the door. *Maybe that's a good thing,* he thought. Surely they would put up a fight if any Shadowhand tried to arrest them.

After more than a minute, Rolf piped up, "Sh-should we check on 'em?"

"No way," Sloane growled. "Dex wanted us to stay put."

"But what if–"

"If it is the boys in blue, you know the drill," Sloane snapped. "GTFO. Back door. Save yourselves, meet up in the woods later."

As if heeding her own words, she rose from her chair. The others followed, even Vincent. He kept his gaze on the door to the shop, his heartbeat loud in his ears.

Suddenly the door sprung open. A massive man stepped through–a stranger. A stranger wearing a police uniform.

"*Run!*" Vincent snarled. He grabbed two kitchen knives from the block beside him, standing between the others and the policeman. He heard his companions scramble behind him, Sloane shouting orders–

"Wait!"

That was Dex. Everyone froze as he pushed his way past the stranger.

"It's cool, it's cool–they're friends."

"Sorry," said the stranger, holding up his hands placatingly. He was truly huge, with very dark skin and a shiny bald head, his beard neatly trimmed. He looked so serious and imposing that Vincent's instincts kept him poised for an attack while his brain caught up. But as soon as the man moved further into the kitchen, Casey and two more strangers followed–a woman and a boy no older than thirteen. When Vincent saw the latter, he finally relaxed.

"This is Virgil," said Dex. "And this is his wife Hadley, and their son Roman. They're gonna crash with us for a while."

"You–you're one of us," Sloane said, surprised.

Virgil nodded, but the woman, Hadley, answered for him. "No need to be shy! Yes, we're werewolves. Sit down, will you?"

She strode into the kitchen ahead of her husband. She was pale and heavyset with long, curly brown hair and thick eyeliner that made her green eyes unsettlingly bright. She aimed a glare at Vincent in particular, who realized then that he was still holding kitchen knives. He slotted them back into the block sheepishly.

"Pancakes, Roman?" said Casey, following Hadley. The kid crept after her, his eyes wide. They were the same color as his mother's, with a mop of similarly curly hair atop his head, but the rest of him more closely resembled his father in a slightly lighter shade. He was in that awkward stage at the very dawn of adolescence, the soft features of youth giving way to sharper angles and lean muscle carried with the hesitation of unfamiliarity.

"Is that bacon?" he said, eyeing Sloane's plate where it lay abandoned on the table.

Sloane wandered back to it, her usual smirk sliding back across her face. "That's mine, kiddo. You wanna fight me for it?"

"Ignore her," Casey growled to Roman, grabbing the remaining bacon from the oven. "Sloane came from a puppy mill."

"Lying to children! Like you're any better," Sloane cackled.

As soon as the plate of bacon was in Roman's hands, he began devouring it. He stayed where he stood, shoving piece after piece into his mouth.

"Hey! Save some for your father," Hadley snapped, walking over to bop her son on the head. "He just got off a long shift."

Roman turned and bared his teeth at her. They were sharp, inhuman. Vincent blinked in surprise.

Hadley nudged him again, a little more sharply this time. "Watch it, young man! You're a guest here and you'll act like it, I don't care if it *is* the full moon!"

Roman backed away from his mother, holding the plate covetously. After a moment, though, his lips slowly pulled back over his fangs, and he seemed to remember himself. He handed the plate back to Casey, looking at the floor.

"That's better," Hadley grunted. Casey offered her the plate and she brought it to her husband before helping herself to a seat at the table. "Sorry about him. His full moons have been getting worse lately," she said to Dex with a sigh.

"Teenagers, ah?" he chuckled. He offered Roman an easy smile. "You're one of us now, man. Don't sweat it. Your folks and I go way back."

"Then how come it's taken them this long to show up?" Casey asked. "I thought you put the call out to shelter here as soon as we warned you guys about the Shadowhand."

As Virgil crossed the kitchen to eat at the table with his wife, Vincent caught a grimace on his face.

"Doesn't matter now." Dex went to sit with them, looking as casual as ever. Only Vincent's familiarity with him told him that he was still unsettled. "They're part of the pack. Treat 'em that way."

Sloane gave them a wary glance. "I'm still beta, right? You're not replacing me, are you, Dexy?" She batted her long eyelashes at him.

Dex smiled. "Don't push it."

"We'll play nice, girl," Hadley told Sloane. "After all, you're doing us all a huge favor. We can't thank you enough for this." Sloane returned her friendly look, seemingly satisfied.

"You didn't get caught by the Shadowhand, did you?"

Everyone looked at Casey, who appeared to be the only one hung up on the issue. After a tense moment Hadley answered.

"We didn't lead them here, if that's what you're asking. We're not stupid."

"Then what happened? Why are you here?"

"It doesn't matter," Dex said again, more sternly this time. Again they locked eyes, but Casey didn't look away.

"We were just talking about how we're already stretched thin. How much longer are we gonna make it work if we have three more mouths to feed? Let alone a growing teenage boy?"

Even Terry and Rolf began to murmur amongst themselves, throwing uncertain looks between the newcomers and their packmates.

"I told you, we can hunt," said Dex, his patience wearing thin.

"And we can help with that," Hadley added. She seemed unbothered by their imposition. "We're not thrilled to have to do this, either, but none of us have got much choice right now. I figure you know that."

Casey glared at her in a way only she could. Vincent was happy not to be on the receiving end of it as much these days.

"And we have money," said Virgil. Vincent realized this was the first full sentence he had spoken so far. His voice was rich and deep, a soothing contrast to his wife's harsher rasp. "We can help."

"There you have it." Dex leaned back in his chair with his arms crossed behind his head.

"Pig money," Casey muttered, turning her back on them.

"Casey," Dex warned. But before he could lay into her, Virgil spoke up again.

"I'm not a cop. I won't cause any trouble."

"He's a security guard," Hadley added.

"Sorry if the uniform spooked you folks," said Virgil.

Looking at it more closely, Vincent realized it was different after all.

"Safety in numbers," Dex said. "And besides, now we have our very own personal security. How's that?"

"There's our alpha," Sloane preened.

"Well, I'm not babysitting," Casey growled. She stalked off back to the couch and draped herself over it.

"Great, 'cause I'm not a baby," Roman piped up, glaring at the back of the couch. Vincent couldn't help but like the kid's spunk.

"The pack looks after each other," Dex reminded her, in a tone that invited no argument. He drew himself up importantly. "Now, who's got morning patrol? We're late already. Wasn't it you, Vince?"

"I'll go with him," Casey offered quickly.

"Me too," said Roman.

Casey threw Dex a look that said *See?*

Dex gazed back at her, unfazed. "It's Vincent's patrol, he can take who he likes."

At first Vincent felt like saying no—he didn't want to play babysitter any more than Casey. But he couldn't help feeling compelled by the burning defiance in Roman's face.

"Yeah, sure. Why not."

Roman's determination burst into a grin, and his chest swelled with pride. "I won't let you down. I know all the best scouting places around here."

"We have our own perimeter we survey," Vincent said lightly, trying not to quash him entirely. "But we could use sharp eyes."

Roman didn't seem to mind. He nodded.

Casey heaved a sigh. "You're an idiot," she told Vincent, heading for the back door.

"So I've been told," he muttered. He glanced back at the others. "Be back soon."

Dex nodded at him. "Be safe out there."

Outside, the world was as gray and silent as it appeared from the window. The bitter cold had softened, new leaves had sprung forth like verdant fireworks, and blossoms crowded every bush. Yet, somehow, their brightness simply wasn't bright enough. An unnatural gloom hung in the still air. No animals scuffled in the undergrowth or fluttered through the trees or filled the air with song. They had all sensed the shift in the world.

These days, Vincent always felt a pressure at the back of his skull, like a hum too low to fully hear. It was much harder to ignore out here, especially as they made their way into the woods, drawing closer to the source of it all. He glanced over his shoulder more than once, convinced he could still feel those black eyes he had woken to watching him. Or perhaps more.

Soon a pillar of pure void appeared over the treetops, lancing the sky and disappearing into the clouds. The space around it distorted inward, as if light itself was being sucked inside. It stretched impossibly upward; Vincent wondered if it even had an end. Grimacing, he skirted the area around it.

"My mom says you guys made that portal thing," Roman's eager voice cut through Vincent's thoughts. "Is it true? How did you–"

"We didn't *make* it," Casey growled. "We just couldn't stop the guy who did."

"So it was your fault still," said Roman. "Which means you made it."

"I thought you were supposed to be traumatized or something," said Casey. "Why are you such a little shit?"

Roman shrugged, grinning. "So how did it happen? Did you really go to Hell?"

"I wish you would," Casey muttered.

"Sounds like you've heard the whole story already," said Vincent.

"Not from the horse's mouth! I know how *Telephone* works."

Vincent sighed. "Well...yeah. It's true. A man named Benjamin Warwick broke open the portal between the mortal world and Hell. It was already there, technically, but he wanted passage between the two worlds to be free."

"Why did he wanna do that?"

Vincent's heart twitched painfully at the memory of his last confrontation with Benjamin. The desperation in his eyes still haunted his nightmares–his hand outstretched, begging Vincent to help him. To make things right.

"He thinks the way people are judged after they die is wrong. He thinks souls who are trapped in Hell deserve a second chance, because they were dealt unfair circumstances in life."

Roman's face screwed up in thought. "That sounds pretty fair. Mom always says people think we're going to Hell, because we're cursed. I think that's stupid."

"You'd be right," Casey grunted. "Who the hell thinks that?"

"I dunno. People. There's all kinds of weird reasons for being damned, isn't there?"

"Can't argue with that."

"But there are some good reasons, too," Vincent insisted. "Very good ones. For people who live violently, or selfishly. People who added nothing to the world. Those people deserve to be in Hell."

"So that's why everything is all crazy now?" Roman gestured to the air around them. "Because some of the damned got out? Are they like, going around axe murdering the *vibes* or something?" He said it with a cheeky smile that annoyed Vincent. He wasn't taking this seriously.

"Have you ever met a ghost before, Roman?"

At once Roman's expression darkened. It took him a moment to answer. "Sometimes I see these...things."

"Things?" Vincent prompted, softening slightly at the trepidation in the boy's face.

"Like...like curtains, almost. Something flickering between the trees, or in doorways, or on the street. I can barely see them at all, but..." He stopped, shaking his head. "I more...*feel* them. They don't feel right." He looked at Vincent warily, as if he expected him to think he was crazy.

Vincent nodded. "I know what you mean. I've felt things like that, too. Is that all you've seen?"

Roman seemed to shrink into himself. His brow furrowed deeper than anyone's should, at his age.

"Sometimes I'll have these dreams. *Bad* dreams. Dreams where I die. And...sometimes, they follow me after I wake up."

The memory of that shadow looming over Vincent returned with a vengeance. He shoved it away, but his skin continued to prickle.

"Did that only start recently?"

Something seemed to click for Roman. "Are you saying it's because of the portal? That's why everything is all strange now?"

"Yep," said Casey. "Thanks to that bastard Benjamin, everyone who ever died and went to Hell is just roamin' around the mortal world now, doing whatever. Sucking the life out of everything."

If only she knew.

"They're lost," said Vincent. "They're long dead, so they don't have bodies. Even if they did, they wouldn't be...right, anymore. Things change after death."

Roman frowned. "So this Benjamin guy just...what, released all the ghosts from Hell, and that was his big plan?"

Vincent shrugged. "Yes and no. I'm...not actually sure what else was supposed to happen. I stopped him before he could finish, and made sure he was imprisoned in Hell for good."

Roman's eyes widened. "*You* did?"

"Take all the credit," Casey grumbled.

"I didn't see you jumping into the abyss with me," Vincent retorted. He turned back to Roman. "I had to do it. I'm, ah..."

He hesitated, not wanting to admit the truth. But if this kid was going to be one of their pack, it was better for him to know now rather than leave it as a surprise.

"...He was my charge, once. He went to Hell when he died, and I was supposed to guard him. But he escaped and came back here. That's when all this started."

"*You* were supposed to guard him? So he got past you?" Roman didn't let him answer, too overwhelmed with questions. "But how is he doing all this if he's just a ghost?"

Vincent ignored the first part, trying to push away the guilt gnawing at his ribs as he recalled his greatest failure. "Benjamin was...he felt more *present* than most souls do, by the time they get to Hell. Something in him was determined to cling to life, to make things right still. So he found a portal and made it back out." Vincent carefully skirted the fact that he had been the one to show Benjamin the portal. He would never have found it on his own. "He found a vampire, who turned him so he could occupy his original body...and he started his work." He closed his eyes, suppressing a heart-deep sigh. "And I was sent here to retrieve him."

Roman stared at him in awe. "Damn, he's a vampire? No wonder he's so powerful!"

"It's not cool, you little brat," Casey snapped.

He paid her no mind. "But...if he's trapped in Hell now, why are you still here, Vincent?"

A familiar cold thrill coursed through Vincent's body. "Because I ran."

"You *ran?*"

Casey cracked a smile. "Greatest runaway in history. His dad's a bigshot in Hell."

"Can you do that?"

"He *did* do that, dumbass."

"But why?"

"Would *you* wanna live in Hell?"

Roman considered this for a moment. "I guess not..." He eyed Vincent curiously. "Then...you're not a werewolf, are you?"

Vincent flashed him a crooked smile. "I'm close enough."

"What does that mean?"

"You'll see soon."

They continued on through the trees. All around them Vincent caught those same flickers Roman spoke of–pale shadows between the trunks, barely a ripple out of the corner of his eye. But they carried a gravity that tugged at his very core, each one of them trying to tear some part of his life force away as if to make it their own. None of them were strong enough to manage it, but Vincent could only imagine what might happen to a mortal who was not so willful. He had seen it himself once before.

Again he ripped himself away from the memory, feeling as if he left pieces of himself behind. He fingered his tie, but didn't tighten it.

Soon the little group came to the edge of town, taking cover in a narrow alley that opened onto the main thoroughfare. It was as gray here as the woods, if not more so thanks to the streets and buildings. However, it didn't feel quite as gloomy. Cars crowded either side of the road, a general din hovering in the air as people scurried here and there, talking and calling to one another. Many of them were well-dressed, some clutching bouquets of flowers.

Even mortals could sense something was deeply wrong about the world, even if most couldn't see or even properly feel the specters among them. Among the superstitious, rumors of anomalies grew–haunted homes, possessions, curses, demons. Some people even changed entirely, as if they had lost some imperceptible part of themselves. That was the most disturbing of all.

At least, that was as much as the pack could gather. Firsthand observation only went so far. On patrols Vincent overheard Shadowhand Wardens discussing these things in hushed tones. For their part, news reports in the area had been attributing it all to radical climate change and electromagnetic disturbances. Some things could be measured with the right tools, but no one seemed to have any definitive answers.

And yet, despite the darkness, everything seemed almost normal here and now. Why?

As if sensing his confusion, Casey leaned closer to Vincent and said, "Graduation. It's gonna be impossible to spot Shadowhand in this mess."

Graduation. Right. Again Vincent's heart twisted, even more painfully this time.

Determined to ignore the feeling, he scanned the crowds for anyone that looked out of place. After a minute, he spotted someone. The man was dressed a little too casually to fit in amongst the families attending graduation, and he wore sunglasses despite the lack of sun.

"There," Vincent murmured, gesturing towards him.

Casey scoffed. "Sunglasses might as well be their fucking trademark. What numbskulls. You'd think they'd learn by now, no one else is wearing 'em."

"They have to cover their faces somehow," Vincent pointed out. Casey only grunted in reply.

"So what do we do now?" Roman whispered. "Just watch the dude?"

"Pretty much," said Vincent. "Just wander the perimeter and make sure there isn't any unusual activity. If they seem to be keeping watch and nothing else, we don't have to worry."

"Have they ever made a move?"

"Not yet," Vincent said darkly.

"We've been lying real low," said Casey. "Too low, if you ask me."

"Man, you guys are determined," Roman remarked. "These sunglasses dinguses don't look so tough."

"That's rich, coming from you," said Casey. "You and your folks are the ones who came crawling to us after five months' no-show. What even happened, anyway?"

Roman suddenly began fidgeting. "Ah, nothing, really."

"Oh, cut the shit. We know your parents gave you a hush order."

Roman shot her a glare. "I'm not s'posed to jeopardize our sanctuary." To Vincent he sounded like he was parroting something his parents said.

"And you always do what your parents say?" Casey challenged.

Roman chewed his lower lip.

Vincent gave him a hard stare. "What did you do?"

Both of them looked up at him in surprise. The guilty glint in Roman's eyes confirmed Vincent's suspicions.

"It's not that big a deal, alright? I just...it's just hard to control right now." Roman's words ended in a mumble.

Vincent's brow furrowed. "Did you transform in front of someone?"

"No. ...Not *really.*"

"*Not really* or no?"

"Okay, fine!" he burst out. "I just got a little wolfy, that's all! Not even, like, that bad. The bastard just got butthurt I won..."

"Who's the bastard?" asked Casey.

"Just some asshole at school," Roman grumbled. "Mom keeps trying to get him in trouble, but nothing sticks. He's a kiss-ass."

"You beat him up?"

Roman nodded. Vincent didn't miss the glimmer of satisfaction in his green eyes.

Casey broke into a grin. She clapped him on the back, hard enough to make him stumble. "Atta boy. Maybe you don't need babysitting after all."

"And that was enough for your parents to go into hiding?" Vincent pressed.

Roman's pride melted slightly. "Well, uh...the bite marks were a bit suspect, I guess. Didn't look human enough."

"You *bit* him?"

"He deserved it!" Roman insisted.

"Hell yeah he did," Casey crowed.

"And he's bigger than me. I had to use what I got."

Vincent couldn't argue with that.

"Sloppy though," Casey added. "If you'd done it right, he wouldn't've told anyone. Next time tell him you'll go for his throat–"

"Well, it's too late for that," Vincent cut in. "Did the Shadowhand actually get involved?"

"I don't think so," said Roman. "But it uh...made its way around the school. Since you guys warned 'em, they figured it's only a matter of time now."

"Man…I don't envy you, kid," Casey said. There was a shadow in her face that surprised Vincent. "Turning that young. Being a teenager's hard enough as it is. Have you always been a werewolf?"

Roman nodded.

"Shit." Casey's words seemed to run out. Vincent couldn't blame her. It wasn't too long ago when he was that age, too, buckling under the weight of what he was and his place in the world. Well…the Underworld.

Except he didn't stand up for himself, back then. Roman had more fire than he ever did.

They moved on from their hiding place, making their way along the edge of town, parallel to the crowded road. The dull ache that always tainted Vincent's heart grew sharper as his eyes followed those cheerful families, all preparing to watch their loved ones graduate college. It was so simple and so bright, it almost usurped the hollowness that hung in the air. He found his thoughts slipping back to his dream.

Was Henry graduating today? Would Henry's family be here now? Was this his last day in Alderwood?

Vincent hadn't truly seen Henry in almost half a year, since that terrible day when the portal had shattered. When he defied his duties and ran away from Hell itself. The face that haunted his dreams, Henry at his most tender, was never as clear in his mind as the expression he wore when he denounced Vincent for the last time.

The ends do not *justify the means, Vincent! I…I thought you were better than this.* Henry's voice echoed in his head.

But I'm not.

Vincent had been so close. So close to true happiness. He had only known it for a precious moment, in the dark of Henry's room, hidden from the rest of the world above and below as they shared their first and only kiss. In that moment, nothing else mattered. In that moment, he knew he was worth something. That he deserved to be happy…because if Henry loved him, it had to be true.

Henry, the first person to look at the beast who crawled from the depths of the earth and show him kindness. The first person who loved Vincent for who he was, not for what he could do for him.

But Vincent wasn't the kind of person who deserved someone like Henry. That much, he now understood. Henry was true, and good. He deserved the world, and he would get it. He was the hero of the story. Vincent was only *necessary*–the one who did what had to be done, regardless of the methods. He didn't care if he had to sully his moral standing–someone had to. He didn't want it to be Henry.

And that meant they were fated to stand against each other. Vincent knew that, in the deepest places of his heart. Now, the only place he could feel that happiness again was in his dreams.

And I deserve it.

But even with that resolution, one final question remained, dogging Vincent's thoughts every day: *What happened to Henry?*

The last time Vincent saw him, he was disappearing into the forest, trying to divert the Shadowhand after calling them to clean up the chaos. Trying to buy Vincent and Casey time to hide. *I'm sorry,* he had said. *For everything.* Those words had haunted Vincent ever since.

Sorry for what? For meeting me? For loving me? For betraying me?

Henry had changed his mind after summoning the Shadowhand...but that didn't prove anything. More than anything, Vincent ached to see him again. Even one last time, just to ask what he meant.

And, moreover...he wasn't sure where Henry was now. Had he gotten in trouble with the Shadowhand while trying to lead them away from his friends? The only comfort that kept Vincent from going after him straightaway was Henry's father being a high-ranking member of the organization. Surely any trouble Henry stumbled into wasn't likely to be life-threatening.

But it didn't stop Vincent from wondering. It had been months now...if anything, Henry would be at college still, finishing up his senior year. Graduating.

And here amongst the graduation attendees, an idea flashed across Vincent's mind. It brought guilt with it, an ever-present comrade. But something inside him clung to the thought all the same with desperate, selfish claws.

"What time is the graduation ceremony?" he asked.

Casey's pace faltered. "Should be in the evening. Why?" Then she said, "Oh god, you're not thinking of going, are you, Vincent?"

He grimaced. "I don't know."

"Yes, you do. You *know* we can't do that. The place will be crawling with Shadowhand–especially if Henry's dad is going!"

"Why do you wanna go there?" Roman asked.

Vincent was quiet for a moment. "It was supposed to be our graduation."

"Yeah, but it's *not* anymore," Casey growled. "We had bigger fish to fry. You don't regret that, do you? Y'know, saving the world and all?"

"Yeah, I do," Vincent snapped, more sharply than he intended. "Because we didn't stop Benjamin in the end, and we gave up everything for it. We failed. *I* failed."

"We *did* stop Benjamin!" Casey's temper flared right back at him. "You trapped him in Hell, so he can't fuck anything else up! Who knows what he might've done otherwise?"

"Melanie's still out there," Vincent argued. "And Jake. And Hunter. They know the rest of Benjamin's plan, and they'll keep trying to achieve it."

"That's bullshit, and you know it. Benjamin was the mastermind. You think those three can pull off something as crazy as that on their own? Please." Casey sighed, deflating a little. "Just...give it a rest, would you? We've done our part. Nothing has changed in months. We just need to keep lying low until this passes. Which it *will*," she insisted hotly.

"I thought you wanted us to ease up on the hiding."

"I do, but...going to graduation is another thing entirely."

"It's not like anyone would notice me in the crowd! I look normal!"

"This is about Henry, isn't it?"

Something exploded in Vincent's chest.

"*No,* it's *not,*" he snarled.

He suddenly noticed Roman was staring at him with blank shock—almost in fright. It was enough for him to falter, if only for the moment. He had no idea what he looked like right now, but he had a feeling it was anything but "normal."

He heaved a deep sigh, trying to calm himself. But it felt like his fury had left a burn on his heart. "Fine. Forget it."

Casey eyed him warily, but seemed to accept this. "Just...put it out of your mind, alright, Vincent?" She dared to rest a hand on his shoulder. It wasn't comforting. "That's not our life anymore. It never really was."

Then why have I never been happier than I was then?

CHAPTER 2

THE LAST PARTY

The night before graduation felt like a blur of color, a bright echo of better times. Times long before Sierra Pechman had to battle her own head.

Then again, that was never really true. She was always a weird girl, and she knew that. Her mother had told her that when she was little, her voice filled with a sweet laughter. Other kids had told her that later, in adolescence, tripping her because it was easy with her long, gangly legs she hadn't quite grown into yet, because she snorted when she laughed and she laughed too often at inappropriate times. She had forged all of it, every word, into armor. Maybe not just normal armor–like, maybe armor made of rubber, or moss, or something that absorbed everything thrown at it and made it stronger. She would work on that metaphor later.

Right now, she was at a party. Enchanting as the idea was, it was Melanie King's party, which meant a lot of things under the surface. She hadn't been throwing as many parties lately as she used to. Thinking on it, the last one Sierra went to was way back at the beginning of the fall semester. And she never liked to think about that one–because that night, she had almost died.

But now it was too late–she had thought about it. Not for the first time, a burst of frustration and sadness found her, mingling in her chest like a knot that couldn't be untangled. If it weren't for Henry and Vincent, she would have drowned trying to grab a treasure and impress her ex-boyfriend. She had put her life and her friends' in danger for that stupid turquoise necklace–but she still couldn't find it. She had lost it, somehow, because she was clumsy and careless, as always. One day it was sitting safely on her volleyball trophy, and the next it was gone. She had to have put it on, or picked it up, or done *something* with it, but she just couldn't remember. Because she was stupid and irresponsible and sloppy.

"Hey," a familiar, warm voice broke into her reverie. She blinked, pulling herself back to the party and its chatter and its colored lights and its thumping music, and found the most radiant smile in the world breaking through it all. "Everything okay?"

Henry wrapped his arm around her, firm and gentle both. Protective. She didn't miss that he chose to wear lavender to match her dress. She liked the way it stood out against her own dark complexion, but it wasn't his color. He didn't seem to care, despite how well-groomed he always kept. Tonight was no different; his sandy hair was carefully combed back, his heather sportcoat perfectly tailored. Anyone would be instantly taken with him.

And yet, he had picked her, for some reason. She still had no idea what she had done to deserve someone like him. To this day she couldn't imagine a word of judgment or pettiness coming out of his mouth. She had to keep it that way.

So she pulled together a smile for him. "Nothing! It's a great party." Again, she swore to herself: *I'll never tell anyone I lost that necklace.* If they knew, she was sure they would hate her. Even if she deserved it, she couldn't bear it. At least she didn't have to worry about avoiding the subject with Vincent—he had dropped out of school.

Sticky shame immediately washed over her at the thought. It was partly because of her, she was sure. Henry had told her time and again that it wasn't her fault, but she hadn't seen him since the night she had gotten involved in all this mess. It had to be because of that. And here she was, worrying about what he would think of her?

"Sure doesn't look that way." Henry's voice again burst the bubble of her thoughts, and she struggled back to the present. He looked at her with an unfailing concern that nearly brought her to tears.

"S—sorry," Sierra said, swallowing thickly to keep them down. *What is wrong with me today?* "It's fun, really. It's just...it's hard, y'know? It's our last day."

She didn't think Henry's face could soften any more, but as always, he made the impossible possible. His hand slid to her back, rubbing between her shoulder blades to soothe her.

"I know. It's strange. It feels like college has lasted forever." He turned his gaze back towards the thick of the party, the pretty glow of string lights reflecting like stars in his clear blue eyes. "I'm gonna miss it, too. It feels like standing on the edge of a cliff, doesn't it?"

In spite of herself, Sierra let his comfort relax her. She nodded weakly, leaning her head against his broad shoulder. They were silent for a long moment, together.

Finally Henry spoke again, gently. "I want you to know...even while we're figuring things out, I'll wait for you. As soon as I can, I'll bring you along wherever I go. Everything's gonna be okay."

Sierra closed her eyes, drawing in a steady breath. Was that what she was so worried about?

Maybe she should just accept the reassurance. He was being so sweet. She didn't want to bother him. But...something restless gnawed inside her gut, something that somehow didn't feel quite like her usual self.

"So what, I'm just gonna sit around back home and twiddle my thumbs until you...until you what?"

Henry blinked at her in surprise. That first wave of guilt became a torrent, but instead of drowning that strange, alien feeling inside her, it only seemed to aggravate it.

"I...I'm not sure what else to do, Sierra," he said. "I have to go back home too, and talk to my dad more about being initiated. It's all pretty secretive, I guess, but I can't really go on any official assignments until I've passed the Shadowhand's tests."

"And then what?"

"I don't know," Henry answered, growing more flustered. "Like I said, they might send me anywhere. Some Wardens travel, some get more permanent stations."

The more he talked, the more desperate Sierra became. It was all building in her chest, tightening and tightening until she felt like she was going to burst.

"And what does that leave for me? What am I supposed to do? I have to get a job–we have to start our lives! How are we gonna do that if–"

Suddenly, a new voice broke in:

"A lovers' spat, at *my* graduation party?"

Both of them turned to find none other than Melanie King flouncing up to them. She was dressed to the nines as usual, if not to the tens. Her shiny brown hair was full-bodied and delicately curled, her makeup perfectly accentuating her pretty hazel eyes and plump lips.

Sierra tensed, her heart quickening as their eyes met. That strange instinct inside her began to growl.

"Come now, can't you save all this nastiness for later? It's supposed to be a celebration," Melanie said, smiling delicately at them.

"It's nothing," Henry said, his tone carefully neutral. "Great party, Melanie. Your best yet, I think. I've missed these."

Invisible strings seemed to tighten around their bodies. They looked at each other like predators assessing each other's weak points before a fight.

"I guess you'll just have to stay in touch," said Melanie smoothly. "I'm sure post-grad parties are just as good."

They all knew this was her last invitation. The first chance she got, she would cut all contact with Henry Wellfellow.

"Yeah, how does that even work? Do you just pick a nightclub and invite all your contacts?"

For the first time, Melanie seemed caught off guard. Her taut smile faded some, and she shrugged. "Depends on where I end up. I'll invite anyone who wants to come."

"Well, where are you headed? I imagine a lot of people will go back to their hometowns and start their adult lives there." Henry shook his head. "It's funny, no one really hands you a manual for these things, huh?"

Melanie's smile returned, but it was painfully manicured. "I'm not sure where I'll go yet. Probably New York, or Chicago, or L.A.–somewhere worth my talents."

"What are you planning on doing there?" Sierra forced herself to join in. *You can't scare me. I won't let you.* Her instincts growled in agreement.

The strain in Melanie's face grew. "Oh, whatever suits me, I imagine. A lot of places will be dying to have me."

"That's gonna be a big leap for you," said Henry. "You know so many people here. You'll have to start from scratch, huh?"

"Well, I did it here. I can do it again. It's really no trouble for me."

"But school life is so different. Now you're gonna have to get a job, work your way up from the bottom, find places to meet all-new friends, make time to keep up with them outside of work...none of it seems glamorous enough for Melanie King," Henry chuckled.

Melanie's expression was almost grotesque now. As Henry caught on, his false friendly air faded to concern.

"Melanie?"

"You'll be sorry if you get in my way, Henry Wellfellow. You know that, don't you?"

Henry's mask slid from his face in an instant, replaced by something almost cold. It made Sierra shiver. He had never once looked at her like that.

"I don't think you're in the position to make threats, Melanie. Do you have any idea how many Shadowhand are watching us right now?"

Melanie's nose wrinkled in distaste, but she glanced around furtively, almost too quick to catch. But Sierra didn't miss it, and neither did Henry.

"You've got nothing on me, and you know it," Melanie murmured, leaning in closer. "As far as you can prove, everything was Benjamin's fault. And since I didn't do anything, the Brethren vampires are happy with the deal we made. Even your little friends with all their power can't justify taking me in. They know people will ask too many questions."

"Maybe not once everyone's graduated."

Melanie recoiled slightly.

Henry shrugged. "Just saying. You could be anywhere, at that point."

"People still care about me," Melanie spat. Her composure was slipping. "More than they care about *you*. You don't get it. I'll keep up with them. They'll notice."

"Don't kid yourself." Henry shook his head in mock lament. "I know I'm popular now, but I've seen it all go away before. Loads of times. I had to move a lot as a kid. Once you're out of people's everyday lives and have to start all over...it's not that simple. You're a nobody again, every time."

"*Fuck you*, Henry!"

For a split second, the mask came undone. Fortunately for her, the music was too loud for her voice to carry. Maybe she knew that, or maybe not. Either way, it only took her a moment to recover, lassoing her anger and letting it carry her forward.

She turned to one of the nearby party-goers and snapped her fingers. "Escort these two out, would you, Charlie?"

A boy even taller and wider than Henry stepped up on cue. He was also stupider. He waved a hand at Henry, who composed himself properly and offered Charlie a polite nod as he led Sierra away towards the gate.

Soon the lights and music were far behind them, leaving the night to swallow them. Moonlight filtered here and there through the dark clouds, dappling their bodies and quickening Sierra's heart.

Not yet.

"I've never seen her like that," she finally spoke, hoping to distract herself. "You must've really gotten to her."

"I don't care," said Henry, which didn't sound like him at all. His mouth was set in a firm line.

Sierra tentatively reached out to touch his forearm. He stiffened for a moment, then softened. She saw him breathe a silent sigh.

"You did everything you could with her," she told him, as gently as she could. That *something* was still roiling inside her gut. It almost felt like claws clutching at the base of her ribs, tugging at her, egging her on.

"I guess so. But she still got away with it."

Sierra squeezed his arm, unsettled by his anger. "She's not your problem anymore. Don't worry about her. Benjamin is gone, and Jake is..."

She stopped herself. *Shit.*

"...Where he belongs," Henry finished for her.

Sierra risked a glance at him. He was stone-faced, utterly unreadable.

"I'm sorry," she murmured.

Henry shook his head. "Don't be." He rested his own hand over hers on his arm. "I mean it. He earned his place in custody."

They both knew it wasn't that simple. If Henry knew what the Shadowhand would do to his former friend, he never dared to speak of it. Sierra had a feeling it was far worse than being "in custody."

"...And you think *I'll* be okay, if I come with you?"

Henry finally looked at her, his beautiful blue eyes searching the worried lines in her face with deep concern. She could feel it radiating off him. He wanted the best for her. He wanted her to feel safe.

I can take care of myself, growled that *something* deep inside her, warring with the rest of her.

"Of course. I'll make sure of it."

"How?" Sierra dared to ask, allowing only a flame of that dark defiance to flare up.

Henry broke her gaze. "We'll take care of it as it comes. Just like we have been. They won't suspect a thing. I promise."

Sierra fell silent. She didn't know what to say, other than the one thing she knew she couldn't: *You can't promise that.*

"Y'know, I think I'm ready to leave all this behind."

Sierra looked up at him in surprise. "Yeah...?"

Henry nodded.

She wished she could say the same. But if she wasn't here, she didn't know where else to go.

She realized all at once that she didn't have any other choice but to follow Henry. Nobody else could help her now. She couldn't keep herself safe anymore. And she hated it. That, both halves of her could agree on.

Sierra was quiet for a time, her thoughts churning loudly in her head. But louder still was that feeling in the pit of her stomach, brooding, growling to itself. She suddenly ached to run across the campus gardens, through the corridors, all the way to the forest beyond. She needed to move. Only then would she feel okay again.

"I think I'm ready, too."

CHAPTER 3

THE PLACES YOU'LL GO

By the time the sun began to set, everyone in the little house other than Vincent was restless. Roman had shut himself in the bedroom he now shared with his parents, the thud of music reverberating through the walls. Terry and Rolf started up a wrestling match to vent their nerves, while Casey set to pacing the kitchen. Sloane sat at the table, vigorously filing her nails and glaring at them like they had personally wronged her. Even Dex was on edge, waiting by the window with his arms folded, gazing out at the dying light with a worried expression. The only ones with enough patience seemed to be Virgil and Hadley, being the most senior of the wolves. They were lounging on the couch, talking quietly together.

Finally Dex turned to the others. "It's almost moonrise."

Everyone looked up at once. "I'll get Roman," said Hadley, disappearing upstairs.

A minute later the music stopped. Roman thumped down after his mother, an unmistakable trepidation in his face. Vincent swore he could see his eyes already yellowing in the half-light.

"You're sure the area's clear?" Sloane asked Casey.

She shrugged. "Should be. We didn't see anyone past town. They all must be staking out the graduation ceremony."

"Well, might be an easy night then," said Dex, stretching his neck. "Let's hope. C'mon."

He led the way out the back door, holding it open for each of them as they moved into the yard. He paused when only Vincent was left, standing alone in the kitchen.

"See you in the morning." Vincent offered him a half-smile.

Dex nodded, returning it. "Good luck, Vince. I'm sure it'll be quiet tonight."

Vincent caught a last glimpse of his companions jogging into the dusky woods before Dex shut the door behind him.

The house felt much darker in silence. Almost immediately, by his imagination or not, Vincent felt spectral eyes following him, digging into his mind.

He whirled around suddenly, as if expecting to see something behind him. Nothing was.

"Mira, if you're there, enough already! I *remember* you, god damn it! How could I ever forget?"

Nothing answered.

"I know it's my fault you're here. I know it's my fault he killed you. I know *all* of this is my fault. Okay? You or anyone else haunting me isn't going to change anything. I can't help you."

Nothing. The feeling remained.

Vincent left all the lights on as he moved to the living room, throwing himself onto the couch with a sigh. It did nothing to help his nerves.

The circumstances weren't new–he had guarded the house during full moon hunts a few times before, each month he had been living here. Nothing bad had ever happened on his watch, or to the others while they were out. But each time his worries only seemed to grow. His dreams intensified. The silent house grew louder.

Even now, that feeling had changed–like *more* eyes were on him, more than ever before. The shadows in the corners of the room were just too deep to be shadows. They were moving.

He again beat back the urge to mess with his tie. His gaze wandered to the door.

It was barely sundown–he had all night to himself.

He didn't want to be here. But there was one place he did want to be.

No one will be the wiser, he told himself. *Not even Casey.*

He felt a little thrill in his heart as he pulled himself to his feet. He paused by the door for just a moment. Then he opened it and stepped outside.

The evening air was crisp, practically humming with dark energy. It always seemed to strengthen once the light had faded. Even as Vincent strode through the backyard, he caught flashes of pale shapes out of the corners of his eyes. *Like curtains,* Roman had said. It wasn't inaccurate. They moved almost like fabric, folding over on themselves in an unseen wind before disappearing again.

Somehow, seeing them so plainly was easier. It was nowhere near as disturbing as being trapped inside with them—as if they couldn't follow him so closely, couldn't pick him out and corner him and siphon away his energy.

He tried to ignore them as he reached the road, pushing away that instinct that tugged at his heart with cold fingers: *Help them. They don't belong here.*

I can't, he asserted again, this time silently, this time only to himself. *That's not my duty anymore.*

He glanced back at the building only once. The garish neon glow of the sign above the bike shop had not disturbed the night for months now. He could barely make out its silhouette: "DEXTER'S LABORATORY." It seemed to glare down at him, disapproving. He turned away from it, pushing away the grip of guilt.

The street was quiet as Vincent began following it away from town. Only his shoes made any sound, tapping against the pavement. He realized all at once that he missed the chirping of insects in the trees that bordered the road. They were a near-constant companion, before the portal had broken. Better yet, their song had warned him of danger, or lack thereof. Now, they seemed to think there was always danger.

Maybe they weren't wrong.

Soon the first lights of the college filtered through the trees. The sight of them lanced Vincent's heart through the middle. He hadn't seen the dim yellow glow of those lampposts in so long. They had once welcomed him home in the dead of night, the first time he ever visited Dexter's Laboratory. He could almost still hear Casey yelling at him for following her. Back then, he hadn't even known the others were werewolves. And when he returned home, he brought news of the third person Benjamin had murdered. The memory sent a chill up his spine.

He was glad *some* things were different, now.

As he took his first step back onto campus, he finally allowed himself to sink into the nostalgia. It felt like hot, sticky mud filling his ribcage all the way up to his throat. It was as comforting as it was heavy, pulling him in with a slow greed. His heart settled there as he passed through the garden paths and the archways lining the empty corridors. They still felt like they belonged to him, at least in the dark. He had seen more of this place at night than during the day, back when he used to patrol every evening with Henry and the rest of their team, hoping to catch anything nefarious going on before more students turned up dead.

For a moment, Vincent's guilty heart felt lighter. Casey was right–they had stopped Benjamin. No more students had to live in fear of being murdered on their own college campus. The spring semester had been peaceful, he was sure. That was all his doing.

But it wasn't enough. Four people were dead because he had let Benjamin escape Hell. More, he realized, counting all the people Benjamin had made into vampires alongside him.

Where are they now? he wondered as he wandered, his footsteps echoing between the pillars in the corridor. The Shadowhand had surely found all the vampires and taken them in. He suppressed a shiver when he recalled Henry's expression the last time they talked about the Shadowhand's methods. Even he didn't know what they did with the dangerous creatures they apprehended. Supposedly they tried to play peacekeepers as long as the Others–their term for the supernatural–stayed in line and kept their heads down. But whenever they started causing trouble for mortals, the Shadowhand were unforgiving.

All except for Henry. Even if he wasn't a full member yet, he wanted to be–and he wanted to be better than that. He *was* better. All he wanted was peace between mortals and the Others, by his own hands.

Finally, a new sound reached Vincent's sharp ears: the echo of a microphone, the words it carried lost as they bounced between the walls of the corridor. He hurried forward, following the noise as it grew louder, until he reached the central quadrangle.

The entire space was ringed with bright lights on posts, illuminating the lawn and the many hundreds of people seated there. Rows of chairs were arranged in a great semicircle facing a stage, decorated with lush flower garlands and strands of glittering string lights. On the stage stood the University of Alderwood's president in her best suit, her voice ringing out over the crowd:

"–my greatest pleasure and pride to present the University of Alderwood's class of 2018!"

She lifted her hands and the crowd burst out in wild applause. Vincent's gaze fell upon the rows at the front, marked by the distinct black robes and odd square-shaped hats their occupants wore. His heart seemed to sink even deeper into the mud.

It submerged completely when a familiar figure stood and made his way onto the stage.

"Thank you all for being here tonight!"

As always, Henry Wellfellow's smile was brighter than the lights surrounding him. It had been so achingly long since Vincent had seen it outside his dreams. He looked no different–tall, broad, muscled but modestly, so he would have to move in just the right way to see them. Even from here Vincent knew his dimples, his curves, his strong jaw, the softness in his face, so perfect and steady he always thought him carved of living marble. This was a man who knew his place in the world, what he wanted, and brought no arrogance along with it. Self-importance, perhaps...but never at anyone else's expense. It was no surprise at all that it was him standing on that stage.

And I should be there with you.

"And what an incredible four years it's been. Give or take, for a few of you," he added, earning a chuckle from the crowd. Then his smile faded into something far more serious. "But before we go too far, I need us to take a moment for something deeply important to me. Because I...I expected more of my friends here with me today, even if they wouldn't be graduating yet. And I will never attend their graduations, either. This is...the last thing we share."

He sounded so hollow now, so small. His big act was slipping. He had no doubt rehearsed this speech dozens of times, but it didn't matter in the face of what he had lost. What *they* had lost. Vincent's heart twisted painfully–because he knew exactly what Henry was feeling, what could break that perfect facade.

A solemn hush had spread over the listeners. Henry closed his eyes, bowing his head. He cleared his throat before speaking again, struggling through the words: "I–I dedicate this moment to the friends we've lost this year. It can only be a moment–as short as their lives will feel compared to the future they could have had. Percy Quailheart, Mira Walker, Ava Mistral."

The rest of the onlookers bowed their heads as well. Vincent took the opportunity to creep closer, standing at the very outskirts of the seats. He joined them, closing his eyes, and was taken aback by the fresh, cold wave of grief that washed over him.

Grief, and guilt. Always guilt.

He didn't truly know Mira, but he had held her body as its final warmth leached out into the frigid waters of the Devil's Maw. Hers was the first corpse he had ever seen. Ghosts were commonplace for him, but death itself was another matter entirely. They had shared something dark and intimate, in that.

Percy and Ava, on the other hand, he knew well. At least, as well as he could. Percy was already dead when they met, nearly consumed by his own loneliness, his shattered mind. Ava was hardly more than a shut-in, despite her witch's powers...but her refusal to help them stop the murders on campus never endeared her to Vincent. The only thing she ever did was let Percy possess her, thinking she could retain control–but instead he piloted her body until she was murdered to finish Benjamin's ritual. She wouldn't have died if

Vincent could have just convinced Percy to let her go, somehow. If he had been a better friend to him.

He was the reason they were dead, all of them. If he hadn't let Benjamin escape Hell...none of it would have ever happened.

Before he knew it the moment of silence had passed, and everyone lifted their heads again. He tore himself from his own sorrow, fixing his gaze on Henry's visage like he was the eye of a hurricane.

"Thank you all." He stopped as his voice cracked. Cleared his throat again. Vincent watched with aching familiarity as he fought to scrape up his scattered bravado. When he started again, his voice came strong and bright—too bright.

"It's through your courage and solidarity that we forge on through this darkness. The world has never been more fraught with danger. We are still so young—they tell us that, over and over. Undoubtedly, we will have to face even more throughout our long lives. War overseas, changing technology, climate crisis, political divide, corporate greed...there are so many battles for us to fight. But I believe we will stand through them all, just as we have through this very moment. I know we will be the generation that believes in something better, and fights to make it real. We've already begun. And I for one can't wait to see what we can do."

The crowd leaped up, cheering wildly. As if nothing was wrong—as if they couldn't see Henry battling through the pain. It baffled Vincent. Henry beamed at them all, signing that invisible contract with his audience. Then, just like that, he was gone again, lost in a sea of black robes as they lined up to receive their diplomas.

A familiar feeling returned to Vincent as he stood at the very back of the clamor. No one noticed him—not even Henry. And it was better this way. Even if he should have been up there with them, receiving his commendations. Being recognized for his achievements at being exceptionally ordinary.

Except he wasn't. He didn't belong here. He shouldn't be here. Now he knew Henry was safe...

Suddenly, the hairs on the back of his neck began to prickle. He turned, scanning the crowd with rising alarm. Someone was watching him.

Then, he saw her. His blood ran cold.

He needed to leave. *Now.*

But before he could so much as turn, Melanie King broke away from the crowd. She made straight for him, cutting him off before he could disappear into the night.

"Well, hello there, handsome. Fancy seeing you here."

She planted her palm on his chest to halt him, right over the scars beneath his shirt. He growled deep in his throat.

"Let me go."

"But I haven't seen you in *so* long, Vincent!" Her hazel eyes glittered maliciously in the half-light. "How have you been? Or, more importantly," she added, looking him up and down, "*where* have you been?"

Vincent tried to push past her, but she shuffled back into his way, tangling herself up with him. He recoiled, his growl strengthening as his confidence waned.

"Why are you here, hmm? Last I heard, you failed your classes. You can't be graduating."

"I'm not. I was just leaving."

"Oh, but we have so much catching up to do!"

"Don't make me get Henry." Vincent locked eyes with her, willing himself to exert his hellish dominion. He knew his eyes were burning, embers against the void itself.

But it didn't work—not on Melanie. "Please. He doesn't want anything to do with you now. You and I both know that." She sneered at him, making his gut wrench. It wasn't true. It couldn't be. She was just trying to get under his skin.

"Want to try me?" he countered.

"More than anything." She licked her ruby-red lips, her gaze tracing the curve of his shoulders to his collarbone quite deliberately. Vincent's skin began to crawl.

She blinked, looking back into his eyes. "But let's cut to the chase, shall we?"

Of course. She wanted something. She always did.

"You know how to get Benjamin out of Hell, don't you?"

That, he wasn't expecting.

"What?"

Melanie gave him a knowing smile. "I know you broke him out last time."

"You actually think I would do it again? I took him back myself! Why would I–"

"Because we need him. You think he wanted the world to look like *this?*" She gestured around them vaguely.

"Like what? It's just dark out."

"Don't be a smartass. You know what I mean. Everything's a mess. We can't leave things like this, or everyone's screwed."

Vincent studied her curiously. "So you're saying Benjamin didn't leave you instructions? You don't know what to do without him?"

Melanie's smile vanished. "No, of course not. It's just that he knows the magic, and–"

Vincent couldn't help a laugh. "You're useless without him. He didn't even trust you enough to share his plans with you." It was hard at that moment to understand how he had ever been intimidated by this woman. She had always seemed so self-assured, beguiling everyone around her with a flick of her wrist and a pretty smile, but now...

Melanie finally scowled. He had struck a nerve. *Good.*

"He didn't expect you to lose your shit and ambush him like that," she snapped. "Or he would've told me more. I guess I underestimated myself, huh?" she added, suddenly flipping back to a smirk. "All I had to do was show Henry what you really are, and everything came crashing down."

Vincent's throat tightened. The memory broke in again–Melanie leading Henry to the shed where Vincent was breaking Jake's fingers, trying to get him to reveal Benjamin's plans. Trying to stop the murders. Trying to protect Henry.

But that didn't matter to Henry. Because Vincent was too brutal. He was a monster, through and through. Even if it meant saving everyone.

Despite his best efforts, Melanie must have seen his expression. Now that they were on equal footing again, she pressed: "I know you don't know another way to fix everything, or you'd have done it already."

Vincent fought back a grimace, for the sake of his dignity. She wasn't wrong, but... "It doesn't matter either way. Anything Benjamin does will only further his own plans. Did you ever consider that maybe this *is* what he wanted?"

"It isn't," Melanie insisted. "We were going to keep going. Farther than anyone's ever gone before."

"You just don't know how to get there."

Melanie's eyes narrowed. She had had enough. "Stop playing games with me, Vincent. I know you can bring Benjamin back."

"Even if I could, why would I help you?"

That awful smile returned. "Because I have a deal for you."

Those words hit Vincent suddenly and hard. He bared his teeth at her in a warning. "I'll never make another deal with you."

This time he shouldered his way past her with all his strength, nearly knocking her over. He didn't care anymore about making a scene–he just needed out. But before he could leave, her voice reached him from behind:

"If you don't help me get him back, I'll reveal what you are to everyone. Right here, right now."

Vincent stopped in his tracks. *She's crazy.*

"Good try," he said over his shoulder. "You'd never do it. That would be putting yourself on the line, too."

"I promise. I will. I need him back, Vincent. Otherwise all this has been for nothing."

Vincent snorted. "I thought you'd be happy to have him out of the way so you could take over yourself. But I guess the only power you ever had over people, you cheated your way into. Before you were a vampire, no one would even look twice at you. You want to know who told me that?"

Her silence told him more than she ever could. A thrill of satisfaction coursed up his spine.

"Benjamin did."

He began walking away again. This time, Melanie didn't stop him. He almost couldn't believe she would give up so easily. Maybe he had hit her where it hurt, after all. He remembered what else Benjamin had said about her, just before Vincent had left him in Hell: *I haven't had much luck with guiding her on a better path, yet.* Even she must have her limits.

Just then, he heard her name ring out over the speakers: "Melanie King!"

He didn't stop. It was perfect timing, really—now he could get away while she was distracted.

He had just reached the edge of the grass when the screech of microphone feedback jolted his ears. It was followed by something so much worse.

"Hello, everyone. It's such an honor to be here tonight."

She won't do it. She can't.

"Like my friend Henry said, it's been a hard year for all of us. But we made it through, and I'm so proud of us for doing it. We shouldn't have had to face such horrible things just to get an education."

Maybe that was it. She was just jealous Henry was picked as the speaker for the evening.

"And that's why I believe you deserve to know the truth."

A murmuring rose from the crowd, and Vincent's stomach dropped.

"I'm sure you've all seen that black pillar in the sky, coming from the forest. The one they keep telling us is a government test, and to keep quiet about it because of foreign intelligence, blah blah blah. Well, it's not.

"You've seen how things have changed since the pillar appeared. *Smoke*, they say. Some kind of government project gone awry. As if. The sky is always dark, the air is always cold, everywhere you go you feel like someone's watching you. None of this is normal. You're not stupid—you've put two and two together, haven't you? Even though they tell you it's nothing to worry about?"

Suddenly there was a jostling onstage, followed by another shriek of feedback from the microphone. Vincent finally whirled around, alarmed, to find Melanie gripping the microphone stand for dear life, wrestling with two of those strangers in sunglasses. They were trying to lead her away without outright grabbing her, but she was giving them a difficult time.

"See? They're trying to silence me! It has to be true!" she shouted into the microphone, yanking herself away from the nearest man's hands. "Don't touch me!"

Before the strangers could escalate, the university's president stepped forward. She said something to Melanie that Vincent couldn't hear, but Melanie shook her head and turned back to the microphone.

"You all know me, don't you? You trust me? Well, here's the truth: that black pillar is a portal to Hell!"

The murmuring grew stronger. The president frowned. The two men seemed hesitant to step in again, as if wondering if it would only confirm Melanie's claims.

"Hell is real! You can go and see it for yourselves! And so many other things are, too—they've been hiding them from you, trying to keep control over the supernatural underworld. And I know it sounds crazy, but ask yourselves—have you been satisfied with their explanations for all this?"

At that moment, the men finally had enough. They reached for her again, and she narrowly ducked out of the way. Vincent cringed against the screech of the microphone as she dragged it to the far end of the stage.

"Remember those rumors about the big three-headed dog that ran through campus last semester? I *know* some of you saw it! It was a hellhound, and it's real—I can prove it!"

Melanie's wild eyes found Vincent's, and he froze. *Don't.*

But before she could say anything, Henry moved between Melanie and the Wardens. They halted at once.

The microphone barely picked up his words to her: "Please, stand down, Melanie. This isn't the time."

It was a carefully neutral statement. Vincent was impressed–but Melanie was having none of it.

"Oh *no*, look who's come back to play the hero again!" She looked back to the crowd. "Well, guess what–your valedictorian is in on it, too. He's been lying to you this whole time! He's one of the people that keep the secrets. Aren't you, Henry?"

Henry set his jaw, but said nothing. Even from the edge of the quad Vincent could sense his remorse. He knew Melanie was digging her own grave, and there was nothing he could do about it now.

Suddenly, someone jumped onto the stage and flew at Melanie. In a blur of color they were lying flat on the wood, wrestling wildly. The microphone fell beside them and clattered onto the stage with a horrible wail of feedback.

"How *dare* you?" The attacker's voice rang out through the speakers. "Leave Henry out of this, you jealous bitch!"

Shit. It was Sierra Pechman.

Melanie let out an unpleasant laugh as she clawed at Sierra's face. "What, gonna fight all your boyfriend's battles for him?"

Vincent's heart dropped into his stomach. *Boyfriend?* Did she mean that, or was she just taunting her?

"Don't worry–it's too late already!" Melanie crowed. "Now everyone knows what he is. Now he's–"

"Sierra, don't–"

Henry moved for her, but he was too late. He and Vincent both saw it happening at the same moment. Only Vincent could hardly believe it.

Sierra was changing. Her flailing arms grew, her body swelled and cracked. Her clothes tore and fell in tatters around her. Her coiled hair spread down her back and then beyond, changing texture until it covered her dark skin in black fur. Her face twisted and elongated, and her mouth swung open in a horrible scream–then a howl.

A monster stood in her place. Hunched, clawed, fanged, furred, with eyes that flashed in the half-light. All in front of everyone.

For that half-second, the world stood frozen. That was all the time Vincent had to realize just how bad everything was going to get.

The uproar slammed into his senses like an avalanche. He staggered back as the crowd leaped to their feet as one, swarming in a desperate attempt to flee. People tripped over the chairs and each other, sprawling across the aisles. Others fumbled for their phones, the glow unmistakable–they were trying to catch it all on video. Proof.

But the Shadowhand had their hands full already. They were the only ones making for the stage, swimming upstream in the crush of people. Melanie scrambled backward, away from the werewolf, her face contorted in terror. Vincent couldn't tell if it was real or not–whether or not she had planned this.

Just in time, someone dove between her and the beast. It was one of the Shadowhand Wardens that had accosted her onstage, lifting his handgun to the werewolf's head.

Vincent's heart jolted. *No!*

"*Stop!*"

Henry was suddenly there, throwing himself against the Warden's arm. The shot fired into the trees at the edge of the quad, sending a fresh shockwave of panic through the frenzied crowd. New screams punctured the tumult.

Vincent had to move. He raced along the edge of the quad towards the stage, skirting the worst of the chaos. A couple people almost tripped him as they flashed past. His heart pounded in his throat–he knew he shouldn't be here. But he couldn't leave Henry or Sierra to face this alone. He would never forgive himself.

"Get out of the way, Wellfellow!" One of the other Wardens brandished his own gun at the rampaging wolf. "We have to stop it!"

"*Her*, damn you!" Henry grabbed his arm, again forcing the barrel away from Sierra. Thankfully, this Warden didn't fire. "Please, you have to listen!"

"Someone grab the kid!" the man shouted, struggling against Henry's bulk as he tried again to take aim.

Henry's fist connected with the Warden's face, shattering his sunglasses. He staggered back, blood spurting between his fingers as he clutched his nose.

"*Sierra, run!*" Henry rounded on the next man like a bull, ready to fight to the death. Vincent could see it in his eyes, even from here.

But Sierra was in no state to listen. She was facing down four Wardens, her terrible fangs gleaming in the stagelight. In another moment either she or they would be dead.

Vincent leaped forward, and suddenly four paws carried him. He was no longer human—instead, a massive hellhound mounted the stage in one swift bound and charged the Wardens, barreling three separate heads into them and tossing them in all directions. Their cries of alarm cut short as they fell, and Vincent knew he only had a single moment to act.

He twisted and sank his fangs into Sierra's wolf body, each of his three hound's heads finding an arm or a shoulder to grasp. He tore her off the stage with all his strength, letting gravity do the rest. They tumbled onto the grass, the fall dislodging Vincent's grip enough for Sierra to rip herself free.

Her shadow loomed over him. He rolled over, teeth bared as he prepared to defend himself against her moon-addled wrath.

But then, swift as a shadow, she fled. By the time he stood she was halfway across the quad, bounding for the trees beyond. In another breath she was gone.

Vincent turned back to the stage, expecting a fight. But the Wardens weren't looking at him, veiled in the deep shadows beneath the stage. Instead they were busy with another target.

Henry was tangled in the clutches of the two largest Wardens, his arms splayed out on either side of him. His once-perfect blonde hair was mussed, stray strands draped over his forehead, and his chest heaved from his efforts— but he had stopped struggling. The other Wardens closed in around him.

"You lied to us, Wellfellow," one of them growled, advancing on him. "You never told us about that girl when you reported the rest."

"She wasn't gonna hurt anyone," Henry insisted, his blue eyes blazing.

"Wasn't that your girlfriend, Wellfellow?" another Warden asked, a woman with a hard voice.

"She was *fine* until that girl Melanie started on me. Why aren't you worrying about her right now? Where'd she go? She's gonna get away!"

"Leave that to us," the man spat. "Right now, we have to sort out a *traitor.*"

Vincent's blood turned to ice. *What does that mean? What are they going to do to him?*

"Get a call out to the kid's father," the woman said, ushering a couple of the others away. "He'll want to ship him back home first thing, I'm sure. Best let Nathan deal with it."

Vincent's shoulders sagged in relief. His father wouldn't kill him. He wasn't sure what he would do, but from the way Henry talked about him Vincent was certain he was, at the very least, safe.

"The rest of you, search the forest. Find the girl–and find that werewolf."

Vincent's heart leaped back into his throat in an instant. Not only was Sierra in danger–but the rest of his friends were too. That forest was crawling with werewolves tonight.

But first, he realized as the Wardens began dispersing, *he* had to get out of here.

He flattened himself against the side of the stage, willing the black shadows cast by the stage lights to continue shielding him. He waited until he heard the footsteps leave the platform before he dared peek one head up over the edge. No one was looking this way.

Now.

Vincent bolted. He heard shouts rise behind him, but didn't look back. If they caught him, he was sure they would show him no mercy either.

His paws pounded blindly across pavement, grass, garden beds, until they found the loamy forest floor. He lifted one of his noses to taste the crisp night air, trying to catch any trace of his companions.

Nothing. He growled to himself, slowing his pace. The darkness beneath the canopy was deep, more so these days than ever. Even his sharp night vision couldn't penetrate every shadow. He wandered between the black trees, more to keep himself moving than anything. He didn't know what to do. How was he supposed to find the pack *and* Sierra–let alone convince a pack of moonstruck werewolves to follow him?

A rogue thought pierced his mind, one he hadn't had in a long time. He hated and reveled in the pain of it.

What would Henry do?

And he knew, almost instantly.

He lifted all three of his heads to the sky and howled.

The eerie, tri-tone sound rose over the treetops, louder even than anything a werewolf could muster. It would reach the Shadowhand, he was certain.

He stopped and sat where he was, his chest still heaving from his run. He needed this moment to rest, while he still could.

He waited there beneath the dark trees for some time, his heartbeat loud in his ears. With each passing minute his anxiety swelled. What if they couldn't find him? What if they hadn't heard him at all?

What if they caught someone else first?

Then, he heard footsteps.

He stood, the shaggy brown fur along his back bristling. His pursuer crashed through the undergrowth, closer, closer...

He bunched his muscles, ready to run. But before he could, a familiar voice called out:

"Vincent!"

He froze in shock. A moment later a black-furred beast tore through the bushes, its eyes aglow in the gloom.

"Casey? What are you doing here?" His own voice seemed to come from nowhere rather than any of his three maws, but otherwise sounded the same as it always did. Casey's on the other hand was strange and throaty in a grotesquely wolfish way.

"Finding you," she said haltingly, as if struggling to form thoughts into words. *"Why howl?"*

"You shouldn't be here!" Vincent hissed, throwing a worried glance back into the trees. He couldn't see or hear anyone, but–

No. He smelled gunpowder. They were close.

"Run!" He took off through the trees. He was relieved to hear Casey's heavy pawsteps at his back, trusting him enough as a packmate to listen without explanation.

"Where are the others?" he called back to her without slowing, grateful he didn't need a mouth to talk so he could focus on breathing. He needed to keep a steady pace–fast enough not to get caught, slow enough not to lose them entirely.

"*Not far,*" she grunted between pants, without the same luxury. "*Went ahead. Who chases us?*"

"Shadowhand." Vincent's leftmost head gritted its teeth. "They're hunting us. All of us. We need to get everyone somewhere safe, before–"

Suddenly, another howl pierced the heavy, specter-cursed air. This one was higher-pitched, singular. Vincent nearly tripped as he skidded to a halt, ears pricking in alarm.

"That sounded like–"

"*Fuck.*" Casey pivoted without slowing, racing back the direction they had come. Vincent cursed too, taking off after her as desperation rose to nearly choke him.

They stumbled into a small clearing between the trees. A hole in the clouds let the full moon cast the scene in eerie silver, a spotlight throwing the image before them into sharp relief.

The Wardens surrounded a mass of fur, pinning it to the ground with their combined might. The creature was heaving and twisting, but it wasn't powerful enough to fight them all. Not only that, but the acrid taint of blood filled the still air. Werewolf blood.

Before Vincent or Casey could move, a single glowing eye found them through the chaos.

"*Vincent! Casey! Help me!*"

It was Roman.

CHAPTER 4

PACKING

"S*tupid pup!"* werewolf-Casey snarled.

Some of the Wardens looked up, alarmed when they realized their odds had dropped. A couple scrambled to their feet, cocking their pistols in Vincent and Casey's direction. Vincent was certain that from this distance, they wouldn't miss.

"Shit." There was only one way he could think of to de-escalate this situation.

Vincent steeled himself, taking in a deep breath. It had always been difficult for him to do this before, but lately he had found the best way–as painful as it was.

He imagined Henry standing before him, those always-clear blue eyes trained on his monstrous body, taking in every detail–his scruffy brown fur, his three canine heads, his cruel teeth, his massive form, the flash of unearthly red in his eyes like embers in the dark. Once he had felt Henry's touch, warm and earnest, unperturbed by the beast beneath his hands, and let himself become what he needed to be. But he could not summon that anymore. Instead he pictured Henry reaching for him, remembering the trepidation before the first touch, being seen and raw in a way he never had before, and he couldn't take it.

"Don't shoot." Vincent stepped forward slowly, his hands in the air. In a blink, he was human again.

The Wardens flinched in surprise as he transformed. "What are you, boy?" one of them demanded, his gun still trained on Vincent. "You're no werewolf."

"No, I'm not. Please let my friend go. He isn't the one you're chasing."

"Doesn't matter. A werewolf this close to town is a liability any way you slice it. We have to take it in."

"But he hasn't hurt anyone. He's just a kid." Vincent tried not to vent too much of the desperation squeezing his chest. He needed to keep a cool head, not show weakness.

"It's only a matter of time." The Warden jerked his pistol in a gesture to approach. "You and that other werewolf, come here slowly. We won't shoot if you cooperate."

Gazing at the squadron of Wardens, Vincent's hope dwindled. They were not going to compromise on this. They had the upper hand, and they knew it. He had no idea what to do now.

Then, Casey stepped forward. Stunned, Vincent watched as she slowly crossed the clearing on all fours, her black fur turned silver in the moonlight.

What is she doing? He had never in a million years thought Casey Helliker would turn herself in without a fight. Hell, even *with* one.

Casey seemed to catch his thoughts. She glanced back at him, once, her eyes glowing yellow in the gloom. *Trust me*, they said.

Vincent stayed where he was, his hands hanging in the air, hardly daring to breathe.

The Wardens all turned their guns on her as she slowly approached. She lowered her head submissively, trying to show them she wasn't a threat.

The Wardens hesitated. The speaker broke first, grabbing some overlarge handcuffs from a pocket and starting towards her.

"Thank you. We won't harm you." He glanced back towards his comrades. "Can someone get a muzzle over here?"

He barely got the words out before Casey jerked her head upward, smashing into his jaw.

All hell broke loose. Before the first Warden could recover she had leaped onto the next, scattering the group. Vincent bolted forward to help Roman, but there was no need–he had already wrested himself free in the chaos and was snapping at the Wardens surrounding them, trying to harry them off Casey. A string of gunshots shocked his heart, but his mind ran clear. They had to get away. They couldn't fight them all.

"*Run*, damn it! We're clear!" he shouted.

Thankfully, Casey and Roman both listened. They broke from the throng and charged across the clearing after Vincent. He flinched as more shots blasted his ears, but he didn't dare make himself a bigger target by transforming again. He turned and ran for the trees, putting his faith in their cover as he dove back into the shadows.

Two sets of paws drummed behind him, reassuring him his friends were still with him. He raced on through the underbrush, wincing as branches caught on his human skin and the sting of blood reached his nose. In a few moments the werewolves overtook him, loping on all fours with their eyes flashing in panic. When they were a few yards ahead of him he finally gave in, shifting back into a hellhound. He couldn't lose them again.

God, he only hoped Dex and the others were far away from here.

He risked a glance backward as he ran on. His rightmost head caught the silhouettes of the Shadowhand a ways back, still pursuing them but falling behind fast. His heart soared in relief and he put on a new burst of speed, catching up with the others.

"We're losing them!" he called. "Where are the others?"

"*Don't know,*" Roman panted. "*Snuck away.*"

"*Stupid pup!*" Casey snarled again. "*Told you to wait!*"

"We should lead them as deep as we can into the trees," Vincent said. "Once we lose them we can head back towards home. By then it'll be close to dawn."

Casey grunted in agreement.

"*What about the others?*" Roman asked, his eyes wide.

Vincent gritted his teeth. "We can't risk wandering around out here searching for them. We'll just get caught. We have to trust Dex will keep them out of danger."

Roman let out a soft whine, but for once didn't argue.

After a few minutes, Vincent realized the kid was starting to lag behind. His own chest was burning with the effort of running, so he slowed his pace, glancing over his shoulder again with one head. This time he saw no trace of their pursuers.

Finally he staggered to a walk, all three of his tongues hanging out. The other two followed his lead gratefully, and only now did he notice both of them were limping.

"What happened?" Vincent asked, nosing Roman's fur. He quickly found a bullet lodged in his shoulder, bleeding sluggishly. He was amazed the kid managed to keep running like that. *The full moon is a hell of a drug,* he thought.

"*S'fine,*" Roman wheezed, turning his face away from Vincent.

"We'll dig it out when we get home," Vincent reassured him. "It didn't hit anything major." He turned his attention to Casey, but she bared her teeth.

"*Don't touch me.*"

"I'm not going to, I just wanted to see—"

"*Fine too. Keep moving.*"

The distinct tang of blood in the air around her said differently, but Vincent knew better than to argue with her. Especially during the full moon. He sighed roughly and veered away from her again, pacing forward through the trees. As long as they kept going, they should keep their lead on the Shadowhand.

He hoped.

They walked on as the moonlight gradually faded, replaced by utter darkness. Vincent could only put one paw in front of the other, keeping his eyes trained on the forest floor so he didn't trip on any roots. Finally the sky began to pale between the branches overhead, slowly tinting the woods gray.

"Let's go back home," Vincent said, changing course. "I think it's been long enough. Keep your nose out for Shadowhand, alright?"

He tried to push away the worry thudding in his chest as they started back. He hadn't heard any howls or sounds of distress, which was good. He had to believe Dex was canny enough to lead the pack away from the commotion, whether or not they wanted to help. It would do none of them good if they all got caught.

Please, don't get caught. He cared too much about them—all of them. At one point he would have fought it. But a lot had changed since then.

Everything seemed better somehow in the growing light of day, even with its ghostly gloom always lingering. The events of the night felt like they belonged to another world. After a while, Vincent began to catch the familiar odor of tar and gasoline, and soon they spotted the back of the house through the trees. All of them picked up the pace, eager to put the evening's chaos behind them.

They finally staggered into the backyard. Roman flopped into the grass, panting, while Casey approached the back door.

"Wait!" Vincent hissed. She halted. "Do you smell anything?"

Casey paused, her nose twitching. She wandered along the edge of the house, disappearing around the corner. Vincent half-followed her across the lawn, but stopped beside Roman, not wanting to leave him alone. He waited, poised to run—or fight.

He jumped as Casey poked her head back around the side of the house. *"Safe."*

Vincent let out a sigh of relief, nodding. He took a moment to return to that place in his head with Henry, letting the memory of his anxiety hide his true form behind his human guise. When he opened his eyes he strode to the back door on two legs.

It was unlocked—just as he had left it, he realized with a twinge of guilt. The inside was dark and empty. The two werewolves limped in after him, exhausted. It was only when Casey brushed past him that Vincent realized the dark fur around her neck was stained with blood.

"Casey," he started.

She didn't stop. In fact, her name only seemed to drive her forward as she rounded the corner and disappeared into the bathroom.

Roman leaned against the back of the couch nearest the kitchen, his flanks still heaving. For a moment more he looked like the wounded animal he was, and then a powerful ripple coursed through his body, followed by a snarl and a yelp of pain. Vincent cringed against the cracking of bones as his form twisted and convulsed, rearranging itself back into what was more or less human.

When it was over, he kept his gaze averted. He knew Roman would be unclothed; Vincent's transformation was more cosmetic, fashioned by some principle of old magic he didn't understand and his father did, but the werewolves' was all physical. He went into the kitchen to retrieve a first aid kit from beneath the sink, giving Roman time to find something to cover himself with.

He lingered a bit before returning to him. He had tied a blanket from the couch around his waist, and was looking balefully up at Vincent from the floor. Shirtless, dirty, and bleeding, he looked even more scrawny and young than before.

Vincent softened. He crouched beside him. "Let me see your shoulder."

Roman grimaced, but turned so Vincent could reach. He was lucky he had been a wolf when he was shot–there was no question the bullet would have embedded itself deeper otherwise. As it happened, Vincent was not worried about being able to extract it. He had seen a lot worse.

"Wait here." He went to find some pliers and a knife. He filled a cup with hydrogen peroxide and swirled the tools in it. When they were as sterile as they were going to get, he brought them and a dish towel back to Roman. He answered the kid's confused look: "Bite down on it. It's going to hurt."

He looked skeptically at the towel, but did as he was told. Vincent carefully wedged the knife into the wound, along the edge of the bullet, and began to pry it out. He heard a muffled cry, his stomach clenching in sympathy.

"Yeah. That's why you don't go off on your own."

His point did nothing to stave off the guilt. It only made him feel more hollow. He could practically hear Henry chiding him, as if he were in the room with them rather than...

The memory flashed through Vincent's mind–those guns, the venom in the Wardens' voices. And they were taking Henry–

No. He forced the thought away. Henry was being carted off to his father to be disciplined like a petulant child. He had heard the Wardens say as much. It was no wonder Henry had wanted to go off to college on his own so badly. Then again, he was lucky that was all he was going to face for his insubordination. Anyone on the other side would be in far worse shape if Henry hadn't intervened.

For a moment, Vincent wondered if Henry had seen him, when he tackled Sierra. He wasn't sure if he wanted him to or not.

When he had enough purchase, he abandoned the knife and clamped the pliers around the base of the bullet. He pulled it out delicately, a splash of blood chasing it.

"I'm sorry about this," he said, more gently this time. He then swiftly pressed some clean gauze hard into the hole. Roman squeezed his eyes shut and groaned into the towel. Vincent finished packing the wound as quickly as he could, wrapping up the gauze with medical tape. When it was secure he took the towel from Roman, offering him an awkward pat on his other arm.

"Ah...good job. That should hold you for a while, at least. Maybe you can get your father or someone to take a look at it later." After all, he was no doctor. Henry was the one who had taught him first aid. He tried not to let the memories of their many cleanup sessions flood his heart.

Roman's teeth were still gritted, but he nodded weakly. "Th-thanks." He swallowed visibly, trying to keep his composure. Vincent got up, trying to afford him some mercy.

He didn't put away the supplies yet. Instead he went to the bathroom door, still shut and silent. He knocked on it stiffly.

"Casey?"

No answer. Unease roiled in his gut.

"Are you okay?" he pressed.

"Yeah."

Her voice was normal again, not wolfish. He wasn't sure if that was good or not.

"Please come out. We need to take a look at your–"

The door opened before he could finish. Casey's dark eye peered out from the crack, puffy with exhaustion and too-bright with pain.

"I got it. Stop fussing."

"You did it yourself?"

"There's more than one first aid kit in this godforsaken house."

Vincent couldn't argue with that, but he wasn't happy about it. "Are you sure you got everything? You don't need help?"

She was quiet for a moment. "Actually, yeah. Grab me some clothes, would you?"

Vincent fought back his annoyance and went upstairs to their shared room. A minute later he returned with a set of her clothes, handing them through the crack in the door. She closed it again immediately.

"You're welcome," he called. He sighed, then wandered back to the kitchen, chewing his tongue anxiously. Dawn had broken, filling the little house with filtered gray light between the curtains. Roman had disappeared upstairs, leaving Vincent once again alone in the quiet.

He paced until at last the bathroom door opened again. Casey emerged, fully clothed and subdued, her hair damp. She must have showered. Vincent caught sight of heavy bandaging on her arm and just below her collarbone. His stomach lurched.

"You–"

"Save it," said Casey, waving him off. She leaned against the back of the couch with a glassy look in her eyes. "I knew what I was doing."

Vincent snorted. "Now who has a hero complex?"

For once, Casey didn't rise to the taunt. Instead, she said, her tone blank, "We have to leave."

"What? We're *not* going back–"

"No. I mean, for good. Leave town."

Vincent froze, his brain stuttering to a halt. He simply stared at her.

"What do you *mean*, you're leaving?"

Roman, now clothed as well, thumped down the stairs in a flurry. He hung off the banister with his good arm, glaring at them.

Casey gazed at him numbly for a moment before turning back to Vincent. "We can't stay here now. The Shadowhand knows who we are. They saw you. Roman called our names."

"What? No!" Roman cried, indignant. "That doesn't mean shit! There was so much going on, there's no way they caught that! You can't leave just because I–"

"You really think it's worth the risk?" Casey snapped, finally breaking from her ice. "If they start sniffing around, it could lead them straight here. It's no secret I'm friends with these guys. My bike's loud enough to wake half the town."

"So? They don't know we're all werewolves!"

"Those louts are professional monster hunters–you really think they won't be able to figure it out?"

Roman opened his mouth, but he couldn't seem to find another argument. Casey rounded back on Vincent.

"We don't have much time. Pack your shit."

Vincent shook his head, more out of helplessness than anything. "We can't leave. This is our place." He didn't want to say the word *home*, because it wasn't–not really. They were guests, at the end of the day. But it felt like home to him, as much now as the college had when he lived there. The thought of leaving yet again was almost unbearable.

"Yeah, well we fucked that one right up, didn't we?" Casey turned away, making for the stairs.

"Where would we even go?" Vincent followed her, ignoring Roman as they swept past him up the steps. "Casey, please think this–"

"My parents' house. It's all the way in southern California. They wouldn't follow us there."

"What if they did?" Vincent challenged, stopping in the doorway to their room as Casey began flitting about, throwing her belongings into a large backpack. "You think they'd stop just because we crossed state lines?"

"Well it'd be a hell of a lot harder to find us." Casey paused to face him with a thundercloud looming on her face. "I mean it, Vincent. We're going. I won't put these guys in danger because of our shitty decisions."

"*What* shitty decisions?" Vincent snarled, heat flaring in his chest. "If you think I'm going to apologize for trying to stop Benjamin–for torturing Jake, for–just because it pissed off Henry enough to sic the Shadowhand on us–"

"You went to the goddamn graduation, Vincent!" Casey's outrage pinned him where he stood, his mouth agape. But then the tide of her fury ebbed, turning instead to a flicker of something almost sad in her dark eyes. "And I went to help you."

Vincent's heart dropped into his stomach. He was silent for a long time.

Casey shook her head, finally turning back to her packing as if she couldn't bear to look at him any longer. "So stop arguing. Pack your shit."

A last flame of miserable defiance rose inside Vincent. "Why are you coming with me, then? Why not just leave me to find my own way out?"

She paused, without looking back. "I told you," she said quietly, too quietly for Casey Helliker. "We're in this together, now."

Hot shame swelled inside him, snuffing out that last mote of rebellion. His shoulders sagged, and he watched her for a moment more, as if waiting for her to change her mind. She didn't. She kept stuffing things roughly into her bag, as if taking out her frustration on them.

The only reason he had this place, this pack, was because of her. He knew that. And he also knew she was right–he could never put them in jeopardy because of his mistakes. It had been hard enough justifying staying here before now, knowing his involvement with Benjamin and the portal to Hell would give the Shadowhand all the more reason to suspect everyone living in Dexter's Laboratory. Knowing he was completely indebted to Dex and his packmates and their generosity. Now...there was no question. Now that the Shadowhand had seen his face, heard his name and Casey's, knew their forms...it was only a matter of time before they connected the dots, all the way here.

Moving slowly, as if in a dream, Vincent began to pack his things.

He barely had anything at all. Some clothes and toiletries, some jewelry, his favorite leather jacket, a blanket Dex had given him during the winter, some books. As he packed, a glint of silver caught his eye from inside his bag. Something thick caught in his throat.

He reached inside and drew it out. It was a necklace cast in silver, its pendant a large, oval-shaped turquoise stone with a sizable crack down the middle. It was striking in spite of its condition, and carried a strange aura about it that reminded Vincent distinctly of the darkness in the air outside, filled with shadows half-there, half-gone.

Percy's amulet. Once, it housed spirits. But after Benjamin used its power to break open the portal to Hell, it was empty. It had failed to protect its rightful owner, and now Percy was gone forever.

Or...was he?

Vincent had done his best to keep last fall's events out of his mind, but it hadn't stopped him from wondering what had happened to Percy. He had been a ghost for so long, trapped in his and Vincent's shared dorm room. And after that, he had possessed Ava Mistral. When they all failed to stop Benjamin from murdering her, the last sacrifice he needed to break the portal, Percy had disappeared.

The first time he had died, he went to the place he was most familiar and most comfortable with. Vincent always had a feeling that if he still existed out there as a ghost, that was where he would be found.

But how would he ever be able to face him again, even if he was there? It was Vincent's fault he was dead, twice over.

Maybe it was better to leave Alderwood, after all. Now that Henry was gone, there was nothing left for him here but memories he couldn't bear.

Just as he was stuffing the amulet in his jacket pocket, he heard a commotion downstairs.

Both he and Casey froze. They held their breath, listening. Roman's voice came through clearly, and then...

Dex. Sloane. Hadley. They were back.

Vincent slung his bag over his shoulder, making a break for the door. He hurried downstairs, Casey on his tail, and found their housemates all clustered together in the kitchen. They were human-formed now and in various states of undress as they scrounged for clothes and towels. Scanning the room, he was relieved to count all of them present–Rolf, Terry, Sloane, Virgil, Hadley, Dex. All of them were dirt-stained, but no blood-scent reached Vincent's nose. He relaxed a little.

"Casey! Vincent!" Rolf and Terry hurried forward to greet them. Dex followed more slowly, his eyes wide as he took in their condition.

"What happened to you?" Sloane eyed them dubiously.

Vincent's throat closed before he could answer. Casey on the other hand didn't hesitate. "After we heard Vincent's howl, I found him just outside campus. The Shadowhand were after him, but they found Roman first, the whelp." She cast another glare at the kid.

"I almost lost my goddamn mind!" Hadley thundered, stomping up to her son. "Don't you *ever* do that again! We had no idea what had happened to you! We heard gunshots, and–" She stopped, unable to continue, but her face was reddening with barely-suppressed fury.

"Sorry," Roman muttered, avoiding his mother's gaze. In that moment he sounded just like his father. Virgil himself moved to his wife's side, touching a large but gentle hand to Roman's arm just under his bandages. He winced.

"What were you doing?" Virgil asked in his deep, unflappable voice.

"I–I wanted to help." Roman grabbed his father's olive branch like a lifeline. "I thought it'd be dangerous, Casey going alone..."

"It was dangerous for *you!*" Hadley snapped. Only a quelling glance from Virgil seemed to settle her, however unhappily.

"Well, we saved the little ingrate's life," Casey broke in gruffly. "He got himself caught by the Shadowhand, and we bargained him out. With a little help from our teeth, that is," she added with a flash of a grin, unable to help herself.

"You *what?*" Hadley hissed, looking from Roman to Casey and Vincent and back again in horror. "How did you–how could you–is he–"

"Nobody knows who he is," Vincent finally spoke, keeping his eyes on the floor. "But...Casey and I had to reveal ourselves to negotiate with them."

His words seemed to echo through the kitchen. They were met with a resounding silence as they sank in.

"You're...you're leaving," said Dex, his shrewd eyes lingering on their packed bags.

"We have to." Casey's voice cracked. She cleared her throat softly. "We're going somewhere to hide. I'm not gonna tell you where, in case they catch you and want it out of you. We've done enough to put you in danger."

"Tell them they don't have to go!" Roman burst out. All eyes fell on him as he rounded on Dex. "We can fix this, there has to be a way! Maybe if they hide out really good, and they don't leave the house–"

Dex rested a hand on Roman's good shoulder, but he winced anyway. He held the kid's gaze for a long moment before he heaved a deep, rueful sigh. He looked directly at Casey and Vincent.

"No. They can't stay here."

Roman blinked, thunderstruck. "What? Are you serious? You're gonna kick 'em out?"

Dex and Casey shared a long look, brimming with an unspoken understanding.

"They'll always be a part of the pack," Dex said, both forlorn and resolute. "But if the Shadowhand trace 'em here, we're sitting ducks."

"So you're just gonna leave 'em to die?" Roman's voice rose in outrage.

Dex's hand tightened on his shoulder. From the look on his face, he felt the same way Roman did, but his mind was clearer. "The pack's safety comes first. What use is it if the rest of us get caught, too? Besides," he added, looking back at Casey, "I think they got a good plan, if I know Casey Helliker."

In spite of everything, Casey's mouth twitched into a wry smile. It was a sad look, and Vincent's heart twisted horribly. Looking across at everyone, all the companions he had come to know and rely on and laugh with over the last few months, he felt for the third time in his life that he had committed a terrible, unforgivable betrayal.

Is this what my life is meant to be? One after another? Always running?

But they were backed into a corner. However he felt, there was no other option right now.

"It'll blow over at some point, man," said Terry, clapping Vincent on the back. He offered him a crooked, reassuring smile that didn't quite land. "Then you can come back."

Rolf nodded fervently, but he couldn't quite hide his own regret either. "We'll stay in touch, yeah? Let you know as soon as those bastards get bored and clear out."

Vincent wanted to believe them, to absorb their optimism and let it be a see-you-later rather than a goodbye. But he wasn't that foolish.

"It's not that simple," he said, his expression grim. "Not anymore."

"What do you mean?" asked Sloane.

Vincent glanced at Casey warily, knowing it might make her angrier to discover he had kept this from her. But he owed his friends the truth, after everything.

"Melanie King tried to reveal us to everyone. The whole graduation audience. I know the Shadowhand are all over it, but...I think she might have succeeded."

Everyone stared at him, hard.

"Us?" Dex pressed.

"Us. You know...the Others. She got in an argument with Henry Wellfellow, and...his girlfriend, Sierra Pechman." He still didn't want to believe it was true. That they were together, that Sierra was trapped in this mess with the rest of them now... "She was caught in the crossfire of what happened last fall. I didn't realize it until now, but...she was turned. She's a werewolf. She showed herself in front of everyone."

"How did you miss that?" Sloane frowned.

"I don't know, okay? I just didn't think about it." He had pushed it out of his mind, more like. He remembered considering it, once, in the beginning.

But he had slipped into the routine of this place and its safety, and it had been so long since news of the college and its students had reached his ears...

"But that could cost us–a rogue werewolf roaming around town, calling attention to herself–"

"It didn't until now!" Vincent snarled, flashing his teeth at Sloane. "I didn't think it would be a problem."

Sloane made a hissing sound between her teeth, narrowing her eyes at him. "Any other suspects you'd like to share before you leave us with your mess?"

"Shut up, Sloane." To Vincent's surprise, Casey growled at her packmate without a second thought. "He's been through enough, alright? We're cleaning it up best we can for you, so stuff it."

Sloane bristled, but Dex stepped in. "Leave it." He gave Sloane a hard look until she broke eye contact with him, tutting under her breath. Then he turned back to Vincent and Casey, worry clouding his gaze. "I dunno what they're gonna do about all that. But it's too late now. Maybe, if anything, it'll keep the Shadowhand busy with damage control more than hounding our asses."

"We *should* have found this girl and kept her with us," Sloane dared to say, although she kept her eyes averted.

"Henry knows how to make a potion to suppress the curse," Vincent said. "You remember me telling you that? I just assumed even on the off-chance she *was* turned, he would keep it under wraps. I...just don't understand why he didn't," he added, some of his ferocity fading as he thought harder about it.

Dex frowned. "You got a point there. But there's no point to guessing now. We'll try and find this girl, if we can swing it safely."

"You will?" Vincent looked at him hopefully, a little surprised by his sudden charity. Then again, this was Dex. Maybe he shouldn't be.

Dex nodded, smiling unhappily. "Course. She's one of us."

Some of Vincent's anxiety drained away, without realizing she had been the source of it until now. But there was still plenty left.

"Won't she lead the Shadowhand straight to us, just like Vincent and Casey?" Roman piped up, some of his temper flaring again. Vincent was surprised he had made this strong of an impression on the kid, to earn such a defense. It only made him feel worse.

"I said we'd find her. I didn't say we'd keep her with us."

Sloane made a little snort.

"That's fair. Thanks, Dex," Vincent said. He knew it was unreasonable to expect anything more. "She's a good person. She deserves the help. She was...a friend of mine, for a while."

"Be safe, will you?" Dex moved to rest one hand on Vincent's shoulder, the other on Casey's beside him. He shook them affectionately, despite the cloud of regret in his dark eyes.

Casey nodded. "It's a safe place, I swear it. Don't worry about us."

Despite the tension in the room, everyone–even Sloane–seemed determined to ignore it. They all felt the sorrow as they crowded around Casey and Vincent, each of them getting a goodbye touch in as they murmured their laments.

"Don't worry about us, either," said Rolf, with that half-hearted smile.

"Yeah, we got this safe house shit runnin' like clockwork," Terry grinned.

"It'll be quiet without you two around," said Sloane, with true remorse.

"Maybe you'll finally get enough beauty sleep," Casey teased, her ire dissipating. "Keep these idiots in line."

"Oh, fuck you," Terry laughed.

"Someone's gotta," Sloane sniffed, returning her smile.

"Well, the squirt will make sure you're not too bored without us," Casey sneered.

"What does that mean?" Roman growled, puffing up.

"You've caused enough trouble," Hadley snapped back at him, quelling him. She looked back to Vincent and Casey, her startlingly green eyes carrying a sheen of emotion. "And we can't thank you enough for...for what you did. Saving him. I'm just sorry it led to this..."

Virgil at her side nodded stoically, his expression grave. "We will make sure everyone is safe."

"We'll hold you to that," said Casey. She looked to Roman, who glared back at her defiantly. It was an obvious ruse; his eyes resembled his mother's, even now. "Take it easy, alright, kiddo?"

"Stop calling me shit like that," Roman retorted, but it had no bite to it. Hadley nudged him hard, and he grumbled something to himself.

Vincent approached him, allowing his regret to show on his face.

"Take care of them. They rely on you just as much as you do them."

Roman blinked, taken aback. It was a long moment before he seemed to understand, nodding slowly, uncertainly.

"But...you better come back, alright? Wherever you're going, it's not the same as here," he insisted hotly.

Vincent fought a smile. "Sure."

"Don't be a stranger," said Dex, and one look told them he meant it. He looked miserable. But he knew what had to be done. "Keep in touch."

"Yeah, yeah..." said Casey, awkwardly.

Vincent's heart twisted, reading her sorrow in a way he was surprised to find came easily now. He had let her down, too, even if she was staying by his side. She didn't deserve this.

He didn't deserve her, he realized. It was an awful thought, and he pushed it away glumly for later.

Instead, he met Dex's gaze, holding it for a long, heavy moment. They understood each other. "I'm sorry, Dex." His voice came so quiet, he wondered if any of the others could hear it. "And thank you."

Dex's mouth twitched up into the slightest smile, the smallest sign of his camaraderie, his acceptance, his remorse.

Neither Vincent nor Casey was fond of long goodbyes. They soon ducked away from the crowd, and before they knew it they were stepping out into the trees behind the house again, the way they had come only hours before. This time the gray world beyond was pale, almost ghostly in the morning mist. It seemed just as hollow as it felt in Vincent's chest.

As they walked into the forest, only the sound of crunching leaves under their feet broke the silence. It seemed far too loud; even Casey couldn't seem to withstand it.

"You didn't want to think about Henry, huh." It wasn't a question. "That's why you didn't think about Sierra going wolf."

Vincent didn't look at her. He couldn't answer.

CHAPTER 5

THE DESERTERS

Vincent's first step out of the airport was met with a cool ocean breeze. It was warmer here by far than springtime in Oregon. A fluffy blanket of gray covered the sky, and the faint smell of salt mixed with gasoline. His eyes lingered on the impossibly tall palm trees dotting the sidewalk, their fronds rippling high above. This was entirely new.

He gazed up and down the street outside the terminal, packed with a line of idling cars and passengers loading up their luggage. He had never seen so many people in one place before—well, living ones, that is. And yet, they seemed to pay him no mind at all. He didn't need to try and disappear, here. The airplane itself had been similarly cramped and considerably more discomfiting, relieved only by tiny bags of free pretzels and Vincent's awe at the view out the little window beside him. Casey had even switched seats with him to make sure he got to see it.

As he sat beside her in the backseat of their Uber, his thoughts drifted back to that vast, yet miniscule world he had seen far below. Somehow he had never imagined just how enormous the mortal world truly was—how many countless creatures existed in the hundreds of thousands of miles he watched pass by. It suddenly felt that much more possible to disappear.

As they left the terminal, the view opened out onto the city harbor and the wide, dark ocean beyond. Again that sense of vastness returned to him, and he strained his eyes towards the horizon, imagining where it might truly end. It was almost dizzying to think about, and the feeling settled in the pit of his stomach with a satisfying thrill.

Soon the world closed back up, swallowed by endless buildings jostling each other for space on their blocks. Vincent kept silent throughout the ride, watching as the landscape slowly faded from coastal city to open chaparral. It was the closest thing to desert he had ever seen, rescued only by swathes of low brush covering the hills. The cloud cover thinned until it had burned away entirely, revealing rich blue sky that felt infinite, unbroken by trees or buildings. Vincent leaned his head against the window to look up at it until vertigo forced him to retreat. He wanted to roll down the glass and stick his head out–something he had taken great pleasure in before, when Henry was driving–but he had a feeling the Uber driver wouldn't take as kindly to it.

Finally, after what felt like hours, the car turned off the highway and trundled down a long dirt road through the brush. A house rose into view, surrounded only by rocky hills and open space. It was large and rather impressive, especially compared to Dexter's Laboratory, its facade the color of sand and its roof fashioned of red tile.

Vincent swayed on his feet as he got out, reacquainting himself with his own legs. The car drove off, and both Casey and Vincent lugged their packs up to the front door. Casey took the lead, but hesitated before ringing the doorbell. It had a metal frame shaped like a lizard. Vincent almost smiled at it, despite the nerves roiling in his stomach. He had had a long flight to wonder how well her parents would take their arrival. He only hoped they were more welcoming than Casey was, at first. The grimace she had worn since divulging the plan seemed to say otherwise.

The door opened. A middle-aged woman stared back at them, her short black hair streaked with gray and her narrow, dark eyes identical to Casey's. Her features were rounder overall and her skin darker, but something in her expression was distinctly Casey.

Before Casey could even open her mouth, the woman cried, "Casey?"

"Uh, hi, *má*."

"Come, come in!" Casey's mother ushered her inside with an urgent hand. Casey exchanged a glance with Vincent before creeping in after her, as if she thought her mother had planted landmines on the doorstep. Vincent followed quietly.

The inside was just as vast as the outside. Polished wood met Vincent's eyes nearly everywhere he looked, accompanied by splashes of color from rugs and pottery. Everything was elegant and clean, but with an aura of desert wilderness that felt more welcoming. Vincent decided he liked it.

Casey paused in the entryway to remove her shoes, and Vincent copied her, suppressing his curiosity. Then Casey's mother led them down the short entry hall into the sitting room. The far wall was taken up nearly completely by glass, which opened out into a wide view of the scrubland and mountains beyond. The afternoon sun cast a rosy, golden glow upon the hills, tingeing them indigo in the distance. Vincent chose a spot on a sofa closest to the window, deciding it would be his refuge against the looming conversation.

"I knew you would be back," said Casey's mother, with a note of triumph. She had a distinct accent that softened her words, melding them into one another. It was a stark contrast to her sharp manner of speaking. "You know we would have come to your graduation, though, if you invited us."

Casey stared at the rug, chewing her lip. "Yeah. Well, I'm here."

"Sit up straight. Did you forget your manners in Oregon?"

Casey did so with an obvious air of resentment, but didn't argue. Vincent decided to take the cue, making sure he was as upright as could be. He saw Casey's mother's eyes flick over towards him.

"He is staying too, I assume? Does he treat you well?"

Both he and Casey blanched. They looked at each other.

"Oh–I'm not–"

"Yeah. Yes, he does."

Vincent stared at Casey in shock, but she kept her attention trained on her mother. She donned a happy mask that wasn't able to entirely cover her strain. But her mother didn't seem to notice. She only nodded sharply.

"Good. Better than your last boyfriend. I should hope you learned your lesson, after what happened."

That piqued Vincent's interest, but he knew better than to ask. Instead, he recognized the role he had to play here–whether he liked what was going on or not. He turned to Casey's mother.

"It's good to meet you finally. I'm sorry we couldn't manage the trip earlier." He put on his best smile, all the while thinking, *Be like Henry. Make her like you.*

Casey's mother looked at him discerningly, and then she smiled back. He realized it was the first time he had seen it. It made her look like an entirely different person, someone kindly and warm.

"It's good to know you take your studies seriously. And you are here now. What is your name?"

"Vincent Chálkinos. Thank you so much for your welcome. Please let me know if I can do anything to help you while I'm here."

Her smile stayed. She liked that. "Tell me, Vincent, how are your family?"

Vincent glanced at Casey awkwardly. But she wasn't going to help him out of this.

"Ah...fine. They live far away, in Greece."

Casey's mother nodded appreciatively. "Ahh. Will they come for the wedding?"

Vincent nearly choked on his own breath. He buried his face in the crook of his arm to cough, while Casey said, "Um, probably. There's just a lot of them, so it might be hard to get them here..."

"Has he proposed already?" Casey's mother all but interrupted. Vincent felt her gaze hard on him before he emerged from his coughing fit.

"C-can I have some water, please?" He did *not* want to go down that rabbit hole.

This seemed to work. Casey's mother stood abruptly, saying, "Of course, of course!" She hurried out of the room, leaving them with a merciful minute on their own.

"You didn't tell me she'd think we're together!" Vincent hissed.

"I-I didn't think she would!" To her credit, Casey looked aghast. "I'm sorry! I guess I should've, considering it's her..."

"Why don't we just tell her the truth?"

"I don't know if she'd let you stay too," Casey admitted, hunching her shoulders guiltily. "I mean, I was banking on the chance she would, but...this is so *easy*. She won't kick you out now, no way."

Easy wasn't the word Vincent would have chosen. "What, so am I supposed to pretend we're getting married?"

Casey shrugged, playing with the hem of the couch cushion. "I mean...you don't have to go *that* far. If she asks again, just say you're planning a proposal, or something."

Vincent frowned. His throat was still tight–he hadn't realized he would have to act his heart out in order to stay. He had to wonder how long he could keep this up. *Or how long I'll need to.*

Just then, Casey's mother swept back into the living room, carrying a pretty silver tray laden with tea and water. She laid it down on the coffee table and began pouring drinks for everyone. Vincent drank half his glass of water before deciding to try the tea she offered him. It was mild, but had an herbal, earthy flavor he found very pleasant.

"Thank you, Mrs. Helliker. It's very good."

Again came her smile, although it was barely suppressed this time as she dipped her head to him graciously.

"You are welcome here. Casey will help you settle." She looked to her daughter expectantly. "He can stay in the room across from yours."

Casey stood abruptly. "Thanks, *má*."

Vincent did the same, but before they could leave, Casey's mother stopped her. "Casey?"

Casey turned to face her nervously.

Her mother almost smiled, but in the end it fell like a shadow to a more complicated expression that flitted over her aging features.

"I'm happy you're home."

Casey offered a smile back, just as complicated but distinctly unsure.

Neither of them seemed able to hold the moment. "Your father will be home soon. I have dinner on the stove. I will call you when it's ready."

Casey made a noncommittal grunt. She couldn't leave the room fast enough, and Vincent followed her awkwardly.

The shadows in the hall swallowed them, offering them some respite. Vincent felt like he could finally breathe again.

"She's not going to make us share a wedding bed?" Vincent said dryly.

Casey cast him a glare over her shoulder as she stopped beside two doors. "Not until you marry me. Consider yourself lucky."

Vincent sighed, trying to force away his annoyance. He knew he should be grateful, having a safe place to stay like this. It just wasn't at all what he expected.

What did *I expect?* He didn't really know.

Casey opened one of the doors, revealing a guest room decorated simply, but in the same elegant style as the common areas. Vincent gratefully set down his pack on the bed's blankets, feeling suddenly very weary.

"Make yourself at home, loverboy," Casey snorted from the doorway. "And don't bother me."

She turned and disappeared through the door just across the dark hall.

Vincent wanted to close his door, too, but he wasn't sure if it would seem rude to their host. Instead he lay back on the bedspread, gazing up at the ceiling numbly. What had he gotten himself into?

Soon the muffled thud and shriek of heavy metal music began drifting from behind Casey's door. It became a strange backdrop to his exhaustion, until finally Casey's mother's voice broke through it, calling them for dinner. A new thrill of nerves coursed through his stomach as he thought of meeting Casey's father, too. But he knew there was no way around it, so he pushed himself up and knocked on Casey's door.

"Casey? Your mother says dinner–"

"Yeah, I heard!" The music stopped, and moments later Casey emerged, looking just as put out as he felt.

She led him to the dining room, where a large table was already filled with a spread of what looked like serving bowls of rice, grilled vegetables, and meat, alongside a deep brown vegetable soup and plates of leafy salad. Her mother was just finishing arranging things while her father sat at the head of the table, still dressed in his business clothes. He looked nothing like Casey, rather a tall, ashy-haired white man, and Vincent recalled her mentioning a stepfather. But he offered Vincent a polite smile nonetheless, and a much wider one for his daughter.

"Casey!" He stood, holding his arms out for her, and she reluctantly went over to give him a swift hug. He patted her back awkwardly at the end of it and let her go. "It's so good to see you. Your mom tells me you're staying with us now, is that right?"

"Yeah. If that's okay."

"Of course it is! I'm so glad you decided to come home. And that you got your degree–we're very proud of you."

Something in Casey's face told Vincent she didn't quite believe it. But she kept up appearances regardless, and the two of them sat down next to each other at the table.

"Good degree means good job," Casey's mother put in as she took her own seat and started passing the rice bowl around. "Ryan is starting his own business in Temecula, did he tell you? He just got a loan."

"I haven't talked to him in a while," Casey said quietly.

"Maybe you can help him," said Casey's father. "I'm sure he needs it, getting off the ground."

"Don't I need to make money? I assume he needs all of it for whatever it is he's doing..."

"Financial analytics. And that's what the loan is for. I'm sure he's accounting for payroll needs in his startup costs."

"Sounds thrilling." Casey pushed some of her vegetables around in her bowl.

"What are you planning to do?" Casey's mother interjected, giving her a hard stare.

Casey shrugged, not looking up. "I'll figure something out."

Vincent tried to tune out the conversation to focus on his rice bowl, which almost made up for the rest of the awkward experience–vegetables and pork in a glistening sauce, punching his senses with a salty, spicy, earthy flavor. He quickly decided it was one of the best things he had eaten in the mortal realm so far.

"What does Vincent do?"

Vincent started. "Ah..."

"Nothing, yet," Casey said, to his relief. At least, somewhat. "He's only just graduated too, y'know."

"Well, do you have a plan?" Casey's stepfather asked.

Both of them sank lower in their seats.

"We'll start applying for places in town," Casey said finally, glumly.

"Not very good prospects," Casey's mother warned.

"It's a start," Casey countered.

"You should ask Ryan."

"I don't want to step on his toes."

Vincent had a feeling Casey wouldn't actually mind doing just that, literally or figuratively.

"If you have no plans, you should rely on family!" Casey's mother insisted.

Vincent could already tell an argument was brewing. Apparently, so could Casey's stepfather.

"Casey, would you take some dinner to your grandparents?"

"They aren't ready yet," Casey's mother protested. "I gave them food at four."

"Well, we shouldn't let it get cold. Maybe they'll want some now."

Casey grunted and left the table. An unnerving silence descended over the rest of them. After a moment she returned with more bowls and began serving up portions, then disappeared down the hall.

"What did you study, Vincent?" Casey's stepfather asked cordially as he ate.

"Philosophy."

Both of Casey's parents frowned. Vincent had no idea why. Casey's stepfather recovered first, but that was the end of the attempt at conversation.

"I'm, ah...going to go help Casey," Vincent said quickly.

He stood up and wandered down the hall, feeling more alien than he had in some time. He heard voices behind a door just off the living room, and quietly opened it. He was surprised to find another hallway this direction, opening out into what felt like a second, smaller house. He made his way through another living room towards another hall and a bedroom larger than his, where he found Casey.

She was bent over one side of a large bed, spooning rice into the mouth of an ancient-looking woman. She might have borne a striking resemblance to Casey's mother were it not for the copious folds and lines in her face, as if her visage were a riverbed that had long since cracked and run dry. Her rheumy eyes lifted to Vincent when he entered, as did those of the tiny man with wispy white hair beside her.

The man spoke in a slow, halting drone, in another language: "Who is this?"

"I'm Vincent," he answered immediately, before realizing his error. The man's narrow eyes widened slightly.

"He speaks Vietnamese?" he said to Casey in shock.

"Is he yours?" the woman croaked out, half-chewing still. Some rice was sticking to her upper lip. "Is he handsome?"

"Ah...yeah." Vincent wished he could see Casey's expression. All he got was a quick glance over her shoulder, a warning look.

"I studied languages in college," Vincent spoke in Vietnamese again, approaching the bed gingerly. He hoped it wasn't too late to tack that onto philosophy, for Casey's parents' sake.

"He's Greek," Casey added.

"I like him," the old woman said, the corners of her mouth twitching into an effortful smile. "Have him feed me."

Her husband scoffed, but it was filled with amusement. Casey exchanged a questioning glance with Vincent, but he didn't want to be rude. He took her place awkwardly, carefully lifting spoonfuls of food to her grandmother's mouth. Her appetite seemed to pick up, somehow.

"You look happy," the old man said to Casey.

Casey blinked in surprise. She too looked uncomfortable. "Do I?"

"We're happy you're home," said her grandmother between bites. "Are you staying, now?"

"...Yeah."

The old woman's smile widened. "Good. Home is where you belong. Will you come and feed me my meals? We missed you. Your mother is such a drag."

Finally Casey managed a grin.

The two of them spent some time with Casey's grandparents during their meal, before returning to their own. They excused themselves the instant they finished, making for the hall; they were only stopped for a moment by a:

"Separate rooms, Casey!"

"I *know, má*," Casey growled, flushing. She ducked into the shadow of the hall. Vincent followed helplessly, also feeling rather awkward. He felt Casey's mother's eyes boring into his back until he closed the door to his room behind him.

He laid on the bed for a while, tired but unable to sleep. He watched as many YouTube thinkpieces he could find on his phone before he could no longer justify staying up. He then dragged himself through the motions of cleaning up and arranging his personal effects, although he didn't unpack too much. It still didn't feel like much of a home, despite the nice decor. He wasn't sure it ever would.

Finally he shut the light off and crawled under the covers, preparing for a long and restless night. Just as he was beginning to drift, he heard the clunk of his door opening.

He shot upright, but instantly his keen night vision picked out Casey's form slinking across the room.

"Keep your fur on, it's just me," she hissed.

"What are you doing here?" Vincent asked, baffled.

"Don't worry, my parents are asleep by now."

She sat on the bed at his side, her expression unreadable. Silence fell; she didn't seem eager to get to the point.

"You didn't answer me," Vincent prompted.

Casey shot him a glare, but it was half-hearted. "Can't sleep."

Vincent sighed. "You too, ah?"

Casey shrugged. "Just...weird, being home."

"Do you really think they'll let us stay?"

"Yeah. Long as we get jobs."

"I had a feeling." Vincent was quiet for a moment. "But I don't know how to do that."

"Well, I don't either."

"Your mother said something about your brother's business, right...?"

"No," Casey snapped. "I'm not gonna be a goddamn coffee monkey for my *illustrious* big brother. My parents can go to hell."

Vincent couldn't exactly blame her. "What if it's the only way to stay?"

Casey shook her head sharply. "We'll figure something else out. They won't kick us out right away anyway. You heard 'em–they want us to stay and *provide for the family*," she said in a mocking voice.

"I mean...I think it's fair, considering."

"Well, fuck that. I'm not just gonna play housemaid or breadwinner or whatever because they tell me to. I don't owe them shit."

Vincent looked at her dubiously. "They *are* sheltering us."

"So what? I'm their kid. They chose to have me–I didn't choose to be born."

That left an echo in the silence between them.

Eventually, Casey let out a rough sigh. "Just...don't worry about it. I'll tell them we're applying places."

"What *are* we going to do, then?"

"I don't know!"

Casey stopped, gritting her teeth.

"...I don't know. Okay?"

Even if Casey wasn't one for planning, it was a strange thing to see her looking so lost. Normally she at least pretended she didn't care about anything, that everything would turn out alright. But now she felt like a hunted animal, unsure of her steps, waiting for something to spring from the shadows and capture her.

Vincent could see she needed reassurance. More than that, she *deserved* it–she had gotten them this far. He had no idea where he would be now without her.

Fighting through his own uncertainty, he rested a tentative hand on her shoulder. He felt her tense under his palm.

"You grew up here, right? There has to be some old haunts nearby. You can show me around tomorrow–make a vacation out of it. I think we've earned it, don't you?"

Casey looked over her shoulder, meeting his gaze in the dark. She studied him for a long moment before her lips twitched with the faintest smile.

"Yeah. Alright."

At first Vincent thought he was imagining things, but then it registered– Casey had leaned into his touch, ever so slightly.

Then, just as soon as she had, she moved away again. She stood.

"Get some rest, yeah? I feel like I haven't had any since before the full moon."

Vincent nodded. "I'll try."

But as soon as she left, he felt peculiarly alone. He stared up at the dark ceiling for a while, fighting off the dim, nagging hope that he would see Henry again in his dreams. Even if it staved off that loneliness for a little while...he knew he would only feel worse when he woke.

The next day, Casey announced that she was taking Vincent into town. As she led him down the lone road out into the scrubland, the rising sun bore down on them with a cruelty Vincent had not expected. Out in the open air, his eyes quickly began to water and his nose dried, until Casey made fun of him for sneezing too much. He found himself missing the forests and fog in Alderwood that kept the heat at bay as spring turned to summer.

The journey took them at least a couple miles from the house, which gave Vincent some comfort that it would be difficult for any Shadowhand to track them out so far–if they even made it here. The town proper was charming, most of its buildings in a similar style to Casey's house, all red tile and brick and stucco surrounded by rolling hills and plains of farmland. Casey took him on a tour, showing him the teeming farmers market, the old-school movie theater, the winery with a giant barrel outside that she used to climb with her friends, the antique car museum they used to sneak into, the old repair shop she used to work for as a teenager during the summer. She stopped there the longest, hovering just outside the closed-up garage with a complicated expression.

"So…that's why you made friends with Dex and the pack, ah?" Vincent guessed.

Casey shrugged. "Convenient, really. They got me into motorcycles. My parents would never let me have one."

"What they don't know won't hurt them, right?"

Casey flashed him a lopsided grin. She took a piece of gum from her pocket and shoved it in her mouth. Then she kept walking past the shop.

"Can I have a piece?" Vincent asked. She was always chewing gum–he figured it had to be good.

"Fuck no." Casey threw him a smirk. He wasn't sure why until she said, "It's nicotine gum."

She began chewing fastidiously and almost smugly as they passed more buildings. "And there's the liquor store his cousin owned. Never carded us, the crazy bastard."

"*His?* Who's 'him'?"

Casey faltered. Vincent realized instantly that he had struck a nerve. She stood there for far too long. He was beginning to wonder if she would ever move again, when she finally did. She strode off so quickly he almost had to run to catch up.

"Casey?"

"My ex."

Vincent was surprised she answered at all. But she didn't slow down. After a minute he had enough of it.

"Casey, wait up, will you?" he panted.

To her credit, she listened, although with a grimace.

"I'm...sorry I asked," he said.

"Me too. I'm damn well ready to forget the asshole."

"I wish it was that easy." Vincent wasn't sure if he meant it, though. Not for who he was thinking about. After a moment a tingle of shame coursed through him—he could hardly call Henry an "ex." He had no right to relate the two.

"C'mon, dumbass," Casey said, taking his wrist and dragging him on. "I want ice cream. And not 'cause of the ex thing."

They stopped at a dilapidated little building with walk-up windows. The neon sign above it said "Northern Lights" in green and pink. Casey stuck her used gum on the lid of a nearby trash can before ordering. They got soft serve cones dipped in chocolate, which hardened on the outside and created a satisfying crunch. Vincent hardly registered where he was walking as he followed Casey through town, blissfully lost in his cone. At least, until she halted so abruptly on the path he nearly crashed into her.

"Hey! I almost dropped–" He stopped when he noticed her gaze trained on something just ahead. He could practically see her fur bristling, even though she was quite human at the moment.

It was an older man, leaning against the wall in the shade of a brick building. His graying hair was long and unkempt, his skin leathery and sun-baked, overgrown with body hair that his patchy clothes couldn't seem to tame. Nothing quite fit on him. Even his eyes were sunken deep into his skull, so deeply shaded beneath his brow that they were little more than a glitter. He was watching them, too.

"Casey?" Vincent murmured, nudging her. "What–"

His touch seemed to unfreeze her. She lurched ahead, her stride quickening. "It's nothing. C'mon."

He had no choice but to follow, but he watched the old man out of the corner of his eye as he passed. The stranger didn't move or even speak. Soon they had left him far behind.

"Casey?" Vincent said again, as soon as they were clear. "Is everything okay? Who was that?"

"No one," she answered stiffly. But Vincent caught a puzzled note there, too. "Just some hobo, I guess. He just...reminded me of someone."

"Who?"

"Doesn't matter," she snapped. "Everything's fine, so drop it."

Vincent bit his lip to stop himself from pressing. He was tired of being at odds with her. She seemed to share the sentiment; a moment later she added more gently, "Your ice cream's melting."

He grudgingly returned to it as they walked on. The cool rush of sweet cream soothed his senses, and after a few licks he decided he owed it to her to trust her word.

Finally they reached a little square with benches and manicured trees. A miniature clock tower at its center showed eleven o'clock. A man sat on the steps at one end, plucking at a guitar with practiced ease. A couple of families with young children sat nearby, chattering and enjoying their lunches. A warm breeze lifted Vincent's hair, as if to help him keep it away from the mess he was making of his ice cream. Here, it was easy to forget his anxiety–and not just for Casey. This place may have harbored some ghosts from her past...but it had a lot more to offer, too.

In fact, for the first time since they had gotten off the plane, everything felt...okay. Good, even. Maybe they could make this work, after all.

"Your grandparents seem to like me," Vincent said, following his thought. "I don't know about your parents..."

Casey sighed. "You really can't just let us enjoy the day, can you?"

Before he could reply, though, she went on:

"I think they do. At least, in their own way. They're just mad I went off to college without telling them."

Vincent looked at her with sudden interest. "You did? Why?"

Casey gave him a pointed glance. "You tell me."

He had a pretty good idea. "I guess I can relate..." Then, he realized something. "You know, you helped me run away from home, too, in the end...but now you're back where you started."

Casey scowled. "Don't remind me."

Guilt nipped at his ribcage. "I'm...sorry about that, Casey. I didn't mean..."

"I know."

Vincent could sense she was finished talking. Instead he looked around at the square again as he finished his ice cream, trying to picture a teenage Casey charging through the place with her gang of cronies. It was a far better look for her than this lonely figure sitting beside him on the bench. He supposed wolves were meant to be with a pack.

Where does that leave me? he wondered.

When the sunlight began to fade, the two of them made the trek back to Casey's house. They saw no more of the strange man, and Vincent did his best to put the encounter out of his mind. Casey's parents thankfully didn't grill them about job-hunting during dinner. Casey later gloated that she might have taught them a thing or two about scaring her off. Once she had kissed her grandparents goodnight and her parents had gone to bed, she and Vincent grabbed some beers from the fridge and went out to the pool. It and the gibbous moon alone illuminated the night, the house dark and silent behind them. The water's shifting blue reflections played over their bodies as they sat at the edge, making ripples in the surface with their legs.

"Where is that lousy ingrate, anyway?" Casey was saying of her older brother, flicking droplets across the pool with her foot. The more she drank, the more she seemed to talk. "Some big hero. I bet he's staying in town. I bet he's paying 'em off, so he doesn't have to take care of 'em himself."

"You mean your grandparents?" Vincent guessed.

"Yeah," Casey said, brandishing her bottle at him. "Easier to throw money at the issue. Actually, he's not even doing that! He's got a business loan, doesn't mean he'll make anything. Doesn't mean he'll send 'em anything, either. But no, *he's* the hero!"

Vincent gazed out at the wedge of moon rippling on the water's surface. "My older sister's the same way."

"Oh, yeah. I think you mentioned her once." Casey took a swig of her beer.

Vincent did the same. "Yeah. I gave Benjamin up to her. I guess she'll get the credit for that, too."

Casey snickered bitterly. "Figures. I guess she's a hellhound like you, ah?"

Vincent nodded.

"She anything like you?"

"Not really. She's always been good at everything."

"What, and you're not?"

Vincent flashed her a meaningful glance. "I mean, I failed at my only duty."

"So? Does that make you a forever-fuckup?"

"Yes."

Casey's brow furrowed. "Seriously?"

Vincent hesitated. "...My father stripped me of my name, when I let Benjamin go. I could only earn it back if I recovered him."

Casey leaned back, propping herself up with one hand on the concrete behind her. "Shit, man." After a moment she said, "What was your name before?"

Vincent answered reluctantly; to Casey, it sounded like *Anendotos.*

"It means 'unyielding.' Now, they refer to me as *Ntropi*–'disgraced.'" He gritted his teeth. "My sister's name is *Superbia.*"

Casey snorted. "More like *Disturbia*. Those don't even sound like names."

"Well, hellhounds are all named in Latin and Greek."

"I doubt I'd run across a normal dude in Greece named Entropy."

"*Ntropi.*"

"Whatever."

"Also, I'm not a *normal dude*. I'm...well, a guard dog."

"A pet." Casey straightened up suddenly. "Well, there you have it–it's a pet's name. It's just a word, right? Not a real name."

Vincent shrugged. He didn't want to answer. He didn't want to think about it, either.

"You talk like your dad's the one calling the shots. Doesn't *Cerberus* mean 'Spot' in Greek? I think I heard that somewhere."

"It means 'flesh-devouring.'"

Casey blinked. "Ah." She was quiet for a moment. She finished her last gulp of beer. "Standout quality. Well, I like Vincent better."

He wasn't sure why or how, but something warmed in his chest. He caught himself smiling at her, and he looked away quickly before she could notice and make fun of him for it.

"I like your family better than mine," he responded.

"I think I do, too," Casey smirked. "Although yours might take me in just as easily as mine did for you. I doubt I'd be able to meet them all–there must be a lot of 'em, if you're supposed to guard all of Hell."

Vincent nodded. "I don't even know all my siblings."

"Sounds more like a breeding program than a family."

Again, Vincent didn't like where this was going. He decided to take a risk, banking on Casey's buzz. "Does your ex still live around here? We're not going to run into him, are we?"

Right on cue, Casey's face fell instantly. But it was far stonier than Vincent had expected.

"No."

Her bottle made a rough *clink* on the concrete as she pushed herself to her feet.

"And don't ask me about him again. I don't want to talk about it."

Vincent wasn't sure if the distraction had been worth it. It brought the otherwise nice evening to an abrupt end–and left him wondering just how bad things had been, to make someone like Casey react like this. There were only a handful of other things that put her on edge so swiftly: Hunter, the man who had been stalking her at college and whom she had attacked, inadvertently turning him into a werewolf as well; Percy, after he possessed Ava and refused to leave her; and...

He realized all at once–Casey had never mentioned exactly how she had been turned into a werewolf. And now, he had a feeling he knew why.

CHAPTER 6

WHISTLEBLOWER

The days melded and blurred with the summer heat as it spread over the land. Vincent and Casey spent much of their time in town or in the pool, artfully dodging her parents and their questions of job applications. However, family dinners were unavoidable. They were always filled with amazing food and obvious care, which left the atmosphere hovering halfway between awkward and cozy.

There was just something about having a somewhat normal family around that made Vincent realize just how different his own was. Even if Casey's mother was strict and proper, he caught the glimmer of concern in her eyes when she looked at her daughter. When Casey's stepfather was home, he encouraged her to pursue some kind of goal, to which she responded vaguely. Despite the tension, there was a familiarity between them all that suffused the home and seeped into the cavity in Vincent's chest, making him feel a nostalgia for something that was never his.

Sometimes his gaze lingered on Casey, wondering how she felt about all this. She always folded in on herself around her parents, despite their care. The only time he really witnessed her unbridled affection was with her grandparents. She dutifully brought them their dinner every evening as requested, chatting with them about the movies they had watched or the news they had read that day or whatever else they felt like reminiscing about. They didn't seem as keen on grilling her about her life goals, and she took to that.

They appeared to enjoy Vincent's company as well, asking him about his own family and his studies and marveling at his near-flawless command of their native tongue. For his part, he filled in the edges of his answers with half-truths, which seemed to appease them. After a few weeks of this routine, he even began to feel like he might have some kind of corner here, in this house. One day, he finally unpacked his things.

And yet, as the days passed and the heat bore down, it slowly began to feel like it had in Dexter's Laboratory. Even though the house itself was bigger, it felt just as small somehow, out in the middle of nowhere with only Casey and her elders to talk to. He wondered more than once if this was why her older brother Ryan had never appeared. It was easy to understand why Casey had left in the first place.

And, nearly every night still, Vincent returned to that golden forest. To a home all his own, that didn't exist. To a Henry that didn't exist. A reminder of everything he could never have. And yet, he couldn't bring himself to hate his dreams–at least, not until he woke.

One evening, as he and Casey were returning from the pool, they caught something on the news her parents were watching that made them stop dead.

"–the whistleblower, so to speak. Miss King, could you tell us a little more about what you saw?"

"Oh, yes. The government has been trying to cover it up for weeks now, but it's impossible to ignore. Everyone around town has seen it."

It was Melanie King. The screen shifted from her face to footage of the pillar of void surging into the sky over Alderwood's treetops.

"I've been telling everyone. They say it's just smoke from some kind of project, but it isn't. Does that look like smoke to you? No–it's a portal to Hell. I've seen the things that come out of it. Hellhounds and vampires and ghosts– they're all real."

The interviewer's eyes widened above her smile, both incredulous and alarmed. "That's quite a claim. But there you have it–whatever that black pillar is, it's causing quite a stir around the little town of Alderwood, Oregon. There is obviously secrecy surrounding it, which makes it a concern for everyone in its proximity. What are your worries for the town?"

"It's not really the town, so much as the world. The sky has been dark ever since it appeared–even in Oregon, it's not normally *this* cloudy, especially in the summer. Well, it's not even clouds!" Melanie laughed lightly. "It's like the portal is tainting the air around it."

She looked directly at the camera now, and Vincent almost felt as if her stark hazel eyes were boring into him. "I know it sounds crazy. But all of you watching out there–pay attention. Things are changing. This is undeniable proof of the supernatural. They've been hiding for a long time now, but it's time for that to change. There's a whole new world of possibility out there, now that we know they exist."

The interviewer took the microphone back. "I understand you've been gaining a lot of traction on social media about this. People are sharing multiple clips of your college graduation speech, and the supposed 'werewolf' that attacked you. Now, there's a lot of skepticism, too–what do you have to say to the people that are claiming you faked the incident?"

Melanie let a sly, humoring smile spread across her face. "Well, Katie, it's like this. I can't force anyone to accept the truth. Some people are always going to scream 'liar.' It's a terrifying thing to accept. It changes everything about the world we know. And I admit, there are a lot of ways to fake videos nowadays. But I will say–wouldn't it be very difficult to fake multiple separate videos of the same event?"

She shook her head. "Really, it's not for me to decide. It's up to all of you. But that's why I encourage everyone to look more closely into things for yourselves. It's going to be harder than ever to hide, now. Sooner or later, you'll see something you never thought was possible before. And when that happens, all I ask is that you consider it. Maybe all those fairy tales came from somewhere."

The newscaster gave an approving nod, turning back to the camera. "Well, there you have it. An extraordinary statement from an extraordinary girl. When–"

Melanie suddenly reached out, bending the microphone back towards herself. "Oh, and one more thing. Follow me on social media at mel-a-drama, with an 'A.' I'm going to keep posting, every day. I'm going to keep tabs on everything. If I stop posting, that means the government found me, and is trying to keep me from spilling their secrets. Then you'll know for sure it's real."

She smirked at the camera. She had it all figured out.

"Ridiculous," Casey's mother muttered in Vietnamese. In English, she said to Casey's stepfather, "Do they think we will believe that?"

"There's always some hoax or another these days," he grunted. "I'm just surprised this made it to national news. Must be a slow summer."

Vincent and Casey exchanged a glance. They continued on their way across the living room, ducking into the hall before Casey's parents could notice them.

"What was *that?*" Casey said, closing the door to her room behind them. "I can't believe she's on the *news!* I thought the Shadowhand would take care of her!"

"I guess she's right after all, about the risk of disappearing her," said Vincent. "She must have been able to avoid them long enough to go viral. Now it's too late."

"What's she doing this for? I thought she just needed Benjamin back." Casey began to pace back and forth in front of her bed, leaving a trail of damp footprints on the rug.

"I don't know. But she's doing it."

"This is gonna make *everything* worse for the guys back in Alderwood. Do you think people are gonna take her seriously?"

Vincent shook his head helplessly. "I don't know. Do you?"

"You're the one who's met people right after they die. What do they do, when they realize it's all real?"

She had a point. Vincent thought hard. "I...I'm not sure it matters. By that time, they're...different. They're dead. They don't behave like living people anymore. Think of Percy."

With a grimace, he remembered: the only dead soul who almost felt alive still was Benjamin. But not enough.

Casey nodded slowly. That seemed to sink in. "Well...what do we–"

Suddenly, the door flew open.

"*Separate rooms, Casey!*"

Vincent scuttled out of the room past her mother, avoiding her gaze. His ears burned at the idea of what she thought the two of them were doing together in Casey's room.

That night, sleep refused to visit Vincent. He shifted over and over in his bedding until at last he decided the four corners of his room were not enough to contain his thoughts. He crept out into the dark hallway.

The house was silent, to his immense relief. He padded out into the living room, flooded with silvery moonlight from the wide windows overlooking the scrubland. The moon was almost full, he realized with a twinge of dread. Most of the landscape was consumed by deep shadow, making it feel like an alien world. Or maybe someplace that belonged deep underground—somewhere Vincent might call home.

It almost made him feel that way, these days.

But he had no choice now about staying—that much was obvious. If Melanie had made national news, her proof had to be significant enough. People were listening to her.

Please be safe, Dex, Vincent prayed, his thoughts flitting towards their werewolf companions. Would they all be able to hide out in Alderwood safely? What if they had already been caught? What about when the moon turned full?

But there was nothing to do about it now. Vincent had warned them—that was enough. It was up to Dex now. At the very least, Vincent had no doubt he was the best man for the job.

Suddenly, a strange sound pierced Vincent's worry. He froze. It came again—he couldn't quite place it. *Where...?*

He took a nervous step towards his room, then realized all at once what it was.

Shit. He hurried into the second part of the house, where Casey's grandparents lived. In moments he made it to their bedroom and knocked urgently. A horrible wheezing sound greeted him.

"Come, come quickly!" Casey's grandfather's voice drifted through the door. Vincent burst through.

Casey's grandmother was bent over the side of their bed, coughing. What breaths she managed between were ragged and weak, her dark eyes rolling with fear in the moonlight.

"*Bà*, what is it?" Vincent darted to her side. "Are you alright?"

"She was snoring a lot," Casey's grandfather said, worried. "I think she needs a doctor. Her lungs are bad today."

"Was she like this earlier?"

"A little...I thought she was fine."

Vincent bit back a curse and bent close to Casey's grandmother. "*Bà*, I need you to take deep breaths. I'll be back with help."

He hurried out, making for Casey's room.

Vincent waited for hours at the hospital with the rest of the family. They had brought Casey's grandmother in as quickly as they could—he only hoped it was quick enough. He passed the time anxiously scrolling through his phone, searching for evidence of Melanie's influence. *Nothing here, nothing here...*

And then, about an hour in, *something.* It was a shaky video of a scene Vincent recognized—the graduation speech.

He watched again as Melanie grappled with the Shadowhand agents, Sierra transformed, Henry tried in vain to stop it—and then he glimpsed himself, a monstrous flash of three canine heads barreling towards the stage. The onlooker fled from him, taking the camera with them, and that was the end of it. The poster said it was the clearest footage from the incident, and that it was impossible to fake. It had nearly a million views. As he scrolled down, he saw some comments linking other versions, other videos. Some of the commenters were skeptical still, but most of them seemed to agree with the poster: it had to be real. It was all too suspicious. There were too many strange things going on in the world. One thread stood out: there were so many congruent tales of odd occurrences and creatures, it was impossible for them all to be wrong. The more Vincent read, the more his entire body grew numb.

"Helliker family?"

The nurse's voice startled Vincent out of his reverie. He looked up with the others, his chest clenching.

Thank *god*—the nurse was smiling.

"She's stable. She has pneumonia, which is quite common among folks her age. We have antibiotics for her, which should help going forward. We have to keep her on a breathing tube for a couple days until it clears up, and then she should be free to go home."

Then, the smile disappeared.

"But...we did find something concerning on the imaging. We're going to have an oncologist follow up with you, just to be certain. It may be nothing, but at her age it's important to check."

Oncologist. Cancer.

Vincent glanced at Casey. She looked as numb as he felt.

Slowly, he inched a hand towards hers. He rested it there, his heart jumping the moment they touched. She didn't move away.

When they finally got home, Vincent helped Casey's grandfather back into his empty bed. It was nearly daylight now, and no amount of worry could fight the old man's exhaustion. Vincent tucked the sheets around his legs and made sure he had water, then followed Casey out.

Her parents were murmuring to each other in the living room. Casey and Vincent passed them, making their way out into the yard to watch the cresting dawn. They sat side by side on the low wall beside the pool, shivering in the chill of morning. The sun slowly tinted the sky pale purple and then pink, the yawning shadows retreating into their hollows all across the plains.

Ever so slowly, Casey leaned her head against Vincent's shoulder. Something panged in the depths of his heart. He almost didn't believe it. He sat frozen, hardly daring to breathe, as if she were a wild animal he was trying not to spook. He didn't dare speak.

Somewhere, a mourning dove cooed.

A few days later, Vincent woke to find Casey's room empty. Alarm rose in his throat, but he fought it down. He crossed the house, looking everywhere–the living room, the kitchen, the bathrooms, her grandparents' room.

Her grandmother had returned home a day ago, laden with medication and fatigued but sound. When he peeked his head in, both grandparents were sleeping peacefully. It was a small comfort. He left quietly, his worry mounting.

There was no way she would abandon him here–was there? No, of course not. That wasn't Casey.

After checking she wasn't outside, Vincent finally relented and asked her mother in the kitchen.

"She left early for an interview."

"Interview?"

"A job interview." Casey's mother scrubbed the plate she was working on with undisguised pleasure.

It took a moment for Vincent's brain to catch up.

He waited for her, trawling the internet for more mentions of the Others. He didn't even get up to eat–he wasn't hungry. After what felt like hours, he finally heard the front door open and close. He put down his phone and hurried out of his room, meeting Casey in the entryway. She almost ran into him and startled.

"Watch it, dumbass." She carefully avoided his gaze as she skirted him, making for her room with her bag in hand.

"Where were you?"

"Out."

Vincent followed her into her room, uncaring of the golden rule. She didn't acknowledge him as she began putting away her things.

"Out where?"

"None of your beeswax."

"I thought I was your boyfriend," Vincent said mildly. "Don't boyfriends get beeswax privileges?"

Casey finally turned to him, scowling. "Don't."

"Then tell me where you went."

Casey sighed heavily. "My mom told you, didn't she?"

Vincent didn't reply.

"Yeah, okay. I applied for a job. So stuff it." She turned away again.

"Why?" Vincent pressed, sitting on her bed so she couldn't ignore him. "You've been so adamant about it since we got here..."

"So? It was bound to happen eventually."

Vincent fixed her with a look he was sure she could feel, even if she wouldn't face him. She sighed again.

"Look...my family needs the money. My grandma's not a U.S. citizen yet, she doesn't have health insurance. And we *are* living here, like you said before. I can't just not help, considering..." She trailed off.

A grim shadow settled over Vincent's heart. "You think it's cancer?"

"My mom told me yesterday."

"And you didn't tell me?"

"You're not my boyfriend," Casey snapped, with more venom than Vincent expected. "It doesn't matter. Just shut up and lie low, okay?"

"What, freeload off you and your family while you work?"

"You can help my mom peel vegetables if it makes you feel better."

"Did you even get the job?"

Casey grimaced. She nodded.

"Where? Not your brother...?"

"God, no. The ice cream place."

"Northern Lights?" Vincent considered this. "Well, that's not half bad. Do you get free samples?"

"Probably." Casey shrugged. She didn't seem cheered by the thought. "I start tomorrow."

They were both quiet for a long time, the air between them heavy.

"What kinds of jobs could I get in town?"

"Who fucking knows. You barely know how to be a person."

"Thanks," Vincent growled. "You know, your mother won't like it if I don't get one."

"She doesn't like most things anyway."

"Stop acting so noble," Vincent retorted. "It's not like you."

Casey shot him a glare. "Oh, fuck you, Vincent. You have no right to tell me what's noble. You'd be strung up on a mantelpiece somewhere if it weren't for me."

Vincent smarted. He couldn't think of anything else to say before she shoved him off her bed and ushered him out.

The two of them seethed on their own for the rest of the day. Casey left for work early the next morning, conveniently neglecting to tell her parents where exactly she was going. She simply called it "work" and "the office" when pressed. Even they seemed to know better than to press Casey too much. Or maybe they were just that distracted by the news about her grandmother's health.

Vincent, on the other hand, had no such qualms. He brooded in his room most of the day, starting out bitter in the morning and gradually settling into loneliness towards the afternoon. It was too quiet now without her, too dull without their visits to the pool and town and the hills. One day turned into another and another, lagging on mercilessly, the sun dragging itself across the sky.

Every night, he went back to the false home in his dreams. His forest, with his Henry. Every morning, he awoke desolate.

Slowly his thoughts began to slip away from him. What was he doing here, really? When was the idle waiting going to end? How was this any better than the home he had run from?

No, that was going too far. This was nothing like Hell. Here, people cared about him. He wasn't only as good as what he was good for.

...Right?

Maybe not to Casey's parents. In which case, how long did he have left?

By the end of the third day, the worst of his stubbornness had boiled away, leaving something thick and soupy behind. He walked alone down the road in the blue dusk, following the streetlights all the way into town. The vast quiet seemed to distill his thoughts, changing them from a churning river to a glittering stream.

He found his way to the little square just outside the ice cream parlor and waited there for a while, sitting on the edge of a fountain. He fingered his tie, watching the shadows of people moving behind the shop's windows.

Finally the lights flicked off. Casey and a couple of her coworkers emerged from the back door, their uniforms slung over their shoulders. It took them a moment to notice Vincent. The other two girls startled when he moved.

"Vincent?" Casey's eyes narrowed. "What are you doing here?"

"Ohh, Casey, is this your boyfriend?" one of the girls cooed.

Vincent blinked at her in shock. *Did she tell them that?*

"Yeah," Casey grunted, still looking at him expectantly.

He shrugged. "I wanted to walk you home. Is that okay?"

Any other girl would have smiled. Casey paused.

"Alright."

Her coworkers whispered something to one another, both of them grinning. "See you tomorrow, Casey!" one of them called as they walked off.

They both waited until the girls had gone before setting off down the road leading back to the house. They were quiet for a time before Vincent finally said, "You told them?"

"Word gets around in a place this small. Gotta keep up the story. Not like my parents don't have friends in town."

"Ah." After an awkward beat, he tried again: "So...how was work?"

Casey didn't answer. The air around her seemed to press down heavier with each step she took. Vincent finally risked a glance at her, and was startled to find her eyes shining with unfallen tears.

He stopped dead in the road. "Casey? What–"

Casey swiped her sleeve over her eyes to clear them. "It was *fine*. It was *work*."

Vincent looked around, unsure what to do. The scrublands stretched all around them for miles, crickets chirping steadily in the dusk. They were utterly alone.

Slowly, gingerly, he crept an arm around her shoulders. She let it linger for half a second before she snatched herself away.

"I said it's *fine!* Are you deaf? Don't Henry me!"

Vincent winced. He drew away. That only seemed to fuel her anger.

"That's what you're doing, and you know it. You're not Henry–he abandoned you. Remember that, Vincent? So save it. Grow up and fucking do what I tell you, or you're gonna get captured by those secret agent freaks and tortured and probably killed, and then what will all this be for?"

Vincent said nothing. His innards had turned to ice.

I'm nothing like Henry.

Then again...would the Vincent who had first emerged from Hell try to console her? Sympathy had always been an unwelcome and persistent guest. But somewhere along the way, he had stopped trying to force it out the door.

He started walking again. Casey growled to herself and surged ahead until she was several yards down the road. Then she seemed to think better of it and slowed down, falling into pace with him.

At last she broke the silence. "Just...just let me do this for you, okay?"

"Why?" Vincent finally said.

It took her a moment to respond. When she did, it didn't even answer the question. "It sucks, okay? It fucking sucks. It *fucking.* Sucks." She paused, gathering herself, and then stormed on. "They won't let you sit. How do people do this all day, every day? My feet *hurt*–they shouldn't feel this bad! And they're just gonna get worse, aren't they? How am I gonna do this for years on end?"

"You could always work for your bro–"

"*Shut up!*" Casey snarled. "I'm just as capable as that know-it-all chode! I'll chew my feet off before I go crawling to that bastard begging to be a dead-end receptionist! And what does it matter, anyway? Huh?" She shook her head sharply. "Food or files, I'm just another goddamn circus monkey jumping when some low-life snaps their fingers! I thought being an adult meant you got some *respect* for fucking once. I feel like I got more of it in college. And if my parents knew I was working somewhere so *stupid–*"

She cut herself off. The full picture had slipped into the light.

"What happened today?" Vincent dared to ask.

Again she rubbed her face with her arm. "It's whatever. I probably deserve to get yelled at anyway. What kind of nitwit can't get a scoop of ice cream into a cone?"

Despite her fury and misery, Vincent couldn't help it–he laughed. It was just too absurd, picturing Casey of all people wrestling a little lopsided ball of ice cream into a cone.

He was ready for her to tear him apart, but they looked at each other and then she began to laugh too. She laughed raucously until the tears threatening her eyes finally fell, and she wiped them away less aggressively. She barely looked like herself at all.

"Shut–shut up," she breathed out, shoving him aside. She tipped her head back to look up at the stars, just beginning to wink into view across the vast evening sky.

No–she was looking at the moon. Only a tiny sliver remained untouched with silver. Her eyes were wide.

"All my life came down to this. Putting food into a container. Every hour of school and growing up and everything I've ever done and worked for. I could've done this fucking job when I was three. But it's all I'm worth, now, to my family."

"That's not true," Vincent insisted. "They love you, Casey. Not just because of what you can provide for them."

Casey shrugged. "Sure, they love me. But only because I'm their daughter. If I were some rando in the street, they wouldn't give a rat's ass."

Vincent didn't know how to argue that. The words seeped in like poison as they walked on. Was it true? Did anyone only ever matter because of circumstance? The thought made him feel cold, from his fingertips to the very depths of his heart. His own father, his own family...none of them were shining examples to the contrary. They were quick to throw him out the moment he screwed up. And Henry...

He suddenly felt very alone, even with Casey walking beside him.

But then, his and Casey's circumstances hadn't been favorable at all. By all accounts, she shouldn't even like him. He still had no idea why she did. And yet...

"Why do you care about me, then?"

Casey blinked. "What?"

"You made it pretty plain when we first met that you hated me. You didn't appreciate me meddling when Hunter tried bullying you into a date. And then with all the werewolf stuff—I *fought* you. We almost killed each other."

"I didn't mean to," Casey muttered. "I wasn't myself."

Vincent shrugged one shoulder. "I guess so, yeah. But before that...and after...I mean, Henry and I blackmailed you into helping us solve Benjamin's murders."

The word *blackmail* came freely, before he could find a better way to say it. When he realized it, guilt trickled in again. This time he ignored it, letting it stay—because it was true, anyway. That was what they had done, for better or worse.

"But now, you're...you're doing all this," he went on, gesturing back towards town, "just to make sure I have a safe place to hide. You could have left me for the Shadowhand to clean up. Honestly, you'd have the right."

Casey growled softly. "I wouldn't."

"Why?" he asked again, sharply.

"Because you wouldn't do that to me."

Surprise coursed through Vincent.

"But I told you–"

"You didn't *do* it. I was just more trouble for you, in the end, but you still didn't."

Vincent had no idea what to think. Was that even true? Would he have turned her in, if it had gone that far?

"Henry was wrong about you. He always was."

Something panged deep in Vincent's heart. It was almost too painful to bear, and it left him breathless. He wanted to ask what she meant, but at the same time, he didn't want to know. It was too much.

Casey didn't offer an explanation. Instead they walked on through the night, all the way back home.

The next day was scorching; by the time Vincent left the house to meet Casey after work, the air was still heady with the memory of sun. It left a purple dusk in its wake, stars scattering across its fabric like spilled paint.

Instead of going home, the two of them hopped a low wooden fence, wandering into the orange grove beyond. It stretched onward past Vincent's vision, rows and rows of rich green leaves dappled with bright fruits that had only just begun to sag their branches. The deepening shadows were almost eerie in a delightful way. They were alone out here in the gathering dark, and nothing could disturb or pressure them. They had already all but forgotten their feud.

Casey plucked a small orange from one of the trees as they passed beneath it. She spat her gum out on the ground and began peeling her new prize as if she enjoyed the act of it more than she would the fruit. When she tasted it she pulled a face, dropping the rest of it beside the corpse of her gum.

"Nope. Not ripe yet."

"You've probably ruined your taste after all the gum," Vincent teased. "I bet it was fine."

"I have not," Casey scoffed.

"You could have at least given it to me."

"I thought dogs didn't like citrus."

Vincent rolled his eyes. "Well, I'm not covering for you now."

"Covering for what?"

"Grand larceny."

"It's an orange, dipshit. No one will miss it. It wasn't even good."

"It's still stealing."

"Not if no one catches you."

"They don't have night watchmen out here?"

"We never got caught before."

Vincent glanced around at the grove. "So you used to come out here with your friends, too?"

Casey's expression tightened, as it always did when they mentioned her friends. "Yeah. We used to drink and smoke here at night." She kicked a loose piece of wood, sending it skittering along the ground. "And steal oranges, I guess. It's been a while."

"Maybe they've posted a guard since–"

Vincent stopped. He had caught a glimpse of a silvery glow at the edge of the horizon, filtering between the leaves.

"...It's almost time."

Casey didn't stop. Her pace quickened as she followed the row of trees, deeper and deeper into the grove.

After a few minutes, Vincent couldn't take the silence any longer. "Are you sure you don't want to go into the hills instead? What if someone's–"

"It's fine. We won't be spotted here."

Vincent wasn't so sure, but he knew better than to argue with Casey tonight. Instead he followed her onward, until the shadows swallowed the world whole.

Steadily the full moon rose like pale fire in the indigo sky. When the last leaves had relinquished their grip on its edges, Casey jerked.

She stopped in the center of the path, doubling over with a hiss. Vincent heard something snap.

"Casey?" He took a step towards her.

"Back off!" Casey clutched her body with fingers so tight they looked like they would break.

Suddenly her head shot up and back, straining against an invisible force. Her mouth gaped in a silent shriek as her bones began to crack, her skin boiling, her body reforming. Even in stark shadow and moonlight the shift was horrible to behold. Vincent flinched away, taking cover behind one of the trees with one hand on its trunk like a shield.

This was the first time he was with her during her transformation on the full moon—the most unpredictable time to change. He had seen her near it, when she had lost control of her emotions, and later on the night itself under the suppressing influence of a potion...but never like this, unfettered and alone. Tonight there was no pack to guide her—there was only Vincent.

A howl pierced the hot night air, tearing through his nerves. He cringed against the tree trunk, praying no one could hear her this far out, hating the agony she was fighting.

Then, silence fell.

Vincent timidly peered out around the trunk. Wolf-Casey was standing there, chest heaving, muzzle upturned towards the full moon as it drifted slowly higher, the bright eye of a titan holding her captive. Her sleek black fur shone silver in its light, her long arms hanging limply at her sides as she balanced on her muscular hind legs, her spine hunched in an inhuman way. She was as beautiful as she was terrible.

"C–Casey?" Vincent finally crept out from behind the tree, one slow step at a time.

Her head snapped around, and he froze. Her eyes gleamed yellow-green in the gloom.

A low growl crossed the space between them.

"She doesn't recognize you, boy."

Vincent's heart slammed into his throat. He spun around, glimpsing the same image in the shadows beneath the trees–two glowing eyes.

CHAPTER 7

OLD DOG, NEW TRICKS

asey's growl grew louder, but it was no longer directed at Vincent. They both stared into the darkness, barely picking out a slender silhouette.

"Who are you? Show yourself!" Vincent demanded, trying to stay steady. He wasn't sure why he felt so weak. A strange instinct was blooming in him—one uncomfortably close to what he felt when he was around Percy's ghost. Something was horribly wrong.

"Are you sure?"

Before he could reply, he realized Casey was backing away. *Werewolf* Casey. He had never seen her look so spooked, especially like this. Her gaze was fixed on that shadow, her ears flat against her skull, her growl weak in her throat—a warning.

"Who are you?" Vincent said again, more forcefully this time. It took everything in him to stand his ground.

"Not the right question," the figure said. It had a man's voice, rough and lackadaisical. "If I told you my name, would it make any difference?"

Vincent's anxiety congealed into ire. "Fine—what do you want? It's dangerous here."

But the stranger didn't seem to think so. "You're still not askin' the right question. Maybe I should spell it out for you, how's that?"

Vincent's fingers curled into fists at his sides. "You know what? I don't care. Get the hell out of here, or you'll regret it."

It was his last scrap of bravado. He used it up just as the stranger stepped forward, out of the shadows and into the moonlight.

Vincent was wrong—this wasn't a man. He was man-shaped, but nothing else quite fit. His graying hair was overgrown and tangled, his eyes so sunken they couldn't overcome the shadow of his brow. He wore no clothes, but he didn't need to–his skin was more a *pelt*, thick in patches and scraggly in others. His nose was longer than it should be, and so were his teeth, poking out from between his dry lips–

No. He recognized this man. This was the stranger they had passed in town.

His body jerked. An odd gulping sound tore from his throat. Vincent took a step back, his heartbeat surging.

"You know me, don't you, girl?" The stranger's voice struggled from his mouth as he turned his attention towards Casey. "You may not know him, but you'd know me anywhere." He chuckled. "Even when I looked and smelled human, that day in town...you recognized me, didn't you? I could hardly believe my eyes. But then, I knew you'd come home someday."

He began to circle her along the edge of the trees. He was much smaller than her, but it didn't seem to matter. He was the predator here. She followed the edge of the circle he drew, keeping him carefully in her sights, her growl rising.

She was afraid. But she was also Casey Helliker, and she wouldn't back down. This was about to get ugly.

A sharp crack sounded as the man convulsed again, stumbling forward through the leaf litter. He sucked in a breath through his teeth, but kept his twisted smile. "We can still run together, you and I, y'know. Is that why you came back?"

A snarl erupted from Casey's maw. If it weren't for her fear, Vincent was sure she would have lunged for him. But she didn't.

The stranger snorted. It ended in a cough. "Still holdin' onto the human part, huh? Thought you'd be farther along by now. 'Specially if you're back here. Wonder what happened."

His body fell forward as if something had struck him from behind. He bent over on all fours, kicking up leaves as he writhed in his own flesh. Saliva spewed into the dirt as he cried out, his yell slowly morphing into a howl of both immeasurable pain and unbridled ecstasy. Horror sucked at Vincent's stomach as he watched the stranger contort into shapes he had never thought possible, shuddering and groaning as what little monster remained inside clawed its way to the surface.

"*I always wanted a daughter,*" the beast said, its voice grotesque in a way that dwarfed every other attempt at wolf-speech Vincent had heard. And yet, it was more controlled, too. He was both man and beast, at the same time, always. "*Lone wolves ain't nature's way. You'll come around, won't you? You hate the humans as much as I do. I saw it with my own two eyes.*"

"*Don't!*" Casey burst out. She was right in front of Vincent now, her back to him. It was as if he didn't even exist. He could see her trembling with fury—or fright. Maybe both.

A hoarse, strangled laugh found its way out of the monster that faced her. "*You do, don't deny it! You let that boy of yours die no problem. You know he deserved it. He was a mean son of a bitch. I did the world a favor. 'Cept maybe the buzzards, haha.*"

Whatever was holding Casey back, those words broke through it. She lurched forward, jaws snapping—but the stranger was ready for her. He ducked aside easily, agile and practiced, and suddenly Vincent could see his full, horrible splendor in the moonlight. He was bigger than Casey, his dark gray fur ragged and scarred, his claws and teeth crueler.

Vincent's blood roared in his ears and he braced himself, ready to leap to her defense. But before he could, he recognized something in her adversary that made him hesitate.

The stranger's flashing eyes saw with an instinct Casey lacked. When Casey's claws found his pelt, it was because he let them. His teeth locked on her shoulder in the same instant, tossing her aside with her own momentum. She skidded through the leaf mold with a yelp and a snarl, her rage drowning her instincts. She lunged for him again, and again he bundled her away harmlessly, leaving her to scramble in the dirt. This was going nowhere.

Again the werewolf laughed, a dry and brittle sound. He was having fun. "*I don't wanna fight you, y'know. 'Less it makes you feel better. Y'know, you're the first one I ever met who feels how I do. You'd be doin' a lot more good out there if you just embraced yourself, the way you really are. Why do you keep lyin' to yourself? What's it costin' you?"*

"She's worth a hundred of you," Vincent spat, forcing himself to advance. "Whoever the fuck you are. For the last time, just leave us alone! She's not coming with you, no matter what you say!"

Finally the stranger's eyes rolled with a flash of danger. *"Who are you, huh? You ain't one of us, boy. Go on, get."* He flicked a clawed hand towards Vincent dismissively, which sent a surge of outrage through his body.

But before he could retaliate, Casey was already there. She snapped at the stranger, and for a split second he was too distracted to catch it–her fangs closed on his collarbone, blood spraying between her jaws as she hefted him off his feet. He snarled as he lurched aside, reaching for her with his awful claws. She flinched as they found her face, digging in until she had no choice but to let go.

She snatched herself away, but was too slow–in an instant he was on top of her, driving her into the dirt. Fur and teeth flew as they grappled, kicking up dead leaves–but there was no question who would win this matchup. Casey was pinned.

A rush of heat broke through the last of Vincent's composure. He finally leaped, his own body shedding its form far easier than the others'. Two canid heads sprouted from his shoulders as he grew, sharp teeth flashing in the light of the full moon. His powerful limbs carried him across the battlefield in two bounds. The older wolf barely had time to glance over his shoulder before his new enemy was upon him.

The stranger let out a strangled cry as he was barreled into the dirt. He kicked out, but Vincent angled his body out of reach. He fastened his teeth in the werewolf's shoulder, pressing down on his spine with a heavy paw.

But he wasn't heavy enough–in a flash the stranger's claws hooked around his hind leg, yanking his balance away. The world lurched around Vincent as he fell, tearing pieces of his enemy's pelt with him.

But the werewolf didn't care. He was up in a blink, chest heaving as he surveyed his new opponent.

"*Look at* you!" He forced Vincent down, grinding him into the leaf litter with impossible strength. "*Guess you had a trick up your sleeve after all, huh, boy?*" He spat on the ground contemptuously. "*Sadly, no room in the pack for mutts. Beat it, kid.*"

"She's not *your* pack, asshole!" Vincent snarled, struggling to right himself. "She's *mine!*"

But the weight bearing down on him was far too great—this werewolf was nearly twice his size. For the first time, fear flared in his chest.

The werewolf's maw opened wide in a silent laugh, his curved fangs dripping in delight. Then they lunged straight for his throat.

Vincent flinched away—but then, all at once, the weight lifted.

Freed, he rolled away. The grove was a black-and-silver blur before his eyes focused again, picking out what had happened. What *was* happening.

Cold shock gripped his heart. Casey had tackled the stranger. Now she struggled madly with him again in the dirt and the leaves, so entangled Vincent could hardly tell where one wolf began and the other ended.

"My *pack!*" she snarled. "*Stay away from him!*"

Suddenly, the stranger broke away. It was like a switch had been flipped. Casey rolled wildly on the ground, still searching for something to shred—but he backed away out of her reach. His head tipped to one side curiously.

"*You...remember him?*"

Casey finally righted herself, the fur along her spine bristling. She advanced on her enemy, teeth bared, head low as she prepared to leap again.

A bark of a laugh tore from the stranger's throat as he watched her, unbothered. "*Well, I'll be. You're better off than I thought. Guess you're both full of surprises.*" He glanced past her towards Vincent. "*Y'know what? I'm feelin' generous. If he means that much to you, I'll take both of you. No harm done.*"

"Is that seriously what you want?" said Vincent, uncertainty creeping in.

The stranger flashed him a wolf grin, all teeth. "*I'm tired of running alone, kid. Wolves belong in packs. Your friend here knows what I mean. Didn't expect her to swap her shitty old one for a stray dog, though. Hehe.*"

Vincent narrowed his eyes. "What do you mean? She had another pack here?"

"*In a manner of speaking.*" The stranger seemed too smug for comfort. Something crawled just beneath Vincent's skin. He looked to Casey, unsure if she was clear-headed enough to even understand what he was saying.

"*You killed them.*" Her garbled voice was so quiet, for a moment he didn't register that she had spoken. "*You killed* me."

Suddenly, horribly, it all clicked—her ex wasn't the one who had turned her into a werewolf. It was *this* man. This stranger from the wilderness, just as much monster as man.

He snorted. "*Oh, come on, girl. It's been* years." He took a threatening step towards her, capturing her in his ominous, glowing gaze. But she didn't back down—a warning growl ripped from her lungs. He ignored it, suddenly serious for the first time that evening. A strange chill coursed through Vincent at the realization.

"*I saved* you. *I made you better. Your buddies maimed a motherfucking cat, for god's sake. And you think that was the first time? They used to come out here to shoot whatever they caught breathin', even before you. I used to see 'em around. They just finally picked the wrong goddamn night. But you?*"

The stranger drew himself up to his full height, towering over her, his massive lupine head haloed perfectly by the full moon, as if he were its emissary and it his beacon.

"*You wanted to kill 'em for it, didn't you? That's what you said. All ninety pounds of you, rounding on that boyfriend without a care. They would've picked you clean. Your boy had a look in his eye. I see it a lot. I see it everywhere.*"

His voice was dark now, the shadow on the other side of the moon. He looked up at Vincent, too, across the way. "*You've seen it—I know you have.*"

He had. Horribly, he knew exactly what this stranger meant. He had seen it lingering in the gray eyes of the dead, vibrant and malevolent in the eyes of the living. He had seen it in Casey's eyes, when she nearly murdered Hunter. But the worst of it—he had seen it in his own reflection in Jake's eyes. In Henry's eyes.

"Everywhere I look in those streets, I see it lookin' back at me." The stranger jabbed a claw back towards the road, towards town. *"Everywhere I've ever been. 'Cept these hills. 'Cause out here, there's only two things–runnin' free, or dyin'."*

Casey let out a sudden snarl, jerking her head forward to bite–but the stranger lurched down at her, his own snarl overpowering hers. He stopped himself before reaching her and they both stood frozen, his glowing eyes boring into hers.

A tense, horrible moment passed. Then, slowly, Casey ducked her head. But her growl still rumbled in her chest.

"Don't deny it! You hunt 'cause you have to. You live for what's in front of your nose. You're the real *you, like this–the* best *you. Right now, you can be happy."* Again the stranger jerked his muzzle in the direction of civilization. *"They've never been happy a goddamn day in their lives. They think too much. They want too much. They don't know who they are anymore. They hunt, but whenever they catch somethin', it never satisfies 'em. They hurt things just 'cause they can. 'Cause it makes 'em feel better. It makes 'em feel alive."*

Everything in Vincent's body felt cold. Everyone he had ever met flickered through his head in a blur, one after the other. Was it true? Back home, among only his own kind and the dead, everything was so simple–keep watch, do as you're told, maintain your dignity. Cold, fierce, composed. Loyal. And everything and everyone there was just that.

It turned out, he was none of those things. At least not where it counted.

Maybe instead he was everything the old wolf was talking about. Never satisfied. Always hungry. Always ready to hurt someone for his own gain. Maybe it did make him feel better. Maybe he really had become human, where it counted.

"I can help you," the stranger's voice broke through Vincent's doubts. His monstrous eyes were gleaming eagerly, eerily. *"Teach you how to be a real wolf."*

"What does that mean?" Vincent demanded, before his thoughts had caught up. "How?"

The werewolf grinned. "*Stop hidin' the real you. The whole desert is your playground. We'll hunt wherever and whatever and whenever we please. Even the moon can't control us.*"

"*And kill people?*" Casey's snarl devoured the space between them.

The stranger's gaze flicked to her. "*If we feel like it. If they deserve it.*" Before she could do more than open her maw, he said, "*Tell me what's wrong with it! They're not our people anymore, don't you get it? We're better now—we've gone back to nature, the way things were meant to be. We ain't bogged down anymore by this silly human decorum—draggin' each other down and down. We're different. We can be better.*"

"You think killing humans will make them better?" Vincent growled.

The stranger shrugged. "*The cat sure appreciated it.*"

Vincent glanced over at Casey, troubled. *The cat...* Her friends, her *boyfriend*...they were torturing a cat. And she had stood against them. It was all too easy to imagine—he had seen her righteous fury many times before. He had also seen it go too far. In the end it had almost killed her, after she attacked Hunter and turned him into a werewolf as well. His newfound strength and hatred became the deadliest weapon, perfectly crafted to destroy her.

But it wouldn't have, if she had just killed him that night. If Vincent had let her.

No...if *Henry* had let her. It wasn't Vincent's might that had stopped her—he was no match for her in a fight. Henry had called out to her, pleaded with her—the *human* in her. Vincent's conversation with her the night before echoed in his mind:

We almost killed each other.

I didn't mean to. I wasn't myself.

"Casey isn't like those people," said Vincent. "The wolf is what's been strangling her. Turning her into someone she doesn't want to be. What right do you have to kill them? To decide that's what they deserve?"

The stranger smirked. "*You're right. She's not like those people. But people don't change, kid. My wolf knows that. It sees that, and it takes away all the bad those people will do in their lives.*"

Something horrible and familiar twisted deep in Vincent's heart. *No*–he couldn't let it in.

"I've seen what death does to people," he countered. "It doesn't make them any better. It makes them into husks. It makes them want even harder. There's no *cure* for...for being a person."

"Sure. But at least they ain't hurting anyone else anymore."

"They *are!*" Vincent burst out. "They're ghosts–they're loose in the world now, they're out of their place–and they're draining the life out of everything! Every terrible thing they ever faced or did or saw became them, they're trapped in it forever with no way to make it right! My friend got a girl *killed* because he couldn't stand being dead and alone anymore–"

He stopped himself. He couldn't let the blaze consume him. He shook his head sharply, trying to clear it.

But he couldn't. The stranger chuckled, without a care in the world.

"Well, shit. Guess even death can't stop 'em."

His beast's eyes fixed directly on Vincent again, and some deep, terrible instinct inside him sensed a shift.

"Well, I tried my best. Guess I really am the last of my kind. Damn shame."

Almost before the final word left his teeth, he lunged.

Vincent didn't think–his instinct carried him forward. Their jaws collided, snapping at each other's teeth in a strange and violent kiss, finding no purchase on each other. Claws ripped out clumps of dark fur, brown and gray, muscles bunching and straining as they grappled, each trying to gain ground on the other.

And in only a heartbeat, the stranger found it. With a burst of inhuman strength he forced Vincent back and down, his back arching desperately as he fought against the werewolf's might. He was bigger and older and meaner, and there was nothing Vincent could do about any of it. A flash of cold fear rippled down his spine as he realized–the stranger was no longer holding back. He had decided Vincent was a lost cause, too–no better than any other human, hungry for the whole world, striving to swallow it whole. The stranger was going to kill him.

But Vincent was not alone. At the same moment he slid backwards in the leaf litter, Casey surged forward. Her claws slashed across the other werewolf's face and he flinched back, long enough for Vincent to wrench himself free. He ducked aside and the stranger stumbled forward.

Casey was on him in an instant, snapping at his throat. The old man was canny—he caught her muzzle with both clawed hands. She tossed her head powerfully, but he held fast. He brought his own jaws down, clamping onto the side of her neck—

Vincent charged him, sending them all sprawling in the dirt. Limbs and teeth flashed in the wicked moonlight as they struggled, the night alive with snarls and yelps. Vincent found matted fur and bit down as hard as he could, until blood rushed out thick and hot between his fangs. He heard the crunch of bone and a howl, felt the sting of fur torn from his body. The world heaved around him as the body beneath him bucked and twisted, but still he did not let go.

Then something caught him in the side of the head. He reeled back, his other heads releasing their grip from the shock of it. He staggered, his hind paws slipping in the leaves, and then another blow found his snout. He skidded back, planting his feet to keep himself from falling over. When his spinning vision returned, he saw Casey holding the stranger fast from behind, her monstrous arms clamped around his chest, baring his neck as she fought to keep him still. Her eyes glowed in the darkness at his back, showing none of the humanity and all of the wolf.

"Kill him! Now!"

Vincent lunged for him, desperation driving him forward. He only had one shot to end this, before the stranger killed them both—

He stopped. His middle head's teeth hovered just inches from the stranger's bare throat.

"Get him!" Casey cried. *"What are you doing?"*

Vincent's eyes met the stranger's. He saw no reflection, but he knew it would be there, if only it were daylight. He closed his jaws.

"No." He looked so deeply into the wolf's glowing eyes that he was sure his enemy could see straight into his heart. "You're not dying by my teeth."

The stranger blinked. "*What? You're crazy, kid. You know I'm gonna kill you if you let me go, right?*"

Vincent did not blink. "No, you're not."

"*If you don't, I will!*" Casey growled, jerking the stranger back as she kept her hold on him.

"He's not going to kill us. And I'm not going to kill him."

"*You have to–*"

"I'm done pretending I'm something I'm not!" Vincent burst out, his gaze finally shifting to capture Casey's. "*You* taught me that! You and Henry." His name almost felt like a dirty word in Vincent's mouth, something he wasn't meant to say, but he forced it out anyway.

Casey shook her head, baffled. "*What are you?*"

"I–I don't know." He felt like he was...something halfway between. "But I won't be this. I won't be a killer." He looked at the old creature, and something he hadn't felt in a long time seeped into his heart.

"*Don't look at me like that, pup,*" the stranger spat, heaving against Casey's grasp. She gripped him tighter, hefting him back again with a growl. "*Don't you* dare *pity me!*"

An echo of his own voice, long ago, returned to Vincent, mingling with the stranger's. It suddenly felt like he was in two places at once–both here and not, young and old, man and monster.

"Then don't give me a reason." Vincent held his gaze, unyielding. "You don't have to be like this."

The stranger stared back at him. "*What–what do you mean? Don't you talk down to me, you–*"

"Fine–if you've truly lost yourself to that beast inside you, go for it! Kill me. Kill everyone you think deserves it, everyone who's just a stain on the world. Justify it however you want, because it makes you feel better." Vincent stepped back, spreading his arms in a helpless gesture. He realized a moment too late that he had transformed back into a human. The shock of it gripped his heart for only a second. "You're no different than the rest of us. You're just as hungry."

The stranger didn't move. He had stopped struggling. He just stared.

Vincent jerked his chin up in Casey's direction. "Let him go, Casey."

Casey bared her teeth in an ugly snarl. "*No! Crazy!*"

Vincent narrowed his eyes at her. His stomach clenched for a wild second as he recognized that beast behind her eyes, even more than the hulking silhouette she now bore. But he didn't let it stop him—he started towards her, human-shaped still.

Casey recoiled in shock, but her fur bristled and she warned him off with a growl. He ignored her, his stride unbroken. He reached up with his human hands and tugged her claws away from her captive's chest.

He wasn't strong enough to pry them off—he knew that—but it didn't matter. Casey let him do it.

The stranger stumbled forward. He half-turned to look back, his eyes flicking between them as if he still couldn't reconcile what they were, why this werewolf so like himself could break through the haze of beasthood for someone like Vincent.

Then Vincent stepped forward, closing the distance, leaving Casey behind. He stood between them, helpless and small and human.

"I mean it. If you're really going to keep hunting and punishing humans, make me your first victim. This is your last chance. If you don't...I'll hunt you down myself."

For a long, dreadful moment, they all looked at each other—the two werewolves in the moonlight, the hellhound wearing human skin.

The smallest twitch, and the stranger crossed the gap in a blink. All Vincent saw was teeth, eclipsing the sky—

—a massive shape leaping over his head, barreling into the beast, banishing those teeth into the night. The two wolves melded into a heaving, snarling mass of dark fur. Then something crunched, and everything stopped.

Cold rushed through Vincent's body. All he could do was stand there, eyes locked on that heap. Waiting for *something* to move.

Then, finally, the shadow split, and one wolf rose on its hind legs. Turned back to him, gold eyes in the dark.

At once the chill washed through him, down to his feet. *Casey.*

They both stood there, waiting, as if somehow the silence would break itself and relieve them of the burden. But nothing happened.

Vincent crept to her side. The old werewolf lay motionless at her feet. The hot summer night smelled like copper. It filled his senses completely, choking him, swiftly turning to vertigo.

But then, he realized—it wasn't just the stranger. Casey was bleeding, too; shiny in the moonlight, seeping through the dark fur at the base of her neck. That broke him free of his stupor.

"Casey..."

He reached for her, but in the same moment she spun and charged off deeper into the grove.

"Wait! Casey!" But it was too late. Her black form had vanished among the shadows beneath the trees.

Cursing, Vincent started after her—but then he stopped. He could easily track her by scent, but when he found her, what would he do? What would he say that she could understand, like this?

Somehow, he felt both closer to and farther from her than he ever had.

His gaze pulled back to the stranger's body. He had died as he had lived—how he wanted to. He would be a wolf forever, now, without a shred of life left to fuel his transformation. Just another animal, marred by animal claws. No one would recognize him—or trace it back to his killer. It was fortunate in one way...and sickening in the rest.

Unable to look any longer, Vincent fell back on what was second nature to him—the only thing he could think to do. He turned back, walking to the fence at the grove's edge. He began following it along its curve.

Moonlight grasped for him between each tree as he paced through the rows, silent. The crickets and other nighttime insects had long since stopped their song. Slowly, though, as the moon made its graceful journey across the inky sky, each one returned until their harmony rose again through the warm night air. Gradually Vincent's heart slowed and his stomach settled, even as the storm inside his head swirled on.

I won't be a killer. His own words echoed again in his mind. Why did it matter so much? Death was inevitable. If it meant he kept someone from doing so much harm during their lifetime...why shouldn't he cut it short?

Maybe it was because he had seen what it meant to be dead. It was too final, too terrible to be trapped in the Underworld forever, chained to a husk of one's old self with only regrets like cinders left within. In all his time there, he had only once seen otherwise. Only Benjamin had somehow clung so viciously to life that his regrets still burned inside him.

And even then, being dead wasn't the final word. Hell made them worse, torturing them, imprisoning them in their own loneliness forever. Even people like Percy, the lingering dead in the mortal world, were not much better. Left with so little will of their own, unseen by most, trapped someplace familiar and yet trapped all the same, willing to do anything to feel alive again...and now, Benjamin had unleashed their suffering on the living.

It made Vincent wonder: what was Heaven like? Were the dead any different there?

He didn't know. Despite being a hellhound, knowing Lucifer Himself, he knew nothing of Heaven. Perhaps this was intentional.

Henry would make it there, he was certain. He was good. Vincent couldn't begin to imagine what anyone could find fault in. The only thing he had ever done wrong was opposing Vincent, when he tried to torture Jake for information to stop the murders at Alderwood. When he tried to stop Vincent from dragging Benjamin back to Hell.

And yet, even that wasn't wrong. That's why Vincent had to do it— because he wouldn't let Henry lose everything, and he wouldn't let the murders continue. No one else could do the wrong thing but Vincent himself.

Except now, Casey had. She killed someone to protect him. And to protect everyone else that would have been hunted–because Vincent had given a murderer another chance.

For the first time in so long, something got past the armor in his heart. It stabbed its way in, an agony so real he stopped in the shadows beneath the trees, clutching his chest. The dark grove, the distant mountains, the scattered stars swam in front of his eyes.

He *had* cut someone's life short. Even if Benjamin had already died once, Vincent had sent him back to Hell. He could have done it again–*should* have. He had almost died, almost set another murderer loose on the world, all in the hope that the old werewolf might prove to him there was something good left in him–something that could change. All because he decided to do what Henry would have done.

What would he think of me now?

For once, he had no idea at all. Nothing was simple anymore...if it ever was. He had caused so many terrible things, all because Benjamin made him think about how unfair it was, condemning a kid to an eternity of darkness just because his life had already been too dark to bear.

I should have just stayed in Hell, his heart cried. He should have done just what he was doing now, the only thing he was ever meant to do–guard. The moment he played judge, everything fell apart at the seams.

And now, what was he doing? Hiding, while everyone else suffered the consequences. Dex's pack, Percy, Ava, Sierra, Henry–and now Casey, most of all. Killing for him, sullying herself in his stead. Even here, she wasn't safe. She wasn't happy. None of them were, because of him.

He was much worse than a killer.

Vincent patrolled the perimeter of the grove until the first milky light of dawn crept into the sky. He found no further sign of danger. It was hardly a comfort; he knew it was all useless anyway. The last true predator in these hills was dead.

He finally allowed himself to draw in the scents in his surroundings, relieved to find the wind had swept away the worst of the cooling blood-scent. He was even able to pick Casey's trail out of the dust and the leaf mold and the oranges. He let his feet carry him on, until at last he found Casey curled up beneath a tree near the grove's center. She was unclothed, her black hair mussed and her skin scuffed with dirt and dried blood. The worst of it was a chunk taken out of her neck, thankfully closer to where the shoulder connected rather than anything vital.

She lifted her face to him, marred by wide scratches where her adversary's claws had dug in. Her dark eyes made the journey back from wherever distant place they had been, and when they reached Vincent they carried misery back with them. She was sad. She was *afraid*.

"I should've known he'd be here. I should've known it was him."

She spoke before Vincent could. Wordlessly he handed her the tank top and shorts he had saved for her in his jacket pockets.

For a moment he was back at college, watching Henry hand Casey his jacket to cover herself the first time they had seen her transform. The rogue image made his breath catch. He forced it away, but he felt it settle somewhere soft in the pit of his stomach.

He turned away so Casey could dress herself.

"...He's dead, isn't he?"

Vincent's heart sank to the base of his ribs. "You...you don't remember?"

"I think I do." Silence. "I think he is."

His words swelled up in his throat. All he could manage was:

"Casey, I...I'm sorry."

She was quiet. Both of them were. Then:

"Don't be. I'm glad he's dead. I'm glad I got to do it."

His gut twisted. "Casey, I–"

"You can turn around now."

He did, and he found Casey's eyes shining with unfallen tears, for the second time in two days. His stomach clenched at the sight. When he looked at her, she finally cracked.

"He killed Connor...my friends...and then he...he *bit* me, he *changed* me, he stole my *whole life!* He wanted me to be..."

For once, she couldn't seem to finish her sentence. She didn't need to. But Vincent didn't know what to say. How could he? So he let his thoughts spill from his mouth.

"You *saved* me. You–you shouldn't have had to do that, Casey. I'm *so tired* of making the wrong choice. I was never made to kill people...I was made to keep them safe. I don't want to make that choice anymore. I don't want you to have to make that choice for me."

"I don't care," she rasped. "I'd do it again. To avenge them. *Me.* To keep him from doing it all again."

"No," Vincent growled. "He's done enough to you. You shouldn't have that on your conscience, Casey. I could have done it for you–I *should* have. Just like I did for Henry. But I...I just *had* to know...because I always hesitate, when it counts."

"Vincent–"

He bowed his head, unable to look at her any longer. "I can't do this anymore, Casey. We have to go back. Back to Alderwood."

CHAPTER 8

GOOD THINGS

Casey stared at him as if he had grown an extra head. Maybe two.

"You...you want to go back?"

"Yes," said Vincent, quietly. "I'm done hiding here like a coward, pretending none of it ever happened. Pretending it isn't all just getting worse back there, for everyone we left. Pretending you and I aren't miserable here. This isn't the life I left Hell for."

Casey blanched. Then she flared up. "Oh. Is everything really *so* bad here, with me?"

Vincent realized too late the nerve he had struck. He opened his mouth, but she carried on:

"I'm *so* sorry for sticking my neck out for you, for *subjecting* you to this horrible place. I should've known living with me and my family would be worse than Hell for you."

"That's not what I meant, Casey! I can't thank you enough for–"

"But what? There's always a *but!*" she hissed. She pushed herself to her feet, wincing against the strain on her wounds. "No, I get it. I never wanted to come back here, either. Even without the dead werewolf, it's fucking desolate. I'm twenty-two and I'm wasting every day working at an ice cream parlor, for god's sake. My parents are constantly up my ass, and my boyfriend's a deadbeat, in their eyes. As if being made into a werewolf wasn't bad enough. I have no future at all. What am I supposed to do with all that?"

In spite of everything, Vincent couldn't help a spark of defiance. "Exactly. Why are you throwing your whole life away for *this*? I'm not even your boyfriend!"

"Because you're the first person who ever really cared about me!"

Vincent stopped in his tracks.

"That's...that's not true, Casey. Your family–"

"Yeah, so what? Like I said before, they're *family*. They have to care about me, because I'm a part of their picture."

"Henry cared about you." The words came before Vincent could really think.

Casey scoffed loudly. "Yeah. He cares about everyone."

"And that's a bad thing?"

"Yeah. To him, I'm just another thing to fix. And so were you–until he gave up on you."

Vincent bristled. "That's not true! Just because he wants to help as many people as he can doesn't mean he doesn't actually care about us!"

"Oh, yeah. How noble. Perfect principles. But I guess that's what makes the difference to you, huh?"

"What do you mean by that?"

"You know what I mean. No one else was ever good enough for you, were they? Because he's so *perfect*, he's as far away as you can get from your old life."

Vincent smarted. He opened his mouth, but no sound came out. Everything inside him had run dry.

Casey brushed past him, heading for the fence. "Yeah. That's what I thought."

"*Casey.*"

Vincent wasn't sure she would stop. But she did.

"This summer has been...incredible. I feel like I'm in a movie, or a dream. I never thought I'd just get to...to be normal. Like this. Pools and ice cream."

Every word hurt like a nail tearing from his chest, coming undone. But he deserved it.

"You've given me your best. I mean that. I...I don't know how to say it, and I'm sorry for that. I don't know...a lot of things, right now. Maybe I never did."

His words failed and silence took over, bearing down on him harder and harder with each breath. Finally he managed to go on:

"All of this is more than I deserve. *You're* more than I deserve. But...none of this is real." He gestured to the grove around them, beyond. "No matter how much we try to glue these pieces together, they don't fit. You knew that, didn't you? When you left home for Alderwood?"

Casey didn't answer.

"Come *on*, Casey. You know that. I know you hate it here. Why did you even want to come back? We could have stayed anywhere, we could have gone into the wilderness–"

"I don't know!"

Casey didn't turn around. Didn't look at him. He waited, sensing the gravity of the words just behind her teeth. Hearing the tears she was barely choking back.

"I–I thought everything here would be better, somehow. I failed at college. I have no future out there. So...so what else is there? What else am I supposed to do? At least this is my birthright." She shook her head sharply. "Everything went wrong when Connor and the others died. When that *monster* took everything from me. But maybe with you here...with you..."

She fell silent. Vincent's heart went numb. His feet burned, filling the footprints someone else had left in this grove long ago.

Does she...?

"I'm fucking stupid," Casey growled suddenly. She started off again in long, angry strides. Breaking from his stupor, Vincent took off after her. He grabbed her arm, expecting her to round on him, kick him, bite him–but he did it anyway, throwing his arms around her, clutching her fiercely.

And she didn't stop him. She let him. He felt her trembling against his chest. Felt something damp on his shirt.

"I'm sorry, Casey," he said, his voice cracking. He could feel the force of her despair like it was seeping through her very skin, into his core. "I'm sorry I can't fix it."

She didn't reply. She didn't make a sound at all, even as more teardrops speckled his shirt. Her arms stayed limp at her sides as he held onto her, as if trying to crush the pain out of her body.

But he couldn't. That was the worst part of it all–*nothing* could fix this.

They stayed there as the sun slowly rose, warming the land gently and then all at once. It felt like an entirely different world from the dark valley that had seen a monster's last moments. The blue shadows across the grove finally fled, chased by the wash of gold spilling over the hills. When they did, Casey finally drew away, her dark eyes filled with sunlight and ghosts.

"This was never going to be our life. My life." She spoke so softly, it didn't even sound like her.

Vincent's heart ached. "No. Thanks to you, we're safe here, but..."

"We're not happy."

He didn't answer. He didn't need to.

"...So what are we doing, then, Vincent? We're just gonna go back? Turn ourselves in to the Shadowhand? Is that better than this?"

"No. I need to go back and fix everything I broke."

Finally the flame returned to Casey's eyes. "Fix ev–you can't fix everything. Is that all this is? Is the guilt finally catching up with you? You *know* you only did what you had to–"

"No," said Vincent, so strongly that even Casey went silent. He softened, but only just. "This summer...it was a good thing. And so are you."

He moved past her and hopped over the fence. He turned back to look at her from the other side. She was no more than a shadow against the morning sun.

"You can come with me or not. If you really think you belong here, that's up to you. But my time for good things is up. I've already gotten far more than I deserve. It's time for me to face what I've done, now."

She just...stared at him. As if she had forgotten how to argue. So he turned away, starting back down the road towards the house. The last thing she needed right now was more pressure. More people telling her who to be.

Footsteps crunched in the dirt behind him.

"How are you supposed to fix anything, Vincent? Where would you even start?"

In spite of everything, his heart felt a little lighter. She was still with him.

"The portal."

"What? How are we supposed to do that?"

"I don't know. So I think we have to find someone who does."

"And who could that possibly be?"

"The one who broke it."

The footsteps halted. "You're shitting me."

Hands suddenly gripped his shoulders, forcing him to turn around. Casey's dark eyes looked back at him, flickering as she searched his face. He let her.

"You risked everything to put Benjamin back in Hell. To get *yourself* back out again. You can't possibly be thinking of going back."

"It's my responsibility, Casey. I accept that now. Whatever happens."

"What if they capture you? There has to be another way."

"We don't have time. The portal has been broken far too long as it is–we have no idea how much worse it's gotten since we left. And Melanie's obviously on the move."

"What does Melanie have to do with anything?"

Vincent hesitated. He knew she wasn't going to like the answer, but he was tired of hiding things. "She was the one who suggested finding Benjamin for help."

Sure enough– "Oh my god, *please* tell me you're not that stupid."

"I know what you're going to say, but–"

"If you do this, you're playing right into whatever she wants!"

"I'm not going to do exactly what she wants. I'm just going to talk to Benjamin, not release him. Besides...she wants this ghost mess cleaned up just as much as we do. It doesn't help anyone the way things are now."

Casey eyed him dubiously. "But you realize she *must* have an ulterior motive, right? It's Melanie King we're talking about."

Vincent sighed. "Maybe. But what other choice do we have? If the portal's corruption keeps spreading..."

They were quiet for a moment.

Then Casey said, "So what, you're just gonna waltz straight into Hell and then back out again? Isn't Benjamin being imprisoned there? You'd have to break into–into Hell Prison! How does one even *do* that?"

"You're forgetting–I'm the prison guard."

It was bullshit. He knew it. There *was* no plan for getting into Hell and back unscathed. There was only one failsafe–and that was Vincent himself. If he belonged in Hell, he was going to dedicate the last of the life he had built for himself to fixing everything he had broken along the way. Now all he had to do was convince Casey that everything would be okay. Otherwise…she would never let him do it.

"And the *other* prison guards won't recognize you?" she countered.

"Of course they would. I just have to avoid getting caught. I can blend in enough, from afar. And I know my way around." *Please, Casey. Just trust me.*

"Oh, it's that easy, then." She crossed her arms and immediately winced. Her neck was still bleeding sluggishly. Vincent frowned at her.

"You need to get patched up. You don't look so good."

"Shut up. I'm fine."

Vincent didn't bother protesting. Instead, he started off again down the road, forcing her to follow. He had run out of arguments–better to distract her, for now.

The sun continued to rise, bringing its heat along with it. By the time they made it back to the house they were more damp with sweat than blood. Casey looked especially pale. They managed to sneak inside and grab a first aid kit from the bathroom before retreating to Casey's room.

She pulled her shirt collar down enough for him to get good access to her neck wounds. Despite their oozing, they had already begun to heal–it was clear the stranger hadn't meant to truly hurt her. Vincent wiped them clean and began dressing them. Casey's jaw clenched tight, but she didn't complain.

"Did he get you?" she asked.

Vincent shook his head, still focusing on his work. "Not too bad. Thanks to you." He hadn't even paid much attention to it; only now did he realize his nose ached, and patches of his skin felt raw where his fur had been ripped away. He had been spared the worst of it.

As soon as he finished with her neck, she lifted her shirt to expose her side. His heart skittered in surprise. Her skin was soft, the curves of her muscles and ribs graceful–all but the jagged scar that tore down her side, all the way to the hip. It was almost merciful; it gave Vincent something else to focus on, other than his own awkwardness.

"Did–did that just happen?"

"Yeah. Clean it, would you?"

Dimly Vincent realized there was a fresh scratch across her ribs, just beside the scar. At the same moment, Casey followed his gaze, her expression tightening.

"Oh. Yeah. No, that was...before. When he changed me."

Silence persisted for a long moment.

"Are you gonna patch it up, or what?"

Vincent quickly reached for the antiseptic. He stayed quiet while he worked, unsure what to say. He kept his eyes carefully fixed on the spot.

After a while, Casey couldn't seem to take it. "Never noticed it before, huh?"

"...No."

Casey snickered lightly. "Too polite to stare? What a gentleman."

Vincent grimaced. "You never let me get that close before."

"Yeah, yeah. Well...I can't reach this one myself."

It was a weak excuse, and they both knew it. It struck Vincent how different things were from the last time they had to do this. Before, they were all but enemies. Now...

Everything went wrong when Connor and the others died. But maybe with you here...with you...

He was sure of it now. Against all odds, Casey...had feelings for him.

The familiar tide of guilt swelled again in his gut. He *liked* her, of course he did. Not at first, but...now, after everything...

She was clever, funny, courageous. Unfailingly loyal, more than he had ever imagined. He had been wrong about her—she was guarded and hostile, yes, but there was so much more to her than that. She didn't hold back, because that's what the world had taught her to do. And he loved her for it. He loved *her*. She was his pack, just like he had told the old werewolf.

For a split second, he wondered what would happen if he did reciprocate. This place was too small for them...but if they went somewhere else. Back to Alderwood...

The idea of it struck his heart like lightning. And he knew that it was impossible. Because he had too much to fix. And...because Alderwood meant Henry. When he thought of Henry, the entire world tilted on its axis. His insides lit ablaze. That gravity in his heart returned ferociously—that sixth sense that had once tethered him to Benjamin as his hunter's mark, that pulled on him whenever he neared the portal to Hell. But this time it was for Henry.

The only difference: he didn't know where Henry was.

He ached for those clear blue eyes, those strong and soft arms, that steady voice, those tender hands. They made him feel small, but not weak. They made him feel safe. They not only touched him—they held him.

He wasn't alone anymore—not with Casey by his side. She had staved off the darkness in him for one wonderful moment. He had almost forgotten how it felt to be known. But it wasn't the same. Something empty still yawned in his chest. He was still lonely. And he hated himself for it.

I'm just like those people the stranger talked about. Nothing is ever enough for me.

Henry probably hates you, another, more vicious voice inside him piped up. *He never wants to see you again.*

But it didn't matter. The feeling didn't stop. Maybe it never would.

And in that moment, the idea that had been brewing in his mind finally settled. He knew what he had to do. None of this was fair to Casey. He had asked too much of her, time and again. Ignored her advice, her warnings, her feelings. He had promised her he would listen, going forward. But he didn't, and now she had to clean up another mess for him—because he was too weak.

And even after all that...here he was again, asking for another sacrifice. Even if she had left her home the first time on her own, this was different. Especially now, because of her grandmother.

She deserved better. He had promised her.

That night, Vincent crept out of bed with his pack hefted over his shoulder. As he stood in the doorway, his gaze lingered on his room one last time–the bed made, the decor pleasant and warm, for all the world as if it had always been a guest room. Then he tore himself away. He didn't let himself look into the living room, out the picture window towards the pool and the wide plains beyond, or anywhere else for that matter. He was tired of last looks.

He approached the front door like a prisoner walking to the gallows. Every step seemed to stretch the distance between. What felt like minutes later, he grasped the door handle and slowly, carefully pushed it open.

Its soft creak sounded like a wild howl in the silence. He glanced over his shoulder, just to be safe–

A silhouette stood behind him. His heart leaped into his throat.

"I'm s–"

Then he caught the scent, and realized who it was.

"Are you leaving without her?" said Casey's grandmother.

Vincent stared dumbly. "Y–you shouldn't be out of bed, *bà*. What if you trip–"

"I know this house well enough. And I also know when you are trying to distract me, *cháu*."

Guilt lanced his heart. *Grandson.*

"I...I'm not taking her from you. I can't."

"I know she is not meant to be here. She has always had a restless soul."

"But–"

"Listen to my words," Casey's grandmother said sternly. He shut up. "She belongs with people her own age. With you. I am cared for here, and that is what matters. Casey needs to discover her own path in life. She will not find that here, so she must go."

"If she leaves, you may never see her again." Vincent's voice cracked. "I can't do that to her. But I can't stay here. Your family has been nothing but kind to me, and I'm so grateful...but I have other things I have to do. Important things."

Casey's grandmother nodded slowly, patiently. "I know. And so does she."

A long silence took hold. Then, softly, a new voice broke it:

"Are you sure, *bà?*"

Casey stepped out from the hallway. Vincent's heart jolted, but she didn't seem angry to catch him here. Her eyes were only for her grandmother.

"Yes, *cháu.*" The blind old woman felt for Casey's hands, taking them in her own. "Your mother may disagree, but I know you should be out there, in the world. There are so many opportunities for you. I want you to find them, and be happy."

Vincent couldn't see her expression, but he knew what Casey must be thinking. She had no idea what was in store for her out there. But if she was coming along...she had to save the world.

"Thank you, *bà*, thank you," Casey breathed, staunched tears heavy in her voice. "I'll visit you as soon as I can. I promise."

"I know you will. Do not worry for me–I am stronger than I look."

She embraced her grandmother, and Vincent looked away, leaving them their moment. He wandered out the front door, his gaze fixed on the impossible spray of stars glittering across the vast sky. He would miss them. He would miss a lot of things about this place, despite its shortcomings.

Most of all, he would miss the idea of *normal.* A home. A family. All of a sudden, he couldn't blame Henry for wanting that *normal.* It was easy.

But it wasn't.

Finally, Casey joined him. She had her own backpack with her now, as if she had already been ready to leave. She didn't look at him, didn't say a word. Instead she started towards the road. Discomfort roiled in Vincent's stomach.

"You can't do this for me."

She stopped. "I'm not."

"Then what are you doing it for?"

"Me, stupid."

"But your fam–"

"I know they love me, Vincent."

He paused, mouth half-open, thought half-finished.

"And I love them. I do. But there is *so* much more out there than what they want from me."

"You can't do this for me," he said again. Insisted.

Casey finally looked back, and the moonlight revealed a wry smile. "I'm *not*. I *came here* for your sorry ass. Besides," she added, turning back to the road, "there are too many ghosts here."

Vincent wanted to smile back, but he couldn't. This wasn't what he had wanted, but...he couldn't stop her. And some part of him didn't want to. He followed after her.

"Then let's put a few back where they belong."

CHAPTER 9

OLD HAUNTS

Returning to Alderwood was somehow even more overwhelming than Vincent had expected. Heavy as it was with memories, he had forgotten just how dark the air felt, sodden with the runoff from the portal to Hell. At first he thought it had simply been so long since he felt it, it was no wonder he was so affected. But as time wore on, he realized that it had gotten far worse.

This place was desolate. Every step was leaden. His heart felt numb and sticky, caked in the ethereal muck from each shadow that flickered across the edges of his vision. Even the daylight was gloomy, making it easier to see that every corner seemed to house another evanescent curtain. The spirits were *everywhere* now.

Worse still, as Vincent and Casey crossed town, the phantoms began to drift nearer and nearer, closing ranks around them, fizzling with dark curiosity.

No—with *hunger*. A shiver coursed up Vincent's spine. He could feel it, almost as if it were his own. He knew what they wanted. What they *needed*.

Casey's own gaze shifted constantly, growing more anxious every minute. She was puffed up, brave, but she was afraid. She had always hated the dead. But she kept her mouth shut tight; it gave her away, because Vincent knew she wouldn't be able to keep the reality of it at bay if she spoke. It was all she could do to pretend it wasn't happening, to close everything out. He gave her that gift. It was the least he could do, for bringing her back here.

As Vincent and Casey walked across campus for the second time in so many months, they kept a wary eye out for Shadowhand, or anyone else who might recognize them. Fortunately it was the height of summer, weeks before school would start up again. They only spotted a couple people wandering the grounds from afar, and made sure to give them a wide berth.

They reached Vincent's old dorm, Walden Hall, without any trouble. By then his heart was in his throat. He jumped when Casey elbowed him.

"Alright, why are we here?"

"I forgot something back in my old room."

Vincent dug through his pocket for his keys. Casey eyed him dubiously.

"You still have your keys?"

"Yeah."

"Don't you think they might've changed the locks?"

He froze, his heart sinking. *Why didn't I think of that?*

"There's no way they'd want to spend that much money redoing all the keys," he reasoned, hoping it was true. "People lose theirs all the time..."

He fumbled with the lock, trying to steady his hands. There wasn't much time to linger without attracting suspicion. He couldn't afford to waste any more of it trying to figure out another way in—especially without being seen. That was a risk they couldn't take. His only hope was–

The key turned. Vincent opened the front door, turning to Casey smugly.

"After you."

Casey snorted, but ducked inside. Vincent followed, and soon he was overcome with the familiarity of his old home. The pleasantly musty smell of old wood filled a hole in his heart. It was half-dark inside, an alternating pattern of overhead lights turned off for the summer, on for the cleaning crew. The gloom felt more oppressive here, too. It seemed to creep around the corners of the lobby into the hallways, broken only by the eerie luminescence of the vending machines in their nook.

They slunk down the hall, passing rows of dorm room doors, all of them shut tight. It was so silent it almost seemed like the air itself was muffled. The closer they got to the end of the hall, the heavier it felt, until finally Vincent stopped in front of his old room.

Once the door had been adorned with stickers of motivational phrases and dinosaurs, but now it lay bare. Not even names were affixed to it now, leaving only the metallic number "139" shining on its facade. Vincent's heart twisted at the bleakness of it. He unlocked the door, relieved yet again that his key worked.

Immediately the darkness hit him like a hurricane, nearly sending him staggering backwards. Casey too cringed against it. It was so powerful, it felt physical. Both of them hovered in the doorway, shellshocked.

"Is he–"

Suddenly, another door swung open just down the hall. The noise sent both of them scrambling into the dark room.

Vincent closed the door swiftly behind them, and all light disappeared.

He paused, listening. No shouts or sounds of pursuit. A moment later, Casey's voice reached him in the dark.

"He's...he's still here, isn't he?"

Vincent turned away from the door, the murk engulfing his senses. A shudder traveled up his spine. The presence here was achingly familiar, but also not. He was used to something smaller, localized; this was oppressive, oozing into every corner of the room like quicksand, hoping to drag anyone who dared enter into its depths.

And yet, it wasn't vengeful. It tasted like despair.

Vincent tried the light switch. It didn't work. Casey had backed up against the door, only the whites of her eyes visible in the gloom. He could hear her shaky breaths just beside him. She must have felt it just as acutely as he did, for even her to cower–but unlike him, she wasn't used to the feeling. Forceful as it was now, Vincent had grown accustomed to its essence many months ago.

"W-whatever you're getting, do it fast, damn it," Casey growled.

Vincent scanned the corners of the ceiling, grasping for any variation in the blackness. He took another step into the room, tentative, searching. His skin prickled with cold. Something terrible had been festering here. He could sense it in his very soul.

"Where are you, Percy?" he called softly.

Something stuttered in the darkness. Vincent cast his eyes towards it, seeing nothing, but feeling it like a vibration in the air.

"What happened to you?" His voice came barely above a whisper, like an inviting hand outstretched. It was very different from the Vincent who had first spoken to this miserable being long ago. "Why are you still here? I thought you might have moved on..."

"*No.*"

The word came more as a sensation than a sound, like a winter wind driving him back. Again he shivered, but held fast.

"Do you remember me? It's Vincent. Your roommate."

No answer came. He gritted his teeth. Maybe this was more of a long shot than he had realized. When he first met Percy, the specter already had trouble collecting his thoughts and memories. After the trauma of what had happened last, he could have easily slipped even further into the void of death...

"*I killed her.*"

Vincent blinked in shock. He felt something coalescing in the corner. He could almost see it, even–the gray light filtering between the closed blinds in the window seemed to reach the room now where it hadn't before, but only just. There was a formless spot of shadow just above Percy's bed, impenetrable by the light.

"Percy...?"

"*I killed her.*"

The words came stronger this time, laced with a gravity that sunk into Vincent's bones, weighing him down. He could feel it–that despair, that misery, that agony, like particles in the very air that absorbed into his lungs and became a part of him.

All at once he knew what had happened here.

"You didn't kill her, Percy," Vincent said, fighting through the mire. "Benjamin killed her. Melanie and Jake and Hunter killed her."

"*I brought her there. I walked her to her death.*"

Vincent didn't know exactly what had happened, but he knew Percy reliving it was a bad idea. What else could he say to him? He pawed through the roiling thoughts in his head, grasping for something, anything. He had spent so long pushing it all away, it was all a jumble now—one he hardly wanted to relive himself. But he had to.

"I'm sorry I wasn't there," he said at last, settling on what shone through the murk inside his mind. The guilt followed like a knife wound, but he weathered the pain. "I should have been there. I should have stopped them."

But instead, he had been with Henry. Sitting by his side, guarding him, tending his wounds, kissing him, murmuring the soft, aching contents of his soul in the dark of his room, indulging a part of himself he had always kept locked away somewhere deep inside the stone labyrinth of his heart. All the while, Ava was dying. Percy was dying, for the second time.

And now, Henry was gone. It had all been for nothing.

His own darkness was so thick, it was difficult to tell where it ended and Percy's began. He tore himself from it just enough to speak again.

"What are you going to do now?"

At first, he wasn't sure Percy was going to answer at all. But then:

"*I deserve this room. I deserve to stay here, forever. It's the only place I belong, now.*"

He was so resolute, Vincent could hardly recognize him. The usual tremor in his voice had disappeared—but in the worst way.

"How is that helping anything?" Vincent challenged.

He felt the slightest tingle of interest in the air, emanating from Percy. It was enough to egg him on.

"You're just wasting away. Eventually they'll just put more students in here, and you'll have to watch them going about their lives without a clue you even exist."

"*I deserve to be forgotten.*"

Now Vincent felt a prickle of annoyance—his own, this time. "You deserve a lot of things, but being forgotten isn't one of them. You should come with us, instead."

"What?" Casey finally spoke out, incredulous. "You came here to *invite him along?*"

Vincent already knew she wouldn't be happy. She had no love for Percy. "I'm not leaving him alone here to wallow for the rest of his days. Sooner or later someone will find him, and then the Shadowhand will exorcize him, or whatever it is they do. Henry isn't here to protect him anymore."

He realized that, without thinking, he had known that fact all along. Of course Henry had protected Percy. He protected Sierra. He always protected his friends.

He had even protected Vincent. Despite everything he had done.

"You don't think he deserves that?" Casey spat. "He possessed Ava, he lied to us, he got her killed!"

"He didn't mean to get her killed, and you know that."

"But it happened anyway! Because he was stupid and gullible enough to walk into it, *twice!*" Vincent could feel the room darkening again with every word she spoke. "And you know *none* of it would've happened if he had just given up possessing Ava when we asked him to!"

She was right. He couldn't argue with that–in fact, he didn't want to. He was angry with Percy too, but more quietly so.

"It's too late." He fought to keep his voice steady. "It's happened, so we have to decide what we want to do now."

"Well, I don't want to be responsible for his sorry ass. I'm leaving."

Vincent rounded on her. "Then what about me? None of this would have happened if I hadn't let Benjamin escape from Hell. Do you know how many deaths are on *my* shoulders? Not just *one*, that's for sure. And yet you've stuck with me all this way."

Casey paused, her hand on the door handle. He realized a moment too late what he had said.

When her voice came, it was cold and quiet. "*You* didn't take over someone else's body."

"No. But he didn't hurt her, either. Me...I've hurt people." He forced it out, barely holding the memories of Hell beneath the surface, suffocating them. "And so have you. None of us are blameless." It was too late to pretend it hadn't happened.

Casey was silent. It was so unlike her—and yet, he had seen it too many times now. Standing in the orange grove, bloody and tear-stained in the cresting dawn...

Suddenly, he understood. That old werewolf had taken her life from her. Her friends, her body, her future. All in the name of his own ideals—all in the hope that she shared them, and would stave off his loneliness. It was too close—too raw. The old man and Percy were so very different, but...they also weren't. Not enough.

With a painful twist of his heart, Vincent drew close to her. Laid a gentle hand on her back. "We can't forgive him for what he did to Ava. We *won't*. But he's already dead. I don't want to let him be destroyed forever just to prove a point, Casey."

But before she could answer, to Vincent's surprise, Percy spoke.

"*No...she's right. You should leave me here. But...please, take Ava with you.*"

"You know where Ava is?" Casey demanded.

"*Across the hall. In her old room.*"

"Have you talked to her? Do you think she'd come with us?" Vincent pressed.

A gloomy air descended upon them. "*If it's between that and disappearing...*"

Obviously Percy and Ava weren't on the best of terms. He couldn't blame her. But he couldn't imagine she would be thrilled with him and Casey, either. After all, they had failed to help her, and she was never too fond of them to begin with.

"I'm gonna get her," said Casey urgently. She shot Vincent a glare that even pierced the darkness in the room. "Do what you want with that lowlife. But he's your responsibility."

Before Vincent could reply she opened the door, the light in the hall assaulting his eyes. He flinched against it, and when it gave way again to darkness, she was gone.

Left alone with the remnants of Percy's misery, an uncertain awkwardness settled over him. His fingers itched to pull his tie taut. He kept them still. His thoughts churned, haunted by the shadows of his own guilt, gooey with the residue of Percy's. How was he supposed to convince the poor kid to come along with them now?

Before he could try, Percy spoke up again, his voice more feeble this time. *"I...I miss you guys. I really do. I-I'm glad you're safe, Vincent."*

His heart clenched. This sounded a lot more like his old friend. It was almost too much to bear, seeing how far he was now from who he used to be. Both of them.

"I'm not really safe, Percy," Vincent said grimly. "The Shadowhand are hunting me, too."

He felt Percy's presence swirl in the corner, as if trying to collect its thoughts.

"W-what happened? Where's Henry? Y-you said he's gone now..."

Again Vincent's heart caught in his throat, and he had to steel himself before the pain overwhelmed him. He knew he couldn't lie to Percy–he didn't deserve that, after everything. And, more than that, Vincent deserved his shame.

And so he told Percy everything–everything except what he and Henry alone shared. When he reached the moment Henry found him torturing Jake for information about Benjamin's plot, he choked. In the end, all he said was:

"He hated me, Percy. He still does. It was...the moment he realized just how different we both were." Vincent squeezed his eyes shut, as if that would block out the ache of it. "Until that moment...he thought he finally found a kindred spirit. He told me that." *And so much more. But it wasn't true.*

Percy hesitated, his discomfort like a scent in the air. He didn't like what Vincent had done either. Vincent almost laughed at the irony of it. Finally the ghost said, *"W...why? Why did you do it?"*

"Because people were dying, Percy. I did it for them. For *you.* Jake had helped Benjamin hurt so many people, and I couldn't figure out why... It was the easiest way to put the pieces together. To stop them."

"D-did it help?"

Vincent gritted his teeth. "No. He didn't tell us anything before Henry let him go."

An echo of Henry's voice broke through the walls in his mind: *The ends do* not *justify the means, Vincent!*

"I would have had him, though. Someone had to do it. I just...I didn't want that person to be Henry."

Something familiar settled in the space between the two of them. Vincent recognized it immediately, resentfully. *We both deserve what we got.*

He continued his story, until he finally dragged Benjamin back to Hell. Percy's shock tingled over Vincent's skin.

"Th-that's why you were here in the first place? For Benjamin?"

Vincent nodded wearily. "I...I failed in my duties as a guard. I let him escape. I let him trick me."

It was so much more complicated than that—so much worse. But for everything he deserved, he couldn't bring himself to divulge the details of his greatest shame to Percy like this. His hand reached for his tie reflexively, and he forced it back down. *No more collars. They won't fix you.*

"I...had to bring him back to Hell, eventually. My father set me up here so I could, with all these resources and a cover. I wasn't supposed to just charge in and alert all the mortals, obviously."

So much for that... He wondered how difficult it was for the Shadowhand to cover *that* up. He realized all at once that he might have given Melanie a leg up on revealing the existence of the Others to the mortal world.

"But Benjamin is crafty. He made sure he had bodyguards, and a good cover, and a plan...something strange I didn't understand."

"B-but...did you need to know what he was planning before you could take him back?" Percy asked.

Vincent hesitated before deciding to give him the truth. What was the point in lying to him, or himself, now?

"Not really...no. But I wanted to know. It was enough for Benjamin to fight so hard to escape Hell for. And I thought...maybe I could do things a better way. Henry's way." *He thought I was good, once. I thought maybe I could be, too.* "And..." He sighed. "I liked it here. The food, and the trees, and the fresh air, and the fun things I could do. I liked having friends. I liked choosing things for myself. I liked being a person, instead of a guard." *A tool.*

The chill in the room warmed slightly. "*Y-you liked us that much?*"

"...Yeah. I did. And...that's why I decided to stay."

Chasing away his awkwardness, Vincent went on, to the very end. When he had finished, he felt Percy's essence trained on him with palpable awe. "*Y-you ran away from Hell? Wow...that's really brave, Vincent.*"

Warmth crept up Vincent's neck. "Well...not really. Thanks, though." *I'm a coward. I ran. I'm hiding, even now.*

"*B-but...what happened to Henry? He was around for a while, I-I remember seeing him... Sometimes he would come in here and talk to me.*"

Vincent froze. "Really?"

"*Yeah...I-I mean, he couldn't see me or hear me or anything...but he would sit on the bed and just kinda...talk at me.*"

Vincent's heart tightened in his chest. "Did he...what did he say?"

Percy paused, thinking hard. "*I...I don't remember much, I-I'm sorry. It's hard, like this...*"

Figures. Vincent was honestly surprised Percy was this lucid, with how far he had sunken into misery. It was hard enough for him to collect his thoughts before he had possessed Ava, but now...

"*I...I remember, though, he was...lonely. He felt lonely. I-I don't think I saw him smile once, in all that time.*"

The news wasn't as satisfying as Vincent had hoped. Instead, it only felt hollow. They had both lost so much, and for what?

"I only saw him once, after I returned from Hell," Vincent murmured. "He told me he was sorry. For everything. And...then he left." His voice cracked at the end, and he didn't even have the heart to hate himself for it. He cleared his throat. "He said he called the Shadowhand here to help, but...he changed his mind. Only it was too late. He went to stall them, give us a chance to hide. I don't know what happened to Jake, or Hunter, or the other vampires Benjamin made. I guess Melanie managed to avoid blame. I saw her at graduation, just–"

He stopped, his thoughts finally catching up with him. Was he ready to talk about what happened at graduation? No, but he knew he wasn't getting out of it–he had to tell Percy about Henry's capture. He owed it to him.

When he had finished, Percy was quiet for a time.

"He's...he's not coming back?"

"I...don't think so."

Suddenly, the door swung open. The room flooded with light.

Vincent flinched away until the door closed again. Casey jostled against him in the dark–and something else seemed to press against him as well, without truly touching him. It was like another source of gravity had entered the room, tugging his soul in a different direction. This one, however, wasn't dripping with despair–instead it felt lighter, buzzing with energy like a storm before a lightning strike.

"Ava's coming with us," said Casey. "But we gotta go. There's people around."

"Ava?" Vincent said gingerly.

A familiar voice, one he hadn't heard in even longer than Percy's, drifted to his ears like the first bite of autumn wind. *"I'm here."*

A tide of guilt and unease swept over him. "It's, ah...good to hear your voice."

She didn't reply. Instead, Casey said, "So how were you planning on getting Percy out of here? The amulet?"

Vincent nodded. He dug the necklace out of his pocket. Even in the half-light he could make out the glint of silver.

Instantly the air in the room changed. Both ghosts drifted closer to it, as if drawn by its presence. But Percy broke off.

"Ava...I-I know you don't want to hear it, but before you go–"

"You've said it enough already. 'Sorry' isn't going to change anything for me, Percy."

A dark silence settled over Percy's essence. Ava's, however, continued towards the amulet. Vincent felt the edge of her spirit brush like ice against his fingertips.

But then, just before touching the stone, she paused.

"*So you really aren't coming, then?*"

"*...No.*"

They all heard a soft *tch*.

"*What will you do, then? Waste away in here? Give yourself up to the Shadowhand?*"

The room seemed to warp with the weight of even more melancholy. "*I-I guess so. I don't know. Whatever happens, happens.*"

A sudden pulse of rage almost made Vincent stumble backwards.

"*That's how you're leaving things? You're giving up?*"

Vincent felt Percy's presence tremble. "*I–I deserve it, you said so yourse–*"

"*I said 'sorry' isn't enough. I didn't say you're off the hook just because you're wallowing in self-pity.*"

Nobody else seemed able to speak. Whatever Vincent had expected from Ava, it wasn't this.

Finally Percy stammered, "*W-what else am I supposed to do? I–I killed you, I tried to help and I–*"

"*You're pathetic!*" Ava spat, halting Percy in his tracks. "*You think that was helping? You poisoned my mind! You made me feel like I needed you! All because you had to help your friends make a werewolf potion, and then you had to help your friends catch a murderer–you had to feel alive again for just a little longer!*"

"He *did* help," Vincent broke in, unable to keep quiet. An ember of his own resentment was burning in his stomach. "More than you did. I'm sorry for what happened to you, but...you could have stopped so many people from dying."

Another burst of fury coursed through the air. "*How dare you! I'm dead because of you!*"

For once, Vincent's anger outmatched his guilt. "And you might not be if you had just helped us when we asked you to! I told you anyone could be next to die! But you only cared if it was *you*, not anyone else. And you were so sure it couldn't be."

"*I* did *help*," Ava hissed. "*When* you *losers asked me to do a seance to talk to* that *loser, I did it!*"

"Only after it was too late! You strung us along for *weeks*, promising to ask your super-magical famous grandmother how to help Percy remember his death, catch his killer–and what did you do? *Nothing.* Not until we needed help getting Percy out of the amulet."

"And then you bragged about being able to withstand a possession," Casey pointed out dryly. "Even when Henry and Vincent warned you not to. It wasn't their fault this happened."

Casey's defense warmed Vincent in a way he didn't expect. Even if he disagreed that it wasn't his fault, at least in part.

The air jolted with Ava's outrage. But then, slowly, the blaze faded.

"*Well, none of it matters now, does it? I'm dead,*" she said bitterly. Vincent felt her focus shift sharply to Percy. "*But* you *aren't getting out of this that easy.*"

"*W-what?*"

"*You heard me. You're coming with us.*"

A stunned silence followed her words.

"*I–I can't, I'm–*"

"*Yes, you can. You owe it to me, after what you did. You have to at least try to make it right.*"

Percy's aura sank. "*How could I ever make it right?*" It didn't sound like a question at all.

"*You can't, really,*" Ava admitted. "*But I still think you should try. I couldn't stand it if I knew you were just rotting in this stupid room, throwing yourself a pity party.*"

"*I–I'm not throwing a pity party!*"

"Yeah, you are! You held me hostage, then you got me killed, and now you're playing highlight reels in whatever's left of your mind!"

"I-I'd never do that! I love you, Ava...I still do. I can't even tell you how sorry I am..." Vincent would have thought Percy was about to cry, apart from the fact that he no longer could.

"That wasn't love. It was desperation." Ava sighed before he could argue. *"If you're really sorry, then prove it. Don't just sit in your room. Help me find a way out of this."*

A current of interest passed through the air. *"H-help you...?"*

"Out of what?" Vincent asked.

"This. I want to move on. I want to go to the afterlife."

"I thought you knew how to help ghosts move on," Casey said.

"I told you, I don't. My grandma does."

Vincent and Casey exchanged a glance.

"Magdalena. You think we should find her?" asked Vincent.

"If anyone knows how, she does."

"Where does she live?"

"A few hours from here, just south of Newport."

Casey groaned. "We *just* got back!"

"Well, she probably won't be there anyway. Not if the Shadowhand are crawling around as much as you say."

"I thought she was friends with them?" said Vincent.

"Not really. Acquaintances. They're always trying to recruit her for favors. She says they're worse than solicitors. She's gone camping before when they got too persistent."

"So you want us to go gallivanting about in the woods, trying to find the old broad?" Casey looked to Vincent incredulously. "We don't have time for this."

Vincent cast his gaze about for Ava, finding nothing but the barest feeling of her presence nearby. "I'm sorry, Ava, but she's right. Everything is messed up right now. We need to fix the portal to Hell before we can do anything else. Otherwise, with all these spirits pouring through..."

He wondered if there was even anywhere for Ava to move on to. He had no idea whether she would have ended up in Hell, or if the portal being broken had disrupted anything else about death's natural roads.

"*I-I can hear them, sometimes,*" Percy spoke up in a small, hollow voice. It sent a shiver up Vincent's spine. "*T-they whisper, in the dark...down the halls...along the walls outside...*"

"They're everywhere," Vincent agreed quietly. "They were stalking us, on the way here..." He exchanged a glance with Casey. "I can't imagine what it must be like for mortals living here."

She only grimaced.

"*I-I wonder when they'll finally break in here...take my room...they're getting closer every day...*"

"Which is why you need to come with us," Vincent insisted. "It's only getting worse. Maybe Magdalena can help you move on, too."

Percy didn't reply. Vincent felt his muggy uncertainty in the air around them.

"*How long is it gonna take for you guys to fix this portal?*" Ava broke in, annoyed.

"I don't know. We don't know how," Vincent admitted, equally annoyed. "We have to go back to Hell and talk to Benjamin."

"*Y-you what?*" Percy exclaimed, horrified.

Vincent sighed. "Yeah. I know. But we don't know what else to do. He broke it, so...hopefully he knows how to fix it."

"And will tell us," Casey muttered.

"*Fantastic. I'm never gonna get out of here,*" growled Ava.

"You don't have to do anything but wait," said Vincent. "We're going to leave you both with our friends for a while, until we come back. You'll be safe with them."

"*W-we're not coming along to help?*" Percy asked.

"What could you help with? The last thing I want is for more people to be in danger for no reason."

Vincent was surprised by a sudden burst of indignation in the air. "*I-I helped before! I helped save Henry, I followed Hunter and told you he met up with Benjamin–*"

"You don't have a body now, Percy," Vincent interrupted. He couldn't fully keep the coldness out of his voice.

"*You were using mine!*" Ava spat. "*Or did you forget?*"

Percy's determination died away silently.

"*Take me away from here,*" Ava said suddenly. A frigid breath crossed Vincent's fingers again, approaching the amulet he still held. "*I'll stay with your friends. But you'd better come back for me, and soon. You owe me that much.*"

"You have my word," said Vincent.

The cold washed over Vincent's hand like freezing water, and then it moved inside the amulet. It felt like ice for a moment before it ebbed away, leaving the turquoise indistinguishable from any other stone, apart from a faint hum of energy emanating from within.

"...Ava?" Vincent tested.

"*I can hear you.*" Her voice seemed to come from inside Vincent's own head, but Casey also looked around for the source of it.

"Everything okay?"

"*Yeah. It's a luxury hotel in here.*"

Vincent suppressed a snort. "I'm glad."

Suddenly, the distinct padding of footsteps reached them through the door.

For a long moment no one breathed. It was easier for some than others.

The sound faded, traveling down the hall.

"We need to move," Casey hissed, grabbing Vincent's arm.

"Percy," he said urgently, almost pleadingly.

"*W-won't I have to go into the amulet? Ava w-won't want–*"

"*It's whatever. I told you, you're gonna help me move on. You can't do that if you're stuck in this room.*"

Vincent could feel Percy grasping for more excuses, but there weren't any.

For a moment he thought he was going to have to wrangle Percy into the amulet himself. But then he felt the telltale chill run up his fingers and into the stone.

Immediately the air inside the room lightened. It was easier to breathe. The gray light from outside found its way between the blinds properly. It struck Vincent just how much worse, how much darker and more powerful Percy's essence was compared to Ava's. He was surprised to find a shiver coursing through his bones. Meek as Percy had always been, he had somehow become something formidable without realizing it. And not in a good way.

You need to move on, too, Percy, he thought. *All of these spirits do.*

Casey cracked the door, peering out. After a moment she ushered Vincent into the hall. He didn't look back at his old room, but he felt a tug at his heart as he left it behind. Some part of him was still tethered to it, just like Percy.

If I became a ghost, where would I be trapped? he wondered briefly as they hurried down the hall.

They burst out the back door into the fresh air. No one pursued them. Vincent and Casey exchanged a breathless look that turned into a grin. They made it.

"Well, that's step one," said Vincent.

"*I* thought step one was finding the pack," Casey growled, but it was mostly for show. She led the way across the parking lot. "You're lucky that went well, or else."

"Oh, come on, Casey. Would you really feel okay leaving them both to fester in there?"

Casey grunted in reply.

"Yeah, that's what I thought. Do you think Dex and the others will still be at the Lab?"

"I sure fucking hope so. Otherwise we've got a whole new problem on our hands."

This time, as they crossed the gray campus, they didn't see another soul—living, anyway. The specters were always there, drifting, watching, grasping. They were the most eerie on the empty road leading into town, starker against the deep shadows beneath the pines that bordered the pavement. Vincent and Casey walked in the center to avoid the worst of them, trying not to look. A few times they had to narrowly sneak past one to avoid passing straight through their ever-shifting forms. Neither of them wanted to know what would happen if they touched.

Finally they spotted the familiar sign suspended over the buildings ahead. The neon was off, despite the daytime gloom. So was the music that normally spilled from the garage. And yet, everything looked just as they had left it. This fact seemed uncanny, somehow. They hesitated outside the shop's front door.

After a moment, Casey said to him, "Coward." She stepped up to buzz the doorbell.

Silence.

They waited. No one came to the door. Nothing moved.

Casey pushed the button a few more times. She waited. Then she began banging on the shop door.

"It's me, damn it! Let us in, dickheads! You're freaking us out!"

Nothing.

"Maybe they had to move out," Vincent suggested, dread slowly filling his stomach. "Maybe Dex thought it would be safer somewhere else."

"He loved this place too fucking much," Casey argued, still pounding on the door. She then tried the handle, shoving with all her body weight as if she thought that would help. She growled and stepped back a few paces, craning her neck to try and peer through the upper windows.

"Casey..."

"Fuck this. I'm breaking in."

Casey strode off around the side of the building, all the way to the backyard. Vincent followed helplessly. They hopped the fence and found the back door just as stuck as the front. The curtains were drawn.

"You fucking bitches." Casey grabbed a hefty branch off the ground near the back woods. Before Vincent could protest or help she jabbed it like a javelin through the back window, smashing it. Vincent winced against the sound—it felt ten times as loud in the uneasy hush.

Casey continued muttering insults under her breath as she reached through the window and unlocked the door from the inside. She stepped through, seething too hard to be cautious.

"Wait!" Vincent hissed.

But it was too late.

Footsteps thudded behind them. From the trees, just beyond the yard. Something was coming. Hunting.

Vincent spun around—something *big*, its eyes flashing in the shadows—

"*Don't go in there!*"

CHAPTER 10

STILL HERE

"**R**oman?"

The young werewolf stood in broad daylight just beside the fence, flanks heaving. His eyes were wide with fear and shock as he looked at them, as if he couldn't quite believe they were real.

"*Not safe! Stay out!*"

Thankfully, Casey had halted in the doorway. She stepped back out, her own face a mirror to Roman's. "What do you mean? What's going on, Roman?"

Before he could reply, another familiar face appeared behind Casey from the gloom inside the house. Casey spun around, alarmed–Vincent could sense the shadow of her own wolf slipping over her, ready to defend itself. But this time it didn't need to.

Vincent could hardly believe it. It was Sierra Pechman.

Unlike the last time he had seen her, she was human. But her dark skin looked strangely ashy, a more prominent shadow hanging beneath her eyes. Still, when her smile emerged from her surprise, it was unmistakably Sierra.

"Vincent?"

She stumbled forward, brushing past Casey to envelop Vincent in her arms. They were as strong and fervent as he remembered, and his heart instantly settled into her touch with a weary gratitude. It was so warm and earnest, he couldn't help it. It had been so long since he had felt any close contact like this, apart from Casey's–and hers was far more complicated. It felt like being caught up in uncountable tangled strings, and even on parting it was impossible to extricate himself from them all. This, on the other hand, was a simple comfort.

"Sierra!" he greeted her warmly. When they pulled apart he found himself smiling up at her. He had almost forgotten how tall and built she was.

"*Sierra!*" Roman called, and she tore her gaze away from Vincent.

"It's okay, Roman! They're all in their rooms. Everything's locked up."

Roman visibly relaxed. He padded closer to them, but kept his wolf form.

"Is someone gonna tell us what the hell is going on?" Casey broke in.

"Not here." Sierra, glanced around the yard furtively. She waved them all inside.

Roman nudged the door shut behind them all, and the murk swallowed them. All the curtains were drawn. The only light came from a battery-powered lantern set up on the coffee table in the living room. Its bright white glow threw strange, stark shadows on the walls. Everyone gathered around it like moths, letting it guard them from the worst of the dark.

"Sierra, I can't believe you're here," said Vincent. "I saw you–" He stopped himself, realizing she had no idea he was the giant three-headed dog that had tackled her off the stage at graduation.

"It's okay. I know what you did."

Vincent blinked in surprise. "What do you–"

"Dex told me you saved me. We kinda had to figure out what happened. That *was* you, right...?"

Vincent bit his tongue. He nodded.

"It's okay. I'm *so* glad you were there. I...I lost my head." Everything about her dripped with shame. "I'm just so sorry. You shouldn't have had to do that. And Henry..."

"Nobody can blame you," Vincent insisted. "You're a werewolf, for god's sake. They aren't exactly known for their self-control."

Sierra looked up at him just as miserably as before. "That's the problem! I should've–"

"Henry knew you were a werewolf, and he let you go up there during a full moon. I have no idea what he was thinking. There's no way you could have stopped yourself, Melanie doing what she did..."

"I–I took a potion."

"You did?"

Sierra nodded. "Henry made it. It's been helping me during full moons."

"You took it that night?" Casey broke in.

"Yeah...well, a couple days before. I always do."

"Then you shouldn't have been able to transform at all. When I was taking it, I couldn't–even when I wanted to."

Sierra's brow furrowed. "Are...are you sure? Sometimes I couldn't fight it..."

Casey exchanged a glance with Vincent. "Guess wonderboy isn't a master chemist like he thought."

"He had Percy to help before," Vincent argued. "It's not like he studied it himself. He was doing his best."

Casey jerked upright suddenly. "What? Oh, don't you *dare* defend him now! After everything he's done–and now, he almost got Sierra killed, or anyone else there–"

Sierra winced.

"Just drop it," Vincent growled. "It doesn't matter now."

"Like hell it doesn't!"

"He just wanted me to have a normal life," Sierra said, her voice breaking. She was about to cry. "I-I didn't want to miss graduation..."

"Well, neither did I!" Casey snapped. "But sometimes life shits in your cereal! You wanna know what *I* had to do because of your little blunder?"

"*You* didn't graduate because you skipped class," Vincent said icily. He didn't like how she was suddenly targeting Sierra–or Henry, for that matter.

Casey rounded on him again. "Oh, *you* should talk! No, you're right–I didn't graduate because *you*–"

A horrible shriek tore through the house. All of them jumped, their heads snapping towards the stairs.

"What was that? Was that *Sloane?*" said Casey, alarmed.

"What's going on here?" Vincent demanded, turning back to Sierra. She looked despondent, but strangely unruffled.

"Everyone's okay, I promise."

"*For now,*" muttered the wolf-shaped Roman. He was curled up on the rug, his ears perked towards the stairs and his body tense.

"I...I had to lock everyone else in their rooms. I'm guessing you've seen the, um...the ghosts around here?"

Vincent nodded grimly. Casey just stared at her. "Are you saying they're *possessed?*"

Sierra's face turned desolate. She couldn't meet Casey's eyes. "I...I don't know. Maybe. They're just...not themselves anymore."

Vincent's heart sank into his stomach. "All of them?"

Sierra nodded miserably. "W-we've been trying to avoid the...the ghosts. But they're everywhere now. They're closing in. We were keeping them away with salt and sage and things, but..."

"*Full moon,*" Roman growled.

"We had to go out. We didn't have a choice." Sierra's voice hitched with guilt. "Th-the ghosts were everywhere, out in the woods. Dex, all of them, they told me and Roman to run..."

She couldn't seem to finish. Roman let out a long whine.

"Are they all here?" Vincent asked.

Sierra nodded slowly. "W-we finally managed to lure them inside, after a while..." Desperation shone in those once-warm brown eyes. "We have no idea what to do now. Please, help us."

"Of course we will," Vincent said at once. Worry battled with determination in his heart. Now he was even more certain that he needed Benjamin's help. They didn't have time to figure out anything else.

"Those fucking idiots." Casey gripped her head with both hands, curling in on herself. She clawed her fingers up her scalp, messing up her hair. Vincent had never seen her quite so bereft—not like this.

A sudden stab of guilt pierced through everything else. All of this was his fault. He had forced her to leave her family, twice, and now she was supposed to deal with this, too?

"We'll figure out how to exorcize them," Vincent insisted. He made himself lay a hand on Casey's shoulder, trying to comfort her. To his relief, she didn't move away. To Sierra, he said, "How are they? What are they doing?"

Sierra glanced towards the stairs. "It's...it's hard to describe. They're kinda...erratic. They'll scream like that, or they'll act weird...creepy..."

"Creepy how? Are they, like...aggressive? Violent?"

Sierra and Roman looked at each other again helplessly.

"N...nothing we couldn't handle, but..."

"Can I see them?"

Sierra looked simultaneously relieved and worried. "O-okay. Yeah...maybe you should."

She handed Vincent the lantern, and the two of them started upstairs. They ignored Casey's call after them:

"What are we supposed to do down here, huh? Sit in the dark?"

The darkness clung sudden and thick at the edges of the lantern's glow, as if it was made of something more material than just the absence of light. It reminded Vincent of Hell–far too distinctly. It seemed to take forever to reach the top of the stairs, and then the first door on the left. Every room was shut tight, but Vincent could hear the thump of footsteps pacing behind the doors. Mutters came from inside, the words too muffled to make out.

Sierra produced a little brass key. They both hesitated by the door.

"What am I going to see in there?" Vincent asked.

"It's...hard to explain," Sierra admitted. "I'm not even sure. It changes... Just keep your wits about you, I guess. And don't let them out."

"Are they dangerous?"

"Not as much as they were. When they were wolves, I mean. But...I don't know what they can do, now. Maybe you can get through to them..."

She was resting her hopes on him. He could tell by the way she was looking at him–a little like she always had. He suppressed a sigh, his nerves beginning to flutter in his stomach.

They're just spirits, Vincent. You know how to deal with the dead.

But he knew he didn't–not as much as he had once thought.

He unlocked the door and cracked it open.

It was too dark to see inside. But nothing rushed him.

Steeling himself, he opened it a little further. He lifted the lantern, casting its eerie white light into the room.

It didn't penetrate far, but it was enough to outline a familiar figure sitting on the bed. Only the whites of his eyes were visible in the gloom; his skin and hair and clothes were all too dark. The lack of movement and expression, only the suggestion of a human sent a shiver crawling up Vincent's body.

"D...Dex? Is that you?"

"It's you."

It was so quiet, Vincent almost didn't catch it.

"Ah...yeah. Are you alright? Sierra says something happened..."

Ever so slightly, the silhouette's head tilted. "It did..."

Vincent stayed frozen in the doorway. Something wasn't right. It was Dex's voice, but it was too subdued. Too hesitant.

"What was it? What happened to you?"

"I died."

Suddenly, the door moved under his hand.

Something whispered in his ear.

He looked. Only an inch from his face, crowded in the crack behind the door: a shadow. A person.

He leaped back, slamming into the door frame. Sierra called out his name, but he hardly heard her over the roar of his own blood in his ears. His eyes were fixed on that figure behind the door—he couldn't pull them away.

That is, until Dex moved. Vincent backed into the hall, every nerve ablaze with dread as the silhouette of his friend paced calmly towards him, one slow step at a time.

"Close the door! Close the door!" Sierra squeaked, grabbing his arm.

"What's going on? Dex, answer me right now!" he demanded, trying to keep his voice from shaking. His gaze darted towards the door handle, but it was too close to that shadow behind the door. If he reached out to slam it shut—

Dex stopped. He looked straight at Vincent. Straight through him. His eyes were black and empty.

"You...forgot about me, didn't you?"

Vincent stared at him with blank shock. "What are you talking about, Dex? Of course I didn't–"

"That's not my name."

Frigid realization trickled into Vincent's head. *No. It can't be...*

"...Mira?"

An expression finally twitched across Dex's face.

Vincent nodded slowly. He tried to relax, but his heart still pounded against his ribs like a prisoner, begging to flee. "You...you've been haunting me. Before I left."

Dex gazed at him, searching him. For what, Vincent wasn't sure.

Another close murmur grazed his ears. He jumped. Fingers curled from the crack between the door and the wall, slender and graceful and gold-brown–

"Sloane?"

The murmuring grew fiercer. Vincent thought he saw an eye flash from the darkness.

"Vincent..." Sierra's warning came as a whisper at his side. Her fingers squeezed his arm so hard it hurt.

He ignored her and looked back to the false Dex, suppressing the shiver that found him. "Why are you in Dex's body? Are you controlling Sloane too?"

Dex's head shook slowly. "Not me. Someone else."

"Who?"

Dex's shoulders shrugged. He–*she* didn't seem to care.

"And the others? Are you and the other spirits just...drifting around, possessing people?"

Dex's gaze was hard and cold. "I'm still here," he said simply.

The door began to rattle. Sloane was scraping her nails against it, shredding the paint.

Vincent clenched his teeth. "I *know*. And I'm sorry. You shouldn't be here."

He suddenly realized–Mira must have gone to Hell. He could only wonder what the poor girl had done in her life to warrant such a decision. Benjamin's words from long ago began to float to the surface, and he swiftly pushed them back down.

She must have deserved it, he thought. *She must have done something wrong.*

"I-if you leave Dex's body, I can help you move on. The way you're meant to. I can make all of this go away."

Again Dex tilted his head, in a very un-Dex-like way.

"You...want to push me away. You want to forget about me." It was phrased like a question, but it sounded too matter-of-fact. Too dismayed.

All at once, the air around them began to sag. Vincent recognized the feeling–it was just like Percy's.

"V-Vincent!" Sierra squeaked, tugging at his arm.

He grabbed the amulet from around his neck and brandished it at Mira. "Please–use this stone instead! I'll take you with me. I don't want to forget about you. I could *never*," he insisted, and he meant it. He could still see her, feel her limp body cold in his arms, in the water–

Suddenly, she was closer. Only a breath away from his face, those black eyes gazing deep into his. He could feel the chill emanating from her very soul. She could see the memories swimming inside him. He stood frozen there, unable to breathe, unable to move, trapped with her.

"You held me when I died."

Vincent felt himself nodding. All he could see in Dex's dark eyes was Mira's, so deceptively bright even after the life had left them. Hers was the first true death he had ever seen, and that above all had stricken him: her body was heavy, but her eyes looked the same as they did when she was alive. It was nothing like the spirits he was so used to in the Underworld, mere shadows of the people they had once been. At least, not back then.

160

He had held her in his arms, before he had ever held anyone else. The shame of it returned afresh, pooling low in his gut.

"I–I'm sorry–"

Mira shook Dex's head. She smiled, ever so slightly.

"I knew you wouldn't forget me."

"Never," he said again, the word barely a whisper.

Gingerly he held out the amulet.

"Come with me. Please."

She reached for it with Dex's fingers, their gazes holding one another still.

Her fingertip grazed the cool stone, and something tiny shifted in those black eyes.

Vincent's hand retreated–in the same second, Mira's flashed out to snatch it. She missed.

A horrible scream shattered the silence. It echoed through the room and the hall, down the stairs, rattling the house. What sounded like a dozen others joined it, desperate and keening. Vincent flinched away, scrambling backwards into Sierra, into the wall.

"I'M STILL HERE! I'M STILL HERE!"

Dex's body reared back, spine snapping as fangs grew from his jaws. *He was growing–changing–*

"*Vincent!*" Sierra cried.

She and Vincent lunged at the same moment, pulling the door shut. The slam reverberated through the house, but it was drowned by the shrieking and howling that now rose from every bedroom. Sierra held the door closed while Vincent shakily locked it with the little key. Only the overwhelming noise convinced her to let go and back away. The door trembled as the bodies on the other side threw themselves against it, but it held fast. Dex had designed it to withstand assault from a werewolf–just in case.

"Fuck," Vincent breathed. Guilt roiled in his stomach. He looked at Sierra helplessly, and she at him.

They hurried downstairs.

"What the hell did you guys do?" Casey greeted them, her form emerging from the darkness as their lantern light approached. She sat close to Roman in the living room still, her fingers tangled in his bristling fur in some attempt at comfort. The young wolf's eyes were wide with fright.

"Dex is possessed," Vincent said breathlessly.

"Uh, yeah. We know."

Vincent ignored her attitude. He knew she was just spooked. "It's Mira. The girl Benjamin killed. At least, Dex's is. I-I tried to get her to leave him, to go in the amulet, but..."

"I thought she was gonna," Sierra said in a small voice.

"No. She...she wants to be alive again. She'll never leave Dex's body. None of them will. Why would they?" Vincent's heart twisted, in spite of it all. *Percy proved that.* "They have nothing left. They don't belong anywhere."

"I thought they belonged in Hell?" Sierra asked, but she didn't seem too happy about it. "At least, that's where they came from...I can't believe that poor girl ended up there..."

Vincent's chest tightened as she echoed his thoughts. "It's not our place to judge," he snapped, a little too harshly. "We just have to get them back there. They can't keep leeching off the living."

"I know." Sierra eyed him strangely. Guilt immediately crept back in.

"Is it safe to crash here?" Casey asked, glancing dubiously at the stairs.

Sierra looked surprised. "You want to stay?"

"Just for a bit. We're going through the portal to fix this."

"You're *what?*"

"Why does everyone say that?" Casey said dryly.

"Won't your father capture you?" Sierra asked Vincent.

He frowned. "I guess the others filled you in."

"I–I'm sorry, I didn't mean to pry–"

He put up a hand. "It's fine. Then you'll know I used to be a guard down there, so I know how to get around. We're just going to talk to Benjamin, and see if he knows how to reverse the damage."

"Oh, Vincent, you can't–you just can't."

"I'm the only one who *can*."

Sierra looked at him miserably. Roman on the other hand stared at him in amazement.

"*I'm coming too! I can scout–*"

"No fucking way," said Casey, glowering at him. He bared his wolf teeth at her.

"*Why? I'm a good scout! You two saw, I helped–*"

"That was a pity invitation, you whelp. Vincent's a bleeding heart." Vincent glared at her. "Do you remember what happened *after* that? Y'know, when you got *captured* and we had to drop everything to save your ass? Yeah, that's not happening again."

Roman growled at her, but couldn't seem to find any good arguments. Casey raised her eyebrows at him until he looked away.

"That's what I thought."

"Well, Roman and I need to guard these guys here anyway." Sierra threw Roman a sympathetic look. "You and Vincent are welcome to stay if you like. Can't guarantee peace and quiet, but..."

"It's enough," said Vincent. "Thanks. We just need some rest before we go. And..."

He drew the amulet over his head, holding it out to Sierra. "...a safe place to keep this. Would you...?"

Sierra reached for it, then stopped. She stared at it in shock.

"Wait. Is...is that...?"

Her eyes began to glisten. Vincent's heart lurched.

"Sierra? Are you okay?"

"That's my–you found my–oh, god, I'm so sorry!" She burst into tears, covering her face with her hands.

Vincent stood there stupefied, awkwardly holding up the amulet. "You're *sorry?*"

"I-I didn't mean to lose it, I just–I don't know what happened!" She barely got the words out before she broke down entirely.

All three of them stared at her dumbly, unsure what to do. Finally Vincent stepped up and wrapped an arm around her shoulders, gently guiding her towards the kitchen. She didn't protest.

They sat together at the dining table, the lantern light barely reaching them from the living room. Vincent kept one hand on her arm, hoping it provided some comfort.

"It's okay, Sierra," he said lamely.

"No, it's not!" she cried, still hiding her face. "You and Henry almost *died* to save me, all because I wanted that dumb necklace! A-and then I *lost* it–I'm so fucking stupid! I'm sorry, Vincent, I'm so sorry!"

Oh. A fresh wave of guilt washed over Vincent. She hadn't lost it–Vincent himself had stolen it from her, after she refused to give it up when they needed it.

Should he tell her? He *really* didn't want to, especially now. But here she was, crying her eyes out, hating herself for it...

I've done enough damage as it is. I deserve this.

"Sierra...please, stop. It's not your fault."

"It *is!* It is, I'm–I'm so careless, I couldn't even–"

"Sierra, I took it."

It took her a teary moment to register what he had said. She finally looked out over her hands, her brown eyes wide in disbelief.

"You...?"

Vincent sighed deeply, his stomach churning in shame. "Yeah. I took it from your room when I was visiting. You didn't misplace it, or drop it, or anything like that. So please, don't cry."

Sierra gazed at him for the longest time. Then she *giggled.* It ended in a hiccup as Vincent stared at her, dumbstruck.

"You really took it? You?" She wiped her damp face with her sleeve. "All this time, I–thank god!"

"You're not mad at me?"

He appeared to have given her the thought for the first time. She paused, thinking. Then she shrugged. "Not really...I'm just glad it wasn't me! I felt so awful, after everything you guys went through for it, for me..."

"I'm...sorry, Sierra. I didn't mean..."

Sierra gave him a watery smile, shaking her head. She took his hand in both of hers and squeezed it. "It's okay. I mean it."

Vincent grimaced. The guilt gnawed on, through his ribcage and into his heart. "You shouldn't forgive me so easily. I *stole* it from you. Don't you even care?"

Sierra's brow furrowed. "Why did you do it?"

Vincent fingered the amulet in his pocket. "Henry and I needed it, and you didn't want to give it to us. It used to belong to Percy...we thought it would help him remember how he died, so we could catch his killer."

"Seriously? Well, why didn't you say so? I didn't know it was that important! God, now I feel even worse...I stole it from Percy..."

"You didn't," Vincent insisted. "You didn't know. And we couldn't tell you why we needed it. You weren't one of us back then." He hoped she understood what he meant. It felt strange calling her *an Other*–or anyone, for that matter. He wondered who chose such an ungraceful name.

"Yeah...I guess you're right. Well, that makes it even more okay. I'm glad you took it. Did it help?"

Vincent shrugged one shoulder. "Yes and no. It's a long story...if Henry didn't tell you already."

Sierra's face fell after Henry's name. "Yeah...he did. At least, most of it. Once he figured out what I was. It was weird...he seemed kinda relieved, but also sad..."

Vincent was quiet for a moment. "He didn't want you to get involved in all this."

Sierra frowned. "But...I thought he liked me. Why wouldn't he want me to know?"

"He wanted you to have a normal life," Vincent replied, echoing her words from earlier. Her expression tightened; she noticed. "That's what he wanted for himself, too. But he could never manage it."

In spite of herself, Sierra laughed softly. "Yeah...he could never mind his own business, huh? Always had to help..."

The more Vincent thought about it, the darker he felt. "He covered for you, when he found out you were a werewolf. I didn't even know you were turned."

Sierra's mirth faded fast. "When...when Hunter took me...when Jake fought him...I-I tried to fight back, too. But he got me." She squeezed her eyes shut, as if that would keep the worst of the memories at bay. "I owe Henry everything. He was there for me, the whole time."

"I'm sorry I wasn't," Vincent said quietly.

Sierra looked back at him and squeezed his hand again. "No, no–don't. It's alright. You had to go. Otherwise, the Shadowhand would have got you, too." She broke off suddenly, a distinct shadow of pain flitting across her face. Vincent had a feeling he knew why.

He wished he didn't.

He said nothing. But Sierra didn't let the thought pass.

"Henry...he's gone. They took him away."

Vincent nodded, not meeting her eyes. "I saw."

"I can't believe he's gone. I miss him so much. When he was around, everything felt...okay. Or, like it would be."

"I bet he took great care of you." Vincent couldn't keep the bitterness out of his voice.

Sierra drew herself up, indignantly. "I mean...yeah, but I can take care of myself, too, y'know. He helped, but..."

"He lied for you. To his own family."

"I'm not the only one he would do that for," she blustered.

"Yes, you are. He was the one who called the Shadowhand here."

"But he kept them away from you," she insisted. "They got Jake, and Hunter, and tracked down most of Benjamin's vampires...but he led them away from this place."

Vincent's heart panged. So Henry had kept his promise after all. He knew he would, because he was Henry Wellfellow, but...

"That doesn't change how he feels about me now. He hates me."

She fixed him with a gaze too serious for the Sierra Pechman he knew. "He doesn't hate you, Vincent. I don't think he ever could."

"How do you know?" he snapped. "Did he tell you that? Because he made it pretty clear to me–"

"Because he never talks about you!" she burst out. "Every time I asked about you, or anything even came close to referring to you, he got so...quiet. I could see it in his eyes."

Vincent's fists were so tight he felt his nails digging into his palms. "You weren't there," he growled. "You don't know anything." He finally turned away from her, ready to get up from his chair. "At least if I never come back from Hell, he'll be happy. Then we'll both be back where we belong. I bet he's already settled back into all the monster hunting, now that he doesn't have to deal with my mess."

"He's in *prison*, you idiot!" she barked. "They captured him! They're probably brainwashing him, or something crazy like that...the way he talked about them..."

Her eyes began to glisten with tears again. Vincent's exasperation warred with a dozen other feelings he wished he could never feel again.

"He knew the risks, covering for you like he did. It's his own damn fault."

"So you think he deserves it?" Sierra snarled, hot tears racing down her cheeks. "You think *I* deserve it? You think he should've let them take me?"

Vincent gritted his teeth. "No...of course not. That's not what I said."

"Then what *are* you saying?"

He hesitated a moment too long. Sierra shoved herself up from her chair. "We need him back."

Vincent bristled in alarm. "What?"

"We need to rescue him. Break him out from wherever they're keeping him."

"Go ahead." He stood too, sweeping a dismissive hand towards her. "I'm going to Hell to fix everything else."

"You think you can do that by yourself? Just you and Casey?"

"Of course."

"You don't think Henry can help?"

"I don't want his help. He wants me gone. And I'm happy to be gone."

"No, you're not. You're miserable."

Vincent smarted. Frustration flared hot in his chest.

"Don't pretend you never cared about him," she pressed.

"What do you want me to say?" he snarled. "That I loved him? None of it *mattered*, because I'm not good enough for him! I'm not you!"

A resounding silence followed. Embarrassment crept into his stomach the longer it lingered, bringing anger with it. He broke her gaze.

"*You...*" Sierra stopped. "But...you were the one who told me he had a crush on me...why would you...?"

"Like I said. He didn't want me. He always wanted a normal life."

Shocked as she was, she broke off with a snort. "If you think that, you didn't know him at all."

Annoyance cut through him. *I knew him better than anyone.* "You said so yourself."

"He could never mind his own business," Sierra repeated. "He could have had a normal life, if he wanted. He could've left all the supernatural business to someone else, after he moved to college. But he literally sought it out. You can't deny that."

The truth trickled in like cold water. He hated it, but she was right.

"After I became a werewolf, he didn't give up on me. He tried to help me get a handle on everything. He made me feel like...like I'm not a monster. Like I could still be *me*. If he just wanted a normal girl, he would've dropped me. But that's not who Henry is."

She ducked her head, angling herself so she could recapture Vincent's gaze. She looked sad. Insistent. He hated it.

"He didn't abandon me, and he didn't abandon you."

"He did," Vincent growled, but his voice came weak. "Even if you're right, even if he couldn't stay away from this life...*I* was wrong. That's why he left me." *Because I* am *a monster.*

Saying it aloud let it resolve into a clear image, for the first time. Henry was right about him—but Vincent hated it. He hated that he was so *wrong*, that he was unworthy, that he was alien. He was a dark thing, meant to make dark choices even for the right reasons. Those reasons didn't matter here. He didn't belong in this world, no matter how far he tried to run from the truth of it.

Henry had seen that, in the end, and Vincent hated him for it, too. Like maybe if he could have proven he was good, if Henry of all people could have loved him...he could have belonged here, after all.

But he didn't, no matter how much anyone else told him otherwise. Sierra, Casey...the people he had somehow fooled into caring for him. Henry, it seemed, was the only one who could face the truth.

And, seeing that image in its entirety at last, Vincent realized what he had to do.

He wouldn't drag Casey into this. Or Sierra, or anyone else. Not only because they didn't deserve it—but because they wouldn't allow him to sacrifice himself. Henry was the only one who would. The only one who understood. Someone had to get Benjamin's information back to the mortal world, to fix everything...and it had to be Henry.

Sierra had been saying something, but Vincent missed it. When he returned to the moment, she was looking at him expectantly, indignantly.

"You're right, Sierra. We have to save him."

She blinked, dumbstruck. "What?"

"Do you have any idea where they took him?"

After a moment she recovered enough to say, "Um...I got a letter from him, once..."

"How recently?"

"Maybe a couple weeks ago? He said he was near Klamath Falls, at some kind of training camp...but they might have moved him by now."

"How far is that?"

"It's about a five-hour drive south." She was looking cautiously hopeful now. "Are you really gonna go get him?"

"*We* are," Vincent corrected. "I'm going to need all the help I can get."

"I'm coming."

"Will Roman be safe here on his own?"

Sierra frowned. "I don't know...it helps to have someone else to change watches with, during the night..."

"Then maybe he should come, too. He'll want to come."

"I don't know, Vincent...he's so young. This is gonna be very dangerous. I mean, if the Shadowhand catches us..."

"He's a werewolf," he insisted. "He'll be fine. We shouldn't leave him behind to deal with all this on his own, anyway."

She held his gaze dubiously. Before she could protest again, he said, "Will the others be okay in their rooms until we get back?"

"Well, they need to eat..."

"Have they been eating?"

"We just kinda shove food in there real fast...neither of us have wanted to check."

"Then I guess we can do that. We won't be gone long, if everything goes as planned."

"And what *is* the plan?"

Vincent shrugged, walking backwards towards the living room. "It depends on what we find there."

He found Casey and Roman on the couch, sharing Casey's earbuds as they watched something on her phone. Roman was finally human again, relaxed enough not to be on constant alert. Both of them looked up when Vincent returned, followed a moment later by Sierra.

"So, ah...we're going to go get Henry."

CHAPTER 11

BENEATH THE SURFACE

asey looked at Vincent as if she had never met him before in her life. She stared at him so long he wondered if she had even heard him. He could faintly hear her phone's audio buzzing from her earphone.

"Casey...?"

She blinked at him. "What?"

"Are you, ah...coming along?"

Casey tilted her head ever so slightly to one side, and Vincent instantly knew he was in for it.

"Oh—you mean, am I breaking into a top-secret supernatural security compound to bust out the man that betrayed you when you needed him most?"

Vincent's heart sank into his stomach. "He didn't tell the Shadowhand about me. Or you."

Casey's eyes narrowed to slits. They shifted from him to Sierra and back again.

"So? He still betrayed you. You tried to solve his mess when he didn't have the balls to do it himself, and he threw you under the bus for it. Did you forget all that?"

"No. But...he regretted it, in the end. He doesn't deserve to rot in prison for it."

"He's not rotting in prison for it—he's rotting in prison because he covered for his werewolf girlfriend!" Casey jabbed an accusatory hand at Sierra, who winced.

Vincent bristled. "He covered for *all* of us! That's just the one he got caught for."

"Well, if he cared so much about their stupid rules, maybe he should've been on our side from the start!"

"I'm not here to debate his morals. I've already made up my mind. Are you coming or not?"

"You're insane. You're insane!" She suddenly stood, her earphone dropping out as its twin kept it tethered to Roman. She kicked the coffee table as hard as she could, scooting it along the floor a few feet. Roman shrank away from her fury.

Vincent stepped forward, a fire blazing in his chest. "I'm trying to do the right thing, damn it! He wouldn't leave us there–"

"Yes, he would!" Casey shouted, rounding on him. A shadow had fallen over her form–something wolflike. Her eyes flashed in the lamplight. She was close to changing.

Shit. With a stab of dread, Vincent realized just how close it was to the full moon still. If Roman couldn't control himself while he was agitated, Casey was only a step behind.

"Casey–"

Suddenly, Sierra brushed past him. Casey snarled at her, but she ignored it and instead wrapped her arms around her.

For a moment, everything was frozen in shock–even Casey.

"I'm here," Sierra said, just loud enough for Vincent to hear, as she pulled Casey in close. "You're here. I don't want to fight."

Nothing moved. Then, slowly, Casey's shoulders relaxed. Her sharp edges faded away, along with the wolf.

Sierra rested her chin on Casey's head. "It's okay, Casey. You don't have to come with us. You don't even have to like it. But I want Henry back. I convinced Vincent to help me. I wouldn't ask you to put yourself on the line for Henry's sake. Especially after everything."

"Of course I'm coming," came the growl, pressed into Sierra's neck. "I'm not gonna let you stupid fucks get caught trying to save his sorry ass."

Shock coursed through Vincent as he stared at the two of them, still locked in their embrace. It was a strange stalemate–it was tender, although he had no idea how or why, but if he looked at it from a slightly different angle it felt like a battle all its own, two combatants holding each other hostage, neither one daring to break in case the other one gained an opening. It was...wolfish, he decided. Even though Casey had calmed down, he could almost see them both in their canine forms, pressed against one another in this dance of wills.

Stranger still, Sierra broke away first. A look both gentle and sorrowful lingered on her face. Casey gazed back at her. Vincent had never seen her look so hapless.

"Thanks, Casey. That's really sweet of you. I'll feel a lot safer with you there," Sierra said, and Vincent could tell she meant it. She finally turned back to him, a little brighter. "We'll head out tomorrow morning, yeah? You guys need some rest."

Vincent shook himself out of his stupor and nodded.

"What about me?" Roman finally piped up from the couch. He still had one of Casey's earbuds in. "I wanna–"

"Come, I know." Sierra caught Vincent's eye again. Her expression said *I don't want to be responsible for this.*

"You're coming, too," Vincent told him firmly. "We need everyone's help."

Roman grinned. "Yes!" he whispered, jumping up to hand Casey's phone back to her.

"But he's just a kid," she argued. "What if something happens to him?" Sierra nodded at her side.

"He's strong," Vincent insisted. "And he's helped us plenty. I mean, I was guarding prisoners in Hell at his age."

"I can scout," Roman added, trying to sound stoic. For a moment Vincent could see the shadow of his father over him. "And I can fight. I want to save my parents."

"Getting Henry back isn't saving your parents," Casey growled.

"It's one step closer!" Roman shot back. "And he'll help us stop the ghosts, won't he?"

Vincent nodded. "I know he will."

"Then I'm coming."

Neither Casey nor Sierra looked fully convinced, but for once they relented. There were more important things to worry about.

That evening they built a rudimentary fire in the backyard, since the power was out. They cooked canned chili in a big pot, keeping a wary eye out for wandering ghosts as they ate on the lawn. The smell and taste of it burned a hole in Vincent's heart. He couldn't help but recall the last time he had eaten it, out in the woods camping with Henry and Casey and Percy when he was in Ava's body. Even if they had been chasing down a murderer at the time, it had felt...nice. Camping with friends. Sitting by the fire together, playing games to try and embarrass one another, eating together, sleeping huddled in their tent...

A memory crowded in: waking pressed close against Henry's sleeping bag, allowing himself to savor his warmth for just a moment. He had felt so safe there, even if Henry was just a human and he himself a hellbeast. So much was different now, but he found himself wishing for that feeling here amongst the darkness and the ghosts.

He closed his eyes, drawing in a long breath, relishing the warm scent of the chili and the woodsmoke and the grass beneath him. It had to be enough to last. He wouldn't let himself forget.

They turned in early, setting watches for the night. Vincent went first, so he wouldn't be woken up so abruptly in the middle of the night. He sat alone by the lantern in the dark living room, watching the shadows move in the corners of his eyes, his rushing heartbeat far too loud in his ears. More than once the room seemed to sway around him, his nerves threatening to take over his senses.

But he steeled himself and rode it out. He was born to guard. This was his duty. His friends needed him. And as he sat there, waiting with bated breath, he realized nothing was happening. No ghosts reached out from the shadows to claim his mind. If they were there, they stayed hidden, biding their time.

The next morning they left some packaged food for their possessed companions, taking turns shoving it into each bedroom and locking the door as quickly as possible. Then they packed up the rest of their supplies and piled into Sierra's Jeep.

The drive left plenty of time for nerves. They kept them at bay with loud pop music, per Sierra's choice, which quickly devolved into squabbling with Casey about changing it to metal. Sierra won by badly singing along loudly enough to drown out Casey's complaints. Strangely, though, Vincent could tell Casey didn't mind as much as she pretended to. She stuck her head out the window, letting the wind assault her face and whip through her jet-black hair.

"Are you a werewolf or a dog?" Sierra joked between songs.

Roman copied Casey gleefully, until Vincent had to wrench him back inside by his shoulder.

"Don't hang half your body out the window. You're going to get your head chopped off."

"Killjoy," Roman said, but listened.

Being the disciplinarian left a bad taste in Vincent's mouth. He wasn't sure why, at first; but then he realized everything about the car ride felt wrong. Last time, and the time before that, all the way back...they were cramped in Henry's sky-blue Mini Cooper, and Percy was there, and Ava was alive, and Casey was bickering with Henry about the radio instead, and Sierra was just an ordinary human somewhere else living an ordinary life, and Henry was leading them, and even though people were dying around them, everything felt like it belonged. He didn't hate Sierra for it—in fact, he enjoyed her company. But she also felt like a cheap imitation of Henry, with her car and her optimism and her pop music, all of them too different to reach Vincent's heart. It was the realization that nothing would ever be the same again.

So Vincent kept his window up as he stared through it, watching the pines flicker past.

Several hours passed like this, until at last the trees opened out into a vast lake. The water was black against the dull gray sky, seeming to charge upwards on the horizon as it transformed into great jagged peaks of dark stone. The road led them along its edge until the city swallowed them.

There was just *more* about this place, in every way, than the little town of Alderwood nestled among the trees. The buildings of Klamath Falls wandered and rambled, some places relenting to nature's bravado, others clamoring for space between the streets and lone, stubborn firs. Always the mountains kept a dark, watchful eye on their concrete children below. Cars slid through the streets with a practiced confidence, and there were always more of them.

"How are we going to find Henry in all this?" he piped up eventually, gazing out at rows of industrial-looking buildings as they slid past. "Did he happen to mention in his letter where he was staying?"

"Not really," said Sierra ruefully. "But he talked like it was comfortable...and high security. He never got to leave the facility."

Vincent bit back the *obviously* that rose in his throat. He was being too irritable, and Sierra didn't deserve that.

"So what, are we gonna wander around the whole damn city until we find a big neon sign saying 'Shadowhand Here'?" Casey drawled.

"Definitely," said Sierra. "Ah." She suddenly pulled over to the side of the road, making everyone jump.

"What–"

"C'mon!" She got out, leaving the others no choice but to follow.

She led them to a coffee shop at the end of the block. A bell tinkled as they entered, and the warm aromas of coffee and pastries rushed to greet them.

"Really?" Casey snorted. "You know this is a serious mission, right?"

"Just trust me," was all Sierra said as they got in line.

It was modestly busy. People lounged on chairs and benches in open common areas. Some of them chatted with one another quietly. It was a far more casual environment than Vincent was used to in places like these. It reminded him of the lobby in his old college dorm hall, except the furniture was in far better shape.

Sierra bought each of them something and they sat in one of the cushioned corners. Vincent lost himself in the buttery layers of his croissant—at least until Sierra's voice brought him back.

"Hi! Hi, sorry—I just love your jacket! Where did you get it?"

Somehow she had managed to insert herself into a conversation between two girls who looked about high school age. Both of them wore distinctly dark clothes adorned with a copious amount of spikes, their necks and fingers and faces heavy with metal jewelry. They were seated at a low table nearby, poring over a spread of what Vincent recognized with a jolt as tarot cards.

"Oh, thanks!" one of the girls said, sounding genuinely pleased. "I don't really remember."

"Aw. Well, still cool! You do tarot?" Sierra chirped, leaning towards their table with bright interest.

The girls exchanged a glance that told Vincent they weren't sure if Sierra was being sincere. "Um, yeah..."

"My friend Ava's really good at it," she assured them. They visibly relaxed. "I don't really have the gift, though, haha. Oh, don't worry, I'm not gonna ask for a reading. I bet you get that way too much."

"Mostly fundie moms yelling at us about witchcraft, actually," the other girl snorted. "I'd be happy to give you a reading if you want."

"I don't want to take up your time!"

"It's no big. I love reading for strangers."

"Well, I'm Sierra. So I guess we're not strangers anymore!"

"Oldest trick in the book." The second girl grinned wryly. She scooped up the cards on the tabletop and began shuffling. "What do you want to know about?"

"Well..." Sierra exchanged a meaningful look with her companions. "My friends and I have been trying to track down a buddy of ours. He's fallen in with some weird people..."

"What kind of weird people?" the first girl asked. Both of them looked powerfully curious now.

Sierra scooted closer to them. "Secret agent types. Shifty. They like hanging out in sunglasses, even if it's not sunny. Mostly watch people. Have you seen anyone like that around here?"

The girls looked at each other with wide eyes.

"See, I told you they–" one of them hissed to the other.

"We always call 'em the mibs," the second girl told Sierra. "Y'know–M-I-B, Men in Black, like the movies? Okay, you're right, it does sound lame," she said suddenly to her friend, who nodded emphatically.

"So you see them a lot, then?" Sierra prompted.

"Oh, yeah. Everyone does. People come up with all kinds of dumb origin stories for 'em. Sometimes people from school throw things at 'em or try to fuck with 'em. They always just kinda leave."

Vincent could tell Sierra was trying not to look too eager, but she was doing a poor job of it. "Do you know where they tend to hang out the most? Like, a base of operations?"

"Well, they get really uppity about their warehouses. We tried doing a ghost hunt in one of the old buildings on South Spring Street, but they kicked us out. The place was empty," the first girl pouted.

"You're not gonna go in there, are you?" the second girl asked with wide eyes. Vincent couldn't tell if it was from alarm or admiration. "I bet they have guns. I bet they'd shoot you."

"If we die, that's on us," Sierra insisted. She didn't seem fazed at all–if anything, she was brighter than before. She stood, finishing off the last of her coffee. "Thank you *so* much. We really owe you one. Sorry for interrupting your tarot!"

The girls relaxed slightly, and exchanged a pleasant farewell with Sierra. Then she ushered the others out of the shop, whether or not they had finished their treats.

"South Spring Street," she said smugly. "Let's go."

"It's a start," Casey grunted, crossing her arms. "But they might be wrong."

"And they might be right." Sierra started back to the car, leaving the others to trail after her.

She navigated them to the right street, which was very obviously an industrial block. Work vans lined the curb and little else, least of all pedestrians. Sierra drove slowly down the road, all of them keeping an eye out for anything suspicious.

It didn't take long. Their first glimpse of people included conspicuous sunglasses. A small group of them were busy loading up a large cargo truck behind a warehouse.

"Bingo," said Sierra, and she parked the Jeep on the curb at the end of the street.

"So who's gonna run distraction?" Roman asked a minute later as they peered at the strangers from around the corner of a nearby building.

"Surely we're not taking the front door," Vincent said, glancing at Sierra. She seemed to have taken on leading the operation, and he was glad of it.

"Yeahhh, let's not." She scanned the warehouse's facade carefully. "They sure fortified the damn thing...we'd have to break a window. See the camera by that side door there?"

"They'd hear us," said Casey. "And the whole place is probably swamped in cameras. This is stupid."

"Well, we don't have a choice," Sierra said roughly. "We have to get in somehow."

"Wait." Vincent's gaze was fixed on the Wardens out front. The more he watched them, the stranger their behavior seemed. He gradually realized they weren't loading the truck at all. "Did you see any of those men come out of the truck?"

"What? Who cares about the truck?" Casey growled.

"No—watch them. They're guarding that truck."

"Of course they're guarding the truck."

"We need to get closer." Vincent slunk around the corner, ignoring the hushed protests from his companions. He darted across an open space and into the shadow of a dumpster, glancing up to make sure he hadn't landed in the path of any cameras. It seemed clear...and now he had a better view of the truck.

It was too shaded and too far to see inside properly, but nothing moved within. And yet, he had watched a couple Wardens disappearing inside only a minute ago. He hadn't seen them emerge.

Two Wardens stood on either side of the truck, loitering in that nonchalant yet ceremonious way that screamed guarding. Vincent knew that well enough.

"We have to get into that truck," he said when he returned to the others.

Casey scoffed. "You want us to get cornered in there?"

"Henry's not in the truck, is he?" Sierra frowned.

"No, but...I think it might be our way in." He explained what he had seen. Only Casey still looked dubious.

"Vincent, you're a genius." Sierra beamed at him.

"Okay, say it is an entrance," said Casey. "What happens when we get in there and get surrounded by Shadowhand? Y'know, 'cause we're probably walking right into their lobby."

"I don't know," Vincent admitted, irked. "But do we have any other options?"

Everyone fell silent. None of them liked it, but there was nothing for it. Again Vincent felt his frustration crawling just under his skin. He just couldn't help but feel like if Henry were here, he would have known what to do. If everything was the way it had been before...

Then, he realized: it wasn't as different as he first thought.

He clasped his hand over the turquoise amulet around his neck. It felt unusually cold.

"Percy, can you hear me? Are you there?"

"*I'm here too, y'know,*" Ava's voice broke into Vincent's mind, making his heart jump. He didn't like how close it felt.

"*Y-yes, of course!*" Percy's voice answered right after. "*W-what's happening out there?*"

"Have you been able to see any of this?" Vincent asked him, ignoring Ava and her attitude for now.

"*N-not really...I can hear you, but...*"

"Can you extend your senses any further out?"

There was a silence, filled by the odd sensation of cold spreading up Vincent's fingers. He flinched back, dropping the amulet. The chain caught around his neck, and the chill faded.

"Percy?"

Nothing. He realized then that everyone was staring at him.

"Give me a minute," he growled, turning away from them. He walked a few paces behind the building, then clutched the amulet again.

"*V-Vincent? What happened?*"

"What did you do just now?"

"*I-I don't know...everything's muffled in here...I-I was trying to go further, but I don't have enough energy on my own...*"

"You were using mine, weren't you?"

He could sense Percy balk. He sighed.

"It's okay, Percy. I'll let you do it, for this. As long as you don't try to outright possess me. Got it?"

He felt Percy's nod from within. "*I-I promise.*"

Vincent wasn't entirely ready for it when the cold seeped back into him, traveling up his fingers through his arm, wrapping frigid claws around his heart and something even deeper. But Percy kept his promise—he felt nothing probing his mind. Instead he gradually became aware of a new, numb weariness dragging at his limbs, as if he had been walking for miles in the snow and was just beginning to lose momentum.

Then, he saw it—*him*. No, *them*.

Both Percy and Ava were silhouettes now, just at the edge of his vision. They were barely even that, mere shadows in the gray daylight. Anyone looking at them would only believe they were a trick of the light, nothing more. But Vincent could *feel* them.

"Ava?" he prompted, bristling. She didn't respond, but he saw her shift uncomfortably. "I didn't say you could–"

"*You promised you'd help me,*" she interrupted, her voice icy. "*You can't shove me in a hole and leave me there in the meantime. Especially not after what you did to me.*"

Vincent's annoyance was eclipsed by a dark stab of guilt. Even if he himself hadn't done anything, he still felt responsible. He could have done more to help her. He should have tried harder. He didn't care if Ava was just trying to manipulate him right now–she was right.

He sighed roughly. "Okay...for now. But I only have so much energy. Please keep that in mind. If you drain me too much, we're all in trouble, got that?"

"*Fine.*"

Vincent turned his attention to Percy. He was surprised he could tell which of the shadows he was, considering their lack of defining features. He just felt...smaller, somehow. "You're here now? You can see and hear?"

"*Oh, it's wonderful,*" Percy breathed. "*The wind...the sky...*"

Despite the chill in Vincent's bones, he couldn't help but feel warmed by his delight. He remembered so clearly the first time he himself had seen the sky. It could only be that much better, having known it already and missing it all this time.

But they had a mission to focus on.

"I'll take you out for a walk later, so you can enjoy it. But right now, we need your help."

An eager glimmer passed through Percy's essence. "*M-my help? What do you need?*"

"See that truck over there? I think it's an entrance to their hideout. But we don't know what's inside."

"*Y-you want me to scout?*"

"Yes, if you can. I don't know how far you can go from the amulet…"

"*N-not too far, I think…b-but I can help, I promise!*"

Vincent nodded. "Thanks, Percy. I'll get us into the truck, and try to hide long enough for you to map the place out a bit."

"*You'd better not get us caught,*" Ava's voice tore through his head.

"I don't intend to," said Vincent, exasperated. But he let it go.

He returned to the others, slipping the amulet under his shirt so it rested coldly against his chest. Percy and Ava followed him like shadows.

"Percy's going to scout once we're in," he explained quickly. "Let's go, before anything else happens."

The others looked surprised, but none of them questioned him. Instead, Casey said, "So how are we gonna get past the guards? Anyone think of that?"

Suddenly, something flashed past Vincent's vision. At first he thought it was Percy or Ava, but when he looked, his heart nearly stopped.

Roman had bolted straight for the truck.

"Roman, *wait!*" Sierra cried, but he kept running.

The Shadowhand Wardens' heads turned–they had spotted him. It was too late.

Casey lunged after him, but Vincent managed to catch her arm and drag her back.

"Let him go!" He ignored her protest and turned his attention back towards the truck.

Roman was no longer there–instead, a dusky-brown werewolf charged for the Wardens. They raised their pistols with a shout, but at the same moment Roman veered sharply off, racing into the alley between two buildings. The Wardens hared after him, leaving the truck and its perimeter empty.

"Vincent!" Casey spat, but the plea in her voice was stark.

"Let him do it," Vincent insisted. Something twisted in his gut, but he fought to ignore it. "It's too late now. This is our chance!"

"We can still help him, idiot!"

"He's already running–he'll be fine! Let's go, or it's all for nothing!"

"Damn it, Roman," said Sierra, but before Vincent could argue with her too, she shot off towards the truck. "C'mon! Quick!"

Vincent released Casey's arm and hurried after Sierra. They reached the truck without issue, only hearing distant shouts from behind the buildings. He glanced back, half surprised and half relieved to find Casey with them, despite the thundercloud on her face.

They climbed the ramp into the back of the cargo hold. The shadows swallowed them; it took a moment for Vincent's eyes to adjust. When they did, he made out a square hole yawning into the floor at the back of the truck.

"Knew it," he breathed. As he drew closer he caught the glint of a metal ladder leading down into the darkness. His throat tightened at the thought of trapping himself underground, in enemy territory. It hit a little too close to home–literally. But he had no choice. And he couldn't back down now, not after leading the charge.

So he swung his body down onto the ladder and began climbing.

At first, he could barely see his hands on the rungs. But then, white light faded in from below.

His feet found concrete. He pressed himself against the nearest wall. He was in a little alcove with a hallway stretching past, illuminated by a fluorescent ceiling. Footsteps and voices echoed from somewhere far down the passage. As long as no one passed by, he was hidden here.

Moments later Casey and Sierra joined him, and he ushered them against the wall as well. He cast his sights around until he caught the vague shapes of Percy and Ava hovering near the ladder.

"Guide us," Vincent whispered. Percy didn't need to be told twice–he drifted through the wall and disappeared from view. Ava stayed behind, emanating both annoyance and dread.

Vincent caught his breath as quietly as he could, trying to focus on the cold concrete against his palms, on his back, seeping through his shirt, joining the numbness in his limbs that the spirits caused–anything other than Roman fleeing outside, or the thinnest veil of luck that separated them from being found hiding here. It had only been a minute, surely, but every second that passed felt far too long...

Then, suddenly, a voice hissed in Vincent's head.

"L-left down the hallway. It's clear right now."

He let out a breath of relief, gesturing for the others to follow. Then he slipped out into the bright hallway.

This way was empty, concrete on all sides. They passed some closed, windowless doors with number plates, but fortunately they stayed shut. Then they heard the clack of footsteps ahead.

"D-door on your right! Go in!"

Vincent grabbed the handle, but it didn't budge. At first he thought his fingers were too cold to work, but Sierra couldn't manage it either. Panic rose in his throat.

"Oh—shit—go back one, that's a closet!"

Vincent did, yanking the door open and hurling himself into the dark. Casey and Sierra piled in after him, pressing close and shutting themselves inside.

It was pitch-black now. Even Vincent's keen eyes couldn't pick anything out. Frigid metal bars pressed against his arm—more ladders, he thought, or maybe brooms. But everything else felt cold now too, as the spirits' influence seeped through his body.

The only warmth came on his other side, shoved up against someone. Breath ruffled his hair. It had to be Sierra, based on the height. He was glad—he didn't really want to be so close to Casey right now. A moment later he felt guilty about it.

The footsteps grew louder, then faded as they passed the closet. Silence followed, broken only by Vincent's blood roaring in his ears.

"Safe," said Percy, and they emerged awkwardly and gratefully. *"Keep going left."*

They did, and soon they rounded a corner. The end of this hall opened out into a much bigger space, although they couldn't see what lay beyond. They hesitated.

"There's a lounge halfway down this hall you can hide in while I look..."

They hurried to it, ducking around the corner and crouching against the wall there.

Waiting breathlessly, Vincent's eye wandered. Despite the industrial construction, the lounge itself was shockingly sumptuous. White leather couches, some kind of palm tree in a planter, glass tables, a stocked bookshelf and a flat-screen TV...even a crystal bowl filled with chocolate truffles wrapped in pretty foil.

"What're you–get back here!" Casey hissed.

"Sorry," Vincent mumbled around a mouthful of chocolate. Sierra snickered. Casey stomped on her foot.

"It's a big atrium," Percy's voice returned, making Vincent jolt. *"I-it's kind of a central hub for the place, I think. There's a bunch of floors."*

"Where do we go?" Vincent whispered back. "We need to find where they'd be keeping Henry."

"Uh...I-I think I saw a directory. B-but I don't know what to look for..."

"It can't be that hard," Ava's voice interjected snidely.

"Get me there," said Vincent, ignoring her.

"B-but there's a lot of people around..."

Vincent cursed softly. He glanced back at the others. "Can you hear him?"

They nodded.

"We need a distraction?" asked Casey.

"You're not gonna go wolf and charge 'em, are you?" Sierra's tone was light, but her round eyes betrayed her worry.

Casey threw her a withering look in lieu of an answer. Then she glanced around the lounge. "Hey Danny Phantom, see any fire alarms around here?"

"Um, down the way we came, to the left around the corner. It's clear."

Before anyone could protest, Casey slipped around the corner and disappeared. Only moments later, noise blasted Vincent's ears. He jumped, cringing against it to try and block out some of the sound. It didn't work very well. He suddenly wished he had come up with something different himself. He exchanged a worried glance with Sierra.

"*Fucking idiot,*" said Ava.

Casey reappeared in a rush. "Let's go, assholes!"

They hurried down the hall and out into the atrium. The word wasn't nearly grandiose enough for this room. The walls soared up into a dome made up of glass triangles between metal frames. Lights behind each of the panes created a scintillating illusion of space; it almost looked like daylight despite being so far underground. As Vincent stepped out into the room, a fresh wave of vertigo washed over him—the floor was made of thick glass, showcasing a vast man-made cavern stretching down into countless other floors. He faltered despite the chaos, swaying on his feet until Sierra caught hold of his arm and tugged him along. He barely felt it, his limbs had gone so numb.

They passed several people rushing towards hallway exits, the alarm still blaring painfully against Vincent's skull. Nobody looked twice at them. They reached the directory posted near the center of the atrium, all three of them scanning it as quickly as possible.

"Lounges, living quarters, education center, training grounds..." He could barely hear Sierra over the alarm.

"I don't see 'prison' listed here," sneered Casey.

"What about high security quarters?" Vincent said loudly. He hated yelling, but a quick glance around told him no one cared.

"Yeah, that sounds nice and easy to get into," Casey growled.

"But it sounds right," said Sierra, tracing a finger over the map. "C'mon."

They followed her across the atrium to the elevator, Percy and Ava's shadows close behind. The doors opened, but when they tried to press the button for the high security floor it made an ominous beep.

"Figures," Casey grumbled.

"*Th-there's stairs to the left,*" Percy suggested.

"*You think they're stupid enough to make the elevator restricted access, but leave the stairs open?*" Ava snorted.

Vincent cursed. "We don't have much time before they figure out it's a false alarm." He rounded on Casey, his nerves bursting from embers into flames. "Why did you have to go and do that? Now the whole place will be suspicious!"

"*You* didn't have any bright ideas!" she spat back.

"You didn't give me the chance!" He could feel anger deeper than the moment prickle in his chest, a tangle of thorn bushes feeding the blaze, but he couldn't stop it.

"I'm trying to fucking help, jackass! I thought that's what you wanted!"

"Are you really?" he growled.

Casey's face twitched in shock, then outrage. "You think I *want* to be here? You think I *want* to risk my hide for that two-faced–"

Sierra's hand fell on Casey's arm, halting her. "Both of you, knock it off! We need to move–now."

To Vincent's surprise, Casey obeyed. She looked away, gritting her teeth, but said nothing more. He himself fought off his rising temper, too ashamed to carry on.

"*I-it looks like it needs a key card of some kind,*" Percy put in meekly. His shadow was hovering near the elevator's keypad.

"*No shit,*" Ava muttered.

Sierra glanced back out into the atrium. "I bet someone has one. Maybe we can lift it off them."

A fresh wave of guilt doused the remains of Vincent's fire and left him feeling colder than ever. He certainly had experience with theft. He wondered if Sierra was thinking the same thing.

Then, the alarm stopped.

It left a dull ringing in Vincent's ears, followed by a cloying dread. Everything else felt far too quiet.

"That's it." Casey threw up her hands. "We're screwed. Let's get out before we get captured."

"What? No!" Sierra exclaimed. "We didn't come all this way to give up!"

"I'm not risking a pickpocket now!" Casey hissed. "Everyone will be on high alert!"

Vincent suddenly realized that she had assumed she would be the one to steal the key card. Now that he thought about it, it made sense. With her past, she must have had plenty of experience...

"Please, Casey!" Sierra squeezed her arm with both hands, her eyes wide with desperation. "This is the last thing we need, I know it! He must be down there!"

For a moment Casey wavered. She didn't want to make Sierra sad. It was so sympathetic of her that he again marveled—why was she so soft on Sierra? They didn't know each other that well, and Casey hated Henry. She couldn't think much of someone that loved him so much.

Then again, she cared about Vincent, too. At least, she did before. Now, he could sense the thread pulled taut between them.

As if thinking the same, Casey's eyes flicked to Vincent. Her face hardened. Then she pulled her arm out of Sierra's hands.

"No. I'm done."

"Fine." Vincent lurched through the elevator doors, back into the atrium.

"Wait—Vincent!"

He ignored Sierra's alarm, Casey's snarl, Percy's cry echoing through his head, the frigid protest in his own limbs as he moved. It was obviously up to him, now.

He deserved this.

Wardens were wandering back into the atrium now from the adjacent hallways. For once none of them were wearing sunglasses, their expressions confused. A few of them clumped together, murmuring to each other.

Vincent crouched behind an armchair in one of the lounge areas, his eyes fixed on a nearby group as they ambled past. He noticed jagged bulges in pockets, each attached to a belt loop with an elastic spiral clip. *Those must be the key cards. They have to be.*

He let the first group pass, setting his sights on another. They were farther, but if he could get to that other cluster of chairs...

He glanced around, making sure no one was looking his way. Then he ducked out of his hiding spot, slinking across the floor towards the closest chair for cover. He paused behind it, heart hammering in his chest. No shouts followed him. So far so good.

He peeked around the chair. His marks were on the other side of this seating area. One more dash, and he would be in the perfect spot.

He darted towards the final chair–but as he did, that creeping numbness finally crashed over him, and his legs gave out.

The giant room tilted around him, his skull so heavy it dragged him to the floor. Then he was looking down, down, down, through endless panes of glass into the abyss below.

For a moment, he thought he was home. Then, he was nowhere.

CHAPTER 12

RECOLLECTION

Eyes like clear water gazed back at him, through him. They were searching, penetrating–achingly familiar, but with no trace of the tenderness they once held for him. They captured him all the same, keeping him frozen there, the only bright spot in the murk of his senses.

Slowly, the darkness faded. One by one, he flexed his fingers, his feet, his arms. He was cold, but not like before. He was returning.

He was in a room. On a bed. He wasn't dreaming.

"Vincent Chálkinos, I presume?"

The voice was not familiar. He felt a stab of confusion, then alarm.

He blinked heavily, dragging himself back with an immense effort. That's when he realized–the man in the armchair beside the bed wasn't Henry. The room smelled faintly of clove and jasmine, but this man didn't. It had to be…

"Nathan Wellfellow," Vincent replied.

He pushed himself upright, cringing as his head swam. He knew at once why he had fainted: Percy and Ava had been draining too much energy from him–despite his warning. He had been too busy to notice just how much. He pushed away his frustration and looked around the room.

It was deceptively nice–a bedroom almost like any other, but for its haunting familiarity. Cheerful blues and yellows greeted the eye, the walls adorned with posters of fantasy movies and shelves laden with collectibles. Vincent's heart panged when he recognized some of the model spaceships. Everything was impeccably tidy and comfortable. It was impossible not to recognize the essence of who lived here.

Henry's father smiled, showing off dimples that perfectly matched his son's. But the smile didn't quite reach his eyes. That was the first thing that was distinctly not Henry.

"You're quick on the uptake. I like it. Feeling alright, son?"

The authority in his voice matched. So did his bulk, and his strong jawline. The rest, however, felt like a strange mockery of Henry. His hair was mousy and tousled in a careless way that somehow shouted the care put into it. His skin was unevenly tanned, the beginnings of wrinkles mere shadows around his eyes and knuckles. But the shrewd glint in his eyes was the most alien of all.

"I'm fine," Vincent answered coolly. He decided to choose his words carefully. "You know me?"

"Henry's mentioned you a few times."

How much about me? He wondered as he propped himself up on his hands. His skin prickled with mounting embarrassment as he thought about how specific Henry must have been describing him, if his father could recognize him. He forced the idea away. "Why did you bring me here? Isn't this–"

"Henry's room," Nathan finished. "Well, like most people, we're not overly fond of uninvited guests. We have to keep you somewhere. But I didn't want to treat a friend of Henry's so rudely."

"Can I see him?" Vincent ventured.

One of Nathan's dimples deepened. "You and I both know why he's here."

"That doesn't answer my question," Vincent dared to say.

Nathan laughed, a breezy thing that showed off his perfectly straight, white teeth. "I see why he likes you so much." Then he shook his head. "He's not supposed to leave, you know. He got himself into a lot of trouble back there."

"You can't keep him prisoner," Vincent growled, his patience waning as his unease grew.

Nathan gestured around the room. "Does this look like a prison to you?"

"It doesn't have to look like one to be one." Vincent knew that all too well.

Nathan sighed. "He's my son. I only want what's best for him. I know it sounds cliché, but it's true." He steepled his fingers over his mouth pensively. "He's a fantastic Warden, by all means. A talented fighter. Strong and clever."

"And kind," Vincent added, with perhaps more feeling than he intended.

Nathan's gaze flickered back to him. "Yes, that too. Too much so, I think."

"I don't think so."

That canny smile crossed the older man's lips again. Vincent didn't like it.

"You've no doubt benefited from it. He makes friends easily."

Does he know what I am? Henry can't have told him–he wouldn't–

"It's the best thing about him," Vincent insisted. "It's not just making friends. He believes the best of everyone, no matter who they are."

"Being 'kind,' as you put it, isn't a requirement for Wardens," said Nathan. "But you're right. He has this way about him people seem to like. You know we try to avoid unnecessary harm to those we hunt, don't you?"

Vincent narrowed his eyes. "Define 'unnecessary.'"

Nathan's smile tightened. "We have a duty to mortals, first and foremost. Henry knows that, too. Which is why his actions were unconscionable."

"Mortals can be just as dangerous as Others," Vincent growled.

Nathan shrugged. "That's true, on some level. But we can only do so much. Most mortals are leading peaceful lives. Most Others are driven by strange and often deadly urges. The risk is far greater, especially since most people don't know the first thing about the Others–or what they can do."

"You could change that. The Shadowhand knows those things."

"Do you have any idea what that would do to the world?" Nathan shook his head in lament. "Well, I'll sum it up for you in one word: chaos. Did you ever study the World Wars in history class?"

"Of course," Vincent lied, feeling suddenly more confident. *Maybe he doesn't know where I come from.*

"I know it's different when it's just little words on a page or the odd black-and-white photo, but believe me, chaos on a large scale like that is devastating.

Even if you survive the fallout, you lose a part of yourself. Nothing and no one around you is ever the same again. Modern society avoids it as much as possible for that very reason. Our grandparents remember the World Wars. They live in our cultural DNA. No one escapes it—those who go out on the frontlines only mitigate the damage for everyone else, at their own expense."

"But there are still other wars," Vincent argued.

"Yes, exactly—in places that have gotten so desperate, there's no other choice. And they pay terribly for it."

"And we send our soldiers out there instead, far away from the public eye, to 'mitigate the damage for everyone else.'"

Nathan nodded ruefully. "If we had it our way, no one would have to fight. But unfortunately, there's always someone who needs something, and someone else who can't or won't give it up. We just have to keep trying to solve these things on a smaller scale."

"So quiet evils are better," said Vincent darkly.

"*Necessary* evils," Nathan corrected. "Someone has to go out on the frontlines."

Vincent was silent.

"Henry couldn't pull the trigger," Nathan went on. "And that's why I can't let him leave this place. Not until he's found it in himself to do what needs to be done."

"And what if he never does?"

Nathan's easy expression finally soured. "That won't happen. He's my son—I know he has it in him."

Vincent grew quiet. Then he said, "You're right about that."

Nathan's beautiful blue eyes glimmered with interest. "How so?"

"I watched him nearly murder his best friend. He would have, if I hadn't stopped him."

"Jake Helmer?"

"He was dangerous. A newborn vampire. He had killed innocent people. He wanted to kill Henry. Henry knew what he had to do, and he would have done it. But he didn't want to."

"Yeah, that's the job," Nathan said with a dismissive sweep of his hand. "If he–"

"If he had done it, he would have lost a part of himself."

Nathan paused.

Vincent held his gaze. "I didn't want that for him."

Suddenly, something seemed to click in Nathan's mind. His eyes slowly narrowed.

"I knew his story was missing something. It was you, wasn't it? You're the one that dealt with Benjamin Warwick."

Vincent grimaced.

Nathan nodded slowly. "Then you're the frontliner."

Suddenly, he held out a hand. It took Vincent a moment to realize what he wanted. Hesitantly he reached out to shake it.

The bedroom door swung open.

It was a cruel mockery of his dreams. There in the doorway stood the man who was meant to be dappled in sunlight, his strong, soft hands outstretched to lift him up, to take him in. Those eyes were now so much more like Nathan's. Only in his dreams would they ever again look at him the way they used to. Now they were empty with shock.

"Welcome home, son," Nathan greeted him cheerfully. "I just met your friend, Vincent. He lives up to his reputation."

Henry's blank gaze shifted to his father. "What is he doing here?" Vincent was surprised to find he sounded accusatory, as if preparing to defend him.

Nathan held up a placating hand. "I let him in. I think he wants to talk to you."

Henry turned his attention back to Vincent. His heart sank as he watched in real time as Henry built up the wall behind his eyes again. An awkward beat passed.

Nathan suddenly stood up from the armchair, slapping his knees as he went. "Well. I can tell you have a lot of catching up to do. But first, I have a bit of news for you, Henry."

Both he and Vincent stared at him warily.

"What is it?"

Halfway out the door, Nathan paused with his signature smile. "It's time for your final re-education exam. I'm just about to arrange it. Are you ready?"

Henry blinked at him, stunned. "Y–yeah, I mean–are you sure? I thought..."

"Great." Nathan ducked outside and closed the door behind him.

The silence that followed gnawed into Vincent's guts. The very air felt heavier and heavier with each heartbeat, as if it were Percy's ghost standing there by the door instead of Henry Wellfellow. He felt too big for the room. He didn't even feel real.

"What did you say to him?" Henry finally spoke, his tone reserved.

"I don't know," said Vincent. He was afraid to say anything else. He realized some part of him hadn't even expected to get this far.

Henry's gaze traveled back to the door. "I've been here for weeks...why would he...?"

He shook his head, and those eyes found Vincent again. He wished they wouldn't. He could barely breathe.

"How did you find me?"

"Sierra," Vincent admitted. "She tracked you down using your letter, and asking around town. Casey and Percy and Ava are here too. We broke in to rescue you."

"Rescue me?" A little smile wavered on Henry's face for a moment, then died. "Where are the others? Did you say Percy and Ava?"

"Yeah. They...well, they should be with me." Vincent fished the amulet out of his shirt and held it up briefly. "They're in here." *I hope.* He didn't want to risk letting them feed on his energy again, after what just happened. "Sierra and Casey...I don't know. They must still be in the facility somewhere."

A flash of worry accompanied the thought. He half-hoped Casey had forced Sierra to leave after all. But he also knew she would never do that. She wouldn't leave him behind, no matter how at odds they were.

"Are they safe?" Henry pressed, reflecting Vincent's concern.

"I hope so. They were hiding when I got caught. We have to find them."

He fished in his pocket, surprised to find his cell phone was still inside. He pulled up Casey's number and called it, knowing her phone was always on the vibrate setting.

He held his breath while it rang. Once. Twice. Three times.

"Vincent?"

Relief flooded his body. "Casey, where are you? Are you guys okay?"

"What do you mean, are we okay? Are *you*? Where are *you*?"

"I'm in Henry's quarters. We're both safe."

He heard Casey say something away from the receiver, then Sierra's voice joined in: "Henry's there? Is he okay?"

"Yeah. He's just..." Vincent glanced at him, then decided to hand over his phone.

"Hi, babe," Henry said into it with a grin. He was practically brimming with joy. Vincent looked away.

"Henry! Oh my god, you're–I missed you! Come find us, and we can get you outta here!"

"Where are you?"

"Um, I think the eighteenth floor? We're pretty far down. We're hiding in a storeroom, there's too many people out there."

"In the high security quarters? Shocker," Casey's voice drifted through the speaker from further away.

"You stole a key card?" Vincent asked into the phone, surprised.

"We weren't gonna leave you in here!" Casey snapped, her voice coming through louder this time.

"What were you going to do?"

"Figure it out!"

"Good thing you called," added Sierra. "You're gonna have to meet us here, we can't leave."

"Do you think it matters at this point?" Vincent asked Henry. "After all, your father didn't punish me..."

"I don't know," Henry admitted, his brow furrowed. To the phone he added, "Sit tight. I'll come grab you."

"Hurry up, jackass," said Casey, and she hung up.

"I hope there's only one storeroom on the eighteenth floor," Vincent grumbled.

But Henry didn't seem to appreciate his sarcasm. Instead his gaze trained on Vincent, uncomfortably so.

"I thought you and Casey left town. Why did you come back for me?"

Vincent was quiet for a long, awful moment. He had no idea where to begin, or where to end. It was all too much.

"Because I need your help with something."

He could feel Henry's suspicion without looking at him. "What something?"

"I'm going back to Hell to find Benjamin."

The suspicion burst into shock. "Why? Are you breaking him out?"

"No, of course not. I need him to help me fix the portal."

Henry looked at him dubiously. "You don't think he'd actually help you, do you?"

"I don't know. But I have to try. The world is ending out there."

"What? Has it gotten worse?"

"Every day. People are getting possessed. Melanie is trying to expose the Others. It's getting harder and harder to hide."

Henry's silence was heavy with worry.

"I can't go back to Hell alone," Vincent pressed. "I need backup."

"What about the others?"

"I need to be stealthy. Less is more."

"So you want me?"

Vincent finally faced him, holding his gaze despite it burning him to his very core. "I need you. I don't want to drag anyone else into this."

A shadow of something complicated crossed Henry's expression. He searched Vincent's face, eviscerating him without so much as a touch.

Then, finally, he nodded.

"I'll come."

Vincent didn't even fully understand why. But he didn't need to. The smallest seed of hope cracked open in his chest. He was sure it would be dead before its first tendril reached the surface.

"Thank you, Henry."

He didn't answer, only nodded again. Then he headed for the door.

"Stay here. I'll be back in a minute."

Vincent sat back down on the foot of the bed, threading and unthreading his fingers in his lap. His thoughts and feelings did the same inside him, creating a tangle he could hardly begin to unravel. He didn't try.

Instead, as he sat there, something else slowly settled into place in his head. He grasped the turquoise amulet in his hand.

"Ava."

The stone grew colder in his palm. This time, though, he didn't let the chill spread.

"*What?*" She sounded petulant, but there was a note of something else beneath the surface.

"You sapped all my energy, didn't you?"

Silence.

"Percy?"

"*S-she wanted to stay around...I-I warned her not to go too far, but...*"

"*Why does Percy get to stay and I don't?*" Ava burst out. She just couldn't seem to help herself.

Outrage flared in Vincent's chest. "Because you weren't helping! Percy was guiding us, you were just floating around making smart remarks!"

"*Well, you didn't tell me to go away. You should've–*"

"I didn't realize you were draining me so much! I was a little busy trying not to get caught!"

"*How was I supposed to know I was draining you that badly?*"

"*B-but I can tell when I'm–*"

"*Shut up, Percy!*" Ava hissed, but it was too late, and she knew it. "*You killed me and now you're gonna throw me right under the bus again?*"

Vincent could practically feel Percy shrink back, his guilt oozing through the amulet. That only made Vincent angrier. He gave the stone a sharp shake.

"Like you're any better? If Henry's father hadn't taken mercy on me, you could've gotten *me* killed with that stunt!"

He felt Ava's rage building–and then it suddenly died. A throb of fear coursed through her, into him. He didn't care. He couldn't bring himself to. All the guilt that had tied up his insides for countless weeks finally snapped.

"You've been nothing but useless the whole time I've known you! You have the Sight, for fuck's sake, but it never even mattered! If you ever inherited any gifts from your *decorated* grandmother, you must've rotted them all out binging Netflix. I wish you had just stayed out of the whole goddamn situation from the start. But you just *had* to show off, didn't you?"

"*I didn't want to do your stupid seance! You kept pestering me!*" she argued, but her bravado couldn't recover.

"I warned you not to let Percy possess you! But you insisted you could handle it, because you and your bloodline are so *very* special. You can't blame me for what happened. I tried to help."

"*Fine,*" Ava growled. "*But I will blame Percy.*"

"By all means," Vincent growled back with a sweep of his hand. "He wasn't entitled to your body. And you aren't to mine. You stay in that amulet until we find some way to help you move on."

"*You can't do that! I can't just sit here in the dark forever!*"

"I thought that's what you liked. People were dying all around you and you only cared about playing video games in your room all day. We begged you for help and you only ever gave us a couple tarot cards and false promises. You never even contacted your grandmother. Remember that? Remember when you promised she would be able to answer all our questions and solve all our problems?"

Ava didn't answer. Vincent scoffed.

"I shouldn't even be helping you now. You're not even grateful. Percy's the only one who owes you. But I can't just sit by and do nothing when someone needs help. I'm not like you."

"Then don't help me! What are you trying to prove, huh? That you're better than me?"

"It's not all about you, damn it. It's the right thing to do. It isn't even that hard, compared to this." He gestured around the room.

"Oh, but you'll go to all this trouble for Henry? Even after what he did to you?"

"Yes," said Vincent, without hesitation. It surprised him when his brain caught up, and he fought back the heat rising up his neck. "Because he cares about people. He believes the best of them. He deserves help, because he will always give his."

Suddenly, the door opened. Vincent swiftly tucked the amulet back into his shirt.

"Vincent!"

Sierra stumbled forward to wrap him up in a fierce embrace. Startled, he squeezed her back, catching sight of Casey and Henry over her shoulder. Both of them looked disgruntled.

"Are you guys alright?" Vincent asked Sierra when they parted.

"Yeah! Are you?"

He shrugged. "Been better."

"What happened to you? We saw you collapse..."

"I was letting Percy and Ava use my energy to manifest. I think it was too much for me."

"What? Why did you do that? We only needed Percy!"

"Ava insisted." Vincent knew it sounded lame, but at the time his guilt over her death was still wriggling in his gut. His anger had burned it all away now. He could feel Henry staring at him, and he pointedly avoided looking at him. "I told her not to drain me too much, but..."

Sierra squeezed his shoulder. She didn't berate him, to his relief, although he could tell she didn't like his answer. "Don't do it again. We can get out without Percy's help now that we have Henry."

"I won't," he promised. He finally looked to Henry. "But we're not sneaking out, are we?"

"You and I don't have to. But you two do," he said, gesturing to Sierra and Casey. "They won't let werewolves go scot-free. Especially not after what happened at graduation."

Sierra flinched.

"Wait a minute–they're letting you and Vincent go?" Casey said with the first note of fury. "You mean we didn't have to break in at all? You could've walked out anytime?"

"No, no. I'm not allowed to leave just yet." Henry lifted his chin. "I have a final test. If I pass it, I can walk free."

Casey and Sierra looked at each other.

"What kind of test?"

"I don't know yet. I had to do a lot of...remedial training. But I'd rather walk out of here in good standing if I can."

"Well, goodie for you. I'm so glad we all risked our necks for nothing," Casey growled.

"I'd rather you hadn't come, too," Henry agreed. "It was really dangerous, especially for you both."

That tipped Casey over the edge. "Oh, *sorry*, my liege! Don't you worry, next time we'll let you rot in here!" She looked between Sierra and Vincent furiously. "I fucking *told* you! We should never have done this!"

To Vincent's surprise, Sierra didn't argue with her. In fact, she looked even more outraged, in spite of the obvious hurt that glistened in her eyes as she turned on Henry. "What are you saying? You really wanted to stay in here?"

"Of course not. But I don't want you to put yourselves in danger for my sake. I got myself into this mess, anyway."

Sierra smarted. "By helping me."

Henry blinked, as if only just realizing what he said. "That's not what I meant. It's just...it's complicated."

"Are you regretting not turning me in when you had the chance?" Vincent had never heard Sierra so bitter. It didn't sound like her at all.

"No! I wouldn't have–I just should've handled it differently, that's all."

"How?"

"I don't know, okay?" Henry snapped, which surprised Vincent just as much. "But it's too late now. They think you're unstable, and if they find you they'll incarcerate you. So we can't let that happen."

"What, haven't flipped from all that re-education after all?" Casey growled.

Henry shot her a glare filled with something more pained than true offense. Then he made for the door.

"Come on. We need to get you out of here."

"And how are you gonna do that?"

Suddenly, there was a sharp knock at the door. Everyone froze.

"Hide," Henry hissed. Casey and Sierra immediately darted for the closet. Fortunately it was well-organized, leaving plenty of room for them both to squeeze inside and slide the doors shut.

"Henry? We're ready if you are," came a familiar voice, muffled through the door.

Henry set his jaw. He glanced sideways at Vincent. "Yeah. Come in."

Nathan Wellfellow opened the door, poking his head inside. He gave Henry a once-over. "You don't look ready. C'mon, do I have to spell it out for you?"

Henry gazed at him uncertainly. "Should I get ready to fight?"

Nathan gave him a crooked grin.

"Right..." He started for the closet, then hesitated. "I'll be out in a minute. Where am I going?"

"Arena twelve," said Nathan. "And hit the armory on the way. Anything you like. Oh, and Vincent can come watch. Don't worry about him."

"Thanks," said Vincent, trying not to sound too wary. Nathan left, shutting the door behind him.

Henry's shoulders sagged with relief. He turned back to the closet just as Casey and Sierra emerged. "There's no time. You'll have to wait here 'till I get back."

"What if you don't?" Sierra asked. In spite of her anger, she couldn't seem to help the note of worry in her voice.

Henry softened slightly. "It'll be okay. I'm not in any mortal danger. If something went south, someone would step in to help me."

"But this test is that serious?" Casey grunted.

Henry nodded. "They want to be sure every Warden is fully capable of standing up to supernatural forces."

"But you're not an actual Warden yet," said Sierra.

"No. I'm too young. But this program...it's meant for real Wardens who need re-education. They're not going easy on me. I'm only here because of my dad, anyway...otherwise..."

Vincent didn't want to hear the rest of it. "You've faced worse than most real Wardens, I bet. You'll do fine."

Henry gave him a long, unreadable look. Then he went to dig through the closet for better fighting clothes.

He stepped into the little attached bathroom to change. A minute later he returned, dressed in some kind of padded, segmented armor.

"Lie low until we get back. Then we'll figure out how to smuggle you out of here," Henry said to Sierra and Casey.

"Don't you bark orders at us, King Arthur," Casey growled. "We broke into the goddamn Shadowhand headquarters without you. We're not fucking helpless."

"And I'm the only one who's actually got some sway here," Henry retorted. "So you *will* listen to me. You're in the high security zone now, and you're not getting out easily. I'm your best shot."

"Don't snap at her!" Sierra barged in, bristling. "You could at least show a little gratitude for everything we did for you!"

Henry balked, but Vincent saw him fight to collect his bravado again. "I *am* grateful. I just wish you hadn't done it. Now I only want you to get out safely."

Sierra began to swell with anger. This time, though, Casey stepped in, reaching up to clap a hand on her shoulder. Sierra glanced at her in surprise, her fury ebbing.

"Fine! You win, asshole. We'll stay here like good doggies," Casey growled.

She and Sierra both looked at Vincent, as if they expected him to back them up. He looked back at them blankly for a moment, then said, "I'm going with him. They expect me to come."

"Figures," Casey snorted. Vincent was caught off guard to see just how wounded she looked.

Before he could say anything, Sierra suddenly swept him up in another hug. This one was tighter, and somehow less friendly. The breath was driven out of him, and it took a second to regain it.

"Be safe. Keep him safe," she said close to his ear.

Vincent nodded against her neck. She released him, turning away to rejoin Casey.

Sierra and Casey had been right about the activity in the high security quarters. Vincent and Henry passed a handful of Wardens in the hallways on their way to the armory. Each of their eyes followed them, making Vincent's skin prickle. It reminded him of his first days at the University of Alderwood, before he had learned how to blend in better amongst the mortal students. Yet again, Henry's presence became his only bulwark.

At least none of the students had tried to arrest him.

The armory was its own beast. It was taller by far than it was wide, a vertical warehouse. Its walls brimmed with every kind of weapon imaginable—from archaic to modern, maces to assault rifles. Each was organized by type and accessible by hydraulic platforms along each wall. Vincent swayed a little on his feet as he looked up, taking it all in.

Henry led him to one of the platforms, bringing it up a considerable distance until they reached the section for fist weapons. Vincent wasn't surprised.

"You don't think a gun would be better here? Just in case?" he prompted.

"I'd rather not risk killing anyone," Henry replied.

"As if you couldn't kill someone easy with that thing," Vincent said as Henry slipped on a familiar silver gauntlet, its surface etched with strange runes. He felt his remark should have earned a smile, but it didn't. He kept quiet while Henry moved the platform again to select a crossbow, hefting its sling and a quiver full of bolts over his shoulder. Somehow, it was comforting to see that his methods hadn't changed, despite whatever re-education he had been through.

"Alright. I'm ready."

"Will that be enough?"

"I don't want to be too weighed down. This should cover my bases."

Vincent hoped he knew what he was doing. He had no idea how far the Shadowhand would go.

They made their way to a deeper floor, which felt darker somehow despite the fluorescent lights still lining the halls. It was ominously quiet. Vincent found himself walking close to Henry, and not just because of the narrow halls.

Finally Henry stopped in front of a heavy metal door, its facade marked with the number twelve painted in bold black. He glanced aside at Vincent.

"You'll be safe spectating. Just wait for me. I'll be done soon."

It was awful and strange. He was so matter-of-fact, so solemn. He was nothing like the Henry Wellfellow that Vincent remembered, the proud captain of the football team, thrilled to compete and reveling in his victories, despite his humility. This could have been a street fight, an unfortunate necessity, the way he was acting.

"Good luck," Vincent forced out. He didn't dare touch him, or offer him any further reassurance. He didn't know how it would be received, and he didn't want to test his fears.

Henry gave him a short nod. Then he scanned his key card and opened the door.

Inside was some kind of control room. Wide windows curved along the far wall, looking out over a large, enclosed arena. However, the decor looked more like a lounge than anything. Several other Wardens were draped comfortably over chaises or whispering to each other on cushioned benches.

They all stopped when Henry entered, turning to stare at him. Vincent fell in step behind him warily.

"Showtime." Nathan Wellfellow rose from a seat near the windows. "You ready, son?"

Henry nodded, his expression fierce and stolid. "Let's go."

Nathan smiled. He ushered Henry forward with a hand on his back, handing him off to a couple important-looking Wardens near the arena door. He exchanged a word with them, then returned to his seat, gesturing for Vincent to join him. He reluctantly sat beside him, but a respectful distance away. Nathan himself seemed perfectly at ease, lounging catlike on his chaise.

"I think you'll like this one," Nathan murmured to him, still smiling his Nathan smile.

Henry walked out into the arena, and they closed the door behind him. Vincent had a clear view through the windows as he waited with his back to them, gauntlet at the ready. For a moment, nothing moved. Vincent's heart thudded in his ears.

You can do it, Henry. You've faced down vampires and werewolves.

Then, a door on the other side of the arena opened. From the darkness, another young man entered, unarmed.

Vincent's blood turned to ice.

A voice projected from a speaker somewhere, through the lounge and into the arena: "The test is simple. Kill the vampire."

It was Jake Helmer.

CHAPTER 13

BETTER THAN DEATH

"What? No!" Henry cried, his voice blaring through a speaker in the lounge's ceiling. He spun around, his wild blue eyes beseeching the windows at random. He couldn't see them through the tinted glass. "We shouldn't kill him! What if he has important information?"

He was bargaining. He was panicking. Vincent watched, frozen in horror.

"We've gotten all we can out of him. He refuses to cooperate," said the examiner over the loudspeaker. Vincent couldn't see who it was. "And he is responsible for the current deterioration of the situation outside. We have made our final decision."

Even from here, Vincent could see Jake was in bad shape–even for a vampire. He was even paler than before, his eye sockets dark with exhaustion. His clothes hung limply from bony shoulders. His dull brown hair was shorn nearly to a full buzzcut. He looked nothing like the bulky, vibrant football player Vincent had first met so long ago, the day he first emerged from the Underworld. He looked utterly defeated.

He lifted his sunken eyes to Henry; but even then, Vincent caught a glimmer of defiance in them. "C'mon, Henry. Let's give 'em a good show."

"You have to stop this." Vincent rounded on Henry's father seated beside him. "Please. I told you, he almost killed him once already. He doesn't need–"

He stopped mid-sentence. Nathan seemed completely unbothered. He hadn't taken his eyes off the arena. The realization trickled in.

"You arranged this?"

"Of course."

"Don't you care that Jake's his friend? He shouldn't have to do this himself!"

"Well, considering he almost killed him before, I doubt they're still friends."

Nathan's flippancy sent a jolt of rage through Vincent's body. "He still doesn't want—"

Nathan finally looked at Vincent. He was suddenly and shockingly grim. "Just because Wardens seek peace doesn't mean we never have to aim for the heart. You understand this, don't you? Intimately. You would do it yourself."

Vincent gritted his teeth. "I might, but...Henry..."

"Needs to learn this. You can't be his shield forever."

"He's better than this," Vincent hissed. "He's better than us."

True anger flared in Nathan's bright blue eyes. "Stop lionizing the poor boy. He's a man now. He needs to face the real world—and his place in it. This is what we do. He's one of us, and he can't live with a foot in each world any longer. You're not helping him by coddling him."

Vincent smarted. The room seemed to sway around him. Helplessly he glanced back towards the arena. Henry and Jake were now circling each other, neither of them making a move.

"Just give yourself up!" Henry pleaded. "If you make yourself useful, they won't—"

"It's too late for mercy." Jake shrugged. "I was damned the second I threw my lot in with Benjamin. Just fuckin' kill me, already. I'll even put up a good fight, just so you'll look pretty for your test."

"I don't want to kill you! I never did!" Henry cried, his voice breaking. "You were my friend, I—"

"You're still so fuckin' *soft*," Jake growled. He spread his arms wide. "C'mon. Bring it."

Henry choked. He halted, just standing there in the arena with his gauntlet in a fist, trembling with desperation, not fear. Vincent knew him too well. For him, this was the worst possible thing.

And Nathan was right. Vincent couldn't save him this time.

"If you won't do it, I will." Jake gazed at Henry as if sizing up a piece of prey. "After all, don't prisoners usually get a last meal? I think I've earned it."

Before Henry could react, Jake lunged.

His speed was still astonishing, despite his condition—he hit Henry with all the old vigor of a linebacker, plus his new supernatural strength. It would have been a devastating blow, were it not for Henry's practiced instincts. In half a second the gauntlet was in front of his face, shielding him from the vampire's teeth as he stumbled heavily backwards. Somehow he regained his balance, his shoes skidding across the padded floor as he fought Jake's grapple. He was strong and healthy, but he was still only human.

Vincent's heart caught in his throat. *No. Stop this.*

But what could he do? He was no match for all these Wardens, let alone on their home turf. Henry had to fight this battle alone, and Vincent had to watch.

Duck, damn it! he projected his thoughts to Henry.

But he didn't. Instead, his hand flashed out, gripping Jake's shoulder and pulling him closer until they were nose-to-nose. Vincent froze in horror.

What is he doing?

Jake's fangs were inches from his face—

His mouth was moving—

They parted like waves hitting rocks.

Both of them charged the door into the lounge. Henry halted at the last second and smashed his gauntlet into the locking mechanism. The force of the impact dented it, but it held fast.

Then Jake's shoulder struck the door. It buckled and slammed open.

"Guns! GUNS!" the examiner's voice bellowed through the speakers, but it was too late. Henry and Jake were already through, darting through the lounge for the exit.

Every spectating Warden scrambled to help, but few of them had brought weapons. "Wait! Wait!" Nathan's voice rose over the din, but no one paid any attention. He pushed past a couple others trying to reach his son, but tripped over the edge of the chaise. A knife flashed as one of the Wardens made straight for Henry.

Vincent lunged, knocking the Wardens aside with new strength as he transformed mid-leap. He shoved his hulking hellhound body in the way, covering Henry and Jake as they began punching their way through the exit door. He bared three sets of fangs at the spectators, challenging them with burning eyes.

Some of the Wardens faltered, but more of them rushed him. Two switchblades slashed, but he snatched each arm with jaws from two separate heads, flinging the assailants aside harmlessly. Three more harried him with fists raised, aiming for his faces, but again he snapped and warded them off–

Then something rammed into his leftmost muzzle. That head's vision exploded into static. He reeled, but his other two heads rounded on instinct, jaws closing on the Warden's shoulder and tearing her off her feet to send her flying into the far wall.

"Vincent! Let's go!"

Henry's cry roused him, and he whirled around to duck through the exit. Henry and Jake had already taken off down the hall, making a break for the elevator.

Jake punched the elevator button, and in a burst of luck the doors opened immediately. He and Henry piled in; only when Henry turned and locked eyes with Vincent did they both realize the same thing: he wasn't going to fit inside.

"Change back, Vincent!" Henry cried.

But he couldn't. The Wardens were close behind–everything was happening too fast–

Vincent broke for the stairs. He heard his name shouted after him, and the frantic footsteps of the Wardens right on his tail.

He thundered up the stairs, thankful for his four legs–he was able to clear entire landings in one bound, while the Wardens scrambled to catch up. Up and up and up, as far as he could go–

He burst out of the stairwell and skidded around the corner into the fluorescent hallway. There he stopped dead.

Just outside the alcove with its ladder to freedom, a throng of werewolves clogged the hall. One glance showed two distinct packs—a larger group of strangers closing in, circling their bedraggled captives. The stench of blood pierced Vincent's senses. Two human Wardens slumped against the wall beside him, unmoving. One wolf lay crumpled at the center of the horde, smaller than the rest—

Roman.

Casey and Sierra stood over him, trying in vain to shield him from the others' advance, but there was nowhere to go. It was the two of them against five other werewolves. Still, Casey bared her teeth in a vicious snarl to ward them off, and Sierra stood on her hind legs, trying to intimidate them with her size. But most of the others were just as big as her; in fact, one of them was bigger, and much bulkier—a large dark-furred male, his maw split into a grin—

Wait.

Vincent knew that gloating look. He knew that wolf.

Ding. Just paces from Vincent, the elevator opened. Henry and Jake stumbled out, halting when they spotted the situation blocking their escape route.

At the same moment, echoing footsteps pounded louder and louder from the stairwell behind Vincent. The Wardens were catching up. They were out of time.

Henry and Vincent locked eyes for one wild moment. Then Henry bolted towards him—

—Past him—

—And threw himself at a control panel on the wall. He flipped open the cover, typed something into the keypad, then slammed his hand into the large button below it.

Just as the first shadows of their pursuers reached the top landing, a heavy steel door slid across the opening, sealing it shut. An alarm began wailing in short bleeps, thankfully quieter than the fire alarm but no less annoying. An emergency light accompanied it, flashing from the corner of the ceiling and dazzling Vincent's eyes every couple of seconds. Frantic banging sounded from the other side of the door.

It would have been well and good, except now they were trapped in the hallway with the werewolves.

Said werewolves were now facing them, ears pricked with interest. Several of them were growling as they set their sights on their new targets. The bulky wolf, however, was still grinning that awful grin.

"*Missed you guys,*" he rumbled, flashing his teeth. They were as big and gnarly as he was.

"Hunter? What are you doing here? Did you break out, too?" Henry asked warily, as if he didn't quite believe it.

"No, dumbass. He's on their side," Jake hissed.

"What?"

"He flipped."

"*Better than death,*" Hunter chuckled, licking his chops. He threw a pointed look at Jake. "*Little bitch. Siding with him now?*"

"You're just as big a moron as always," Jake snorted. "You're a fuckin' meat shield. They don't give a shit about you. I'm getting outta here."

"*Good luck,*" Hunter growled, his sneer fading fast. "*My pack says no.*"

The other werewolves beside him advanced as one, their snarls tearing through the space between. For a moment Vincent saw a flash of his own pack in their eyes–they cared for one another. They clung together in this place just the same way he had to Dex and the others.

Sorrow warred with dread in his chest. For all his ills, Vincent held a shred of sympathy for Hunter. He had always been lonely; no more. This new pack of his would tear anyone apart to protect their own. The Shadowhand were smart to cultivate this.

They were guard dogs, like him.

And that meant he would have to stop them.

Vincent stepped forward, baring three sets of teeth at the werewolves as the fur lifted along his spine. He knew his eyes gleamed with otherworldly flame as he let the shadow of what he really was descend over him.

He hoped it would be enough to cover the truth: he was terrified. He had never yet beaten a werewolf, despite his own strength. They were on a whole different level. And now he was facing down six of them. Even with the others at his side, they were still outnumbered.

"You don't have to do this," Henry told them. "Jake's right–you could leave with us instead. You could help us." It struck Vincent as a painful echo of another plea he had once made, when it was Jake on the other side of it. Sure enough, he heard a snort of disdain from the vampire beside him.

"Still on this shit, Henry? Don't make me regret this," he groaned. "Look at him, man. He's–"

He didn't even get to finish as Hunter lunged for him.

With supernatural speed, Jake jerked out of the way just in time. He grabbed the werewolf around the neck, bearing him to the floor–but Hunter twisted in his grasp, raking his monstrous claws across Jake's chest.

Vincent and Henry jolted into action at the same moment as the rest of the wolves. Side by side they met the beasts head-on, Vincent snapping at the closest one's legs, tripping him up, while Henry fired a crossbow bolt into another's chest. He snarled in pain, but Henry hadn't shot to kill, and he continued his charge.

Not today. Vincent abandoned his opponent in an instant and lurched aside, intercepting the wolf's attack and barreling him into the wall with a sickening crunch. The werewolf yelped, crumpling to the floor. A shock of triumph surged through Vincent's body.

Maybe I can *do this.* There was something deeply, intimately right about fighting alongside Henry again like this. For just a moment it felt as if nothing had changed between them at all.

He whirled around, fangs flashing as he readied himself to face the next attacker. Casey's dark form grappled fiercely with a pale-furred wolf just paces away, while Sierra swiped at another to keep him at bay, defending the injured Roman at her feet. Henry had abandoned his crossbow and was now locked in close combat with Hunter, trying to pry him off Jake with the help of his gauntlet. He was impressively muscular for a mortal, but he was still no match for a werewolf, let alone one as big as Hunter. The werewolf's massive jaws were clamped on Jake's arm. In lieu of blood, black smoke rose in a stream from between his teeth. He barely flinched when Henry's gauntlet slammed into the side of his head, trying in vain to make him let go.

Vincent surged forward to help, but something pierced his hind leg, stopping him in his tracks. He snarled as he turned back–the werewolf he had just downed had bitten into his leg, dragging him back with all his remaining strength. His skull was dark and wet with blood, but his yellow eyes burned with fury.

Then a weight crashed down on Vincent's back, driving him into the floor. His lungs burned as all his breath hissed out, leaving him all but paralyzed. Teeth flashed in front of his face and then his vision left the right eye on his rightmost head–red, then black. He felt something hot and damp in its place that sent a shudder through his body. It didn't hurt–*why didn't it hurt?*

His other heads snapped at empty air–the werewolves were behind him now, keeping him pinned, staying far out of reach. He heard their gloating barks as they taunted him, taking turns tearing out pieces of his pelt. He barely felt the sting of it, his heart hammering in his ears.

His muscles surged as he struggled to push himself up, throw his attackers off, but he just wasn't strong enough. He twisted aside sharply, trying to dislodge them, but one leaped off and the other on, keeping him down. He kicked out in a panic as cruel fangs snapped towards his soft belly. One well-aimed bite would tear out his intestines, and then it would all be over. He felt his claws rip into something soft with a shock of satisfaction, but it was short-lived.

Paws clamped down on his hind legs, pinning them, exposing his stomach. Fear coursed through it like lightning, and his front paws scrabbled for purchase on something, *anything* to get him up–

Those teeth lunged–

He heard a sharp *crack*, and a wolf cry. He felt nothing–no teeth in his stomach. Then the weight lifted from his legs, and he was free.

He scrambled to his paws, ignoring the tide of blood flowing from his face. The wolf that had held him down was on his back, kicking and tussling with Sierra as she aimed bite after bite at his muzzle. The second werewolf was slumped against the wall, bleeding profusely from the wounds Vincent had inflicted earlier and new ones from Sierra. But he wasn't out yet. He used the wall to prop himself up, pull himself together, bunching his muscles to leap back into the fray.

"Sierra!" Vincent warned, lurching forward to help. But then something careened into his side, driving him into the wall. Pain shot through his rightmost skull–this time it was deep, too deep for his fighting instinct to quell. Frustration rose with it, and dimly he realized this hallway was too narrow to fight in properly. It seemed everything was against them here.

"Ladder!" Henry's voice rose over the alarm, the banging on the steel doors, the snarls and howls of battling werewolves. "We need to get out, now!"

"*Someone grab Roman!*" Sierra's cry followed, cut short as one of the other wolves snapped his jaws shut on her ruff. She wrenched herself free, leaving a meaty tuft of fur in his mouth like a bloody piece of roadkill. Vincent's stomach turned at the sight of it.

Henry was right–they needed to flee. They weren't going to win this fight.

Vincent tore his senses away from the chaos, finding the alcove that housed the ladder across the hallway. Relief cooled his nerves as he spotted Henry stumbling for it, away from the throng of wolves, dragging Roman's half-grown bulk behind him with immense effort. But he would need help– he couldn't get the young werewolf up the ladder by himself. His body armor lay torn and discarded in the hall, smeared with blood. It might have saved his life, but clearly he hadn't gotten away unscathed.

Vincent heaved himself upright, shoving past the tangle of teeth and fur and claws in a desperate dive for the exit. In a blink he was there at Henry's side.

"I'll push him up towards you! Go!" He nudged Henry towards the ladder with his muzzle.

Their eyes locked for an electric moment, and yet again it was like nothing had changed. They were here as always, helping someone who needed them. It was something only they could do, together.

Then Henry flung himself at the ladder and began to climb.

Vincent grabbed Roman's scruff with his middle head, the one that had sustained the least damage. He hoisted him up the first few feet, struggling with his dead weight–he was young, but he wasn't small.

Wake up, damn it!

His paws trembled with effort as he began to push himself up the ladder one rung at a time. It was *so* hard...he was too bulky to balance properly, and with Roman's body–

"It's closed."

Vincent froze, clinging to the ladder with paws not meant for it.

"What?"

"Vincent, it's *closed*–there's a lockdown hatch over it, like the door–"

Vincent cursed, nearly dropping Roman in his panic. "What do we do? Can you cancel the lockdown?"

"I–I don't know! Not from here–I'd have to get back to the control panel–"

"Then let's go! I'll cover you!"

Vincent scrambled back down the ladder, his paws slipping on the metal. Roman's body bumped against it over and over, but he couldn't stop. He slid the last few feet, staggering when he hit the concrete, but the alcove's wall caught him. He dropped Roman onto the floor, and then Henry was at his side again. Their eyes met, and he caught something dreadful in those beautiful depths.

"What is it?" he breathed.

"If I get the doors open, the Wardens will be on us. That means guns."

"Shit." Vincent's mind whirled. "We have to. We have to get out. Otherwise–"

"I wish you guys hadn't come." Henry turned, his eyes finding the control panel across the hall, his shoulders squared despite the weight that now fell upon them. Vincent didn't like that look about him—he knew it too well. "They probably won't shoot me. Get the others and get out."

"What? No!" Vincent snarled, alarm surging through him. "We didn't come all this way just to leave you behind!"

"And I didn't ask you to!" Henry snarled back, fixing Vincent with that forbidding, arctic gaze. "I deserved this, anyway! You think I want any of you to die for this? For me?"

"I would have!"

It was out of his mouth before he could think. For half a second, the ice in Henry's eyes melted away, and Vincent glimpsed that summer sky for the first time in so achingly long.

And then Henry turned away, and it was gone.

"This isn't worth dying for, Vincent. You know that. Now go!"

And before Vincent could say anything more, Henry surged ahead.

"No!" If the Wardens broke through, guns blazing, and Henry was in their way—

But it was too late. He had ducked past Hunter and Jake and another werewolf locked in combat, making straight for the control panel.

Suddenly Sierra broke away from the fray, abandoning her brawl with one of the other werewolves. She shoved past Henry, toppling him into the wall—and then continued towards Vincent, making for the exit.

Shock pulsed through him. Was she that afraid? It wasn't like her to flee so suddenly while her friends still fought for their lives—

That was when he saw it: just as she flashed past, he caught a glimpse of a familiar turquoise stone trailing from her neck.

His paw jerked upward towards his own neck instinctively, but then he realized he had three now. He couldn't check for it. It would have shifted away out of sight with the rest of his clothes when he transformed into a hellhound. But it didn't matter, anyway—there was nothing else it could be.

Somehow, Sierra had gotten the amulet.

In the same moment, she heaved herself up the ladder with the frantic clang of claws against steel, and the shadows in the passage above swallowed her.

"Sierra?" Vincent called up, fear and confusion pounding through his skulls.

Then, the whole passage exploded into light. Something white-hot like lightning surged just above him, outlining Sierra's body, every hair standing on end. Vincent felt it pulse through his own body, a wave of energy so powerful it nearly flung him against the wall. He flinched away from it, blinded.

Suddenly, everything stopped.

The alarm went silent. The flashing emergency lights shut off, plunging the hallway into darkness. Even the snarls of battle halted, turning to cries of confusion—and rising above that, a metallic grinding noise, both coming from down the hall and above Vincent's heads.

"Everyone, get out!" Sierra yelled. "The door's open!"

Vincent didn't have time to wonder what had happened. A phone flashlight blinked on, illuminating Henry's face as he appeared from the blackness.

"This way!" he shouted down the hall towards the others.

Vincent grabbed Roman again in his jaws as Henry launched himself at the ladder. Together they helped the unconscious werewolf up, Vincent heaving him over his heads and Henry catching him until Vincent caught up, again and again until the gray light of day reached their eyes just above. Henry hoisted Roman up the last few feet, then reached down for Vincent.

The moment froze, and suddenly Vincent was back in his dream again. That same one that haunted him nearly every night. The one that made his heart ache in ways it never had before, and never would again. That hand outstretched, just for him, inviting him into the light.

But Vincent had no hand to take it with, even if he wanted to. And he wanted to.

His heart tearing, he hauled himself, his bulky hellhound's body, over the edge of the hole onto solid ground.

No—fingers tangled in the thick fur around his shoulders, helping him up the rest of the way. They were warm, steady, *real.* He was finally real.

Vincent nearly collapsed on the floor of the truck, but Roman and Sierra were in the way. There wasn't much room in here now that he was bigger—especially with the others now piling in. Jake came next, leaping out of the dark with otherworldly nimbleness and torn clothes. Casey scrambled out of the murk just after, her gold eyes wide and her dark muzzle wet with blood—

She yelped, jerking to a halt. Something was pulling her back.

Yellow eyes gleamed from the hole. Monstrous teeth clamped around her leg, dragging her down. She kicked out, over and over, but Hunter held fast.

"Leave me alone! Just let me go, please!" Casey howled, with a desperation Vincent had never heard from her in all his time knowing her. It sent a shudder through his core.

But knowing Hunter, knowing just how fervently he coveted and despised Casey, Vincent was certain he would never let go.

But before he could even move to help her, Sierra was there. Her claws slashed across Hunter's face, and the shock of it forced him back, his jaws opening. Casey yanked her leg free, throwing herself forward. Vincent caught her, steadying her with his body.

But Hunter wasn't finished. He launched himself after her, shouldering Sierra aside, his pack surging on his heels up the ladder—

Sierra's claws hooked in his fur, wrenching him back. He stumbled and fell into the hole, the cries of his packmates rising from the darkness as his bulk bore them all down, down.

"Out! Go!" Sierra shouted.

Vincent didn't need prompting. He nudged Casey ahead of him, charging for the truck's open doors. They all burst out into the gray daylight, not slowing as they raced across the open lot towards the street. He could see Sierra's Jeep from here.

He put on a burst of speed, reaching it seconds before the others. Sierra came next, flinging herself at the front tire and fishing her keys out of the wheel well with clumsy claws.

"Henry! Would you–"

"On it." Henry grabbed the keys from her and hopped in the driver's seat. He popped the trunk so Casey and Sierra could lift Roman into it. Vincent squeezed in after him, careful not to step on him. He was suddenly thankful they were in a Jeep instead of Henry's Mini Cooper.

Everyone piled in, and in seconds they were peeling out into the streets. Not even bullets followed them. They were free.

The car was silent, breathless. Then, Casey said:

"*We did it. We made it.*"

"Is the kid okay?" Henry called back.

It was dark, but Vincent's eyes were good. Most of the damage came from several bullet wounds peppering Roman's body. His fur was matted with blood.

Vincent's stomach knotted up so tightly that his vision began to swim. Even though Roman took up half of the trunk, he had never looked smaller. He was so young.

"I...I'm not sure...he's still unconscious," Vincent reported, his voice wavering. "He took a lot of bullets..."

"I'll stop to check him over once we get out of town," Henry replied, worry thick in his voice. "It can't wait for home. Keep an eye on him."

Vincent held his breath, expecting Casey or Sierra or someone to jump on the chance to berate him for letting Roman throw himself out as bait for the Shadowhand. But no one did. The silence was somehow worse. It left him with the promise of everything that could still be said, all echoing at once inside his head.

They drove on into the gathering dusk. One by one the lights of Klamath Falls winked on, glowing like eyes in the night. They passed them all by, until they became mere reflections on the inky lake outside town. Then they left them behind entirely.

There was a small commotion as the werewolves in the backseat finally managed to change back into their human forms. They had Vincent pass blankets over from the trunk to cover themselves, awkwardly adjusting their seatbelts.

Meanwhile Vincent turned his gaze numbly to the imposing darkness beyond the car, broken only by the slightly darker silhouettes of hills and mountains and trees slipping past. The pain of his wounds was beginning to creep back in. It wasn't an unfamiliar situation for him, but he could feel his heartbeat acutely in his unseeing eye. The blood had slowed, at least...

Finally they pulled off into a gas station, the only bright spot in the whole world. Henry parked on the outskirts, outside of the light's reach to mitigate any passersby who might catch a glimpse of the car's strange occupants. He rushed into the building, leaving the others to their uneasy silence. Even if they wanted to say something, Jake's presence was too forbidding to allow it.

Henry emerged a minute later clutching a shopping bag. When he reached the car he handed a couple T-shirts and board shorts through the open window for Casey and Sierra, then hurried around to open the back and take a look at Roman. Vincent tried to press himself flat against the back of the seats to give him more room, but he still took up more than half of the cargo area.

After a failed attempt to position Roman so he could help him, Henry met Vincent's gaze. "Can you change back?"

Vincent grimaced. "Can't you work around me?"

"Come on, Vincent," Henry sighed with open frustration. Vincent knew it was just from urgency, but he winced anyway. "I need to stretch him out to get a better look."

Vincent hesitated, trying and failing to come up with a good excuse. He really didn't want Henry to see his rising fear, but he couldn't think of a way around it.

Through his bitterness he finally choked out, "Can you take a look at my eye?"

Henry blinked at him in surprise. He peered more closely at him in the gloom. "Is something wrong with it? It's too dark..."

"I...I can't see out of it."

Henry took out his phone and carefully shone the flashlight over Vincent's three faces until he found the right one. Vincent cringed against the light, unsure if he was glad or not that he couldn't see Henry's reaction.

"It's...not good. I'll look at it after Roman, okay?"

Vincent gritted his teeth. "I can't change back, alright?"

"Why not?"

"I–I don't know what'll happen to it, when I turn human."

Henry was silent for a moment. Vincent burned with embarrassment. If he could, he would have run off into the night. It would have fixed everything–given Henry the space he needed, and fled from this awful vulnerability. Henry didn't deserve to see him like this, after everything that had happened between them–both for his sake and Vincent's. In his mind, all of that was a mutual agreement not to trust each other anymore with these kinds of things.

But above all, he hated that he missed confiding in Henry. And he knew he couldn't run. If someone saw him like this...

"You can't stay like that forever," said Henry. His tone was patient, as usual. But it lacked the empathy he had always afforded Vincent before. It felt like a dagger still protruded from Vincent's heart, and each word only pushed it in deeper. Though the specter of Henry's fingers hauling him out of the darkness still burned in his fur, he knew now that it wasn't enough. That moment was all he would ever get. There would be no more comfort here.

It was all up to Vincent now. He took in a deep breath and told himself that he shouldn't be so concerned for his human form, anyway. After all, it was only a disguise. It wasn't real.

But it was. It was still the only thing tethering him to this life he loved so much. Without it, what was he? A hellhound, through and through. Anything human he had cultivated wouldn't matter anymore.

Henry was right–he couldn't stay like this forever. Not yet.

Henry was still looking at him, and that old shame of what he was rose like a tide inside him. When it had washed over him, it left him human again.

He looked around, and he saw everything. He could still see out of both eyes.

Relief settled like cool water in his core—at least, until he realized there *was* something missing. It was like the night that stalked the edges of the gas station carport; there was only blackness in the corner of his right eye, no matter where he looked. His heart sank into the pit of his stomach.

Without a word, he jumped out of the car and left Henry to tend to Roman. Henry didn't call him back. The dagger sank deeper into his heart, but somehow it felt right. Its presence filled the hole that would otherwise bleed out.

Vincent sat in the driver's seat to wait. It took him a moment to realize that the others had begun talking, despite Jake's presence. Maybe the pressure of silence had finally grown too much to bear. He couldn't blame them—he wanted to feel normal again, too.

"What even happened?" Casey was saying. "One second the exit was blocked, then…"

Vincent craned his neck to look back at her. "Sierra did it. She climbed up, and there was this light… What *did* you do?" he asked her directly, his curiosity crawling back to him. "I've never seen anything like it. It was almost like magic."

Sierra didn't meet his gaze. In the gloom, he noticed her fingering the amulet around her neck.

"Hey—you took my amulet. Why? When? I had it when we got there…"

"She had to escape. She wasn't just going to wait around and bank on Henry talking her way out of there."

Silence descended over the car as her words sank in.

"*She…?*"

Sierra finally turned towards Vincent. But he didn't recognize the look in her eyes.

"It's me, Vincent. It's Ava."

CHAPTER 14

AUTOPSY

Everything clicked the moment the name left Sierra's lips. Vincent stared at her in blank shock.

"Relax. Sierra let me possess her."

"Why would she do that?" he demanded, his anger rising again from deep within. Hadn't he just told Ava not to meddle? Hadn't she almost gotten him killed in there? And now she was possessing Sierra, putting *her* in danger–

"I had to, to get enough energy. I short-circuited the electrical system. That's what made the doors open."

"You...*you*...?"

"How the fuck did you do that?" Casey broke in, sounding nearly as outraged as he was.

"It was...like you said, Vincent. Magic."

"Are you serious?"

Sierra nodded.

"But you're a ghost," said Casey.

"It's about the soul, not the body. I can still do magic."

"Wait–*still*? Are you saying you could do magic before, when you were alive?" Vincent pressed.

Ava balked from inside Sierra's body.

"Well...yeah. Sometimes."

"So you really could have helped us, and you just didn't."

"I can't do that much, okay?" she burst out. Everyone stared at her.

"Come again?" said Casey, with a little note of enjoyment.

"I'm not my grandmother. I don't even really know what I'm doing with it. I just...made it happen."

"But you saved us back there," Vincent pointed out, much as he loathed to admit it. "You could have done any number of things to help, if you had just been there."

"I know."

She sounded so defeated, Vincent thought Sierra might have taken back over. Even Casey was startled into silence.

"But...I was there, this time. So I figured, even if I'm dead, it's not too late."

Vincent gazed into Sierra's brown eyes until he could focus on that profoundly un-Sierra entity within. It was the longest he had ever regarded Ava before, and he was startled to find something familiar there. Something unsure of itself, afraid of the judgment gazing back at it.

He nodded hesitantly. "Thank you."

"Why now, though?" Casey cut in, staring at her suspiciously. "Don't try to take credit for being all selfless. You only cared about saving your own hide. Or, whatever's left of it. And now you're taking over Sierra—get out of her already, will you? I thought you of all people would know better!"

Ava's expression soured. But it wasn't as petulant as they might have expected; instead it carried a shadow, something Vincent could only recognize as *shame.*

"H-hey—let up on her! She's been through enough, don't you think?"

Percy's voice echoing through Vincent's head made him jump. Casey's rancorous expression told him she had heard it too.

"Oh, shut up, body-snatcher. You don't get a say in this," she growled to the air.

"No, he's right," Vincent argued. "I don't care why she did it—she still saved us."

Casey returned his glare. "Fuckin' rich, coming from you. Then again, I guess you really have turned over a new leaf, haven't you, Vincent? I didn't realize you'd gone Catholic on us when my back was turned."

"What?" he said, not understanding the words but hearing the threat in her tone.

"Seems to me you're handing out forgiveness like candy today. First Henry, now Percy and Ava? What's next, Jake?"

"No," Vincent growled. "Never."

"Why? Because he threatened your boyfriend? Why should everyone else get a blank slate and not him?"

"Hey, I'm not askin' for one," Jake finally spoke from the front passenger seat. He sounded amused.

"Good, 'cause you're not getting one," Casey snapped.

"Then leave me out of this, will you?" Jake cranked his seat down and leaned back in it as if to sleep.

"*W-what* are *we gonna do with him?*" Percy asked meekly.

"One thing at a time." Everyone stopped short as Henry came around the side of the car, wiping his hands on a bloodstained rag. He looked troubled. "First, we have to get home."

"How's Roman?" Vincent asked, his heart in his throat.

"Could be better. I think he's in shock."

"Which means...?"

"I don't know when he'll wake up." Henry suddenly let out a growl of frustration. "I wish we could get him to a hospital, damn it."

Everyone but Jake, still lounging in the front seat, looked at each other helplessly.

"We could..."

"Any vets nearby?"

Henry shot Casey a disapproving look. "You really think–"

"No."

"Let's just go." Vincent got out so Henry could take his place at the wheel. He hesitated before deciding to sit next to Sierra instead of Casey. He didn't want to risk it in her current state.

His gaze met Ava's. For a moment they stared at each other through their false human eyes, neither moving.

"Aren't you going to let Sierra go, Ava? You don't need her energy anymore, right?"

"What?" Henry halted, his key in the ignition. He glanced over his shoulder, eyes wide. "Did Ava possess Sierra?"

Sierra's face twisted into something darker. Almost eerie.

"It's easier talking like this..."

"What?" Casey all but shouted from her other side. "Are you for real? After everything Percy put you through–"

"*I need it!*" Ava burst out, an unearthly snarl in her voice. Even Casey recoiled. "You get that, don't you? I'm *dead!* That's the end of the line, forever! He got me killed, and now I have *nothing!* Don't I deserve just a *minute* to be human again?"

"Do you hear yourself?" Casey shot back. "Do you want to be just as bad as Percy?"

"She let me do it! *She let me do it!*" Ava cried. She started fumbling for the car door, but Vincent blocked her exit and Casey grabbed her by the shoulders, throwing what little weight she had into dragging her back.

"You think that's an excuse?" Casey yelled. "Bring her back!"

"Let Sierra go!" Henry's voice joined the fray. "She did you a favor, Ava– and this is how you're gonna repay her?"

But neither approach made a difference. With a sudden burst of desperation, Ava ripped free of Casey's grasp and shoved past Vincent, pelting from the gas station carport into the dark wilderness beyond.

"Fuck!" Casey launched herself across the seats, but Vincent threw his arms out to stop her.

"Stay here! Guard Jake and Roman!"

He pivoted and ran after Ava, not stopping to check if Casey listened. If he did, he was going to lose her. He tried to keep her silhouette in his sights, but Sierra was too athletic–in a matter of moments she turned into the sound of footsteps, then disappeared altogether.

Another set of footsteps remained, however. Vincent glanced back, expecting Casey, and was surprised to find Henry instead.

Vincent slowed to a halt. "Lost her," he panted.

Henry stopped beside him, breathing hard but not nearly as winded. "Can you track her?"

Vincent paused, tasting the air. Sierra's fear scent greeted him sharply. "This way."

Henry followed him through the dark, hurrying but no longer running. They wove between thick pine trunks, their shoes muffled by a carpet of needles. The longer they stayed out here, the more Vincent's skin crawled. He began to notice those ghostly, curtain-like shapes flickering around them. He wondered how many lingered now unseen out of the corner of his damaged right eye. They seemed drawn to the living souls wandering through their woods, drifting closer and closer...

Then, a voice reached Vincent's ears.

"You have no right to tell me what to do! After everything you did?"

It was Sierra's voice. Vincent was about to step forward and confront Ava, but Henry took hold of his shoulder.

"Wait," he whispered.

Vincent cast him an uncertain glance, but the warmth of that hand seemed to dig into his psyche, bidding him to obey. Henry led him towards a dense fir tree and they crouched behind it.

"It's not like that." Silence. "It's *not*. Percy, I haven't felt more like myself in *so* long...it's like I've been dreaming, and I'm only getting bits and pieces of everything going on around me..."

Another pause. "No. She wants this. I can feel it from the inside." A frustrated growl. "I *said*, it's not like that! You did something to me, you made me feel..."

Ava was quiet for some time. Then, finally: "I don't know anymore, Percy. It all went away the second I died. I sure as hell didn't feel anything for you before you went inside my head. But then...well, you know. You know it all. It's like we turned into the same person..."

She broke off, then sighed roughly. "But I feel like *more*, now! Back then, I felt like less! Or, I did, when I look back on it..."

Silence.

"But I can tell...Sierra's been so lonely for a long time... No, Henry's just making it worse. I don't know why she even wanted him back. Neither does she."

Henry winced. Vincent studied him out of the corner of his eye, nursing a peculiar tingle deep in his chest.

"Now that I'm here, she doesn't have to be lonely anymore. Someone finally understands her. So she'll let me stay, and we can both be real for once."

"You sound exactly like Percy."

Vincent stepped out from around the tree as he spoke. He barely made out Sierra's shadow just ahead in a small clearing; she whirled around as he approached. Henry's footsteps followed just behind.

"Don't run, please," Vincent added, holding up his hands. "We just want to talk."

"Well, I don't!" Ava spat. "I'm not getting pushed aside again!"

"Then we have to figure out a better way," he insisted. "You *know* Sierra doesn't want you to keep her like this."

Ava scowled at him, then Henry. "Fuck you guys. You have no right–"

"Percy always said the same things, you know. Back when he was possessing you. He said you were in love."

Ava froze, her mouth still open.

"You were perfectly happy letting him stay, weren't you? But once he was gone..."

"I was *dead*," Ava hissed.

Vincent grimaced. "I know."

He was quiet for a long moment. He realized that his usual mantra was playing again in his head: *What would Henry say?* But he didn't have to wonder anymore–Henry was right here. Instead Vincent waited for him to say something, to come in and make everything better like he always did.

But he didn't. He was silent.

Vincent looked at him pointedly, finding something unusually dark in Henry's expression. He returned the glance, finally seeming to register the prompt–but when he spoke to Ava, it wasn't what Vincent had hoped for.

"Why doesn't Sierra want me back?"

Ava stared at him, equally surprised. Then she cracked a tiny smile. "So you're fine with me spilling her secrets like this?"

"I just need to know." Henry looked pained, but didn't relent. "She won't talk to me."

"No," said Vincent, rounding on Henry. "You should ask her yourself. She's not–"

"You wouldn't understand," Henry snapped. Vincent blinked, shocked. This wasn't like Henry at all. A little flame of anger flared inside his stomach, but before he could speak Henry turned back to Ava expectantly.

She shrugged, fighting a smirk. "Like I said, she's lonely. She's always been lonely. She thought being with you would fix it for her. But you always keep her in the dark, or treat her like she's delicate. She feels like she doesn't deserve you and should be more grateful, but..."

Henry looked affronted. "What? Grateful? I'm not–" He broke off, shaking his head. "I don't treat her like she's delicate. She's a werewolf, for god's sake."

"I'm not here to argue with you," Ava cut in. "I'm just telling you how she feels. Maybe this attitude of yours is the problem. So much for Mister Perfect."

A thundercloud slowly grew on Henry's face. "I'm not *perfect*. Damn it, Ava. I don't know why I believed you. I'm not gonna let you sabotage our relationship. Why do you hate me so much?"

Ava's smugness disappeared. "I don't. And I'm not lying."

Vincent gritted his teeth. This was going nowhere good.

"Ava," he said, as gently as he could muster, "Please...just give Sierra's body back for a minute. We can ask her what she wants, while her mind is completely her own. Then, if she really wants you back, you can do it."

Ava hesitated, chewing her lip. He had cornered her, and she knew it.

Then, quietly, she said, "Alright."

She sat down cross-legged on the forest floor. Her head bowed, silence spreading almost unbearably over the clearing. No insects or night animals stirred. It was a supernatural hush, borne of things that should never have bled into the world of the living.

Then, finally, Sierra's head lifted. She groaned, running a hand over her face.

"What..." She blinked rapidly, looking around with mounting horror. "Where are we? What's going on?"

"Hey," said Henry, rushing to her side and resting a steadying hand on her back. "It's okay. You're okay. We're just on the side of the road, heading home."

"What? Did we escape?" She suddenly got a faraway look in her eyes. "Oh..."

"Are you alright?" Vincent asked, drawing closer.

She focused back on him. "Y...yeah...it's just...I kinda remember, but not really. It feels like a dream..."

"You and Ava got us out." Vincent forced a smile for her sake. "You did great. And now you're back."

Sierra looked around again, more calmly this time, with an air of curiosity. "Uh...why here? Shouldn't we get as far away from that place as possible?"

Vincent and Henry exchanged a glance. Sierra caught it, and immediately grew indignant.

"What? What's that look?"

"It's fine–" Henry started.

"Ava stayed with you for a while," Vincent said at the same time. "She didn't really want to leave you."

Sierra gazed at him, her thoughts catching up. "I...I remember her... It was like both of us were the same person. I could feel her, and hear her thoughts, and they were *mine*, like they always had been. But now, they're not...they weren't... Does that sound crazy?"

"Of course not," said Henry.

"Yeah," said Vincent at the same time. He and Henry glanced at each other again. "But it makes sense. That's what happened to Ava and Percy, too."

Sierra gave a nervous laugh. "Well, at least it wasn't like that..."

"Did you want her to stay in control?"

"Huh? No, of course not. I mean..." Sierra's face softened. "It was kinda nice, having someone with you like that...like...I don't know. For a second, it was like someone finally, really understood me, from the inside out. Like, as well as I understand myself. I...I've never felt that before."

"Never?" said Henry. It was sharper than anyone could have expected from him, and both Vincent and Sierra looked at him in surprise. Sierra's shoulders hunched uncomfortably.

"Well...no, I mean...it's not like that...it's different. She was inside me, like, in a way no one could ever–"

"So she just gets you now, is that right? And no one else ever will?"

Sierra stared at him, stunned. "What's wrong with you?"

"Nothing." Henry suddenly pivoted, starting back the way they had come. "Come on. We need to get Roman home."

Sierra opened her mouth to say something, but then closed it again. She and Vincent exchanged a glance before trailing after him.

As they trekked back through the dark woods, the phantoms drifting by them felt somehow less menacing now. They didn't speak for some time, but eventually Vincent couldn't help himself.

"Sierra...did you actually want Ava to stay?"

She frowned. "It was nice, in a way, but...I mean, I wasn't *me*. It was both of us at once. I missed being me. And even then, I don't want to live my whole life in a dream. I'd imagine it's a lot better for her, considering," she added with a little laugh. A small smile found Vincent against his will.

"It's good to have you back." He nudged her with his shoulder affectionately.

"I'm just glad I helped after all. Besides, I had to get you back for stealing this thing in the first place." Sierra held up the amulet around her neck.

"Yeah, yeah...slick," Vincent snorted. "I didn't even notice. When did you take it, anyway?"

Sierra ducked her head sheepishly. "Well...let's just say that last hug was a good one."

Vincent threw her a fake glare, but he was impressed. "See if I ever let you hug me again."

Almost before he could get the sentence out, Sierra snagged him in a quick but hard squeeze. Immediately both of them cringed against their wounds, groaning.

"Thanks for that."

"Hey, I got instant karma!"

The hug was awkward enough that Vincent suddenly became aware of just how glum Henry was, pacing along quietly ahead of them. A cold wave of guilt lapped at the base of Vincent's ribs.

"If it helps...I think Henry is just worried about you," he murmured to Sierra. "That's how he is, you know."

Sierra sighed roughly. "Yeah. I know. He's always worried about me."

"Isn't it a little nice, to be worried about?"

"I guess it was, at first. But...I mean, I can take care of myself. Now more than ever."

"That's funny. That's what Casey always said about being a werewolf."

"Yeah?"

"Well...I mean, she's not very imposing, as a human. Nobody seems to really take her that seriously. Think of Hunter."

Sierra nodded thoughtfully. Something more solemn settled over her. "Sometimes I feel like I'm different when I turn back into a human, too. Like I never really come all the way back."

Vincent studied her. "I guess I haven't been around you long enough, now, to notice."

"Really? I think it's pretty obvious. Maybe it's just me. Then again, you don't have to worry about that stuff, do you? You're always you, no matter what you look like."

Vincent's pace faltered. It took him a second to recollect himself. Sierra slowed too, staring at him.

"What?"

"Nothing." He fell silent, unable to find anything more to say. He didn't like it. He clawed something out of thin air: "I don't know. I think it's nice to be worried about."

"Maybe it's a wolf thing, not to," Sierra offered.

"Maybe it's a Sierra thing."

She sighed again, softer this time. "Yeah. Maybe you're right." It was her turn to shoulder the silence, and after a moment she said, "I just wanted to do something, y'know? I wanted to help him for a change. I feel like he's always holding my hand through everything, making me feel better, and he won't let *me* help with *his* burdens. It's not fair. I think I did a really good job leading that whole rescue mission. I even put myself on the line with Ava to get us out. And he didn't even thank me. He just fuckin'...scolded me. Like I'm just a nuisance to him."

"Maybe you should tell him that."

"He can hear me." She threw a glare at Henry's broad back. If it was true, he didn't say so.

Vincent shrugged. "Give him time. He's been through a lot."

Sierra turned her glare onto him. "*He* has? I just got my brain hijacked by a goth girl!"

He wanted to laugh, but didn't dare. "Okay, both of you have been through a lot."

"You're just as bad as him. Ungrateful bastard." But he could tell she didn't mean it. "It's weird...I feel like I was pushing away so much of how I've been feeling about...about this whole thing with Henry. But when Ava was with me...I don't know. Maybe it's because she doesn't like him. Maybe she's poisoning me."

"She's out of your head," Vincent insisted. "She can't poison you."

"But what if she did? What if some part of her is still hanging around in there?" The whites of her eyes flashed in the gloom, wide with dread. "What if I'm not really me anymore at all? I'm just some soup of whatever's left of me, and the wolf, and pieces of Ava's ghost..."

Vincent laid a comforting hand on her arm. "You're not. You're still yourself, even if some things have changed."

"That's the thing, Vincent. If things have changed, then I'm not myself. Not fully. They changed me." She let his hand stay there, turning her gleaming wolf's eyes into the night that, even as a human, they could now see. "Even if Ava's gone, I still remember her. All the things that were in me."

"I'm sorry," Vincent said with a note of sarcasm, trying to tease her back to herself. It didn't work.

"She's not as bad as you want her to be, Vincent. She's scared, just like us. She's lonely like us, too. Honestly, we both liked being together, for a bit. Even if it was her more than me." Sierra looked sad, now. Almost like a ghost, herself. "I think both of us feel the same way about Henry, actually. Not fully, but...we both wish we could be like him. We wish people would go to all this trouble to save us."

Vincent took in her sorrow, her wistfulness, her loneliness. He squeezed her arm gently. "I would."

Sierra offered him a weak smile. "Y'know...I actually believe you." She took his hand. Hers was warm, slightly damp. A small comfort.

Finally emerging from the trees, they spotted Sierra's Jeep just ahead. Casey was leaning against it, chewing a piece of gum aggressively. She shot up when she saw them.

"Shit, what took you so long? Is Sierra back?" She looked Sierra up and down suspiciously.

"Y–yeah, it's me!" Sierra offered an uncertain grin. "That anxious to see me?"

"No–your fuckin' vampire ran off!"

"What?" Vincent and Henry said at the same time.

Casey flung an arm towards the car. "How was I supposed to stop him by myself? He took off as soon as you left! I didn't want to leave Roman alone, with how bad he is–"

"Damn it," Henry hissed. "I thought maybe he'd..."

"What, turn over a new leaf?" Vincent growled. He brushed past Casey towards the Jeep. "Forget about him. He's long gone. We need to get back to Alderwood."

"We can't track him?" Sierra asked, wide-eyed.

"Vampires don't leave any scent," Henry said a little too gruffly as he followed Vincent.

"You can't seriously be mad at me for this," Casey called after them. "What was I supposed to do?"

"Nothing," Henry answered flatly, getting in the driver's seat. "Don't worry about it."

"Hey," Sierra said, hurrying over to him. "This is my car, remember? I'm driving."

Henry stared at her for a second before sheepishly getting back out. "Oh...right. Sorry."

Vincent quickly rerouted to take shotgun just before Henry reached it. He didn't miss how Henry hovered just outside the closed door for a moment too long before slipping gloomily into the backseat. Vincent couldn't help the tingle of satisfaction that settled in his chest as they drove off.

"Why was Jake with you, anyway?" Sierra asked. "I thought you wanted him to stay in custody..."

"It probably would've been better..." Henry murmured, sounding somewhere between bitter and guilty. "But I didn't have a choice. They wanted me to kill him."

"He helped us escape," Vincent put in. "I guess that was better than dying." Something squirmed in his gut. It was only out of convenience, of course...Jake hated Henry more than anything. But without him, there was no telling what would have happened to them. Vincent didn't like being indebted to someone like Jake. It went against every instinct he had—both personal and practical.

"What were you gonna do with him, once we got back?" Sierra's query pulled him out of his uncomfortable thoughts.

"I don't know, honestly," Henry admitted.

"You're welcome," Casey muttered.

"It's probably better this way," Sierra agreed.

"It's not," said Henry.

The car went quiet.

"You weren't gonna get him into vampire rehab," said Casey.

"I guess that was already the closest thing to vampire rehab," Sierra added.

"This isn't funny," Henry snapped, his voice uncharacteristically dark. "You have no idea what happens in there."

It finally struck Vincent: Henry was *different*. Not fully...but enough. Something had changed while he was in that facility. He had always thought Henry would get off easy, thanks to his father's influence...but now he wasn't so sure. What had happened to him there?

Or...maybe it was his own fault. Maybe Henry had changed after Vincent betrayed him, and he was only now seeing the full effects.

"Cut us a break," Casey snapped. "We *did* just save your ass. Or did you forget already?"

"*You* saved *me*?" Henry echoed, incredulous. "I was fine! I was about to graduate the program anyway! I didn't need you guys to trample in and risk your lives!"

"You weren't," Vincent argued. "You know your father only arranged that test because of me."

"What do you mean?" Henry demanded. "Damn it, what did you even say to him?"

"Who cares?" Sierra burst out. "Yeah, I risked my life! To save you! Even if you *were* fine, how was I supposed to know that? Last I saw of you, they were dragging you away like a prisoner! And last I heard from you, they were gonna keep you forever!"

"And that's worth getting shot? Or worse?" Henry shook his head sharply. "I had everything under control. I never wanted to be responsible for anything bad happening to you. Any of you."

"Bullshit! You said they were gonna make you kill Jake. What if we hadn't been there to help you get out? You think you two could've taken on all those werewolves by yourselves?"

"Everything would've been different if none of you had come," Henry growled. "Apparently, I wouldn't have even been cleared for that test if it weren't for Vincent's chat with my dad. And I'd love to know why!"

Vincent's throat tightened, but before he could respond Sierra said, "Don't you dare blame Vincent for this! For once, can't you just appreciate the fact that all of us care about you? We *wanted* to do this for you! Not everything is up to you and only you!"

"This should've been!" Henry cried. "All of you got dragged into this because of me! Especially you, Sierra! I wanted it to stop long before it got this far! Why won't you just listen to me and stay out of it?"

"Screw this," said Casey. "Your girlfriend put her life on the line for you and you aren't even grateful?"

"I'd rather she left me to die!"

"Somebody better let me out of this car or I'm gonna kill this man. You useless sack of shit–you remember what I said before about a hero complex?" Casey banged her fist on the back of Vincent's seat for emphasis. His innards churned. This was getting worse and worse. And he was so tired of fighting.

Evidently, Sierra agreed. "Everybody, just shut up and let me get us home," she growled, her fingers tight on the wheel. "If that's quite alright with you, Henry."

"Why wouldn't it be?"

She didn't reply. A heavy silence permeated the car for some time after.

CHAPTER 15

KATABASIS

The only good thing about the tension was that it left little room for anything but sleep. Vincent took the opportunity gratefully; by this point he could barely fight back his exhaustion. He could practically feel his wounds slowly sealing up even as fitful dreams tore across his mind's eye like wisps of smoke on the wind.

When he finally woke, dawn's gray light dazzled his eyes through the car window. He lifted his head, leaving a smudge on the glass where his forehead had been. Familiar trees flickered past, welcoming him home despite the darkness that crept beneath their boughs. Even from here he caught glimpses of phantoms like tattered curtains.

No—like wisps of smoke on the wind. They had finally found their way into his dreams. A shiver traveled across his skin.

He tried to let the forest lull him back into wakefulness, but the thought had already ruined it for him. By the time they pulled onto the street outside Dexter's Laboratory he was wide awake and on edge. His fur would surely be bristling if he had it. Even the familiar storefront felt wrong somehow, like a dark caricature of itself. The neon sign was off. The curtains were drawn. All was quiet.

"Should we be parking right out front?" Casey grunted.

"I guess not," Sierra sighed, passing it by. "Not sure if the Shadowhand know my car, though…"

They found a spot at the end of the cluster of buildings on the little road. They made sure no one was around before hopping out and lifting Roman out of the back. He was still out cold, but at least he was human again.

His dark skin looked concerningly gray. The sight of the young boy like this only made it all worse for Vincent. His stomach churned as he took in the bullet wounds that poked out around the blanket they wrapped him in. He let the others hurry him around to the backdoor, instead keeping an eye out for witnesses–dangerous or not. But the only ones he saw were ghosts, trailing towards them between the trees. He didn't want to find out what would happen if they completed their journey.

Inside was gloomy, but not too dark to see. It was also eerily still. As soon as they closed the door, however, the thud of erratic footsteps from the second floor reached their ears.

"I guess they're still kickin'," Casey muttered, helping to rest Roman carefully on the kitchen table.

"First aid kit?" Henry said shortly, which were the first words he had uttered in hours.

"Yes, *sir*," Casey growled. She disappeared into the bathroom.

Vincent wandered over to the living room and collapsed on the couch, staring up at the ceiling. He tried to count his swirling thoughts, but they all bled into one another. He heard the others murmuring as Henry presumably began truly digging into Roman's injuries. Vincent tried not to think of pliers plunging into the teen's flesh, staining the family dining table with blood. That first bright morning with the pack felt like it came from another lifetime.

Of course it would end like this. Every family he touched splintered.

"Vincent? You okay?"

Sierra's voice dragged him back from the brink. He blinked, straightening up on the couch.

"Mmh. Yeah."

Sierra didn't look convinced. "You're up next. You don't look amazing."

"Thanks." He tried to smile, but it didn't make it past his brain.

"I'm not kidding. C'mon. You want me to do it?"

He hesitated. Then he craned his neck to peer over the back of the couch. Henry was adjusting the blanket over Roman's body, still draped over the table. Vincent swallowed thickly–it *was* bloodstained.

"He's all patched up," said Sierra. "Henry thinks he'll be okay. Like you said, they didn't hit anything major."

"But...the blood..."

"Just from pulling the bullets out. They actually stoppered it all up pretty good while they were in there."

That only made Vincent's stomach lurch even harder.

"Hey–are you–?"

"No. No, I...I need to go."

Vincent tried to stand, but swayed on his feet. Sierra immediately grabbed his arm, supporting him.

"Hey, whoa–wait up, you need some help too, mister! What's going on with you?"

"Nothing. Just let me go."

He didn't fight as Sierra lowered him back down onto the couch. Casey came around the other side quizzically.

"Need mommy to do it for you, precious?" she said snidely, but it was lacking her usual flair. It also wasn't funny–not right now. Vincent glowered up at her.

"Have some fucking decency. The kid almost died. He still might."

Casey's attempts at humor bled from her face. "What, like you have the right? You're the one who let him go out there like that."

Vincent smarted. His gaze fell to his hands in his lap, but he didn't see them. Everything had gone blurry.

"I'm sorry," was all he could say. It was so quiet and so meek that it gave way to a wave of self-hatred so powerful it would have knocked him back off his feet.

Sierra's hand squeezed his shoulder. It gave him no comfort, even though he craved it so badly.

"Damn right, you're sorry," said Casey. "He's only–what, thirteen? He has no business out there dodging bullets for us. We shouldn't have even taken him along. But you really wanted him to, remember?"

"Yeah. I do."

"Casey..." Sierra gave her a pleading look.

"What? He's right, the kid almost *died*. You don't think he should take some responsibility for that?"

"I think he gets it."

"Well, I want to be sure. 'Cause, y'know, a *kid* almost *died*. Why were you so eager to have him stick his neck out like that?"

"You mean, what's wrong with me?" Vincent said savagely. He felt like curling up into a ball so no one could see him. He had never wanted to be human less. "I don't know, Casey. You tell me. You've always been keen on it."

He felt a brutal pleasure as Casey's eyes flashed with anger. "You mean, apart from throwing out a kid's life to bust your ex out of his new bedroom?"

"He's not my ex, for fuck's sake!" Vincent snarled, springing up from the couch. His fury was volcanic–he hadn't even realized it until the eruption came. "I'm *sorry* Roman came! I'm sorry *you* came! I'm sorry I dragged all of you into this shit! I never meant for it to be like this!"

Sierra didn't try to stop him this time, only stared at him with her hand suspended in the air between them, forgetting what it was meant to be doing. Casey however was apoplectic.

"Yeah, you fuckin' should be! I wish we had just stayed at my parents' house! Then everything would still be okay!"

"You were falling apart there, and you know it!" Vincent shouted. "Stop lying to yourself!"

He only caught the first twitch of pain on Casey's face before he turned away. He couldn't bear to look, even as his heart raged on.

"You–you–*fuck you*, Vincent! I gave up *everything* for you, my pack, my family–*twice!* I went back to that place for *you!* I *killed*–"

She stopped suddenly. She didn't need to finish that thought–Vincent knew exactly what she would have said. When she started again, her voice was raw.

"You have no *idea* what that took from me. And now all my friends are gone–possessed, *god*–all because you couldn't let that stupid fucking boy go!"

For a horrible moment, Vincent wasn't in the little house on the empty street. He was home–his *true* home, in the heat and the dark–his father's eyes burning him to ash, those last words echoing through the desolate space between the two of them.

He deserved this.

"You know...I get what Henry means, now," he said. "I never asked you to do any of that. Why put so much on the line for *me?*"

"I told you, and I meant it–because even through everything, you were the one person who was always *real!*"

Casey's voice finally broke. Everything else was left in its wake. Vincent knew if he looked, he would meet her ferocious tears. Those, he couldn't fight against. So he didn't look.

"I'm sorry I'm not good enough, Casey."

He walked away, past the bloodstained dining table, into the dark bathroom. It was not a good refuge–he could still hear the anxious footsteps through the ceiling. But here, no one could see him, and he could see no one.

He sat in the dry bathtub for a while, his arms tight over his knees and his knees tight against his chest. He could barely make out the glint of the gray light under the door reflected in the shower head. He stared at it like the north star. But it brought him no guidance.

And yet, somewhere deep and dark inside him, some tiny thing felt good. No...*right*. He had done what he had to do. Casey would stop following him, throwing herself between him and his consequences. And now the way was clear–nothing left to distract him from the final step he had to take to fix everything. He knew what he deserved, now.

Dimly he listened to the muffled voices of his companions arguing through the door. At least, some of them were. He didn't pay them enough attention to make out their tones. He couldn't bring himself to care anymore.

Eventually they stopped. He stayed there a minute longer, until the upstairs footsteps breaking what was otherwise silence unnerved him too much. He climbed out of the bathtub and cracked the door, cringing against the light.

Roman was no longer on the table–only his blood. Henry sat beside it. Alone, his back to Vincent, his head in his hands.

He looked nothing like the hero now. And that was fine with Vincent. Whatever had changed while he was trapped in the Shadowhand base...it didn't matter anymore.

Slowly Vincent moved to Henry's side. He stood there silently until Henry finally lifted his head.

"Are you ready to go?" Vincent murmured.

Wearily, Henry nodded.

Together, Vincent and Henry stepped out into the morning mist. It was thicker than it had ever been before the portal was broken, wreathing through the trees as if exhaled by some giant, invisible entity. It seemed to draw them in, welcoming them with spectral arms, goading them onward towards the center of it all.

Not long, now, Vincent told himself as he walked on beside Henry. *It's almost over.*

Eventually, something rose through the fog—a chain-link fence, twice as tall as them and topped with curls of razor wire. It stood like a strange prison in the middle of the forest. Henry and Vincent looked at each other.

"They'll be patrolling, I expect," Henry murmured, glancing either way down the fenceline. "We'll have to be quick."

"What will we find inside? Can we stand up to it?"

"We'll just have to make a break for it, before they can figure out what's going on."

Vincent was no longer surprised by how resigned Henry seemed. He jumped up and hooked his fingers and shoes into the fence, hoisting himself up one foothold at a time. He heard the muffled clang of Henry at his side.

He hesitated when they reached the razor wire, but Henry swung his leg up over the top of the fence. His jeans snagged on the little blades and he stalled, grimacing as he tried to unhook them.

"Can we go around?" Vincent called to him softly.

"The gates will be guarded," Henry replied, still struggling. Vincent heard the telltale *shrrrp* of tearing denim.

He looked up, his limbs beginning to ache as he studied the razor wire as close as he dared. The coils were too tight to slip between, naturally. If only they had brought something thicker…

Vincent clambered back down the fence. He shrugged off his leather jacket and slung it over his shoulder. Then he took off one shoe and wedged the tongue between his teeth. He climbed up again; when he reached the top, he flung his jacket over one of the wire coils, trying not to think of the blades digging into the leather.

Still holding the shoe in his teeth, he shoved his left hand inside like a glove. Balancing carefully, he used the shoe to pull apart the exposed coil next to the one covered by his jacket, creating a gap. Swiftly he hauled himself through–

The sound of ripping leather stabbed his heart. He felt blades snag on his shirt, but he kept going until he was safely on the other side of the fence. He climbed down the rest of the way, hardly daring to breathe until he reached solid ground. No new burning greeted him there–only what lingered from his recent injuries.

"You could have let me hold it open for you," Henry said to him through the fence. He still clung onto the opposite side, watching. A little thrill of remorse found the fresh bruise on Vincent's heart. He didn't reply, so Henry said, "Here–throw me your shoe."

Vincent tossed it over without a word. Henry fitted it on one hand like Vincent had. He didn't need Henry's instruction; he hoisted himself back up the fence and reached up with his other shoe. Each of them held one of the coils apart until Henry could slip through the gap–this time entirely unscathed. They both dropped down onto the ground side by side.

Vincent gazed up at what remained of his leather jacket, still snagged on the razor wire above him. One of the sleeves had nearly torn off, hanging by a few threads. The rest of what he could see was heavily lacerated. He sighed deeply.

"C'mon...we don't have long," Henry said quietly.

Vincent instinctively expected to feel his hand on his shoulder, but it never came. Instead, his footsteps crunched away through the leaf mold. Vincent turned to follow.

The forest was quiet here–too quiet. They walked unfettered through the mist, each tree fading into and then back out of its shadowy existence like strangers passing by. The longer they walked, the darker it got–both inside and out. Their innards grew heavy, weighed down by the very air they took in. Despite Vincent's best attempts to ignore it, the knowledge of it grew heavier, too:

The chasm was close. The one that haunted his dreams. Its gravity was real. It wanted him back–it always had. And he knew in that moment, without a shred of doubt, that it always would. It had never left his heart.

Not long, now.

And then, there it was. The roar of water at the edge of hearing, then slowly louder, until it filled their heads and left them uncomfortably deaf to everything else around them.

A rocky bluff rose before them through the mist like a leviathan. A waterfall thundered down into a wide pool at its base, its waters black. But it was nothing compared to the blackness that spliced the sky, that pillar of pure void shooting up from someplace unseen at the top of the ridge. It hovered over them like an omen, staring through them without eyes, its head swallowed by the fog. Vincent avoided looking at it directly, chills rippling across his skin.

"Where is everyone?" he whispered. "I thought you said it'd be guarded."

"I'm not sure." Henry crept towards the Devil's Maw, glancing every which way and finding no one. Vincent followed close behind, every sense straining past the waterfall's tumult, equally in vain.

They stepped up onto the rockfall leading towards the top of the falls. Now they were trapped between the cliff and the water far below. Vincent's fingernails dug into his palms as they climbed steadily higher, watching behind them and ahead, glancing up to the top of the cliffs soaring above them. Two entrances, yes…but also only two exits, not counting the fall only a misstep away. He didn't like those odds. But they had no other choice.

They pressed on.

And then, miraculously, they were at the top. The pillar of darkness loomed before them like a nightmare, far too close and impossibly real—and with it, the chasm that had borne it. It yawned into the earth, a maw with no face, endlessly swallowing water, all of it disappearing down and down and down into impenetrable void…

And still, they were alone. They walked right to the edge, slowly. Both of them felt as if they were dreaming.

Vincent felt a powerful urge to look at Henry, to tell him he didn't have to do this. That was what he should have done. But he knew he couldn't. He needed Henry to do this. *Everything* needed Henry to do this.

He sensed Henry's eyes on him. "We jump?"

Vincent nodded. Henry sucked in a great breath.

He was afraid. Vincent could tell, the way he always could. Henry had always been a sixth sense to him, like the chasm itself. He didn't want either anymore, but it was far too late for that. It had only taken him this long to accept it.

"We have to do this, don't we?"

Again, Vincent nodded. "It's our best chance."

Henry was silent for a moment that could have lasted a lifetime. They both were.

"Will I survive it? I don't…have to die to get there, do I?"

Slowly, Vincent shook his head. "It's a portal. You'll be safe on the other side." He hesitated, then said, "Do you think I would lead you to your death, Henry?"

It might have been rhetorical, but truthfully, it wasn't. Both of them knew that.

"…No. I don't think you would."

Defiance burst in Vincent's chest, and he said, "Good. Out of everything, you should at least know that."

Henry winced, but at the same time Vincent saw it rekindle an old flame inside him. "Should I know that, Vincent? After everything you did?"

"And what did I do?" Vincent demanded, the last of his composure tearing from its leash, the words he had been holding back for months spilling out. He knew this didn't really matter anymore, with what he was planning to do—but he couldn't help himself. "All I wanted was to stop the murders, to protect everyone—" *To protect you—* "—and I was ready to do *anything* to get the answers we needed out of Jake. *Especially* after he tried to kill you."

"He was *done*, Vincent. He surrendered. How far were you prepared to go for those answers?" Henry's tone was dark, his eyes watching Vincent's face so carefully it hurt.

"I don't know," said Vincent, and he meant it, and he didn't mean to let a flicker of dread slip into his voice. "I never found out. But seeing how much he hated you...he was never going to stop trying to kill you. He was obsessed. I've seen people like him before. Those are the things that land people where we're going now, Henry. My job was always to guide people like him where they belong—just like yours is to keep the people of this world safe."

He turned his face away, refusing to meet Henry's gaze. Instead, he looked down into the abyss. It did not look back at him, because it had no eyes. Instead, he felt invisible tendrils reaching for him, clawing at him, pulling him in. *Come home, Vincent.*

"I don't know how you did it, but...you knew we were the same from the very beginning, didn't you?"

Henry didn't answer, but he didn't need to.

"Or, you thought we were. But...we're not. We're two sides of the same coin, I think. Can't have one without the other."

Suddenly, a shout carried across the clearing, rising above the roar of the waterfall. Both of them glanced back down the rocky path. The fog showed only silhouettes, but it was enough. *Wardens.* They were approaching—fast.

"Is that why you asked me to come, instead of the others?" Henry said, with the urgency of a final question.

"Yes," said Vincent swiftly, and he wasn't sure if it was a lie or not. But he could still sense Henry's trepidation, that first question yet unanswered. And they were out of time.

The Wardens had reached the rockfall. Their shoes crunched and skidded through gravel as they clambered up the path, closer–

Henry and Vincent's eyes met, for one wild, desperate heartbeat.

Together, they jumped into the darkness.

Vincent opened his eyes.

He could not recall the descent. One moment there was only void, and the next, a vast, bleak plain stretched all around him. Long grass rippled and thrashed across the hills like an ocean storm, waves gleaming somehow despite the absence of sunlight. Any illusion of freedom was broken by immense, jagged cracks coursing through the earth, reminders of the emptiness prowling both above and below.

This place was a brief respite in the everlasting darkness, and a dreary one at that. The landscape was not so much gray as colorless, as if every iota of life had long since drained away–if it had ever been alive to begin with. The shadows were stark and deep, but none so absolute as the blackness that loomed high above, swallowing the earth's ceiling. The air was thick and hot and stagnant, a stale wind whipping across Vincent's face and filling his lungs with the stench of peat and ash. He stood at its epicenter, every sense soaking in it until they were sodden with its desolation.

It was so achingly and awfully familiar. It was home.

The only difference: it was even more lifeless than usual. No lines of hapless souls trudged across the grasslands, urged by some strange instinct towards the horizon. There a fortress waited like a vast, black animal, its countless spires like jagged fangs poised to swallow the world above.

"Welcome to Hell," Vincent said humorlessly.

Henry stood at his side, gazing out over the plains. His expression was unreadable, carved in ever-shifting lines of dismay and awe and dread. He shifted his feet and the grass turned to dust beneath his shoes.

"I...I don't know what I expected."

"Fire and brimstone?" Vincent guessed dryly, starting down the slope. "Don't worry, we're not there yet."

Henry and Vincent traveled steadily across the plains, leaving a trail of ash in their wake. Hours passed, or so it seemed; and yet, like a cruel dream, they never seemed to draw any closer to the distant citadel. For a moment Vincent wondered if Hell itself was forbidding him with some strange power–or perhaps he had simply forgotten how time worked down here. Everything in the world of the living moved and breathed and changed. Here, nothing did.

Not until Benjamin, Vincent reminded himself, and in spite of everything that had come with it, a tiny flame of hope glimmered deep in his chest. He wasn't sure what to think of it, so he kept walking.

Finally, Henry's voice broke through the wind's roar: "This place is *huge.* Is all of Hell just...this?"

"No," said Vincent, trying not to take so much heart in Henry's presence at his side. His voice was like music here, bright and soft and clear against the dark and the heat and the rushing wind. "These are just the Plains of Asphodel. There's much more out there."

"Asphodel?" Henry echoed, his eyes wide. "Like in Greek mythology? It's real?"

"Yes."

"I thought it was called Asphodel Meadows." Henry cast his eyes across the grasslands, finding nothing but those empty hills.

"Maybe once." Vincent trailed his fingers through the wispy grass as he passed. The stalks crumbled to dust against his skin, and he flicked it off his fingertips. "My father said there used to be little white flowers growing all across these plains. Hence the name–asphodel. But that was a long time ago."

"What happened to them?"

"New management."

Henry was silent for a moment, his gaze crossing the horizon until it came to rest on the black citadel, where it too darkened. "Satan rules here now, isn't that right?"

"Lucifer," Vincent corrected, with a little growl. Henry stared at him in surprise until he looked away.

"Even the Shadowhand barely knows anything about the Underworld," Henry said thoughtfully. He tipped his head back to take in the vast darkness above their heads. "This is amazing…"

"Glad you think so," said Vincent curtly.

"Sorry. I don't mean…"

"I know."

They were silent for a time. But Henry couldn't stay that way for long.

"You never really told me much, either. Back when we were on speaking terms."

"For good reason."

"What's changed, then? You're suddenly okay with bringing me here, after all the secrets?"

Vincent fought the impulse to lie. There was no point in it now. "I don't care what they want me to do anymore."

"But you're still trying to help them," Henry pointed out. Vincent bristled, despite his neutral tone. "Fixing the portal…"

"I'm a free agent now," he snapped. "I'm not doing it for them. I'm doing it for our world."

"*Our* world?"

Vincent's thoughts buzzed in his skull as he tried to untangle that instinct to call this place *home*, to call the mortal world *ours*. Then he looked at Henry, studying his face, trying to eke out what he might be thinking behind those marble features. Did he think Vincent should stay here? That this was his rightful place?

Good. Keep thinking that.

"I gave up everything to stay in it," Vincent said at last. "I think I'm owed that much."

"You really love it that much, Vincent?"

He wished Henry would just shut up. He was making this so much harder than it needed to be. "Obviously," Vincent said with a finality, hoping Henry would take the hint.

He didn't. "But your duty is here. It's what you were made for. Don't you feel...I don't know, lost? Without it? You can't have been doing much else all this time, except for hiding..."

Every word made Vincent bristle more and more. "You're right, okay? Happy? I couldn't hide forever. I was always made for this. That's why I'm here now, because I'm sick of hiding. I'm going to fix the portal and then everything can get back to normal."

"But after that...what are you gonna do, up there? You're back to square one, no duty, no home..."

Instead of answering, Vincent shot back, "What about you? You're in the same boat, aren't you? You think the Shadowhand will let you walk free after that stunt we just pulled? Your career is over. You'll be lucky if they let you live."

That shut Henry up. He kept walking beside Vincent in silence.

Finally, he thought. But it didn't feel as satisfying as he hoped. Instead, it just felt...hollow. All this silence between them, where once there had been *everything.* He couldn't stand it. So he kept going:

"Oh, don't worry. You're Henry Wellfellow–I bet everyone will forgive you if you bat your eyelashes and ask nicely."

Henry halted. "They *won't,* damn it! Why does everyone keep saying–I'm not *immune* somehow, you were right the first time. They won't let me back, I don't know *what* they'll do..."

He cut himself off, looking just as miserable as Vincent felt. And as angry, which didn't suit him. Something roiled uncomfortably in Vincent's gut.

Suddenly, Henry faced him. "Did you tell my dad to pit me against Jake?"

Vincent stared at him in surprise. "No."

"Stop lying to me, Vincent! I'm sick of your lies. I know you hate Jake. And after what happened between us–"

"I stopped you from killing him!" Vincent cried out, his pain and his fury finally boiling over. "Did you forget that? You would have murdered him if it weren't for me! I never wanted that!"

Those clear blue eyes looked black down here. "And then you tortured him. Just like they did."

"Because he tried to kill you!"

This time, Vincent stopped dead. He turned away, his heart and his stomach burning. Now Henry knew...it wasn't just to save the world, or to get Benjamin's plot out of Jake. Vincent expected a rebuke, *something*...but nothing came. Nothing but that awful silence, taunting him with everything he had lost.

He tore his mind away, looking up at last to find the black citadel obscuring the horizon. Its spires seemed to meld with the darkness far above their heads, as if the fortress was and always had been part of the landscape. They were close enough now to glimpse little streaks of torchlight among the towers, glittering like stars against the black of night. Mist curled around the wall of tarnished bronze guarding its perimeter. Beneath it lay a vast expanse of what appeared to be white, flat terrain dotted with rocks, stretching all the way to where they stood.

Vincent's heart ached at the sight of it. He was home. He never thought he would see it again. He never wanted to.

It's almost over, he told himself again. Then he started forward.

The fields sloped downward sharply. He half-skidded down until he made it to the edge of the white ground. Henry did the same, stopping beside him with a breath of surprise.

"It's ice..."

"We've made it to Cocytus," Vincent replied, stepping onto the ice. "We're nearly–"

His shoe slipped. His stomach lurched as the ground slid away–

Something solid appeared at his side. It kept him upright, tugging him away from the ice until he could stand safely.

"Be careful," Henry mumbled. He didn't meet Vincent's eyes. Instead he lifted his gaze to the far side of the river. "How are we gonna get across? It's so far…"

It was an unexpected problem for Vincent. He didn't remember having trouble slipping before…

Then, he realized why.

Without warning, Vincent's human form slipped away, leaving the hellhound in its place. Despite the inexplicable relief it always brought to return to his true nature, for the first time, he loathed doing it. It felt like he was leaving behind the surface world, piece by piece, step by step. But he had to do it.

"Hold onto me," he growled, moving forward again onto the ice. His sharp claws caught on the smooth surface and scored grooves into it, steadying him.

He waited. For a moment, he wasn't sure Henry would follow. But then, familiar fingers curled into the fur at his shoulder. They seemed to burn straight through, down to the skin and further in until the pain and the heat penetrated his very heart.

This wasn't the first time he had felt this. But he was sure it would be the last.

And so they began the arduous journey across the ice of the River Cocytus. It was awkward and slow with Henry holding onto Vincent's canine body to keep from slipping. Moreover, it was *cold*–the further they traveled, the colder it got, until the wind whipping across their faces froze little crystals on Henry's eyelashes and the fur around Vincent's three muzzles. They hadn't prepared for this kind of cold. It was all Henry could do to lean against Vincent's side for a moment and get out the jacket he had brought in his backpack, but it was much too light. This wasn't autumn chill–it was subzero.

"I thought Hell freezing over was just an expression…" Henry grumbled, shivering.

"Not here." Vincent's shaggy coat kept the worst of the cold at bay. Still, it gnawed at his noses and his eyes and the tips of his ears and his healing wounds until they all burned.

"God, I hope this ice is thick enough to hold us...if we fall in, we're dead for sure..."

"It's been here a long time. At least since Lucifer came. It won't break now."

"Seems like a lot of things got worse after Sa–Lucifer..." Henry muttered.

He huddled even closer against Vincent's fur as they moved on, and it only seemed to drive that agonizing stake of heat deeper into his heart. Some part of him still wanted to protect Henry–relished the fact that he was doing it, now. Maybe it always would, whether he liked it or not.

It was some time before they finally reached the first of the rocks scattered across the ice.

"We still have a long way to go...maybe we should take a break–"

Henry stopped mid-sentence, his fingers tightening in Vincent's fur until it hurt. His gaze was fixed in horror on the nearest rock, the one he had been about to sit on.

Only it wasn't a rock at all. It was a human head, and it was staring straight at them.

CHAPTER 16

THE EDGE OF THE WORLD

The head continued to gaze up at them, an unmistakable glimmer of intelligence in its dark, bloodshot eyes. No—not *it*. *He*.

"You are alive." A voice croaked feebly from his crusty mouth. Frost crept up around his ears, his bald head, his gray lips. He blinked with great effort, as if he hadn't opened his eyes in ages.

Henry let out a whimper that sounded more canine than human. His fear wrenched Vincent's heart—he knew how many horrific things Henry had witnessed in his lifetime, but this was undoubtedly the worst of them. Yet another terrible thing that was Vincent's fault.

It will be the last, he vowed to himself.

"W-what are you? Are *you* alive?" Henry choked out, his fingers tugging hard at Vincent's pelt as he held himself steady on the ice. It hurt, but Vincent didn't dare complain.

"No," said the head, bemused. "Do I look it?"

Henry seemed as if he would have been happy never looking at the head sticking out of the ice ever again. But to his credit, he forced himself to, trying to peer below the surface with little success. The ice was thick and nearly opaque. "A-are you...is your body down there, too?"

"I imagine so," the head replied, pausing to consider this. "I cannot feel it anymore. It has been too long beneath." He looked towards Vincent now, with measurable disgust. "You escort this living soul to Tartarus, hellbeast? Shame on you."

Annoyance prickled in Vincent's pelt. "Have you no fear?" He bared three sets of teeth, but to his surprise, the head didn't flinch.

"What more can you do to me?"

Vincent narrowed his eyes. He jerked one head towards the other dark shapes dotting the ice. "There are worse positions to be in. I could have you moved."

"No, no. There are rules to this," the head said with great disdain. "I have seen it. My sins have not earned me such treatment."

"There's still time," Vincent growled.

"There is not. The Devil has better things to do with his time. Especially now."

"What do you mean?" Henry crept closer and lowered himself to better meet the head's eyeline.

"About what?" said the head irritably.

"What is the Devil so busy with right now?"

The head grinned, showing broken black-and-yellow teeth. "You did not glimpse the portal on your way in? It is broken. Sinners have been pouring out into the world in droves. But, of course, I myself remain here." He tipped his head down towards the ice encasing him.

"Maybe we can get you out." Henry reached for his backpack. "Vincent, will you–"

"You cannot," the head told him. "Do not waste your time, or mine. This ice cannot be broken. It has been here for millennia, ever since the Devil's first footfall upon the center of the earth. This is his favored domain, for his most cherished prisoners. Besides, you would not want to release me."

"Why not? Nobody deserves to be stuck here like this," Henry said vehemently.

The head looked at him with a new, powerful curiosity. "Nobody, you say?" He glanced at Vincent. "Neutrality. A tenuous stance."

"I'm not trying to be neutral," Henry insisted. "I'm trying to do the right thing."

"Then why are you here?"

"Why are you?" Henry countered.

The head blinked at him. He pondered for a moment. Then: "I murdered my father for his land. He was old, and very weak. Easy to startle. I grew tired of waiting for him to die, so I berated him until his heart gave out." One corner of his mouth quirked upwards. "I lived well for many years, before the Devil enacted his vengeance. He has a special fondness for fellow traitors. And so, I am here."

Henry stared at him, his mouth half open. His shock melted into outrage. "That's horrible. How did you live with yourself?"

"I simply did. Until I did not. And what of you, do-gooder? Is freeing prisoners your capital sin?"

"Not yet," said Henry. "But maybe it will be."

The head's dark eyes narrowed. "You will not free one so horrible as I, surely?"

"I would, if I could. If you'd let me try."

"No," said the head, thinking some more. "No, you cannot. For your undue kindness, I shall grant you this favor. Do not waste your efforts trying— even if this hellbeast would permit it. I am surprised you have allowed us to speak thus far, beast," he added to Vincent. "Do you wish to torment this man with his own misguided desires for revolt? You must."

"It's none of your business," Vincent growled, nudging Henry gently with his nose. "Come on. We should keep moving."

Henry turned to him, his eyes gleaming with desperation. "We can't just leave him here like this! Look at him...it must hurt so much. Imagine being frozen, trapped, forever..."

"Did you not hear him? He murdered his own father. For some *land*. You don't think he deserves this?"

Henry's gaze darkened. Vincent knew that look, and it made something deep inside him shrivel. "No. No, I don't. *Nobody* deserves this. But I bet you think they do, don't you?"

Vincent hesitated. He knew Henry wouldn't like his answer. But it was pointless trying to hide it now. "Yes. He deserves it."

"And all of them, too?" Henry swept his arm towards the rest of those dark shapes protruding from the ice, all along the river.

"Yes. They all betrayed someone who trusted them. That's the worst kind of sin."

"Then what about you, Vincent?"

Vincent flinched. Everything stopped as the weight of those words sank onto his shoulders. He felt frozen, too.

I might as well be.

"I'm sure they'd put me here, too, if they caught me." He turned away, and whispered, "And I would deserve it."

He wasn't sure if Henry heard, but he didn't care. He started trudging along the ice, back on their path towards the citadel. He knew Henry would have to follow, or he would be stuck out here. But he didn't. Instead, his voice rose from behind:

"If it's really true we can't get you out...I guess we have to go now. I'm so sorry. Can you at least tell me your name?"

There was a pause. "Leopold. I have not used it in a long time."

"Leopold. Thank you. I'm Henry Wellfellow. I won't forget you. If there's ever a chance to free you, I'll come back. I promise."

"I still do not understand. Why go to such efforts, knowing what you know of me?"

Vincent realized his pace had slowed unconsciously. He didn't fight it; he listened.

"I don't think anyone deserves this. No matter what you did. What's the point of it? Hurting you just for the sake of it? Will it fix anything? You won't learn anything from punishment...or ever have the chance to do better next time. You'll just be trapped here, hurting forever. I just...don't see the point."

"And what if I were to pursue revenge, should you release me?"

"Well...I doubt you'd be able to do much. You're dead, after all. But I would hope that you'd take the second chance and make something better of it. I would hope you'd repay me, and try to make my effort to help you worth it."

"...You do not belong here, boy. You belong in the other place. I pity you."

"I'm here to help. So don't worry about me. I hope I'll see you again."

Henry sounded so gentle, now. So much more like his old self. In this little moment, he was at his best again. It was almost easy to forget where they were.

Vincent heard Henry's shoes scratching on the ice, then felt his weight fall against his side.

"Let's keep going."

Vincent nodded one head wordlessly. Then they plodded forward.

One by one, they passed more heads frozen into the surface of the river. Most of them were bowed, their eyes closed against the frigid winds. A low keening sound rose from some of them. Once Vincent dared to look, and he glimpsed tears frozen and glittering on the sallow face. He didn't look again. He swallowed thickly as he passed.

Suddenly, as they passed another cluster of prisoners, Henry gasped. Vincent stopped, against his better judgment.

"What? What is it?"

"They're..."

Vincent forced himself to look again. These heads were frozen not up to their necks, but past their chins. They were completely immobilized. All of them faced the same direction–straight into the wind. Their eyes were wide open, frozen solid, encased in sparkling tears. They had long since fallen silent.

Henry's fingers tightened in Vincent's fur. The sting of it brought him back to himself.

"Oh, Vincent..."

Vincent shook one of his heads, and kept padding on across the ice. "Just keep moving. There's nothing you can do for them."

"They can't even cry anymore..."

Vincent's heart twisted. He had never thought of it, before. They were only prisoners, after all. They had hurt. They had betrayed. Did they deserve to cry?

He realized: he didn't know. He had never cried.

On and on, across the frozen river, as the bitter air grew bitterer still. Their breaths came fast and shallow, their lungs burning. They barely kept their own eyes open, but they caught horrible glimpses of what lay at the center of the River Cocytus. One by one, the faces in the ice turned to bodies–frozen with their backs under the surface, upturned towards the blizzard, shredded by the merciless wind; and then more and more, each contorted with agony in shapes that no human should ever endure, each more grotesque than the last, frozen forever in their final throes of anguish. Every last one of their eyes gleamed with tears turned solid, turned to shackles.

The message was clear, to Vincent. "They did this to themselves," he murmured. That was what he had always been told.

But every last one of them cried, in the end.

"I wish we could help them." Henry's voice was barely audible over the howling wind.

But they couldn't. So they kept moving.

Vincent had been this way before, but it was so much worse than he remembered–as if the land itself had turned against him for his betrayal. Soon their limbs turned numb, and then they were so stiff they could hardly move at all. But they had no choice–if they stopped, they would die. So they didn't. They went on, their bodies burning with cold, each breath letting more in, until they felt they were slowly freezing from the inside out and the outside in, and there would never be an end to the torment of it.

Just before Vincent's thoughts could no longer struggle to the surface, one final thing did: *Why did I bring you here? We're going to die. I'm going to get you killed, after all. Of course I am. Of course...*

And then his mind fell silent. All that remained were shuddering breaths, heartbeats, footsteps on the ice.

He closed his eyes, inviting the darkness. His last instinct drifted to those fingers still gripping his fur. Always holding on. Always warm, even when they had no warmth left.

He didn't deserve that much. But he had it anyway. One last good thing.

Then, his paws scraped dirt.

He forced his eyes open, breaking apart the film of frost that had formed over them. At first, the world was only a blur of light and shadow. Then everything slowly coalesced.

They stood beneath the soaring bronze walls of Tartarus, veiled in mist. Black against white.

They had made it.

Henry coughed weakly. Vincent turned, worry breaking through the frigid shroud of death that lingered in his abused body. Henry was nearly blue with cold, his fingers frozen into Vincent's fur. His beautiful eyes were dull and bloodshot. They struggled to focus on Vincent as he looked up, tearing himself from the brink. Vincent could see the shadow of it hanging over him.

"Henry? Are you alright?"

Henry nodded dimly, but when he shuffled forward he lost his balance. He slumped onto Vincent's shoulder, and Vincent held him steady as they both slid to the ground.

Together they laid on the shore of the River Cocytus, unseeing and uncaring of the time that passed them by. The cloying heat of the underground had instantly returned as soon as they left the ice, and for the first time it felt like salvation. Slowly their nerves reawakened and their burning insides calmed, and then at some point they realized the pain of it had faded to memory. They stayed there for some time, their warmth mingling, soaking in the comfort of each other's presence with all the innocence of death. They traveled back from it side by side. Only when they returned to life did their judgment come along, and following close behind was the sorrow and the bitterness and the awkwardness and the pain. Such was being alive.

Vincent moved first, standing shakily. At last Henry's fingers dropped from his fur, and the spot he left felt colder than anything the river had wrought.

He opened his mouth, but before he could utter a word, the crunch of footsteps shattered the silence.

One, two, three, four. Four feet.

"Surprise."

A black figure emerged from the mist, massive and sleek and canine. The similarities with Vincent ended with her three heads; she was even bigger but also more slender, her noses and ears sharp and pointed, not a trace of scruff on her. Her dark, shiny coat was broken only by a rust-colored underbelly and a dot over each of her six eyes. They gleamed as if fueled by flame deep within her skull. Three matching collars glittered at her throats, polished bronze with heavy interlocking segments, each of them bearing a terrible spike. *Menacing* was the first and best word for her. Anyone under her gaze would feel a heavy darkness descend upon their back, urging them to back away, to run.

But if they did, they would be very sorry.

Vincent resisted the instinct to bare his teeth, but his ears flattened. "Superbia."

She did not smile, but it colored her tone anyway. "Welcome home, *Ntropi*."

Vincent smarted. His lips curled, but his teeth stayed behind them. He felt rather than saw Henry's confused glance in his direction–his rightmost eye was still blind.

"I'm here to escort you back to the palace. I imagine, with so bold an entrance, you will come quietly. You weren't trying to sneak in, were you?" she asked abruptly, barely concealing a sneer. "The sentries saw you crossing the Cocytus all the way from the far bank. Surely you're not *that* inept."

"Of course not."

"Good. Because you know you would never get in on your own. Not after what you did."

He didn't reply. Superbia turned her eyes instead to Henry, and it took everything in Vincent not to bristle.

Don't you dare look at him like that.

"And you brought an offering? Please don't tell me you're here to make amends."

"He's not an offering," Vincent growled. "He's my friend."

Superbia blinked at him, a disdainful theater of surprise. But before she could speak, Henry did:

"I'm Henry Wellfellow. Glad to meet you. Are you related to Vincent, by chance?"

Vincent knew Henry well enough–he was acting his heart out, his cordial display so unshakable he almost seemed naive. But, soft as marble was, stone was stone.

"This is my sister, Superbia," Vincent told him quietly.

"Half-sister," she corrected, wrinkling her nose in distaste. "Lucky me. Lucky *him*."

She began to circle them, agonizingly slow, muscles rippling under her pelt, those burning eyes fixed on both of them like prey. Vincent turned with her, always keeping her in his sights, and try as he may he couldn't keep the fur along his spine flat. He was painfully aware just how bedraggled he looked in comparison. Even with Henry at his side, he wasn't sure he could win if she attacked.

Finally she stopped, pinning them between herself and the towering black wall. One white tooth flashed from one of her maws.

"Walk."

Vincent did not want to turn his back to her. His eyes met hers fiercely, his fur spiked along his shoulders, struggling to keep the growl deep in his throat from breaking free. But in the end her gaze was so savage and absolute that it seemed to enter his skull like an arrow through each eye socket, piercing deep and shredding what remained of his will along the way.

He turned away. They walked.

On through the mist, following the great bronze wall, they traveled the last of the way until they stood before the immense gates of Tartarus. Cast in the solid metal sprawled a relief that both resembled and dwarfed any Renaissance painting Vincent had laid eyes on in mortal books. All the way up, hundreds of feet above his head, great battles were waged between thousands of men, floods and fire consumed the earth, animals were hunted and piled atop sacrificial pyres, the sun and moon rose and set, lovers tangled in verdant gardens, and at the center of it all, a single man fell from the heavens, feathers scattering from his magnificent wings. Vincent had never noticed it before, but now, he glimpsed the tears pouring from the angel's upturned eyes, clinging to his last view of the world once promised to him.

Superbia suddenly threw her heads back and let out a bone-chilling, tri-toned howl. It reverberated against the wall and rang inside Vincent's skull.

At once, the earth began to tremble. With the horrible groan and shriek of tarnished metal, the gates dragged open. Clouds of dust billowed forth, mingling with the mist. Henry and Vincent cringed against them, coughing, squeezing their eyes shut until the awful sound ceased and they could once again breathe.

"Move." Superbia shoved them forward.

They walked through the narrow gap opened between the gates—although "narrow" was relative. It was big enough for all three of them to fit through shoulder-to-shoulder, although Superbia drove them on from behind like the prisoners they were. They were not worthy of the gates opening completely, of course; Vincent had never once seen such an occasion.

As they passed through, still cloaked in dust and fog, he caught a glimpse of a gargantuan, human-shaped silhouette peering at them from behind the gate, its beady eyes flashing in the gloom. A shiver coursed up his spine, and he ducked his head as if that would help him avoid its interest. He did not glance back, even as the gate was hauled shut behind them.

No turning back now.

A narrow ring of solid ground stretched all the way along the perimeter of the wall, miles and miles out into the distance. Beyond it, the earth plunged down into a great bowl, so deep it sloped almost immediately into darkness. Mist spilled eternally over the edge like water, disappearing into the abyss. A single strip of flat earth shot across the chasm, leading all the way to the towering spires of the black citadel that loomed in the center.

"I hope you're not afraid of heights," Superbia sneered, driving them forward towards the land bridge.

Vincent wasn't, but his heart still caught in his throat as he stepped out over the abyss. He offered it one glance, because he couldn't help himself. The world swayed around him, as if the darkness itself were reaching out to drag him into its depths. He snapped his eyes back to the path ahead, forcing himself not to look again—or to imagine what might be lurking just beneath their tiny bridge.

Henry seemed to be having a similar time of it. He stuck close behind Vincent, and immediately began talking as if to soothe himself. "So...half-siblings? I didn't know your family was so complicated."

"It isn't, really," Superbia lilted. "Our father has many mates. But oh, consecrated and fussed over as they are, they're only common bitches at the end of the night. And they die just the same."

Despite his best efforts, Henry couldn't stop the horror from creeping into his voice. "He...he *kills* them?"

Superbia snorted. "Why would he? They bear his precious children. Well...precious *some*." Her eyes flicked towards Vincent. "None of our broodmothers survive the birth. They are mortals bearing demigods."

Vincent felt the heat of Henry's gaze on his back.

"That's...sad. You never get to know your mothers."

"They're just dogs," Vincent said bluntly. But something tiny, almost imperceptible, ached between his ribs. He remembered talking about the very same thing with Benjamin, long ago—how he, too, thought it was sad. How the first kind touch Benjamin had given him had reminded him of his mother, in her first and last moments.

"Why would we ever want to know them? So we can play tug o' war?" Superbia snickered, tearing him from his thoughts. "Keep going, coward human. You deserve to know the fear of the pit of Tartarus. I won't help you keep it at bay with this idle chatter."

So she caught Henry's nerves, too. Vincent gritted his teeth, but this time he couldn't keep the anger from spilling through them.

"Shut up. He isn't a coward."

"What's that? Is someone biting back now?"

Vincent didn't reply. He wrestled his anger back down, pinning it somewhere deeper inside–

Suddenly, the world turned on its axis. He slammed into the earth, and the breath left his body. Pain shot through his healing wounds–

He opened his eyes on darkness, falling away far, far below. His stomach lurched.

He flailed his limbs, but he was pinned–hard. He gasped for air. He heard Henry shout his name from somewhere far away.

Massive fangs flashed an inch from his face. A cruel grin. No–three.

"Watch. Your *fucking* mouth."

Vincent swallowed the whimper that rose in his throat. He was no match for his sister, but he wasn't going to give up the rest of his dignity. Instead he nodded, breathless.

She kept him there for another delicious moment, then slowly lifted her weight. He gulped air and scrambled away from the edge, crouching in the center of the bridge. Shame crept in, coiling low and hot in his belly, grounding him.

He lifted his gaze and found Henry crouching beside him, not quite touching him. Those clear blue eyes were dark with concern, and something else Vincent couldn't place.

"Move," his sister snarled, ramming her middle head into his flank. He fell forward onto Henry's lap with another burst of embarrassment, struggling to his paws.

"Easy," said Henry. His tone was so gentle it startled Vincent. He hadn't heard this voice in so long–not towards him.

His hands bolstered Vincent's chest, helping him stand. His fingers pressed against the huge clawmarks scarring Vincent's flesh. His nerves burned where they touched, and he caught his breath. For one little moment their eyes met.

They turned their backs on Superbia, as if she didn't even exist, and began trudging onward towards the citadel. They heard a low growl behind them– she hadn't missed this gesture. But she followed behind them wordlessly.

At long last, they reached solid ground on the other side. The fortress soared above them, carved of basalt, its tallest towers disappearing into the murk of the underground sky. Tiny windows high above flickered with torchlight, the only spark of color in the desolation. The front gates stood open. Waiting. Arrogant.

Vincent's stomach dropped at the threshold. He stepped through, into shadow.

It was dark inside. Even the sconces and braziers along the hallways felt dim somehow, as if something about this place forbade light from traveling far. The air was heady with incense, the haze bleeding through everything until the darkness itself seemed to move and breathe. The ceilings were impossibly, dizzyingly high. The only thing that moved freely among the halls were echoes. Everything else was a prisoner.

Vincent didn't need to ask where they were going. He led the way through the labyrinthine halls, each smooth, black wall exactly the same as the last. New corridors sliced through them here and there, leading on and on into shadow beyond the torchlight's reach.

Only one bore something unusual; as they passed, they caught a glimpse of a diaphanous curtain, and through it *something* looked back at them.

An eye. A single eye, its iris somehow every color at once. It was far too big, far too close—but no, it was all the way down the hall, in that room, behind the curtain.

That didn't matter. It pierced straight through the distance, the veil, through matter itself, spearing them with a spike of fear so real it was painful. For a single instant, Vincent swore he saw himself in that eye, gazing back at him. And more, just beyond that—*too much.*

He couldn't bear to look. He ducked ahead down the hall, overcome with relief as the wall blocked his view. He willed himself to forget it. He had seen it before, and it had brought him nothing but trouble.

Finally they reached a distant corner draped with vast red curtains, only the smallest sliver of gray light slicing through the crack between them. He pushed his way through. A courtyard awaited them beyond, fashioned of the same dark stone. The walls here were terraced, each row carved with caricatures of monsters from a bygone era. Similar statues ringed the pit in great columns–winged lions, horned serpents, minotaurs, giants with dozens of limbs, boars with tusks so fierce and curled they pierced into their own flesh. The halting glow of the braziers cast their features into terrifying relief. At the very center of the floor, a place of honor, lay a mosaic depiction of a fearsome, jet-black hellhound, its ruby eyes blazing and incense leaking from its three maws. This was a coliseum.

Then, the shadows moved.

A flash of crimson eyes in the smoke. Three colossal heads emerged, as if born of the haze itself. Pure white teeth gleamed in the flickering firelight. A growl rumbled so deep it felt like thunder rolling through the earth at their feet. The darkness had taken form, and it was canine.

Cerberus stepped forward, dwarfing both his children and twice as tall as Henry. He was black as the abyss itself. His coat did not shine and ripple like his daughter's; it framed his body like a lion's mane, exploding from the darkness at its center in a great, imposing ruff that shielded him from both the elements and his enemies. Glittering bronze spikes protruded from his three necks, their collars hidden among the forest of fur. His long tail lashed behind him like a slaver's whip, his claws scimitars mauling the ground they walked on. Smoke billowed from his jaws as if real hellfire lurked in his belly. If Superbia was *menacing*, Cerberus was *monstrous*.

The very sight of him was like a nightmare come true. For Henry, something like him shouldn't exist. For Vincent, he should have stayed a memory.

His instincts took over before he could think. He ducked his head in submission, his gaze low, fixed on those wicked claws. The shame of it burned in his gut, but it was not a battle worth fighting right now. Not here.

"Hello, Father," Superbia purred from behind them. But for once, he ignored her.

"*Interloper.*" The word came as thunder, a curse, quaking the entire arena. Gravel crackled down from the looming statues, landing at Vincent's paws. "You dare show your face underground?"

Vincent's heartbeat was almost louder than his father's voice in his ears. He fought to stay steady. "I...I came to fix the portal." He hated how his own voice quailed.

That growl tore through the earth and air, through his very organs. "To what end? You crawl back to me on your belly? You think you can scuff away the stains of your betrayal?"

He lunged suddenly–Vincent and Henry both jumped back, but his gargantuan paw slammed into the stone floor instead, showering them with grit.

"You are *Ntropi*–disgraced! So you will forever be!"

"I know," Vincent choked out, fighting through the pain and the shame. "I'm not here to deny that. I know what I am. I just need to talk to the prisoner–the one I left you. Benjamin Warwick."

"Ah...you mean the boy Superbia brought me." Cerberus' eyes gleamed. "The one you allowed to escape."

"I need to speak with him," Vincent insisted, a whisker away from pleading. He could feel everything rapidly slipping away from him. "He's the one that broke the portal. I can get him to fix it–"

"The portal is of no concern to you." Cerberus flicked an ear dismissively.

Vincent halted, mouth half open. This time, Henry spoke up.

"But–there are lost souls all over the mortal world, possessing humans... Respectfully, sir, I was under the impression your master cares very much about ensuring the souls in his charge end up where they belong–"

"You think our Lord is not capable of mending His own designs?" Cerberus snarled, and again Vincent and Henry flinched back. "You think He is unaware that it was *your* prisoner who caused all of this chaos? *Your* weakness that sabotaged His order? I loathe to assign you so much credit, pup, but the depths of your pitiful nature are exceptional. You could not stop at one weakness, no–you allowed your prisoner to wander free, devise this little ploy of his, while you amused yourself dallying on morality and playing *house*."

Vincent stood frozen before his father, his thoughts and blood racing.

"How did you know what I was doing?" *Why didn't you stop me?* He knew better than to suggest his father's ineptitude.

"I am not a fool, and your prisoner is not indomitable."

"Are you saying Sa–Lucifer knows how to fix the portal?" Henry dared to ask, bewildered.

Vincent was sure Cerberus did not miss Henry's blunder. His fiery eyes narrowed to slits, and his serpentine tail thrashed.

"The portal between Hell and Earth does not belong to the whims of mere mortals. You dare believe it can be violated or restored by your delicate hands? It has stood since the gods were new. It is being repaired as we speak. It is a matter of moonsets before balance is returned."

Something heavy and cold as iron settled in Vincent's stomach. He stood unfeeling, unthinking, as the reality of it slowly clicked into place around him. When his mind returned, it brought with it a single, hideous truth:

It had all been for nothing.

The journey through Hell itself, across the Plains of Asphodel, across the River Cocytus, their brush with icy death...

Rescuing Henry from the Shadowhand, Roman's sacrifice...

Everything Casey had given up...

Mira and Percy and Ava and the old night watchman, all dead...

Sierra, her life stolen from her and turned to beasthood...

Jake's torture...

Losing Henry, betraying Henry...

And Benjamin. All the people he had turned to vampires. All of his efforts, all of his hope, all of his agony...none of it mattered. It was only a temporary inconvenience for the Prince of Darkness.

It was just as Cerberus had said: they were simply too small for any of it.

"Okay," Vincent said at last. It was all he could do, now. "Alright. I'm sorry for coming here. I'll–We'll leave. You'll never have to deal with me again."

"No. I was foolish to allow you to stray. I will not err again."

The great Cerberus was cold now, his words filled with malice and teeth. He gazed at his offspring as if he were an earthworm wriggling on the concrete after a rainstorm.

"I underestimated the damage you could wreak, given the opportunity. Instead of redeeming yourself, you have disgraced yourself beyond recognition."

Every word pierced Vincent's core.

Cerberus shifted his stance, and the air seemed to crackle like the instant before a storm breaks.

"Anendotos is dead. The unyielding yielded. What remains is the refuse of my blood, which is my solemn duty to cleanse."

CHAPTER 17

THE ONLY WAY

Those eyes blazed, twin embers in the perfumed haze. And Vincent knew instantly, with cold certainty: his father was finally finished with him.

The shadow behind those eyes closed the distance in the space between one breath and another. All at once, Cerberus was upon them.

"Vincent!"

Henry's cry was drowned by the thunder of Cerberus' paws as they crashed down on the spot Vincent had occupied a half-second before. He felt the shock of snapping jaws closing at the very edge of his pelt. It sent a ripple of terror up his spine, carried him like a riptide to the arena's entrance. He dove for the curtains–

No–Henry!

He pulled up short, his leftmost head glancing over his shoulder–

A shadow slammed into his side, bearing him to the ground. He thrashed, knowing it was hopeless–his father was far too big, too powerful. A thousand fears and regrets flashed through his mind, but one rose above it all.

"Henry!" he choked out. "Get out of here! Run!"

He fought to catch a glimpse of him, to see if he was safe, if he was fleeing, but for once three heads did not help. And his rightmost eye was still blind. All he saw was gnashing teeth and dark claws.

So he knew: he had to fight. Even if it was hopeless. Henry had to escape.

He twisted, throwing as much strength into it as he could, and sank his teeth into a limb.

It recoiled. It gave way.

That's when he realized–this could not be Cerberus. He had a chance.

He kicked out, and suddenly his claws connected with something solid. The weight shifted and he dragged himself out of its grasp, just enough–

A sharp thud, then a howl of pain. It turned into a snarl halfway through, and the shape above him lurched—

"Leave the human, Superbia!" Cerberus' voice commanded. "He is not yet judged."

"Let him go!" Henry's voice rang out. He was close by. "Or you'll have no choice but to take me. I won't let you have him."

"Damn you!" Superbia snarled. She reared back, away from Vincent—enough for him to glimpse a crossbow bolt jutting out of her neck.

"Keep him occupied!" Cerberus barked. "Block the exit!"

Finally the weight lifted from Vincent's body. It gave him a split second to pull himself up, to catch Superbia leaping for Henry, his crossbow taking aim—

Despair throbbed like poison through his body. This wasn't supposed to happen. This wasn't how it was supposed to go.

"Henry, *leave me!*" Vincent cried, desperate, too desperate to hide it. It was all he could manage before his father caught him.

Before he could blink he found himself on the ground, that hulking shadow bearing down on him. He rolled aside, just in time to avoid those crushing jaws, but he met a leg like a tree trunk and could not escape. This time teeth caught his ear, ripping through it with such force it was like tearing paper. Hot blood coursed from the shreds, but Vincent didn't let himself feel it. He wasn't going to win this fight, but he was going to do his best to give Henry an opening. He was going to make an impression. His father may have been right about many things, but not this one.

I am still unyielding.

Strength wasn't going to cut it. He took half a second to think, to look—

What would Henry do?

He would find the advantage. There was only one—a single spot vulnerable to a smaller, pinned opponent.

He kicked up with his hind legs. His claws caught in fur, then flesh, then blood, tearing through his father's soft underbelly in one wicked sweep.

But before Vincent could even feel the triumph, those fangs finally found their mark.

Cerberus grasped his scruff, piercing the folds of flesh and fur, dragging him out from beneath him and tossing him across the arena. He skidded onto the smooth stone, feeling the mosaic tiles catch on his pelt and scratch one of his muzzles. He tried to stand, but as soon as the world was upright again it vanished back into his father's shadow.

He hit the far wall, stone crunching against bone. He crumpled at its feet, a whine tearing from his throats as his heads spun. His vision had gone black, trickling back in little spots, but not fast enough. He caught only a glimpse of Henry's silhouette across the arena, harrying Superbia's—not running and not escaping. He indulged a last moment of despair before he was knocked aside.

He fell onto his flank, and this time his limbs would not respond, no matter how he tried to drag himself up. He was beyond pain—he could not feel any of it. Instead, only panic coursed through his body, gripping him, shrieking at him to move.

But he couldn't. His father's power was unmatched. There was nothing anyone could do.

"Henry...I'm sorry," he said, fighting through the gathering darkness, projecting his mind's voice in one last desperate attempt to reach him. If this was it for him, for both of them, Henry deserved to know... "I never should have brought you here...I thought we could do it, I thought..."

His mind was splintering. He struggled through the haze, but he couldn't remember his own words. Fitting, he thought, when he had wasted so many of them. If only he had been a dumb animal, like his poor dead mother. Then he wouldn't have betrayed anyone, he wouldn't have hurt anyone—or, at least, it wouldn't have been his fault... He would have just followed his orders, would never have questioned what the right thing was, and everyone that mattered to him would be pleased with him, because he never would have met Henry, or Percy, or Sierra, or Casey...

At first, he thought his fading mind had summoned an image. A dream. A face that was once dappled with sunlight, cradled by mist tinged gold, close enough to taste. Here it was gray, shaded, streaked with dust and grit, his once-neat hair rumpled and bloodstained. But those eyes...for the first time in so long, the sky lived in them again–bright, clear blue, incandescent with life and vigor, hiding nothing. They gazed at the man from beneath the earth with no fear, no hesitation or shadow of doubt.

It could not be real. Not after everything. From the moment Vincent returned to the Underworld, he knew he would never see the sky again.

"Get out of the way, mortal!" Cerberus snarled. "Your life is not forfeit today."

"No. I won't."

"Insolent little flea!" Superbia hissed. "Kill him, if he allies himself with traitors–"

"Silence! He is our charge. Boy, if you do not stand aside..."

"I don't care what you do to me. This is wrong. Vincent came here to make things right. He may not always make the right choices, in the end, but he *tries*. He's always trying..."

"Do you know what he did?" growled Cerberus. "He befriended a mortal condemned. Abandoned his post, helped him escape. And when I granted him mercy, gave him the chance to rectify his mistake, again he abandoned his duty for *self-indulgence*. Allowed his charge to murder innocents, to crusade against Hell itself! And you think he is *trying?*"

"Yes. I do," said Henry, without a moment's hesitation. "I get it...sometimes it was hard for me to see, too. It's hard to overlook all the harm that's come from what he's done. But...I think you're forgetting to weigh the good, too. The people he saved, doing what he did...and all along the way, too. He saved my life, once. Maybe none of this would have happened, if he hadn't let Benjamin go...but he didn't do it knowing all this would happen. He did it because he cared. He truly thought Benjamin deserved a second chance."

"That matters not!" Cerberus roared. "Any loyal hellhound stands beside Lucifer's judgments! His devotion for his family was eclipsed by a mere shade with a sad tale!"

"Is this what you call 'devotion'? You'd kill your own son?"

Silence. Then, faintly, warmth brushed across the old scars across Vincent's chest. A hand.

"Did you give him these?"

Silence, again. Longer, this time.

"He is no longer my son. As I said before, Anendotos is dead."

A pause. Then: "Does your bloodline not matter to you, Cerberus? He may not be your son in name, that's your right...but your blood still runs through his veins."

No one spoke for so long that Vincent thought his senses must have finally faded altogether. But then, at last, his father said, "You argue so earnestly for him."

Henry did not answer.

"...You are right, mortal boy. He carries my sacred blood. This shall be his only mercy. I will not kill him. He shall be imprisoned for the rest of his days, until perhaps he has remembered his place."

Henry's hand tightened on Vincent's chest, then slowly withdrew.

"Thank you." His voice was barely above a whisper. It didn't sound triumphant.

"As for you...you do not belong here. That much is clear to me. You are able to see the best in such lowly creatures as he...to place your own life between his and that which would see his retribution. Misguided as this is...you carry an empathy I have rarely seen before. Perhaps there is still time in your mortal life for you to stray, but...you deserve the chance. Please, return the way you came. Back to the mortal world above."

Another beat of silence, heavy with shock. "Oh...th...thank you, sir. There's just one thing...I'm not sure I know the way back."

"Very well. Superbia will guide you."

"Ah...well, do you think she'll actually take me all the way? She's made no secret of wanting to kill me..."

"She is loyal. If I tell her, she will obey."

"And you don't think Vincent will? I mean...look at him. I think he understands his place now."

There was another silence, and Vincent could feel their eyes on him. When Cerberus didn't answer, Henry added, "I...I want to say goodbye to him. Properly. Alone. After everything he's done, I know I'll never trust him again, but...we were friends for a long time. We went through a lot together. It just feels wrong to part like this."

A little growl rumbled in Cerberus' throat.

"Even if I allowed it, he is clearly in no state to guide you."

"I will take him."

Slowly, with the weight of death on his back, his ruined body trembling, Vincent pulled himself up. He felt his blood leaving him, trickling hot down his face and matting in his thick fur, pattering to the stone beneath him. Every bone and muscle ached. Some screamed. He was dizzy with it. Darkness crowded him, lingering at the edges of his vision like wild dogs circling, waiting for an opening to deal their prey a final blow. But he was not dead—not yet. Every scrap of him that was not dead yet clung to a single goal: stay up.

"Vincent?"

Vincent ignored Henry. Instead, his eyes met the cinders that were his father's, for only half a heartbeat. Just enough. Then he bowed his head—not in exhaustion, but in submission. He held it there, focusing everything he had left on drawing one ragged breath after another. On channeling that image of utter supplication. He had to be more pathetic, more pitiful than he had ever been before. Only then would his father underestimate him.

The world seemed to freeze for a long, horrible moment. Mocking him. Mocking his efforts. The longer he stood, the harder it became. But then...

"Then go. Prove to us all you are capable of something useful. And if you should stray again...you know what awaits you."

Cerberus lifted his rightmost head towards the arena's entrance. Three sets of crimson eyes glittered from the shadows there—the only part of Superbia that did not blend in perfectly with the gloom.

"Yes, Father."

Vincent squeezed his eyes shut, dragged his limbs forward. Against all odds, they carried him across the courtyard, agonizingly slow. It felt like crossing the ice again: each step achieved only with claws clamped into the ground, pulling him ahead. And with each step, despair leaked more and more into his heart.

I can't make it.

But Henry remained at his side. He took each slow step with him. And so he kept going.

Finally they reached the curtains at the arena's entrance. Still his sister's blood-red eyes gleamed from the shadows, laughing at him without making a sound. Spite surged through his gut like lightning, but it was joined by a shiver.

"You'd better not stray again, little Ntropi," Superbia crooned as they passed. "Or nothing will stop me. I'll be the hunter this time, and I'll find you. No matter where you hide."

Their eyes met for just a moment, baleful. Then Vincent ducked through the curtain and into the dark.

The way through Tartarus was serpentine, hazy with incense. Henry would never have made it on his own, but Vincent trudged on, a stolid guide. They were silent all through the palace, terribly aware they were not alone, although they saw no other soul. They passed the corridor with that horrible eye behind the curtain, unwilling and unable to look at it, knowing its gaze followed them—perhaps even after they had left it behind.

Time bled into itself; any amount could have passed before they at long last glimpsed light again, however dim. They returned to the gray world beyond, the underground stretching out before them into the distant horizon, taunting them with the scope of the journey they had made to get there—the journey they would have to make to get back.

Henry caught his breath, which came in a little shudder. Vincent did not look at him and did not stop, plodding on towards the narrow land bridge across the abyss surrounding them.

"Vincent, wait. There has to be another way back."

"There isn't."

"There *has* to be. You can't...you can't make it all the way there. Not like this."

"I have to. You can't go alone. Not across the ice. Not if my other siblings find you here, or worse..."

"Worse?"

Vincent didn't answer. He kept walking, this time locking his eyes on the ground in front of his paws, refusing to acknowledge the chasm hungrily awaiting him on either side.

"Vincent–stop, just listen to me!"

Vincent finally paused, but took advantage of the narrow bridge–Henry could not force him to face him.

"It's not about that. It's about the distance. You're too weak like this to make it that far–even just walking, forget about the ice or...or whatever else is out there. If I had to, I could figure something out on my own, but..."

He was right. Vincent knew it, deep in his heart. He took in a great, painful breath.

"Then I'll get you across the ice. From there...you have your crossbow."

"What? No, Vincent–"

"If anyone can make it, you can."

"Vincent, I'm not leaving you behind!"

Everything stopped.

No. He can't...

"Yes, you are. You have to. I can't make it."

"Vincent, look at me."

He didn't move.

"Look at me."

Nothing should have made him turn around. But there was so little will left in him, and Henry's voice was filled with such desperation, his body seemed to move on its own. When his eyes met Henry's, he no longer found clear skies in their depths, but a thunderstorm. So many emotions flickered like lightning across the blue–crackling with power, too quick to pin, each of them warring with the others. But Vincent felt their tingle beneath his skin. For the first time, he could no longer see his own reflection in Henry's eyes–the beast standing before him.

"I'm not leaving you here."

Henry's words struck him like hailstones.

This isn't supposed to happen. This isn't how it was supposed to go.

"Look at *me*, Henry," Vincent hissed, searching his face, tracing the soft, strong marble of it, chasing the lightning in his eyes, clawing for some breath of understanding. "I belong here."

And then he caught something, illuminated by a flash: sorrow.

"You don't. You never did."

Vincent stared at him, incredulous, everything slowly boiling over inside him.

"You just told my father you'd never trust me again."

"I was lying, Vincent. I needed him to let you come with me."

"But–when I was taking Benjamin back to Hell, you thought I would kill you. You said–"

"I know what I said." Henry gritted his teeth. He looked moments away from tears, which stunned Vincent into silence. "I was wrong. I was so wrong. I never saw...I didn't realize what you really were."

"You know what I am," Vincent growled, beating back the shame.

"No. *Who* you are. I didn't understand. But now...now I do. I know how you got here, how you got *there*..."

Henry knelt before Vincent, inches from the edge of the cliff dropping away into darkness, his knees barely planted on the land bridge. Their eyes never left each other's.

"I meant what I said to your father. All this time, you were trying. You still are. And...and so am I."

He reached a hand out into the empty space between them, tentatively, imploringly, those beautiful eyes shifting between each of Vincent's three faces equally.

Vincent didn't move. He didn't even breathe, though it ached in his chest.

Then Henry touched it, and it ached even more. Those gentle fingers traced the scars there, the paths forged by his father so long ago...but not long enough.

"How could someone who's only ever known *this* be as good as you are?"

Something burst inside Vincent, more painful than any of his wounds. He pulled away.

"Stop it!" he cried, but it was weak. "Stop taunting me, stop pitying me–"

"I don't pity you, Vincent!" Henry said with such ferocity that Vincent stopped dead. "I never have! I *care* about you! It's like I said, that night–our last one–I stopped being alone when I met you."

Vincent's heart twisted until he felt he had to gasp for air. "You left me, you *hated* me, as soon as you realized what I really am. I tortured Jake, I dragged Benjamin to Hell and left him here for eternal torment. I chose that. I'm not just some kicked puppy following my father's orders."

"You stopped me from killing Jake." Suddenly Henry's voice was much quieter. "When I didn't have the strength to stop myself. I was just as bad as you were, Vincent, in that moment. I...I tried to deny it, for a long time. Even to myself. Especially to myself."

"It's not the same," growled Vincent. "I'm still *bad,* Henry. I'd do it again, and again, every time–because someone has to do it, don't you see? I didn't want it to be you, because..."

He swallowed hard, fighting the tightness in his throats, hating the weakness behind it. "Because you're the best person I've ever met. You're...you're not *perfect.* Jake was wrong. But you're...good. Underneath everything you've ever done, you just want to help people. You want things to be better. You want people to be kinder. And maybe one time you slipped up, because you're human, and he hurt you, and he was killing people, and when you came back to yourself you were horrified by it. *That's* what makes you who you are. And…I never wanted to let a mistake, a side effect of being human, change that."

"And you *don't* want to help people?" Henry countered. "Why did you let Benjamin escape? Why did you promise to help Percy? Why did you help me? Or anyone else, for that matter?"

Vincent wanted to deny it—to tell him he was only following his duty to help the dead. But he was long past believing that. In truth, Cerberus was right about him—he was selfish and treacherous and greedy. His life, the things he cared about, were worth more to him than Lucifer's order, than upholding justice for all living beings. He was no better than Percy, possessing someone out of loneliness, or Ava, ignoring pleas for help to preserve herself, or Casey, running from the constraints of what was expected of her. No better than Melanie or Jake or Hunter, wielding new powers to escape the shadows of mundanity. No better than Henry, arrogant enough to believe he alone knew how to fix everyone and everything, until he himself crumpled under the weight of his own responsibility.

His duty was to be selfless, and loyal, and modest—because if given the chance, a mortal would always do the wrong thing for their own reason. But instead, he was like them. He cared too much. He always had. First Benjamin, then Percy, then Henry, and Sierra, Mira, Casey, the pack, even Ava—they mattered to him, even if they were smaller than all of this.

And yet…he wasn't mortal, either. Caring wasn't enough—not for him.

"I felt something for Benjamin. I let him trick me…and look what happened. And *again*, in California…I gave a murderer a second chance, and he betrayed me. I made Casey *kill* for me. I can't be *good*, Henry, I can't be *kind*. If I ever do it…I let all these terrible things slip through the cracks."

Henry shook his head. Any surprise he held for Vincent's confession didn't make it to his face. Instead his eyes were shining with unfallen tears, glimmering like stars in the Underworld's darkness. "No. All of that just proves it—you're still *good*. We both want things to be better, and people to be kinder. We just go about it in different ways." He gestured towards the half-dead world around them. "The only ways we know how. I still see myself in you, and I *know* you see yourself in me. Tell me to my face that you don't feel the same way I do—that you don't feel so alone anymore."

He was right. Vincent hated it, but he was right. He cared too much. He did terrible things because he cared too much. And he was going to have to do it again.

Vincent held his gaze—steady, excruciating. "I feel more alone than I ever have."

A shadow passed over Henry's expression like a cloud across the sun. Vincent forced himself to witness it for a long moment, because he deserved to. Then he turned away.

It was a lie. He had to lie, because both of them cared too much. If he didn't...Henry would never let him go. He *had* to let him go. Because a new resolve had begun to burn deep in his chest, a blaze catching on a thousand things that had been collecting like fallen leaves in his heart. Only the last ones had been enough to spark:

The memory of Henry's gentle hands against his monstrous chest, his scars. The look on Henry's face when he saw those heads frozen in the river of ice, upturned towards the bitter wind so they could never cry. His own father's eyes searing into him, judging him, reviling him. Deeming everything he ever did *worthless*. And Lucifer's eyes, too, somewhere far away and unseen, always, *always* watching, from the inside out. His master, the god who believed in suffering. Who used him to inflict it.

That was who he was, at his core. And yet, somehow, Henry didn't think he deserved to be here.

Nobody deserves this. His voice echoed in Vincent's head.

Maybe he was right, after all. Vincent could feel the anguish seeping through every particle of earth and air that made up this place. Every soul that suffered here became a part of it, whether they burned eternally in the coal-fires or wandered lost forever among the gray plains. So bereft that even when they left, they brought their gloom and their empty yearning with them, poisoning the living world. It was as if Hell had taken every shred of darkness within them and distilled it, crafted it into something all-consuming, inescapable—something that eclipsed whatever else had once lived inside them.

Vincent's heart twisted sickly in his chest. It shocked him for a moment—how instinctive it was. The sympathy. He had been fighting it for so long, beating it down into a crevice deep inside...but somehow it had crept out, without him noticing. He wondered how long it had been crouching there, waiting for him to notice, wondering if he would pummel it down again.

But it was too late for that. He realized now what it truly was. It wasn't sympathy at all—it was *empathy*. Because he too had been trapped for so long in the cold, in the dark. Except his tears had been frozen so deep inside him that he hadn't even known they existed.

Benjamin was right about him, all along. He couldn't fight that feeling anymore. It was his greatest weakness, and it had ruined him. He had hoped someone else just as vengeful and prideful and hungry and wretched as himself would get a second chance, and somehow be worthy of it. It was the reason he had given Benjamin that chance, even if his father made him regret it almost instantly. Failure after failure, in everyone's eyes, never knowing what the right thing was, because nothing he ever did was good enough for anyone. And still, through it all...he longed for that second chance. Making something of it, finally making someone happy.

You were right, Benjamin. It's not fair. I don't know how to do the right thing. Maybe none of those people do, either. Maybe it's not our fault that we don't. I just want it to stop hurting so much.

The only difference was...he was made for this. Unlike Benjamin, unlike any other person who had ever died and found themselves here, Vincent was a part of this place from the first breath he took. He and his kind alone deserved to be here. He was made of this lonely, all-consuming darkness. Of course he would feel this way. This was what he was made of. And it always would be.

But mortals? They were different. Their suffering here was pointless. And he would be a part of it no longer.

He stopped in the middle of the path. "We still have one last thing to do."

"What?"

He limped along the edge of the bridge, leaning his leftmost head out across the chasm, fighting the vertigo as he scanned the bluff. Then he spotted it–a narrow ledge built into the cliffside, several feet down. Winding along below it, hidden amongst the rocks, was a crude staircase, descending into darkness.

"Do you see that?"

Henry peered at the cliff until he too noticed it. He looked at Vincent in horror. "You're not serious. Why would we–"

"Benjamin is down there. We came all this way. I'm not leaving without getting what we came here for."

"You can't make it down those, Vincent. There's no way. What if you fall? You heard Cerberus–Lucifer is fixing the portal Himself, we don't need Benjamin's advice..."

"Yes, we do." Vincent met his gaze with a cold determination. "I don't think the portal should be restored."

Henry froze in shock. "You...*what?*"

"You're right, Henry. I'm sorry I didn't see it before. There was...a lot in the way." Vincent glanced back at the towering palace, fighting back the guilt with a new ferocity. Even if he was wrong, and his father and his master were right, he didn't care anymore. Because he cared about mortals. His friends. The only ones who truly cared about him, stood by his side. All of them were far too complicated to end up here, wasting away, suffering forever. No matter what... "Nobody deserves this." *Nobody but me.*

Hope flitted across Henry's face. "Vincent...do you really mean that? You believe it, after all this time?"

"Yes." Vincent looked away, starting to limp back along the bridge towards the cliff's edge. He didn't want to justify himself to Henry. He didn't need to give him any more excuses not to leave him behind, if that was what it took to escape Hell. And right now...it was looking more like *when.* "We don't have much time. We need to find Benjamin."

Henry followed after him, alarmed. "Wait—do you really think leaving the portal broken is the right call? What about all the ghosts? You said so yourself, they don't belong in the mortal world. If the corruption keeps spreading..."

"That's why we have to talk to Benjamin. His plans can't have stopped there. He *must* know a way to set spirits free without letting them wreak havoc on the world."

"Like what? Vincent...they're *dead*. They can't stay—"

"I know," Vincent cut him off. "They need something all their own. Some kind of afterlife. But not this one. And I won't leave without at least trying. Not after all this."

He didn't give Henry the chance to question any more. He knew him too well—knew he would follow as he drew dangerously near the edge of the cliff. Every step ached, and every breath burned. But he fought through it, ignoring Henry's protests, standing at the precipice. His vision swayed as the abyss seemed to reach up for him, clawing and grasping at his senses, goading him down into the murk...

Not like that.

He edged his hindquarters over the side, gripping the cliff with his front claws. His muscles shrieked, and it was all he could do to squeeze his eyes shut and promise himself it was almost over.

He began to climb. His long claws snagged in outcroppings, easing him down one pawhold at a time towards the landing just below. His limbs trembled with the effort of keeping him up, bearing his weight after they had already done so much to fend off his father—

And then, without warning, they buckled.

The abyss leaped up to claim him. His organs flew as his body dropped—

"*Vincent!*"

WHAM. He thudded onto solid ground. Pain shot through his ribs, his legs, his shoulders.

He laid there for what felt like ages, tearing ragged breaths from the air, dimly registering the scuffling of Henry's descent down the cliffside.

"Vincent, god—are you alright? Can you stand?"

He knew the answer before he tried to move. He knew Henry could see it too.

"Oh, Vincent..."

Henry knelt beside him. The scent of clove and jasmine wreathed around him, the only balm to his pain. He felt the brush of those strong, soft hands through the fur on his cheeks. Henry moved closer, and then he was cradling Vincent's middle head on his lap, stroking gently between his ears, down his nose. It was so tender and he was so far gone that he released the last of his guard, closing his weary eyes, sinking into Henry's touch, letting himself have this, for once.

They laid there together, fighting the despair. But both of them knew they didn't have much time left.

"It's okay, Vincent. We'll go find Benjamin. We'll see what he has to say, see if we can help," Henry murmured, his fingers curling into the fur around Vincent's ears. "But we have to go now. They can't find us here. I'm...gonna have to carry you."

Vincent's stomach jolted. He lifted his middle head with an immense effort to stare at him. "No. How would you even manage that?"

"You have to transform. Back into a human."

Vincent's lip curled. "You can't carry me all that way."

"I have to." Henry's face was carved with sorrow, but it was still as resolute as stone. He stroked one hand down Vincent's cheek. "Please. Change back."

Vincent hated the indignity of the idea. As if he hadn't had enough of that already. But he knew he was being foolish. Henry was right: there was no other way.

Except...

"I...I don't know if I can."

"You *can*. I know you can. You have to."

"It's already hard for me to do, okay?" Vincent growled. "But...like this..."

"You have to try," Henry insisted, his fingers tightening in Vincent's fur. "I'm not leaving you here. Which means we'd both get caught, and who knows what they'd do to us then?"

Vincent gritted his teeth. *Stop saying that.* "Fine. I'll try."

But his body was too broken. He knew the instant he let his mind drift to it, trying to coax it to assume the alternate form his master's magic had created for him. Every part of him was already too preoccupied with its own damage to dedicate any energy to changing into something else.

"How do you usually manage it?" Henry's voice broke in. He could tell it wasn't working. "Didn't you used to sit somewhere and calm your thoughts? I know it's hard here, but..."

"No...not really." Vincent sighed deeply. He knew now what he had to do.

"Then what–?"

"Look at me. Just...keep your eyes on me. Don't look away."

Henry's brow furrowed. "What? Why?"

"You want me to change, don't you?"

Henry searched his face, grimacing. Then he dropped his hands from Vincent's head. He kept looking–deliberately so.

It was too easy. The longer he stared, the more it crawled up Vincent's spine, boring into his fur and flesh and deeper, bone-deep, organ-deep–

I don't want you to see me like this.

I'm sorry for what I am.

And then, ignoring their own protests, his cells began to rearrange themselves. They battled through the agony, finding ways to splice their wounds together into something smaller and altogether more broken than even before.

Then he was lying on the cool stone, his head in Henry's hands. If he had felt vulnerable before, it was nothing compared to now. Now he was small– far too small for this place and its vengeance.

Blearily he looked up at Henry, fighting back a fresh wave of pain. His limbs trembled with the force of it. This body wasn't meant for this.

"Hold on," Henry whispered. Then he slid his hands under Vincent's body, carefully lifting him to his chest. Vincent stifled a groan, squeezing his eyes shut as pain wracked his ribs where Henry's arms pressed. The dead weight was too much—Vincent had no choice but to wrap his arm around Henry's neck, keeping his head upright.

Warmth crept up his body as he was cradled so close, unable to keep his gaze from Henry's face above him. He was as statuesque as ever, if not more so—a champion carved in the finest marble, the dim light of Hell striking the curves and alcoves of his features in dire shadow. Vincent felt the strength of the arms around him as they bore him down and down into the depths of the abyss, stoic and resolute despite the excruciating effort of it all. There was barely enough room for one person on this staircase jutting from the cliffside, let alone someone carrying such a burden. He knew he could never repay Henry for this sacrifice, nor were there words for it; so he stayed silent and still, trying his best not to cause him any more strife.

But even so, Henry couldn't seem to leave things where they lay. "You...you'll heal, won't you? It shouldn't be long, with how you are..."

"Long enough," grunted Vincent. He really didn't want to talk, but he wouldn't dare deny Henry now.

"That's okay...you'll be alright." He sounded as if he were trying to convince himself as much as Vincent. Still wary of the silence, he soon spoke again: "Vincent...why did you ask me that? To look at you..."

Vincent was quiet for so long that he wasn't sure an answer would come. But then: "It helps."

"Why?"

"It just...does."

"That's not an answer. Vincent...after all this time, please, don't hide this from me too. Just tell me—"

"It's easier to be human for you."

He heard a short breath enter Henry, stopping there. All was quiet for another long moment.

"So you're...still hiding." It wasn't a question.

"I can't hide anymore." A smile forged in irony crossed Vincent's face. "We both know that. But when I'm like this...we can both pretend, for a little while."

"Vincent..."

Henry didn't seem to know what to say.

"Does it make you feel better, to know the truth?" Vincent dared to ask. "Is that what you always wanted from me?"

"Yes."

Now Vincent didn't know what to say. Henry didn't wait for him.

"I just wanted to know you. *Really* know you. That's all. But you could never give that to me."

"Because I knew what would happen if you did *really know me,*" Vincent retorted. "And I was right. I let it slip, eventually, because you got too close. I *let you* get too close. And then..."

He trailed off. He knew he didn't need to finish. It was like a shadow hanging over them both, always.

Finally, it was enough for Henry to stop talking. It was a hollow success. Except–

"I'm sorry."

Those were the last words that fell from Henry's lips, almost too quiet to hear. Vincent's heart missed a beat, and his voice was jolted right out of him. He couldn't get it back.

So Henry carried him down the cliffside, down into the chasm, through the mist and the unending dark, each footstep sapping a little more of his mortal's strength. It was only by the grace and dedication and faith of being Henry Wellfellow that they made it down that formidable staircase, into the deepest reaches of Hell itself; but, more than that, this was the only way either of them would find themselves there, where they needed to be.

The only problem was, just as solid ground came into view several hundred feet below, the stairs suddenly ended.

CHAPTER 18

EMBERS

"**S**hit," said Henry. "We can't make it down that...it's too far. Did the stairs break...?"

"No," said Vincent. "Let me down..."

With a grunt of effort Henry crouched, still holding him carefully. Vincent reached down to the step they stood on and pressed his palm against the cool stone.

Suddenly, the ground began to tremble. A deep rumbling accompanied it, growing louder until it turned into an ear-splitting grinding. Before their eyes, stairs slid out from the cliffside one by one, spiraling down the rest of the way until they reached the bottom. The mist swirled around them as they halted. The earth grew still once more.

"That'll work," said Henry, his eyes wide. He tested the next stair with one foot before lifting Vincent again and continuing on. "What was that all about?"

"It keeps prisoners from escaping. Only the guards can make it appear."

Henry grimaced.

Both of their nerves eased some when Henry descended the final step–at least, in one way. Their adversary was no longer gravity; now it was whatever lurked in the depths of the pit of Tartarus. It stretched endlessly all around them, its edges obscured by fog and shadow. They couldn't even see the way they had come, far above. The only thing they could glimpse beyond themselves were strange, flickering orbs of orange light, their forms scattered by the mist.

"Fires?" Henry guessed. His fingers tightened on Vincent's body. "Should we go to them?"

Vincent nodded. "It's our best shot."

So they crept forward, following the closest of the lights. As they drew nearer, a new shadow rose through the fog, broken by stripes of firelight. Then it resolved into something real: a great stalagmite jutting from the earth like a giant's tooth. A hollow was carved into it, strips of rock crossing the entrance like prison bars. Bright fire burned inside the little cave, dancing with wicked delight–so hot Vincent and Henry could feel it from where they stood several feet away. A silhouette slumped against the bars, as far from the flames as it could get. A human.

Henry caught his breath. "What...? Is this..."

"Tartarus' deepest prison," said Vincent, grimly. "These are Lucifer's personal favorites. Keep walking–we'll find Benjamin here."

"How? This place is massive...it must be miles and miles across..."

"I think I can still track his scent. He isn't a vampire anymore. But I need to be closer..."

Henry nodded, starting off again, although his gaze lingered on the tortured prisoner as they passed. More stalagmite prisons rose from the murk, one by one, little nightmares surrounded by darkness. Most of their occupants were silent, but a few of them stretched their arms out through the bars, their bony, desiccated fingers grasping for help, for human touch, for *something*. Vincent could feel Henry's distress growing each time, and he drifted closer to them more than once before Vincent reminded him not to stray. He trudged on, and soon Vincent could tell he was starting to falter.

No–he had been slowly growing weaker for some time now. It was only just beginning to show. He had been carrying Vincent for so long, and so far...

We have to find Benjamin. Soon. This can't be for nothing. I won't let you win, Father.

Finally, after nearly an hour, he caught a familiar scent lingering in the mist–faint, stale, but unmistakable. It had been so long since it last crossed his senses: the taste of peat and frost, deeply eroded by death, but still there. *Just enough life left.*

"Henry, I have him. Take us this way."

Henry did, his pace rejuvenated by hope. They zigzagged between prisons until they heard a strange clinking sound ahead, accompanied by heavy, plodding footfalls. They slowed, wary, but drew closer still...

Yet another stalagmite hollow appeared through the fog, but it wasn't the only thing. Two short figures approached it from another direction; Henry and Vincent dared to creep closer, until they could see clearly.

They might have preferred not to. The figure in front, guiding the other, was a spindly little creature, only humanoid in its most basic arrangement of body parts. The rest of it was cobbled together in grotesque combinations: leathery skin the color of rust, horny protrusions crowding its joints, clawed feet and hands, curved tusks jutting from its snarled maw, a bony tail curling up its back and tipped with a menacing stinger, much like a scorpion's; and the worst of all, its bat-like face with its beady black eyes. Its features resembled mutilated flesh more than anything living. It only came up to Henry's knee, but nothing would have convinced Vincent to get close to it, much less pick a fight.

The two of them stopped where they were, watching from their distance. For now, thankfully, the imp had not spotted them. Instead it trotted up to the fiery prison with obvious glee. It turned back with an unearthly, garbled growl, sweeping its claws impatiently towards its companion, who was still trudging after it. In a few moments the other one arrived—nearly the same height as the first, even on all fours, but at least as wide as Henry was tall. It appeared at first to be some kind of tortoise, but as they looked harder, they realized in place of a single head and tail it had two gnarled, dragon-like heads with jagged teeth. Its eyes glowed like embers, not unlike Cerberus'. Steam billowed from its thick shell, and as it stood there the rotten stench of sulfur reached their noses.

The imp hissed as it crowded the tortoise, reaching towards its back. As Vincent peered closer at it, he realized: there was a gaping hole in its shell, filled with glowing coals. The imp grabbed a double handful and hurried over to the prison, lobbing one of the rocks at the figure huddled inside. The prisoner ducked just in time to avoid it. It skidded towards the back of the cell, where it caught fire instantly, spitting smoke. The imp screeched in frustration, brandishing its next coal.

Vincent growled deep in his throat. He looked up at Henry. "Take us over."

Henry's expression mirrored his, and he immediately started forward. It only took a few steps for the imp and the tortoise to notice them. The imp snarled at them, shaking its remaining coal in their direction threateningly. The tortoise merely watched them with its two heads and their glowing eyes, steam hissing from the chasm in its shell.

Vincent didn't bother with words. Instead he fixed his gaze on the imp, slipping into that fierce darkness his true self commanded. He felt his eyes burning, his will looming over the lesser demon. Immediately the imp ducked its head, baring its ugly teeth at him and lashing its venomous tail.

"Walk," Vincent told Henry, his tone dark. He did so, and at once the imp scurried ahead, past the prison and out of their way, hissing curses at them in a dead language as it went. The tortoise waited where it was until they had crossed its path, then began plodding a wide circle around them, following after its companion. It stared curiously at them as it passed, but otherwise went on unbothered. Vincent waited until the mist had swallowed them both before turning back to the prison cell.

They drew very close, until the heat of the flames within licked their faces, just on the verge of burning. Only then did they recognize the sullied features of Benjamin Warwick behind the rocky bars, gazing at them in dull disbelief.

"This...must be a fever dream." His voice crackled with disuse. "Am I finally burning away to nothing? My mind crumbling? You, Vincent, maybe...but Henry Wellfellow? Here, in Hell?"

"It's not a dream," said Vincent, countless emotions warring in his chest. "We're here. We came to find you."

Benjamin blinked at him slowly, as if allowing his fractured mind to catch up with the idea. "You...came all this way, back to the deepest pit of Hell, to find me? After all the lengths you went to, to personally ensure I ended up here? Well…" He leaned against the bars, curling his blackened fingers over them, his eyes gleaming in the firelight. "This ought to be good."

Vincent pulled against Henry's arms, and he got the message. He eased him down onto his feet, trembling with the effort of it. Vincent swayed dangerously, but grasped Henry's solid shoulder until he was able to regain his balance. His muscles and bones and *everything* burned as he used them again–too many injuries in too many scattered places to begin to inventory–but he could stand. That was good. The healing must have started.

"We need to know what your plans were," he said, grappling with the wrongness of it. "After you broke the portal."

"Right to the chase, huh? For once." Benjamin's ice-blue eyes were bloodshot and weary, but a glimmer of his old shrewdness remained. "Why do you need to know that?"

"Because…you were right." Vincent loathed every word out of his mouth. But it was true. At least, in sentiment. "We want to stop souls from coming here. We want to stop the suffering."

Benjamin's eyes lit up with a keen interest–so much so that he almost looked alive again. Then his expression melted into a wry smile. "So you went to all the trouble of hunting me for nothing. All of this, just to say I was right in the end."

"That's not true," Henry interjected, his tone cold. "We had to stop you. You were killing people. Sacrificing them for the ritual. And making a vampire army."

"A *vampire army?* You're so dramatic." But Benjamin's lip twitched all the same, the smallest display of disgust. He had gotten to him. "I'm not a goddamn supervillain."

"Then why were you acting like one? Turning innocent people into vampires–"

"They weren't *innocent*. That was the whole point. I was saving them from themselves. Giving them a new purpose in life. They agreed to it–it's not like turning them gives me mind control over them or something. They *wanted* to follow me, because I had a vision for a better world. A world without death."

"Everything needs to die sometime," Vincent growled. "It's a necessary part of the balance."

"Oh, sure. It's not like vampires are immune to it, after all. The whole world would collapse if nothing ever died. Overpopulation." Benjamin waved a hand dismissively, but his gaze was hard. "But as it stands now, death is just a punishment, Vincent. You should know that better than anyone."

"You sent people to their deaths with your own two hands," Henry pointed out.

"And then I released them. I broke open the portal. I sacrificed my own life for it, too, all thanks to your dear friend here." Benjamin gestured towards Vincent, whose stomach tightened unhappily. "And it was all worth it. I freed *countless* souls from eternal torture. I wish I didn't have to take any other lives to do it, but...well, anything worth doing requires sacrifice."

"But it isn't over," Vincent insisted. "Their spirits are restless. Possessing people, poisoning the mortal world with their darkness. They're still suffering. They remember all of their pain—from life, from death..."

"And even then, it all won't last much longer," Henry added.

Benjamin paused. "What do you mean?"

Vincent and Henry exchanged a glance. "You must not know, then."

Then Vincent leaned in closer, the heat from the coal-fire blasting his face.

"Lucifer has been fixing the portal. It's almost finished now. Your plan failed. It was all for nothing."

For the first time, horror froze Benjamin where he stood. Gradually an emptiness descended upon him, leaching any remaining color or shadow of life from his face. All throughout the time Vincent had known him, Benjamin had never lost that rare spark of hope, even when most everyone else did. But now, at last, he looked the same as every other dead soul. Hollow.

Vincent took no pleasure in it. This surprised him. He thought it would feel satisfying to take everything from his greatest enemy, the one who had stolen everything from him. It was Benjamin's fault he had lost his home, his dignity, his family...even his new life in the mortal world. Dragging him back to Hell had cost Vincent everything he had built for himself.

But...it didn't, really. He realized it as soon as he thought it. That final act had been an excuse, nothing more. Vincent had already ruined his new life, all on his own. He had ruined his old one, too. It was his own fault he had ever strayed from his duty. Benjamin was just a tortured soul, like any other. Blaming him was like blaming death itself for its very nature.

And in that moment, something shifted. Like a dewdrop falling perfectly in the groove of a leaf, guided down into a pool waiting below. He looked at Benjamin, and more than feeling like a mirror to that hollowness, he wanted to take it back. To breathe life back into him, to stoke that ember until it returned to a flame. He couldn't take the thought of that final light in the darkest depths of Hell going out.

Ignoring the searing heat from the cell, Vincent drew closer until his fist closed over Benjamin's, trapping it against the rocky cage bar it clung to. It was surprisingly clammy. He gazed hard into his cold, dull eyes. He swore he could see the shadows of his history swimming there still, the terror and agony of that kid who was all but murdered by the mere silhouette of a stranger, whose mother was not so lucky.

Or perhaps death's swiftness was a kindness, and the truest victim was this pale imitation of the child that could have been, twisted by circumstance into something far beyond the mundane. Now he was here, alone, abandoned, and it was all for nothing.

It was all too familiar. In a matter of hours, Vincent could be in the next cell over. He felt a humorless smile tugging at his lips as the realization trickled in. He fought it back.

"I know you don't have any reason to trust me, after everything. But we don't have many options left now, and neither do you. So here it is: if you promise to help us, I'll release you."

Benjamin's glassy eyes widened. Vincent had never seen such innocent shock on his face. The smallest glitter of hope returned to it in that moment, and Vincent's heart quickened in a strange delight.

"You...expect me to believe that? *You* put me here."

"I *know.* I know. But...I don't think you deserve this, Benjamin."

Benjamin blinked at him. "W...what?"

Vincent let out a long, beleaguered breath. "You don't deserve this. No one does. This is...too much. I don't want you to stay here. I want you to rest. So please, help us make a world where no one has to suffer like this. I know you still want that."

That stare remained, frozen between them. It posed a question that could never be answered, a void through which no light could pass.

"Vincent..." Henry had hung back reluctantly, but now he was at Vincent's side, cringing against the heat of the flames. "Asking him what to do is one thing. But...he has no qualms about killing people to achieve his goals. He killed Percy. He killed Ava, and Mira–"

"So did Jake. And you let him go."

Henry winced. His gaze grew distant. "You're right. But...I didn't want to work with him, or to let him loose. He escaped. I know he's just gonna hurt more people. He...he has to, now that he's a vampire." He focused on Benjamin pointedly. "Because you made him one. That was part of your plan. That's what you want more of. People who have to hurt other people to survive."

"No," said Benjamin, his eyes alight. "They were doing that already. Most everyone does–far worse than that, too. That's what you do, isn't it, monster hunter?"

Henry did not reply. His expression went blank.

Benjamin gave a little smile. "I changed their relationship with everything around them. With pain, with hurting, with other people. Life and death. They found a covenant in a way they never had before. I gave them meaning, a new yearning to focus on rather than letting them go on thrashing in the dark, striking everyone in their way."

"What meaning? Attacking people, feeding on their blood? You think that's better?"

Benjamin's smile grew cold. "Don't pretend you have any idea what they were going through. You could never know, because you've never lived it. You've been pampered and groomed to greatness your whole life, Henry Wellfellow. You've always had your path paved for you, long before your feet could reach the mud at the end of it."

"I know." Henry said it so passionately that it caught both Vincent and Benjamin off guard. "I figured that out." His eyes flickered to Vincent for just a moment. "But I don't think turning people into vampires is how to help people out of feeling lost."

"When you put it that way, maybe so," Benjamin admitted, with a note of amusement. "But it was the only way to get my life back. To keep people from dying and coming here. And to build the forces we needed, to do what needs to be done."

"What were you planning, Benjamin?" Vincent pressed, gritting his teeth. "Please. We need to know."

Benjamin leaned close against the bars of his cell, his eyes gleaming in the flickering shadows between them. "If you take me back to the mortal world, I'll help you. But if you don't do things my way...I can't guarantee we'll succeed."

"We'll do it *our* way," Henry insisted, before Vincent could reply. "No more murders."

Benjamin's gaze flicked to Vincent pointedly, a silent question.

"No more murders," Vincent said, without hesitation.

Benjamin nodded quietly, with an empty smile. "Alright. I'll do my best. But only once you get me through that portal."

Vincent and Henry looked at each other, a silent question passing between them. Benjamin seemed to sense it too, and added, "It's not like we have much time to talk plans here, anyway. I can't imagine you made it all the way here without attracting attention."

At last Vincent released Benjamin's hand, sliding it up to grasp the rocky cell bar.

At his touch, his will flooded the stone. A terrible grating sounded as the bars slowly retracted into the walls like jagged teeth. Benjamin staggered forward immediately, desperate to escape the heat of the fires at his back. Henry caught him, half supporting him and half guarding him, as if expecting him to bolt. Against the vibrancy of Henry's living body, Benjamin looked like smoke.

A jolt of alarm gripped Vincent's heart. He forced it back, swallowing hard.

"Time to go. Quickly."

He stood up straight, finding that at last he could walk. The pain still stabbed his joints when he moved, but that he could ignore, as long as his body would support him. So he did as he started off, scenting out their prior path through the mist and trusting Henry to guide Benjamin safely behind. As much as he hated to admit it, he himself wouldn't be any help if it came down to a fight.

Of course, Benjamin was in no state for it, either. He had to count on that.

They hurried as fast as they could through the pale darkness, passing each of the fires glowing ominously through the fog, each one another tormented soul. Vincent felt as if he collected every one on his shoulders as he passed, invisible but weighing heavier and heavier until yet again he could barely stand. His pain would heal, but theirs would continue on, forever and ever, physical evidence of the agony in their hearts, the terror and the anger and the sorrow forever spilling over from the lives they should have left behind.

Was he wrong to go against it? Was it natural? He had always thought it was, but...didn't the seasons run in a circle? Didn't the sun rise and fall? Didn't each and every death feed new life? This place was an ending that never finished. It was a paradox. How had he not considered it before?

The only relief came at the sight of the cliff and its staircase appearing through the mist—and only briefly. The rest of the journey lay ahead of them, and Vincent's remaining vitality was fading fast. He leaned against the wall when he reached it, breathing hard for one grateful moment before Henry and Benjamin caught up to the first step.

But just as soon as they did, Vincent's breath caught in his throat. Something unwelcome had come with it: a scent. Dread coursed through his stomach.

Of course.

Well…then he had one thing left to do. The moment he had been waiting for.

Vincent followed behind the others, taking each stair slower, laboriously, glancing back over his shoulder every few moments. Nothing stirred in the fog below.

When he reached the right step, he paused to press his hand against it, sending his will through it. At once it began to recede back into the cliff, along with the rest leading down into the depths. He leaned against the bluff to steady himself as the ground rumbled and quaked, agonizingly slow. He only dared to breathe again once the lower stairs had fully disappeared.

Then, just as he was about to turn back to his ascent, something gleamed through the mist below.

He froze. He peered down, into the murk.

At first, nothing. Then–

Two flashes of yellow-green. Eyes.

"Run!"

"What?" Henry and Benjamin glanced back.

"Go!" Vincent snapped, casting a desperate glare at them over his shoulder.

Before they could ask anything more, a dark shape leaped from the fog. It flung itself at the cliff, slamming its paws into the rock–

The earth began to roar and tremor again. The stairs were returning.

"She's hunting us! *Move!*" Vincent shouted, standing his ground even as his entire body began to tremble.

He heard footsteps shuffling in alarm, then halting. "Come on, Vincent!"

This was it. He didn't look back.

"I'll hold her off."

"No—Vincent, don't—"

They didn't have time for this. Vincent rounded on Henry, mustering every ember inside him into a firestorm. "Keep *going*, damn it! For once, don't be a fucking hero!"

Benjamin was staring at him with a powerful curiosity; Henry, though, was aghast—a perfect portrait of horror as the realization seeped in.

Seeing that look on his face, Vincent's heart twisted, almost more painful than his lingering wounds. He wanted so badly to soak it in, to wallow in Henry's care for him, to believe it would carry him back to the world he loved and finally make everything okay, like it had for that single precious moment he had stolen the night they kissed.

But he couldn't. That one moment was all he had.

"Don't do this," said Henry. "Don't you dare do this."

Vincent shook his head, ever so slightly.

"You know I have to. You know this is what I deserve. You're the only one who truly understands. That's why you'll let me do it. That's why you're the only one I could have at my side, when I finally went home."

Then he turned back to his sister, surging up the stairs in all her monstrous glory, reveling in her power and her duty, hulking and dark but for those gleaming white teeth and burning eyes.

She had been waiting so long for this. And so had he.

He fell back—

Something *dragged* him back—

Henry appeared between them, his fist raised high—

White light exploded from it, engulfed him—then *everything*.

Vincent flinched away, shielding his eyes with his arm. A jolt of energy tingled through his body. He staggered back, his stomach turning as he felt the edge of the stair at his heel, the abyss plunging into darkness just beyond. He snatched himself away from the drop, pressing himself against the cliffside—

Something slammed into him, shoving him back. He stumbled, but that same something caught him with a strong hand.

"Come on, Vincent! Keep going!"

Vincent blinked his eyes open. The light had gone. In its place stood Henry, jostling against him, his sky-blue eyes wide and urgent. Beyond him, Vincent caught a glimpse of his sister's hellhound body slumped on the stairs, her limbs twitching and paws scrabbling as she fought to get up. Her fiery eyes found Vincent–wild, merciless. Playtime was over.

A surge of fear gripped his heart. He turned and stumbled up the stairs as fast as his battered legs would run, Henry at his side. He felt the warmth of his hand on his spine, urging him on, promising safety if he fell. It was all too much to bear, but he did. He let it carry him, for once. Fighting it would be foolish, now.

They soon caught up with Benjamin, too bedraggled to outrun them. It felt like only moments later when they all reached the top of the stairs. Vincent's chest burned and heaved–every part of him did. But he couldn't stop. He peered up at the final climb before them, the small hand- and footholds that stood between him and solid ground above. It felt miles away.

"I'll help you up," said Benjamin, approaching the cliff.

"You're not going up there alone," Vincent growled, pushing him aside. "We're not stupid."

Benjamin threw him a withering look, so earnest that it shocked him. "I'm not running. I need your help, or I won't be able to finish my work."

"Why should I believe you?"

Benjamin thrust a bony arm towards him, his pale, freckled skin blackened with soot. "I'm dead, Vincent. For real, this time. My body is long gone. I won't be able to occupy it this time, out in the mortal world."

Vincent stared at him. "Then how are you going to help us? You'll just be a ghost. You'll have to possess someone, and I'm not letting–"

"With this," said Henry. Vincent turned–he was holding up a familiar silver and turquoise pendant.

His heart lurched in shock. "The amulet–when did you get–"

He suddenly put two and two together.

"That light you made–Ava? You channeled her?"

"Sierra gave the amulet to me, before we left. She thought we might need the help."

"She knew–you told her we were coming here?"

Henry nodded, without a drop of shame. "Casey wouldn't let it go. She knew something was up with you. She cornered me after you two fought."

His heart missed a beat. *Casey.* She had known...

"Why?" he demanded. "Why did you tell them?"

"Because I felt like it was the right thing to do. I told them you wanted us to go alone, that you said you didn't want to drag anyone else into this. It felt...too Vincent, to me."

"Too *Vincent?* What does that mean?"

"You forget–I know that feeling. It's mine, too. It felt like a sacrifice."

Henry captured his gaze, holding it steady, and for a moment the abyss, the cliffside, the rest of that dark world around them fell away into a clear sky.

He knew me. All along.

"You should have let me do it," the words spilled out as something burst inside him, thrashing against the light that finally reached it. "If you know me so well, you *know* I deserve it. This was meant to be!"

"No. There was always another way, Vincent." Henry finally turned away, looking instead to Benjamin. "Go on. Pull him up."

"But he–"

Without a word, Benjamin hoisted himself up onto the cliff. His fingers trembled as he did, and his feet slid as he tried to climb. Henry immediately went to grab his legs, steadying him.

Vincent held his breath as Benjamin dragged himself the rest of the way up. He disappeared over the top, and everything went silent.

"Ben–"

A pallid hand reached down from the cliff's edge. "Come on, Vincent."

Relief tingled through his body. It brought a prickle of shame with it, followed by a stab of annoyance. He shouldn't feel guilty about it–of course

Benjamin would consider running. Vincent had trusted him before, and he had betrayed him.

But...he couldn't help it. Something had changed in him.

Vincent took in a deep breath, then grabbed onto the wall. Instantly his muscles shrieked in protest, and he almost fell as a wave of nausea crashed over him. But steady arms caught hold of him from below, lifting him up. A new heat rose up his neck, no longer driven by anger or shame, but something far more innocent.

"Take his hands!" Henry called.

Benjamin reached down farther, and Vincent reached up. Their hands met, and so did their eyes—and for the first time in so long, they saw each other.

"I've got you," Benjamin said through gritted teeth.

Vincent cringed against the agony of it as he strained to pull himself up. Benjamin let out a strangled cry of pain as he heaved with all his dwindling might. Henry pushed Vincent up, as high as he could muster, and then his elbows were over the edge—

With a final tug, Vincent fell onto solid ground. His legs kicked precariously over the drop, and he scrabbled in the dust with desperate fingers, trying to claw his way forward. Benjamin grabbed hold of his shoulders and dragged him the rest of the way, until thin air turned to earth beneath him.

They both collapsed on the ground, panting. In moments Henry climbed over the edge on his own, sinking to his knees beside them.

"We should keep moving—she can't be far behind, even after that blast."

Vincent clenched his teeth. Henry was right—Superbia was far too vengeful to let that stop her.

He forced his burning muscles to drag himself to his feet again. Henry reached out to steady him, then to help Benjamin up. Both of them were fading fast.

They crossed the land bridge over the abyss unaccosted, then passed through the great bronze gates Cerberus had no doubt left open for them, thinking Vincent, defeated, would escort Henry straight home. But he wasn't defeated–not fully. Not yet.

But it was getting harder and harder to push down that cold, wriggling despair in his gut–especially as they stood at the gates overlooking the vast landscape before them, the frozen river disappearing into the mist, the slightest strip of gray plains beyond.

They still had to cross it all, again.

"I'll get you across the river," Vincent said between labored breaths as they started down the slope, the mist engulfing them. "And then–"

"Stop saying that," said Henry fiercely. "I'm not leaving you. No matter what you think of me, I will never leave you."

Vincent's heart burned in his chest. Hot shame mingled with a deep ache. "But you did," he choked out, hating how meek his voice came, but unable to fight it. "You left me."

At that moment they reached the bank of the Cocytus, and without even a thought Vincent's human form melted away, leaving the battered hellhound in its place. He limped out onto the ice, digging his claws into the surface as hard as he could. The cold had already begun to descend over them, penetrating his fur and turning his ragged breaths into clouds.

Henry wrapped his arm around Vincent's ruff, steadying himself– steadying both of them. Benjamin took his other side, tangling his thin fingers in the thick fur above his shoulder. Henry's voice arrived warm with his breath against his ear.

"I was wrong. And I'm sorry. I'm so sorry. I thought I understood you, back then, I thought you understood *me*...and then I realized I didn't, and you didn't, I didn't know what to do."

"I thought I did, too," Vincent murmured, dragging the little group across the ice with his fading strength. They were moving agonizingly slow, but it was all he could muster. "I thought you knew...I would do anything to protect you."

"You...didn't want me to have to stoop to that," Henry whispered. "To torture. To sacrifice my morals, even for a good reason."

"Yes, but..." Vincent took in a great, shuddering breath. *One foot in front of the other. Keep going. We'll make it.* "I wanted to protect you, too. Just...protect you. After that night, I felt..." For a moment he was back there, in Henry's dark bedroom, a fierce hunger clawing at his ribs. His senses were slipping. "...Like it was my new duty. Like it mattered more than anything–stopping Jake from coming after you. From finishing what he started. There was no other option for me, not after that."

Henry was quiet for a moment. Only the whistling, bitter wind reached Vincent's ears. For a moment he imagined he heard pawsteps thudding behind them, gaining on them, but they disappeared when he listened harder.

Then Henry said: "Would you have killed him?"

Vincent let out a soft whine as something in his foreleg panged. He buried his claws in the ice, narrowly managed to avoid stumbling. "If I had to."

"...*I* would have. If you hadn't stopped me."

The image of that wild, hungry look in Henry's eyes flashed through Vincent's head. That silver knife plunging again and again into Jake's chest... "You never looked less like yourself, in that moment," he murmured.

Henry's arm tightened around his shoulders. "I never felt less like it. But *you*...you did. You were me, for me. You...protected me. All of me. Who I am."

"Is that why you kissed me?" Vincent dared to ask, before he could stop himself. His vision was beginning to blur at the edges, but he couldn't bring himself to care, somehow. His paws kept moving, because that was what they had to do.

"...I don't know."

A needle of pain lanced his heart, but it was so small compared to everything else, now. He felt an empty smile tugging at the corner of his lips.

But Henry kept going: "I think...that's the moment I thought we knew each other. *Really* knew. You were like me, and I was like you..."

"And then I proved you wrong."

"No—you proved me *right*," said Henry, his desperation finally bleeding through as his grasp tightened in Vincent's fur. "I'm not the hero I thought I was. Jake was right about me. Acting like I'm so perfect, all the time, but I'm *not*...thinking I have the right to save *anybody*, thinking I'm any better than anyone else...but look at me, doing the same things, trying to kill someone, losing control—and I couldn't even see who you were, at your core. I didn't want to look, not really. I couldn't see the pain behind it all—"

Finally Vincent stumbled, his torso falling forward onto the hard ice. Henry grunted as he tried to hold him up, but even with Benjamin's help they couldn't manage it.

"Vincent, no!" Henry pleaded. "Please, don't give up here. Keep moving, we have to keep moving—"

But whatever healing powers remained in his blood, they weren't enough for this. The bitter wind that froze the tears of the damned found every wound, every patch of missing fur, every bruised bone, every weak joint, and it latched on with its cruel fangs and sucked away the last of his strength. Its only mercy was the numbness it breathed into his burning body, seeping in like poison, soothing that wretched pain at last. He wanted to enjoy it, to sink into it and let its darkness wash over him...

No, he couldn't, he *couldn't*—the cold meant he was stopping, he couldn't keep going, he couldn't save Henry or Benjamin, he couldn't stay with them...the pain told him he was still moving forward, and he couldn't leave without it.

But it was leaving him.

"Vincent—Vinny—"

A surge of anguish lapped his heart at the sound of that old nickname. He had never thought he would hear it again—just another name he thought he had lost his rights to. But it wasn't enough, either. He could barely feel the warmth of Henry's fingers now, or his body pressed against him...he would have given anything for it only hours ago, but now it didn't matter anymore.

"Vincent, come on...get up...you can't give in now after everything you've been through," Benjamin's voice drifted through his head. "We were supposed to make it out, together...don't you remember? Even when we first spoke, you wanted to see what it was like up there. You wanted to come with me. And now you finally found the nerve to do it—you won't let your father take that away from you now, will you?"

For a moment a glimmer of that old Benjamin was back with him, the one brimming with life and wit and hope like an ember in the endless gloom of the Underworld—the first one Vincent had ever seen. His heart ached with the memory of it, the bruise of his betrayal that refused to heal...

"I...can't..."

He felt Benjamin's fingers grip his fur. "You could have come with me. You know that. I would have taken you with me. But you said..."

Vincent closed his eyes. *I know.* Was it really a betrayal at all? Or had he himself been the betrayer, in the end, for dragging Benjamin back to his prison after freeing him? If only he had been ready...if only he had fled Hell with Benjamin. Maybe he could have convinced him not to kill those people, guided him to some better solution...

But then he never would have met Henry. If Benjamin was an ember, Henry was the sun itself...

"He's loyal," said Henry, close to Vincent's ear. He was lying against him now. His voice held the shadow of tears behind it. He was trying not to break. "Even when it hurts him... Vinny, please, just hold on a little longer. You'll heal, if we can just make it to the other side of the river..."

Vincent tried again, willing his nerves to fire and his muscles to move, but he couldn't even feel them anymore. They didn't move at all. Everything was cold and heavy and empty.

This was what it was like to die. He finally knew. Dimly he wondered where his soul would go—if anywhere. Maybe he didn't even have a soul.

It wasn't fair, he thought, even as his thoughts began to fracture. It wasn't fair he had been born into darkness, and had finally escaped it, and now he was returning to it—this time, without a single chance at a choice.

And what had his brief life come to? What had he done with it? It was hard to remember, now...only flashes of things, of faces, people he had left behind and who had left a lingering mote of warmth inside his chest, even now...

They had to remember...

"Tell...tell Roman I'm sorry..."

"Oh, *don't* start that." Henry's voice finally cracked apart. "Please don't–"

"And...tell Casey that, too...tell her none of it was her fault, and that she deserved better...better than me, better than everything else she got. She saved me...I owe her the world..."

His mind was filling with dark water, slowly freezing over. But he had to remember, just enough...he couldn't let them forget him, what he thought, what he felt...

"Percy...I'm sorry I couldn't help him...I broke my promise...he shouldn't have died, and it was my fault...and Ava. I failed her. She didn't need to die, either. I was so hard on her. If I had only..."

He swallowed hard, clawing words from his own throat. "And Sierra...she's better than she thinks she is. She's always been there for me, always... You two deserve each other." He tried to smile, for Henry's sake, but he couldn't feel it. "You two deserve to be happy...to live a normal life, safe..."

Despite the numbness, he felt something squeeze harder against his shoulder, clinging to him with a desperation.

"I was never going to live a normal life, Vincent...it was never in the cards for me. It's not who I am, not who I was raised to be, even if I am human. And Sierra...I dragged her into my mess. Even now, I'm dragging her, pretending she's my ticket out of being...myself."

"Then it's too late for her, too. It's too late for all of you. There's no point wishing...so you might as well stick together. Save the world from my father, my master. Protect each other. Be there for each other, like you were for me. All of you...in spite of everything I am, everything I'm not...you made me feel less alone."

And that was his final thought, in the end. The one that lingered after every other flame had flickered out.

I'm not alone. Not anymore.

I'm not alone. Not anymore.

CHAPTER 19

THE RIVER'S END

"Vincent? Vincent...!"

Henry was clutching at the hellhound's crumpled body, tugging with frigid fingers at his great heads, his tangled fur. He touched Vincent over and over, bargaining every time, trying and trying to rouse him, to win one more word from his throat.

Something ached in Benjamin's chest, too. It surprised him at first, but then, it was just too familiar. His own fingers stayed in Vincent's fur, feeling the feeble warmth that remained there slowly fading.

He shouldn't have let himself care. It was pointless. Vincent was just another casualty of this everlasting war, death against justice...

But he wasn't, really. Vincent was the first living soul that had listened to him. Cared about what had happened to him. Sure, he barely understood what he was listening to, and it was too easy to convince him to help, to bend the rules out of pity...

No...*sympathy*. He was always so adamant about pity.

Damn it. Benjamin knew so much. *If only the idiot had come with me...* Maybe everything would have turned out differently. Maybe he and Vincent would have taken on his crusade together from the start, and found a real, lasting solution to this endless train of despair. If they hadn't wasted so much time and energy on their feud...

The wind howled around them as if in mourning; but they knew it was the true murderer, the final stake in Vincent's heart. If it weren't for the river, this damned river filled with its traitors and their frozen tears, maybe they could have made it. Now they were trapped here, in the middle of the ice. Vincent's claws could no longer help them keep their footing. Soon enough, his sister would surely find them, drag them back to Tartarus...and Henry wouldn't be so lucky this time.

But he didn't seem to care about that. He was sobbing now, his face buried in Vincent's fur. His wailing sent a shiver up Benjamin's body, straight through his soul. It *hurt*. God, it hurt. A perfect shot of empathy. Maybe more than that.

Someone had cared about Vincent this much. Despite what he was.

And with it came a stab of guilt. That was more surprising than anything else.

Why?

He was there for you. You used him.

It was an easy answer. Benjamin didn't like it.

"Henry," he said, finally removing his hand from Vincent's body to rest it on Henry's shuddering shoulder. He tried to make his voice as gentle as possible. "We can't stay here. They're going to find us–"

"I don't care!" Henry tightened his grasp on Vincent, all of his bulk tense and strong against Benjamin's attempts to usher him away. "They can take me. They can answer for this. Vincent–god–I let this happen! I just wanted to be good, I–"

"It's not your fault," Benjamin told him softly, solemnly. "You didn't kill him. His father did it. His own determination did it. He wanted to help. He should have known..."

"How can you be so heartless?" Henry finally rounded on him, that marble face of his broken into a mask of pure anguish. "He helped you! He helped me! He just wanted everyone to get what they deserved–he wanted to keep us safe, because he loved us...!"

He broke off into another sob, ducking his head with the force of it, those beautiful features swallowed by shadow. "And we broke him! We broke him...because he was different, he wasn't *perfect*–because of course, of course he didn't see death like we do, or pain...because this place is all he's ever known, because he's a guard dog, he's always been a guard dog..."

Henry's grief was like a tsunami, shock wave after shock wave crashing over Benjamin, bearing him down with its brutal, inescapable might. His annoyance turned to distress and then to heartache, until all his urgency had eroded away. He sat there in the middle of the storm, a grim and helpless witness.

"He gave up *everything* for you, Benjamin–his home, his family, his duty! Because that's just what he does, for people he cares about, people who care about him–he thought *you* cared about him! You were his first friend! Didn't you care about him at all? Even for a single moment?"

"...I...yes. I did."

"But you still betrayed him! You let him give it all up, just so you could escape–"

"It was for the good of *everyone*," Benjamin hissed, finally summoning his bravado. "You can try to blame me for it, just like he did, but he and I are the same that way. We both do things for the good of everyone, even if it means sacrificing something lesser. Sacrificing our moral standing. *Someone* has to play dirty to win for the right cause, because the do-gooders like you can't do it." He broke off with a sigh. "The only difference is...he's always been confused. His loyalty, as you put it, holds him back. He cared about his father, his master, those friends he made...you, and me...enough to let it stop him."

"I don't know what happened to you," said Henry, his voice shaking with the effort of holding back, "to make you think that's a bad thing. Because it's not. Without it...without it..."

He looked back to Vincent's still face, stroking it tenderly, his own melting into such a picture of adoration and devastation Benjamin practically felt the force of it lance his long-dead heart. It didn't make any sense to him, that devotion.

But then...it did. It was how he had felt about his mother, wasn't it?

Suddenly, a sound tore through the howling wind. Benjamin lifted his head, squinting against its bite, listening hard. A trick of the ear? Or...

No–there it was again. This time, Henry looked up too.

"What was..."

And again. A voice, closer this time. And then another, closer still.

As it drew nearer, it became clearer—and hoarser. It belonged to an old woman—then a young man—then a different one—different people, but each of them rasping with disuse. Then, only feet away, an older man called out:

"This way! They are here!"

Benjamin's stomach dropped. He tried to rise, but his feet slipped on the ice and he fell back against Vincent's unmoving body.

"It's the heads," he hissed to Henry, gripping his shoulder. "The traitors in the ice. They ratted us out."

As soon as the words left his lips, a monstrous shadow appeared through the haze.

No—*two.*

Cerberus and his daughter forged ahead through the ice, following the trail of frozen heads as they shouted the way. Even they were not swift in these conditions, forced to pull themselves along with their claws—but they were certainly quicker than the rest of them had been, and it didn't matter now anyway. Without Vincent to guide them, Benjamin and Henry were trapped where they lay. All they could do was watch as their pursuers drew closer and closer—

Henry grabbed his crossbow from his back, loading it. He wasn't going to let Vincent's sacrifice go to waste. He surely wouldn't be able to forgive himself if he didn't go out fighting. But Benjamin just smiled a bitter, tight smile.

It was all for nothing, wasn't it, Vincent? For both of us.

"Here! Over here!" called the head closest to them, only a lump jutting from the ice. The beasts turned, homing in on them, their pace quickening—

They broke through the mist, their forms resolving, and suddenly Benjamin realized—they each only had one head. These were not hellhounds.

They were werewolves.

"Vincent? Henry? Is that you?"

"Casey! Sierra!"

Henry lowered his crossbow at once and almost leaped to his feet, but the ice stopped him. He and Benjamin clung lamely to Vincent until at last the werewolves reached them, nearly skidding into them in their haste. Benjamin flinched back, unsure if the beasts would afford him the same welcome.

He was right—as soon as they recognized him they rounded on him, their hackles rising and fangs flashing.

"*What's* he *doing here?*" the black wolf growled.

"*Look—Vincent! He hurt him! He's hurt!*" the dark brown wolf cried, finally noticing their friend's condition. Benjamin's heart tightened.

"I didn't do this," he hissed.

"*Liar!*" the black wolf snarled. She would have lunged for him, but Henry planted a hand on her chest, urging her back.

"No! He didn't. It was Cerberus—Vincent's father."

Both wolves turned to stare at Vincent now, their bright eyes wide. They broke off to nose at him, circling his body, little whines tearing from their throats as they took him in.

"*He's cold...*"

Henry jerked his face away, hiding a fresh sob. "He—there was nothing I could do. I tried...I..." He shook his head, helpless, his words failing. He could not face them.

"*Come—quick, then.*"

The black wolf nudged her body under Vincent's, hoisting him up with a grunt of effort. Her claws scratched deep scars in the ice as she fought to keep her footing. The other wolf took the other side.

"He'll just slow us down," Benjamin protested, despite knowing the fight that would follow. "We have to leave him behind—"

Jaws snapped inches from his face. He jerked back, but it would have been too late. Golden eyes burned a hole through him.

"*Never!*"

"Casey, stop! He—he's right." Henry's voice caught in his throat, but he pushed through it, even as tears rolled on and on down his face. "We should go. W-without him. They'll catch us."

The black wolf stared at him, outrage descending over her like a shadow. "*You'd leave him? After everything?*"

"*Wait.*" The brown wolf gazed at Henry with a growing realization. "*You think he's dead.*"

Everything froze. Benjamin's heart missed a beat. Henry gaped at her. "He's not?"

"*He's cold,*" she repeated, nudging Vincent's body with her nose. "*He's hurt. Not dead–yet. Have to get him home.*"

The sun seemed to slowly dawn in Henry's eyes, even this deep underground. His arms tightened around Vincent's neck as a shaky breath, almost a laugh, escaped him.

"Thank god...oh, thank god. We–yes, we have to get him home."

The werewolves took their positions again and lifted Vincent up, their claws scrabbling and scraping against the ice. Henry and Benjamin kept handfuls of his fur, letting their strange procession guide them onward. It was nearly as slow as before–but they were moving. It was all they could do. The cold was dogging them, biting into every crevice it could find, sapping their waning strength. Benjamin was only glad he was already dead.

Even so, it didn't take long for Casey to send a glare over her shoulder, towards him. "*Why is he coming?*" she demanded again.

"Because Vincent wanted him to," said Henry. "And because he's gonna help us."

"*You trust him?*" asked Sierra, casting him a wary glance of her own.

"Enough."

This surprised Benjamin. He had expected some kind of caveat, or a justification at least. But Henry gave neither. Even more surprising, the other two accepted this answer. He looked between them all, the werewolves and the human, and then the bedraggled hellhound they had come to care so much for, and for the first time in a long while he felt profoundly alone. It took him startlingly long–a second or two–to push the feeling away reproachfully. He was slipping.

"Thank you guys for coming," Henry said then, his voice thick with emotion and exhaustion. "I wasn't sure you would..."

"*I won't leave him,*" Casey growled, without looking back. Benjamin caught a smile flitting across Henry's face.

"*We won't leave you,*" Sierra added more softly.

That smile tightened, twisted into something more complicated.

"I know that now. I...I really appreciate that. More than I can say. And Vincent does, too. He will, once he wakes up..."

A silence fell heavy over them. Henry forced it away.

"The people trapped in the ice...they guided you to us?"

Sierra nodded. "*One called out to us. Told us to help you. Then the others...*"

"Was he called Leopold?"

"*Yes!*"

Henry smiled again, only for a moment.

Suddenly, a horrible sound rose over the whistling wind: an eerie howl— no, *three*, tangled into one.

"Shit. She's close." Benjamin's skin prickled. "She's hunting us."

"*Who?*" Casey growled, the fur lifting along her spine.

"Vincent's sister," said Henry, grimly. "Superbia."

"*Great. What now?*"

"We hurry..."

"*Can't go faster!*" Casey snapped. "*Ice–*"

"This way!"

An unfamiliar voice broke through the wind. They all turned to peer through the mist, barely making out a small round shape sticking out of the ice. They glanced at each other, then veered off slightly to move in that direction.

As they neared, they picked out the dark head of a middle-aged woman. Her face barely broke the river's surface, frozen in place so she was upturned to the worst of the wind. Her eyes were nothing more than lumps of ice, solidified by tears shed long ago. "Quickly, now! It is hard to track on ice, but the hellbeasts are good. Follow the next voice–they will guide you to the riverbank."

She let out a short, louder shout, and another voice responded through the mist, not too far away.

"Why are you helping us?" Henry asked, leaning closer to her. His face was deeply creased with sympathy.

"I cannot speak for the others," said the woman's head, her expression unreadable under the ice. "But for me...you are one of us. We all battle against the wrath of God and the Devil. We are never good enough, so we must be clever. Now go—avenge me! Escape!"

The other voice hollered again nearby, and they scrambled onward, following it.

"Thank you! Thank you!" Henry called back to the frozen head as they went.

They soon found another silhouette, another head in the ice. The man passed them on to his nearest neighbor, and she the next, on and on across the Cocytus. And all the while, they heard those howls drawing steadily closer behind them.

"She's taunting us," Benjamin hissed. "She wants us to be frightened. She thinks we're easy prey."

"*We won't be,*" Casey promised, with a snarl.

Then, out of nowhere, a dark silhouette appeared from the fog ahead— jagged, horizontal. Benjamin's heart leaped into his throat.

The riverbank.

And that's when they heard the drumming of paws on the ice, the scrape of claws.

It was too late.

"*Slide him!*" Sierra cried, dropping her grasp on Vincent's body. Casey did the same, just as a monstrous shadow lunged from the mist straight for them, eyes like burning coals and maw wicked with the glee of the chase.

Sierra threw herself between the hellhound and her companions, and they collided with a great thud and gnashing of teeth. Casey took the split second's distraction to brace herself, then—

"*Hang on!*"

She kicked out as hard as she could, sending Vincent's body spinning across the ice towards the bank. Henry held on, hunkering close against him, but Benjamin wasn't ready–his fingers slipped off Vincent's fur, and suddenly he was sliding away on his knees, on a trajectory all his own.

"Benjamin!"

Henry reached for him, but it was too late. The distress in his clear blue eyes pierced Benjamin's heart.

Claws screeched across ice, and then Benjamin was yanked into the air. It took a moment for the pain to battle past the cold and the shock and strike his nerves–teeth, teeth embedded deep in his arm, grinding against his bone, freezing fire shooting through every vein all the way up his battered body. Maybe he was used to burning, but this was different. Worse, because it spelled his doom. He was being dragged back across the frozen river, and soon he would be in the deepest pit of Hell to suffer again, forevermore. He almost smiled.

Of course. Why did I think it would be any different?

This was his life, and also his death, and everything that came after.

"*Drop him!*"

The snarl came close to his ear. The world lurched around him as he was flung aside, those terrible teeth holding fast–

The black wolf–Casey–she was grappling with Superbia, driving her back, desperate jaws snapping at three demon faces. Trying to reach Benjamin.

"He's *my* prisoner now!" Superbia cried. "I'm not like my brother–I'll *never* let him go!"

Her words cut in a yelp as Casey's fangs closed around her muzzle. Hot blood spattered Benjamin's dirty face.

Superbia reared back, taking him with her. The head that held him was merciless; the free one clamped its fangs into Casey's scruff, pulling and pulling, trying to tear her off–but Casey was relentless. Superbia lifted her off the ground, but she refused to let go.

Why?

But still she didn't stop—not even when Superbia finally ripped her off, tossing her hard onto the ice, so hard that a sharp *CRACK* resonated across the river.

Casey struggled to her paws, leaning on her front limbs, breath billowing in great clouds.

"Why go to all this trouble for *him?*" Superbia crowed, brandishing Benjamin in her mouth. Another jolt of pain surged through his limbs as he dangled. "My poor little brother is as good as dead and here you are, wasting time!"

Casey lunged, snapping at Superbia, but she jerked out of the way at the last second, pushing her away across the ice with a paw and a snort of triumph. Casey skidded to a halt, her claws shrieking through the ice, and bared her fangs so viciously even Benjamin might have quailed.

"Vincent gave his life for this! I'll finish it if it's the last thing I do!"

That garbled wolf's voice sounded clearer than ever before. Whatever curse had claimed her, both halves of her shared a singular purpose now.

She tore across the river again, colliding with Superbia, but all Benjamin could think was: *She's right.* If they didn't get Vincent to safety soon, his final act would be freeing Benjamin. And that couldn't happen. It wasn't right. Not after everything.

His eyes rolled, grasping for the others—where were they? Did they leave, did they take Vincent away? He couldn't see them—

"Henry!" he choked out, cringing against the pain as he swung wildly in Superbia's battling jaws. "Go, now! Save him!"

There was no way to know if he had heard. Benjamin was yanked aside as Casey's fangs found Superbia's neck, blood surging—but then she kicked out, shredding Casey's pelt, claws tangling and forcing her down.

Casey wasn't going to win this. Her dark fur was already sticky with blood.

"Don't die for me, you stupid wolf!" Benjamin called through gritted teeth. He didn't like the guilt—he didn't want it—he didn't understand. How was this so important to her? Was it really just for Vincent?

His gaze met hers—golden eyes glowing from her black coat—and the moment stuck, suspended in time as he saw what lay within.

Yes. It was for Vincent. Somehow, that was what mattered here. She cared about him, so deeply he almost didn't believe it. How could anyone care so much? Especially this girl, for all her violence and fury? He could see it all the way through, burning a hole in her.

He felt it profoundly, colliding in the center of his chest: he had missed something. He was missing something, all along.

He didn't know what it was yet, he realized. But right now, it coalesced into a single thing: *I'm not going to let you die for either of us.*

The moment unfroze, and suddenly the two beasts crashed together again, Casey surging upward to smash her skull into Superbia's. She snarled, tossing that head as she flinched back, giving Casey a split second to push herself up.

"Damn you!" Superbia spat, her last free head baring its teeth in a wrathful promise.

"*I figured,*" Casey growled, chest heaving, fixing her stance as she prepared for the next assault. Dread jolted through Benjamin's stomach.

She's not going to survive it. Superbia was done playing.

Suddenly the world tilted on its axis—his heart stopped—he was flying through the air—

The icy ground lunged for him, slamming into his already battered body. All he could manage was a grunt as his bones snapped, fire leaping through his veins. His vision went white.

He lay there, cold. He couldn't move. His body wouldn't obey. He felt more than heard the battle pursuing, the vibrations of warring monsters traveling through the ice.

I'm helpless. He didn't have the energy left for anger, but the shadow of it moved through his barren soul. *Why am I* always *helpless?*

He hated it more than anything. Everything good or hopeful in his life was always, always stripped away right in front of his eyes, while he could do exactly nothing. And here it was again.

You're going to die just so I can be thrown back into that cell to burn. It would all be for nothing. Just like all his attempts to do anything just for the world. He had worked so hard, sacrificed so much, gutted his own morals, cut lives short in hopes of saving their eternity–and none of it mattered. The portal was going to be fixed, and then...

Slowly, the shadows began to creep back into his vision. The first of them was jagged and stark–an ugly crack in the ice beneath him. He must have landed on the spot where Casey had been thrown before.

Futile cycles.

No...cracks in the ice.

Had this ice ever cracked before? It had been here so long, it might have always existed. But that wasn't right, either. Everything had a beginning–even a cycle.

Which meant everything had an end, too.

"Casey, here! The ice!" he cried, surprised he had a voice left–and then not. He had never let *helpless* mean *hopeless*.

Their eyes met for the second time, a split second in which everything that needed to be communicated passed between them. In that moment, so grotesquely different as they were, their minds were one.

Casey lurched forward, ducking just in time to avoid two sets of snapping jaws, and grabbed Superbia with both arms. She dug those wicked werewolf claws in deep, squeezing tight, dragging the hellhound across the ice with all her strength, ignoring her foe's claws and teeth and every blow she managed to land, but never with enough power to stagger Casey's resolve.

Not *yet*–she was slipping, and in moments she would be free. But Casey beat her to the punch.

She braced, her claws catching in the ice.

Benjamin closed his eyes, feeling more than hearing as Casey hurled Superbia across the space between, as her massive hellhound body crashed down atop him, as the ice shattered beneath him and freezing water rose to engulf him–

—As teeth sank into his arm, all the way to the bone. As they pulled him up, out of the hungry water.

He skidded through the dirt, lungs burning as the earth drove the air from them. Nothing else held him now—only the memory of teeth, surging up his arm. His head spun, but he fought through it, picking out the vast frozen river spanning his view, the dark crack that was now spreading across its surface like venom through a vein.

Oh, but that *sound*. It was so deep and so jagged that it seemed to splinter through Benjamin's wasted body too, a shiver through every nerve. For a moment the River Cocytus was alive, a creature, a being so ancient it could not remember its birth, groaning in agony.

Superbia was flailing in the dark water, desperate claws scraping against the thick ice—but even she wasn't immune to the merciless cold. Her thrashing grew weaker with each cloud of breath. The ice creaked as she flung herself against it, over and over—

And then, with a horrific crash, the river burst. Water erupted from the fissure like a torn artery, ripping the ice into great chunks and flinging them downstream with the vengeance of boundless ages of restraint. That groan was now a roar, a death cry, as on and on the flood spread, swallowing everything between its banks.

"*Shit*," Casey breathed. She crouched by Benjamin's side, wet with blood and frost.

They watched from the bank as one by one those little dark shapes—the heads, all that was left of those traitors trapped in the ice—disappeared into the black water. They scanned the flood rushing past, frantically searching for bodies, but they found nothing. Not even Superbia. The river was too vast, too vicious. It had consumed them all.

"*What did I do?*" Casey snarled, clutching her own head with her claws.

Slowly, Benjamin pushed himself to his knees. His chest seared white-hot—his ribs were broken. But he didn't care. He stared out over the destruction with awe.

"You freed them," he croaked.

As his words fell, a high, wild sound rose over the roar of the river. For just a moment, Benjamin glimpsed a human shape slipping past, far out on the water. Another answered, beyond sight. And then another.

"They're laughing." A smile broke across Benjamin's ruined face. His eyes began to burn, and then the world distorted. *Tears.* Something was welling up inside him that had been there for so long, he had almost forgotten what it meant. Maybe it meant even more now, after all this torment.

"*Are they crazy?*" Casey growled.

"They're relieved. They don't have to hurt anymore. They get to rest."

"*Doesn't look like rest to me.*" She peered downriver. "*They'll drown.*"

"They're already dead. They can't drown."

"*Then what'll happen to them?*"

"I don't know," Benjamin admitted. "But they have a chance now. Maybe they can escape with the rest of the damned." *Unless he can restore the ice somehow.* He prayed it was impossible–that the river was a force of nature, that its winter had finally broken into spring.

But they couldn't stay to find out. Benjamin looked around, seeing no one else but Casey beside him.

"The others must've gone ahead," he said, struggling to get up. He flinched, hissing as his ribcage flexed painfully. At least his limbs were intact– apart from the teeth marks. "We need to catch up."

Casey grunted. She stood too, shakily, her eyes never leaving the raging flood she had caused.

Benjamin wasn't sure what to make of her; but he followed his first instinct, pacing closer, reaching out to rest his hand on her arm. It was thickly-furred, well-muscled, wiry. It twitched under his grasp, and she turned to look at him, first in shock and then outrage and then paused on a question.

"You did *good.* This is…unprecedented. You saved them." He smiled again, a little more this time.

Those golden eyes burned through him. This time he couldn't read the expression there.

She turned away. "*Come on.*"

They climbed the riverbank, relishing the fading chill from the air. It didn't take long for the cloying heat of the Underworld to return. As soon as they crested the hill, the Plains of Asphodel opened before them, stretching out to the dark horizon, but for a single line of blinding white lancing the black sky. Their way out.

"I can't see the others," said Benjamin, scanning the hills. Everything was too dark, too gray.

"*They came this way,*" Casey answered, pushing ahead. "*I can smell them.*"

Benjamin followed. The grass turned to ash beneath each footfall. The arid wind blasted his face and whipped his hair across his eyes. Each gust brought another hazy memory along—crossing these plains in an endless march, lines of souls just like him, bound with loose ropes and unyielding despair. It was hard not to let his mind slip into the shadows that seemed to creep in through his eyes, his nose, his ears... Every thought from that time was pale and broken, only pieces drifting behind his eyes waiting to be messily glued back together.

That was how it was to be damned in the afterlife. He no longer mattered enough for memory; but he mattered enough to be coveted, collected. He was a trophy, an offering to all the misery in the world. This place was its nexus. He fed it. They all did.

But not enough. Somehow, he had warded the shadows off just enough to keep that flame alive in his heart, however small. He refused to accept this was the end of his journey—trudging on forever with no destination, no reprieve. All the suffering was supposed to mean something. It had to. Otherwise...he would have to accept that the universe itself was designed for cruelty. And he couldn't do that.

His gaze shifted to the black-furred werewolf padding at his side. Her massive paws seemed to crush the grass with relish. Her lean muscles twitched, as if aching to run ahead. But she wouldn't leave him.

"You're in control of your instincts," he said, breaking the quiet between them. "I haven't seen that in a werewolf before. Not that I've known many, but...I didn't think it was possible."

Casey didn't reply. But her expression tightened.

"It wasn't like that before. I remember. I saw what happened that night, when you turned Hunter."

That earned him a glance, an attempt at a glare. But the fear was bright in her eyes. No one else would have seen it, but he knew the look of it intimately.

"*You were there?*"

"You care about him. Vincent."

That stopped her. Her lips twitched, but the snarl didn't arrive. She turned her face away, kept trudging on.

"This was all because of him." A little laugh fell from his mouth. "I honestly couldn't believe it...after everything, he still made people care. You and Henry and that other werewolf, and the ghost boy...even Melanie, in her own way. I thought after me, he would never let it happen again. He was so angry, all the time...so desperate to keep people away. Too afraid to fail anyone again. But something happened."

"*Henry happened.*"

Benjamin blinked. "Is that right? He started it?"

Casey gave a short nod, without looking back.

"Huh." Was that all it took? Henry was so unfailingly kind...he overlooked all of Vincent's barriers and spikes, and disarmed him from the inside.

No...Vincent let him in. He wanted it. It was like something inside his very soul had been waiting, hoping someone would try.

Benjamin had done it first; but Henry did it better. Wholeheartedly. For the sake of it. No ulterior motives.

Did I only use him? Yes, and no. It was hard not to love a dog. They were useful companions, painfully loyal...but they were so much more, too. Vincent had looked at him like he held the sun and moon in each of his hands. No one had ever thought of him like that before. In spite of everything

Vincent was trained to be, the best of his nature always shone through…if you knew how to look.

And Henry did. Maybe better than Benjamin ever had.

"…And what about you? You don't look like you want to care about anyone."

"He's real. He doesn't play games. He knows what he is and that's that. He knows what I am."

She stopped, the howling wind filling in for her.

"And he doesn't expect you to be anything else."

She cast him a curious glance, quickly hidden.

He nodded to himself. "Yeah. I know what you mean. Except somehow it makes you want to be better, anyway."

She didn't have to answer.

"Casey!"

As she and Benjamin approached the portal at last, Sierra, the brown werewolf, rushed to greet her. She pushed her muzzle under Casey's with a whine of relief, tail swishing. Henry sat beside Vincent's crumpled body, stroking between his ears with a shadowed look on his face, his thoughts somewhere far away. It took him a moment longer to collect himself and stand, with an obvious effort. He faced the newcomers solemnly, clutching the turquoise amulet in one hand.

"Ready to go?"

"Glad you're alive, too," Casey growled, accepting Sierra's fussing with surprising patience.

Henry shook his head slightly, as if to clear it. "Right. Sorry. I knew you'd be okay. It's just…we need to get him home." He glanced back down at Vincent, horribly still but for the hot wind ruffling his fur in waves that mirrored the grass all across the plains. He was the largest of them, rivaled only by Sierra, but he looked strangely small now in his helplessness.

"I broke the river."

Henry blinked at Casey a couple times, trying to grasp her words. "You...what?"

"The Cocytus. She shattered the ice, and it flooded over. It's flowing again." Benjamin couldn't help but smile. "The prisoners are free."

Henry met his gaze in shock. "It's..." Slowly something in his face softened, and he let out a long breath. "I wonder if that's as easy to fix as the portal."

"We'll find out." Benjamin turned to it only steps away, squinting against its light with relish. He could almost feel the sun's warmth already–something imperceptibly but unequivocally different from the heat of the underground.

That's when he remembered: he wouldn't be able to feel it anymore. Not once he left this place.

Henry seemed to know what he was thinking. "Are you ready?"

"Yes." He didn't hesitate. "Grab Vincent. Let's go. I just hope you know what you're doing with that amulet."

"I do."

The werewolves went first, heaving Vincent between them. They stepped into the light, letting it swallow them. Simple as that. It was almost hard to believe just how much that little act of leaving meant.

Now it was just him and Henry. Benjamin stepped to the very edge of the pillar of light, his heart aching to touch it. He wanted out more than he wanted anything else in the world. He wanted everyone who had known the horrors of this place to feel the relief and joy of it. But he would have to keep working for that.

That's okay. I'll never stop. No matter how many times it takes, I'll keep breaking your shit, Lucifer. Until you finally give in.

"I'm ready."

Something warm touched his hand, and he flinched. He felt foolish about it at once, but both of them pretended he hadn't.

Of course Henry had to hold his hand–they had to create a physical link. He was all too familiar with rituals. It had just been so long since someone had done it. It made him feel like a different person entirely–someone who had disappeared from the world long ago.

Mom. That was the last time. He remembered now. They used to cross the street like this. She used to keep him safe.

His eyes burned as he shut them, fighting those foreign tears, letting the sunlight bleed through his tired eyelids for the last time. He felt Henry slip the cold stone amulet into his palm, their fingers still interlocked.

"Together," said Henry.

CHAPTER 20

RENAISSANCE

Gray. But...it was brighter, now. Growing brighter.

At first, that was all he knew. But then, slowly, he became aware that he had limbs. He could see them in front of him, feel them. He tried to move them, but they were too heavy. That must mean he had a body still, too.

The next thing that returned was the cold. *He* was cold. Then came the memory of it, colder still. Surrounded by it, out on the frozen river...

The air here...it was warm. It moved. Living things moved through it, breathed it in and out.

He must be alive.

Something drummed against his ears, ever so faint. A voice. Something else, something warm, was pressing against him.

Some*one*.

The voice faded in, until finally he recognized the words:

"Vincent! He's awake! Vinny, can you hear me? Please–"

Vincent dragged his mind back from the brink, fighting the insurmountable weight of his own body and the death hanging over it. He struggled for a single shaky breath, enough for a low groan. Enough to move one of his three heads, resting it against Henry's side. He could feel it properly now–his warmth, the soft curve of his body, the trembling breaths that rose and fell, the rumble of his voice through his chest.

"You're alive! Oh my god, Vincent–" Henry's voice broke, flooded with tears. His hands clutched Vincent's rightmost head, holding it close.

That was when Vincent noticed all his senses were returning to him, little by little. Trees faded into focus just ahead, cold and gray as he had last seen them. But the grayness was so much brighter here, on the surface. There was a whole world beyond, and above, and below.

At first he expected the sound and touch of shifting leaves and wind to follow his sight, merely lagging behind. But they didn't come. He then realized–he wasn't in the forest. He was on a bed. Indoors. No...he was on *his* bed, and the trees he saw were outside, through the wide window overlooking the woods behind Dexter's Laboratory. His friends had brought him home.

Everything that had happened in the Underworld flitted across his mind in a blur, all at once. He squeezed his eyes shut as if that would help. It didn't. Every image lashed his heart with a new feeling, each more complicated than the last.

Father...Superbia...Benjamin...Henry...

It was all too much.

The door slammed open, charging straight through his thoughts. Before he could even lift his heads, he was surrounded by noise and color–familiar faces, all of them clamoring for him–

"Vincent! Vincent!" Sierra laughed through her tears, hugging him tightly.

"You fucking asshole." He couldn't see her, but Casey's voice was unmistakable, close to his ear as she cradled his leftmost head with her cheek against his skull.

"You made it," Henry whispered, those hands like sunlight in his fur. "You're safe now."

Vincent almost believed it.

Finally, with an immense effort, he lifted his middle head. "How..."

"Did you really think we were gonna leave you in Hell to die?" Casey growled.

Guilt and love bloomed into an ache deep inside. "You were there. You came. You knew what I was going to do..."

"Of course I knew."

Her words left so much unsaid, but there was no need for anything more. His chest felt tight as the shame and warmth for her expanded until he thought it would burst him open.

"You shouldn't have..."

"Oh, shut up, Vincent. I'm sick of you telling me what I should and shouldn't do."

"I'm...I'm sorry, Casey. I'm sorry for everything. You deserve better than–"

"Yeah, you should be! You're lucky I had my own plans, or you'd be a doggy popsicle out there right now. When are you gonna learn we're in this together?"

Her grip on his head tightened, then released as she stepped back again. He forced himself to finally meet her eyes, taking in every shadow of grief and resolve on her beleaguered, delicate, battle-hardened face. He didn't understand.

"But...after everything..."

"You're an asshole, yeah. But...so am I." It was her turn to avoid his gaze. "And you cared about me anyway. Despite my best efforts."

Vincent's heart lurched. His thoughts flickered frantically past, darting just out of his reach every time he tried to grasp them. Then he caught one, and with it came a fresh wave of shame:

"Casey...you know I don't..."

She waved a hand at him. "Yeah. Whatever. That doesn't change anything. You and me, we're packmates."

Guilt was the first impulse, just as it always was–but somehow, some way, it cut itself short. In its place came affection, so profound and so blunt there was nothing to combat it.

"You're not alone, Vincent," Sierra added, squeezing him gently around the middle. "We know you don't wanna be, even if you think you deserve it."

Vincent tried to twist one head to look at her, but a jolt of pain in his neck stopped him. "Do...do *you* think I deserve it?"

He felt her shrug. "Who cares? We've all done shitty things. All I know is, if it was me going to Hell by myself...you'd be following me down there. That's what matters."

That warmth between his ribs grew, impossibly so.

"I said I was sorry," Henry murmured, stroking the space between Vincent's ears so gently it hurt. "And I meant it. You were doing what you thought was right. And I left you alone. I...I wasn't myself. Just like when you stopped me from killing Jake."

He glanced up at Casey and Sierra, those beautiful blue eyes so terribly sad and so hopeful, all at once. "I think...we're our best selves when we're together. Looking out for each other."

The silence between them then was not empty, as silence often was; it felt like the hush of dawn, as the first spear of sunlight pierced the gray, promising an end to the cold confusion of night.

Casey's gaze found Vincent's. For a moment they were back in the orange grove, silvery shadows under the full moon, facing down their monster together. "No more lone wolves."

A little smile tugged across Vincent's faces—all three of them. "Welcome to the pack."

Henry laughed, and the sound of it lanced Vincent's heart. He had almost forgotten what it felt like. "Am I allowed in? Or does one of you have to bite me first?"

Sierra giggled, and even Casey let out a snort. A weight seemed to lift from all of them—the sun breaking over the hills. The air was warm again.

But it didn't last. Another thought broke in: "Benjamin—what happened to him? Is he...?"

"He's safe." Sierra held up the turquoise pendant. "Casey protected him until we got to the portal."

Vincent looked at her, stunned. She shifted awkwardly. "*You*...? Why?"

"He's important," Casey grunted. "You risked your life to get him. Henry said he's gonna help us."

Vincent turned to Henry immediately. "Did you tell them...?"

"That we're saving the world from Lucifer now?" Sierra piped up. "Yeah."

"And...and you're alright with it?"

"Well, I sure don't wanna end up in Hell when I die," Casey growled. "But all those spirits–they can't get off scot-free. Not after what they've done to Dex, to the pack."

"They're not trying to hurt them. They're desperate. Like Percy, like Ava...like Benjamin." He could hardly believe the name had dropped from his own mouth.

"*Desperate* doesn't cut it," Casey argued. "They're not good people, Vincent. All of them screwed someone else over for their own selfish reasons. Percy and Benjamin got people *killed*. Who knows what other horrible things those ghosts did to land a spot in Hell? And now they're still doing it."

"You're right. They're not...*good*." That wasn't it. What were they? "They're...sad."

Casey stared at him as if he had sprouted a fourth head. "Sad? Being *sad* doesn't mean they had to do any of that."

"No, it doesn't. I just...wonder if they would have done it, if they weren't."

The old werewolf's words danced across his mind again: *They've never been happy a goddamn day in their lives. They think too much. They want too much. They don't know who they are anymore. They hunt, but whenever they catch somethin', it never satisfies 'em. They hurt things just 'cause they can. 'Cause it makes 'em feel better. It makes 'em feel alive.*

It wasn't true. Vincent knew that now. Not everyone was like that. And the ones that were...it was because they needed something, desperately. They were hungry, just like he had been, deep in the Underworld's darkness his entire life.

Maybe they didn't even know what it was like to not feel hungry. Maybe that was why they kept hunting.

"If you didn't want them free...why did you release them, Casey?" Sierra asked.

To Vincent's great surprise, Casey's anger receded. She looked almost haunted. Almost sad.

"What?" He stared at her blankly. "What is she talking about?"

"Casey broke the ice on the Cocytus River," said Henry. "It started flowing again, all the way down. Everyone trapped there escaped."

A shock wave traveled through Vincent's heart, straight to his stomach.

"You...you can't have. That river has been frozen for...since *forever*. How could you–"

"I did," said Casey. He had learned to read the shadows on her face; he took in the uncertainty, the guilt...but also, a mere glimmer of satisfaction. He knew it was true. "I–I didn't really mean to. I don't know. But you can blame your sister, too. She started it. If she hadn't thrown me so hard into the ice, it wouldn't have cracked..."

"Superbia? She was there? You fought her?"

Something strange crossed her expression. Vincent didn't understand it, and didn't like it. She wouldn't meet his gaze.

"She...she fell, Vincent. Into the water." Suddenly Casey straightened up, looked him dead in the eye. "I pushed her in, when it flooded. I don't know if she or any of the prisoners made it out."

Nothing seemed to register in Vincent's head. It took him the better part of a minute to even think to himself: *Superbia...dead?*

It was unthinkable. She was too ferocious. Too powerful. A world without her malice was impossible.

But then, the Cocytus River was no longer frozen. The portal to Hell had been broken. The impossible was now possible.

It took him too long to realize everyone was holding their breath, waiting for him to do something. In the end, all he said was: "This may not last. Lucifer might be able to fix that, too."

"Then we have to get started. See what Benjamin can do," Henry urged. "Casey, are you with us?"

Casey set her jaw. Looked at Vincent, long and hard. He could feel her sizing up every mote of trust they had forged between them, everything they had shared. Then, at last:

"Do you really think this is the right thing to do, Vincent?"

"If we can do it without hurting anyone? Yes," he insisted. "All of this suffering is pointless. It just leads to more of it. It's time to let the dead move on."

"And how do we do that, exactly? Where would they move on to?"

"I don't know," Vincent admitted. "That's why we need Benjamin. He knows more about all this than any of us. He had some kind of bigger plan, before."

"Yeah...one where everyone either turned into a ritual sacrifice or a vampire," Casey growled.

"Not this time," said Henry. "We won't allow it."

"We may not have a choice, if it's Benjamin's plan."

"Let's just talk to him," Sierra said. "We don't *have* to do what he wants. He's only a ghost now–he doesn't have any power over us."

Casey stared at her for a long moment, her expression unreadable. Then, finally, she sighed.

"If we don't have to become serial killers to make it work...I'm ready to raise a little hell."

A familiar warmth crept back into his chest. Once, Vincent would have never expected such grace from Casey of all people. But it seemed he wasn't the only one who had changed.

"You're not gonna raise hell without me, are you?"

Vincent's stomach dropped as a new voice sounded. His gaze found the doorway, and there...

"Roman," he choked out. Something welled up thick in his throat, behind his eyes. "You're alright...!"

The kid wore a crooked smile–more than Vincent could have asked for. He strode into the room, to Vincent's side. He looked tired, weak...but whole.

"I should be saying that." He touched Vincent's furred shoulder gently. "Guess we both fucked up, huh?"

"Hey–language," said Henry, but without any bite behind it.

"Come on, I think he's earned it," said Casey.

Vincent searched Roman's face, noting the lines where his skin was drawn tight with pain. He looked hollow in a way he hadn't before. The shadows in those once-bright green eyes were darker, their depths deeper. He was young, so young, still...but he wasn't the same kid who had trailed after his parents into this very building. He had seen too much.

But stranger still...there was no trace of resentment, no matter how hard Vincent searched. He couldn't understand it.

"I...shouldn't have let you go out there like you did." He closed his eyes, unable to bear looking anymore. "I'm sorry, Roman. I'm so sorry."

Roman's smile faded in an instant. "I'm not. And you shouldn't be. I wanted to help. If it wasn't for me, you guys wouldn't have been able to get in to rescue Henry."

"We could've sent someone else for it," Vincent growled. "Or figured out another plan. You didn't need to–"

"I know, I'm just a kid!" Roman spat, and finally the resentment showed–but not for the reasons Vincent expected. "I've heard it over and over! But I'm old enough to help! What else am I s'posed to do, just sit in this shitty old building and let my parents waste away?"

"Let *us* do the–"

"As if you'd leave me alone here! 'Cause then you'd worry the ghosts would get me too, and even worse if one of you stayed behind to protect me— you needed *everyone*. You needed *me*. If Casey or Sierra had to run distraction–"

"We would've figured something out," Vincent said again, baring his teeth. But he wasn't strong enough now to let that fire inside him burn any hotter.

Roman's glare burned bright. "And if it didn't work? Bullshit. You wanted to save Henry–*I* want to save my parents. I won't stand by and do nothing."

"He's right, Vincent."

Everyone looked at Henry in surprise.

"I thought..."

"It's stupid trying to pretend he's not a part of all this now, just as much as the rest of us. Whether or not it's fair. I see that now." Henry's eyes locked with Vincent's, and he froze beneath them. "I get why you feel the way you do. Both then, and now. He's like you were, isn't he? When you were that young, and you felt the weight of your father's expectations on your shoulders, and you didn't have a choice but to prove yourself."

Vincent suddenly realized why something in Roman's face had always looked so familiar—even more now than before. Henry was right.

"Roman put himself on the line, the same way you did. To protect the people he cared about. I know he's young...and he shouldn't have to. You shouldn't have, either. But it didn't matter then, and it doesn't matter now. He's old enough to make a difference. This world doesn't wait—not for people like us."

Henry softened then, and he moved to rest a hand on Roman's shoulder, careful not to touch his bandages.

"It took me a long time to see it, myself. We don't get the luxury of avoiding it. We're different. It...it's hard. Knowing what we know. But we do, and that means we have the responsibility to act. To make sure the people who don't know get to stay that way. Safe."

Roman's eyes gleamed in the gloom—a predator's eyes. He belonged in the darkness, too. He nodded, more solemn than fervent now. Something had changed in him.

Vincent gazed into that mirror, seeing that pup he had once been, vicious and clumsy, and something deep inside him cracked. It held together, but the strain of so many years had finally met its match.

Everyone seemed to see it. He wasn't sure how, but they did. Roman curled his fingers into Vincent's fur—affection, reassurance. A promise.

"I'm, uh...I'm sorry I worried you, Vincent. Really. I'll try not to go running off anywhere again like that."

Vincent closed his eyes, breathing a long, slow sigh. "Together, from now on."

"Yeah. You got it. I won't let you down."

Vincent felt as tired now as he had on the frozen river. He felt as if a spotlight shone down on him, laying bare all the twisted little things inside him. He didn't have the strength to hate it anymore.

Maybe he didn't want to.

Somehow...Henry understood. He saw what even Vincent couldn't. He had reached in and pulled that pup out of the mire in his heart. That was real. It felt different than it had before they had ever set foot in the Underworld, side-by-side. When Henry had looked at him before, the image was distorted. Something better, something worse. Not quite right. But this...

Yes. Something had changed.

"Vincent?" said Roman, bringing him back to the present. "The others said the portal is gonna be fixed soon...does that mean the ghosts are gonna leave my parents alone?"

Vincent clenched his jaws. "I don't know."

"But you *have* to know—you're a hellhound!"

"It's not like this has ever happened before. We don't even know if the ghosts will be forced back to Hell right away, or if they'll have to be rounded up. And either way, we should try to fix everything before that happens." He lifted his gaze to Sierra, whose neck bore the turquoise amulet. Henry must have given it back to her. "Give me the amulet. We need to talk to Benjamin."

"What? Right now?" Sierra asked. "Are you sure you're strong enough to handle it?"

"Let me do it," said Henry. "It needs to be someone strong, so he can project his voice for everyone to hear."

Even Vincent couldn't argue with that. "Alright..."

Sierra took off the amulet and approached to fasten it around Henry's neck. He took in a deep breath, closed his eyes. His fingers tightened in Vincent's fur.

The dark bedroom felt suddenly darker. A chill seeped through Vincent's body, radiating from Henry's hand, and a familiar voice whispered from nowhere:

"*Vincent...you made it.*"

"So did you," he answered.

"I'm...glad you did."

Vincent was silent as the idea sank in. *He...cares about me?*

"We have to finish our plans, Benjamin," said Henry. "Quickly. We don't know what will happen when the portal is fixed...if you'll be forced back into Hell somehow, or..."

"Don't worry. I'll be safe in this amulet."

"How do you know?"

"Oh, I know a lot about this amulet. It was the key to breaking the portal to Hell, after all."

"Can it help us again?" Casey demanded. "Without killing anyone, this time?"

"Possibly...although, it would be a lot easier if we pursued ritual sacrifices again. We know that works."

"I told you, we're *not* killing anymore," Henry growled. "Don't you care at all about the lives you cut short? Percy's in there with you, isn't he? Can't you feel what he feels? How horrible everything has been for him since he died?"

"Percy was our first sacrifice to save the world. Believe me, I will never forget that sacrifice–or my mistakes. I wish it had gone differently."

A wave of sorrow washed over Vincent's body, startling him. It wasn't his own. It had to be Benjamin's.

"You know I wanted to make people better. I thought I could help Sebastian control his blood-thirst. I didn't realize it was so powerful, so soon after his Ascension. I didn't mean for Percy to be drained the way he did."

"Who cares how he died? You meant to kill him! You made him into a bone-tower!" Casey spat, glaring at the amulet around Henry's neck. "You're pretending to give a shit about him *now*?"

"I do care about him. Right now I feel him next to me, and his sadness. I'm sorry it all ended up being so traumatic for him, and for the people who cared about him. But it had to be him. When Melanie overheard him talking about his amulet and its spiritual containment properties...it was fate. We had to take

it and study it, and we needed his blood to do it. If there was a way to do it without sacrificing anyone, we would have. But the lines between life and death don't matter anymore. We're talking about the eternal—walking outside the lines God drew for us."

Vincent tensed at the name. "Now we're talking about God?"

"We were always talking about God. He's the one who set all of this up, after Lucifer's betrayal and the fall of mankind. This is just one meager step in the plan to dismantle the cage He built for us, drunk on His own pride."

Vincent stared dead ahead, thunderstruck. But Casey only snorted.

"You think *you* can take on God?"

"Not me—we. This is your fight too, now." Vincent could almost picture Benjamin's smirk. *"And why not? I broke open the portal to Hell itself. You broke the ice of the Cocytus River. We freed countless prisoners. If we can do that, imagine what else we can do."*

"That *is*, like, world-ending stuff," Roman put in.

"Oh, sure," Casey scoffed. "Just as long as someone else is the sacrifice, and he gets to make everyone do his bidding."

"I would gladly be a sacrifice," Benjamin countered, with a ferocity. *"This isn't about becoming a dictator. I'll do anything to stop this fucking torment. Didn't you see what it was like down there, in Hell?"*

Casey hesitated.

"Even if you're as heartless as you pretend to be—which you're not—do you really think you won't end up there when your time comes?"

Casey bared her teeth wolfishly, but didn't reply. Instead, Henry broke in:

"For the last time, we're not killing anyone! There has to be a way to do this without it!"

"Oh, Henry...death doesn't matter. Not really. It's just a state of being, like being alive. You can do some things, and can't do others."

"You're wrong," Vincent snapped. "It matters a lot. Being dead is the loneliest, emptiest thing in the world."

"It can be. But it doesn't have to be. It's just the way things are now—because God made them that way, out of revenge. You only know death the way He made it–Hell, and the purgatory of being a ghost on the mortal plane. Have you ever seen Heaven?"

No, thought Vincent fiercely, looking at Henry without a second thought. *But I felt it, once. For just a moment.*

He didn't realize Benjamin had picked up on this until it was too late. He felt the ghost's thoughts turning, his curiosity prickling, a physical sensation in his own gut.

"If you think this world is wonderful, Vincent, you haven't seen anything yet."

"Why? Have you seen Heaven?" Vincent challenged, blazing with his own shame.

"No, but…we all know what it's supposed to be like. As long as you do exactly what God tells you, in exactly the right way, all your wildest dreams come true at the snap of your fingers. You'll never feel hurt or hunger again, forever."

There are worse things, Vincent thought.

"If only we could break open a portal to Heaven," Casey muttered.

"Exactly!"

CHAPTER 21

REMNANTS

Everyone stopped dead.

"*That's* the plan?"

"You want to–"

"*I don't know how, just yet,*" Benjamin admitted. "*But if we can do it for Hell...well, that's step one. The second part is finding a way to open the door to Heaven, for all those souls. An afterlife where everyone can be at peace.*"

For a moment, a glimmer of hope warmed Vincent's core. But then it dimmed. "Even if we could...what would stop Deus from fixing it, just like Lucifer is doing?"

"*Deus?*"

"God," Vincent explained. It felt strange to be admitting such things to mortals, but...it didn't matter, now. His allegiances were long decided. "He proclaimed Himself *the* God, when He took over. But my master knows the truth–His real name is Deus. That's why Lucifer mounted His rebellion, after all."

Excitement leaped up like flames inside Benjamin's essence. "*Took over? You mean God–Deus–didn't create the world?*"

"No. He didn't. No one knows who or what did. Gods have been squabbling over the place since the dawn of memory. So why should Deus get to rule over everything? That's what Lucifer thought, anyway."

"Really? You know all that?" Roman piped up, amazed.

"So much for philosophy class," Sierra remarked, staring at Vincent as if he had sprouted a fourth head. "You knew the true nature of *gods* this whole time, and you never told us?"

He grimaced. "It didn't exactly come up. And I'm not really supposed to tell mortals these things anyway." He carefully avoided looking at Henry. He had revealed much of this to him alone, long ago. It struck him now how peculiar it was for him to have done that. How foolish he was, not recognizing why he wanted to...

"So you just know all the secrets of the universe, and you kept it from us because *it didn't come up?*" Casey slapped her arms against her sides. "Every time I think you've turned over a new leaf–"

"*This is incredible,*" said Benjamin, alone unbothered by Vincent's secrecy. "*You really know all these things...you're going to be the ticket. Do you think we could convince Lucifer to rebel again? Pit Him and Deus against each other? That would be ideal...*"

"Not after what I did," Vincent growled. "Lucifer doesn't suffer traitors, as you've seen."

"*I'll think on it. In the meantime, the first step is to find a portal to Heaven.*"

"No problem at all," Casey muttered.

"Did you find one before I took you?" Vincent asked.

"*Sadly, no. I'm not sure where to start looking, either. It might be wise to consult someone who knows more about...*"

Benjamin trailed off.

"Uh...Benjamin?" said Sierra.

"*I'm here,*" he said. "*It's just...Ava is speaking to me.*"

"Ava? You can hear her in there?" Casey demanded.

"*She says...her grandmother might know where to find a portal. Maybe even how to break it.*"

"Oh, right!" exclaimed Henry. "She's a powerful witch–I bet she would know!"

"*Start there,*" Benjamin urged. "*I should leave you, for now. I don't want to drain any more of your energy, Henry. But before I go...Ava has another message for you.*"

Everyone waited, curious. But Vincent had a feeling he knew what it would be–and he was right.

"*While you're there...she wants you to make good on your promise. To help her move on to the afterlife.*"

"Fuck, dude–this shit again?" Casey let out a frustrated growl. "Right when we need her help with all this? Are you serious?"

"I remember someone else who didn't want to be involved," said Henry, his words more amused than his tone. Mostly he was troubled.

Casey glared at him. "So what? I changed my mind, alright? You guys are my pack." She glanced away with a snort. "Besides–you think I wanna die and go to Hell? Or let the world get eaten by ghosts? You dumbasses need me."

In spite of his weakness, a smile crossed Vincent's faces.

"I think we can do this by ourselves."

Everyone stopped to look at him, startled.

"Seriously?" said Casey. "If it weren't for Ava, we would've been werewolf chow! And *you* would've been sister chow, from what Henry told me!"

"Exactly. She's done her part. More than enough. We can't keep her chained to us, Casey."

He tore through the fog in his head and found her dark eyes, holding her gaze like a lifeline. As he did he felt Benjamin's essence fading–and suddenly he could take a full breath again.

"It's just like you said before. If it weren't for us, she would still be alive." He let his expression soften. "You were right. We owe her peace, at the very least."

Casey's eyes narrowed to slits as she thought about this. He watched her soften too, even as she crossed her arms. "You think she's gonna get any peace? Is this girl that confident she's getting into Heaven?"

"It's not about that." For a moment Vincent swore he could feel the cold shadow of every ghost drifting around them for miles and miles, desperately grasping for the warmth and substance and purpose only the living had to give. But even that was futile. Borrowed. Stolen. He thought again of his possessed packmates locked in their bedrooms, addled and distraught. He shivered, even as his heart twisted. "Ava is dead. She doesn't belong in this world. None of the ghosts do. They know that. This place has nothing left for them now but memories."

Casey shook her head helplessly. "But they'd rather have Hell?"

"No, of course not...or they'd return on their own. But...they feel a need to move on. Somewhere they belong. It's just a shame Hell is part of that answer, right now..." He sighed. "It's not up to us to decide. It's up to her."

Henry's fingers tightened in his fur, just so. Warmly. They hadn't left him once since he woke. When he looked up, he found Henry's expression softer than it was moments before.

Casey sighed too, roughly. "Fine! I guess you're right. She's stupid as ever, but...that's her choice. I just...I guess I hoped she'd learned something."

That smile was struggling back onto Vincent's faces again. He barely kept it at bay. *Like you did?* He didn't dare say it aloud.

"We'd better get her to her grandmother, then," said Henry. "If anyone knows how to do a peaceful exorcism, Magdalena does. And then we can ask about the portal to Heaven."

"If she doesn't send us there herself, after she learns what happened to Ava..." Casey muttered. "Will she even be at her house? Before, Ava said she goes camping to avoid the Shadowhand..."

Vincent grimaced. "We...we have to try anyway. This is our best shot." He pushed himself up, swaying, his muscles trembling and howling in protest.

"You should stay and rest, Vincent. You can't even walk." Sierra rested a gentle hand on his back, trying to urge him back down.

"Then carry me. This is my responsibility, too."

Sierra and Casey exchanged a glance. "Um...it's not like we can transform again now..."

"Then how did you do it before?"

"You needed us," Casey snapped. "It's different."

"I thought you could control it now." Henry glanced between them in confusion. "You were almost talking normally, Casey, back on the river..."

"What?" said Vincent, shocked. Flashes of that night in the orange grove crossed his mind's eye–Casey pushing through that impossible barrier of instinct, barely keeping a grasp on who she was, who *Vincent* was, to protect him from that old werewolf. *That* was her best. What had changed?

He realized suddenly that Casey and Sierra were looking at each other again. It gave him the distinct impression of looks he often shared with Henry, without even thinking.

Finally Sierra spoke: "I gave her some of the potion Henry made me. However he makes it, it's not enough to stop the transformations...but it helps clear my head, a bit. It was enough to help Casey. Thank god it was. I wasn't sure..."

"It was a really smart idea," said Casey, her gaze lingering on Sierra.

Sierra broke into a sheepish smile. "Well, it wouldn't have been shit if you weren't so good at controlling yourself. I still don't know how you do it..."

"She cares about him," said Henry.

Casey rounded on him with a growl, but it was half-hearted. "Shut up."

Sierra laughed, which mingled with a snort in that Sierra way. Vincent's heart instantly felt lighter at the sound of it. "But you do!"

"Yeah, well, so do you."

"But he's your best friend, isn't he?"

That gave her pause. The silence stretched for a moment too long before she turned away from them all.

"Whatever."

"Is that an admission?" said Sierra gleefully.

Roman cackled. "Maybe she *likes* him!"

"That ship's sailed," Casey growled, so quickly it shocked everyone into silence. She made for the door, but stopped beside it. "And it doesn't matter. He's my pack. You all are, like it or not. So I'm gonna do my fucking damndest to fight *for* you, not *fight* you. Unless you push it."

She ducked into the hallway, and the shadows there swallowed her.

The others all looked at each other. Sierra's smile never left.

"Can you change into a human?" Henry asked Vincent, shifting the air in the room.

The idea of summoning enough energy to do that was almost sickening. But Vincent wasn't going to miss a single moment of his retribution. This was his new duty. That, and sending Ava off. He owed it to her after everything she had done to help them, and everything he should have done to prevent her death. And they couldn't afford to wait any longer.

"I'll try. Just...give me a minute, will you?"

"Sure." Sierra, Roman, and Henry all started for the door.

At that very moment, Vincent realized something.

"Wait, Henry."

The three of them stopped, curious. Vincent didn't look at them. He didn't want to say it in front of Sierra and Roman, damn them. But he did.

"Stay with me."

He could practically feel the knowing looks, the grins, and he silently cursed them. But he heard two sets of receding footsteps, and then the door closing.

Henry crossed the room to his side, sitting on the bed. He was quiet, respectfully so. As if trying not to spook a wild animal.

"...You didn't say *back*."

Henry blinked. "What?"

"You always say 'Can you change back?' But...this time, you didn't."

Henry was silent for a moment. "You're...not a human, Vincent. Changing into one isn't changing back. It's not who you really are. You're a hellhound."

Suddenly, his fingers tangled in Vincent's fur, where it was thickest just below his ear. The touch was rougher than normal, insistent, and it shocked him enough to look Henry in the face, assailed by the earnestness there. The *passion*.

"Just...do me a favor, Vinny. When you change forms...do it because it helps, right now. Not because it's better or worse than any other part of you. Not so you can hide behind it."

Any reply died in Vincent's lungs. He thought of every time he had weaponized the feeling of Henry's gaze upon him, in his most monstrous form, so he could return to being human.

"What does it matter why I do it?" he finally forced out. "It works."

"Because I hate it," said Henry, so softly and so fiercely. "You think I don't notice the way you look at me when you're trying to change?"

Again Vincent tried to argue, but the words didn't come.

"I know you're not human...but it's a part of you now, Vincent. You're more human than your sister, or your father, or any other hellhound ever was. You learned what it's like to be human. But you're still a hellhound, too. You're a lot of different things, all tangled up together. And all of those things together...they make you the person we all care about like we do. No one else could be what you are. You're *Vincent*."

"That's not even my real name," Vincent argued, fighting back the sorrow and the hope. "It was made up for me, to pretend to be human. My true name is *Ntropi* now, because I'm disgraced. I was meant to earn my old name back, but..."

"Did you like your old name?"

Vincent tried to hate the kindness in Henry's tone, but as usual, he couldn't. "It was *Anendotos*," he murmured. "*Unyielding*. But...I wasn't. It was always too heavy for me."

"Then...maybe your dad was right about one thing."

Vincent said nothing. But Henry's words stayed with him for a long time after.

Eventually Henry let out a soft sigh. His fingers loosened their grip and stroked Vincent's neck fur instead, tenderly. They left a trail of warmth in their wake, quickening his heart and easing his muscles at the same time. He tried not to shiver, not to think how much it felt like Henry was savoring it. Surely it was a remnant of a different time, before he had once again ruined everything...

Just like he was doing now.

Why was he trying so hard? What pride did he have left to lose? Death was so close...he could feel it lingering at the edges of his vision even now, lamenting its loss, biding its time. Somehow his friends had ripped him from its frigid grasp. Somehow...they all cared that much for him. Even Henry, who had no reason to anymore. Henry, who had told him he was sorry for leaving him, for only seeing the worst in him, for turning him into a dark mirror. Who had carried him from the depths of Hell itself, until he couldn't anymore. Until Vincent wouldn't let him.

Henry finally broke the silence. "All I mean is you don't need to try so hard to be–"

"Henry?"

Henry stopped.

"I'm tired now." Vincent shifted his rightmost head, resting it on Henry's lap. His eyelids drifted shut, even as his heart pounded in his chest. For one little moment, he let himself feel safe. "When we go...I want you to carry me. Please. Like you did before."

Henry was quiet. Then he laid his hand upon Vincent's head again, smoothing the fur between his ears in a soft rhythm.

"I...yes. Of course I will."

Vincent's heart skipped, almost painfully. Even if everything was too tangled, too much to bear...he was too tired, too wounded in every possible way to fight this anymore. He still wasn't sure what he deserved...but after everything, he just wanted this one tiny thing. So he let himself have it, and nothing more.

His canine form melted away, and his single human head lay warmly on Henry's lap. For a breathless moment Henry's hand hovered above it.

Then he lowered it, until his fingers brushed a soft path through Vincent's hair.

Vincent squeezed his eyes shut even tighter, grappling with the floodwater that rose inside his body, buffeted by the debris of his own heart. He let out a shuddering sigh, and slowly it all drained away, leaving only the bone-deep weariness of a creature forged and touched by death.

They stayed that way for a while, just like they had on the bank of the Cocytus River. Nothing else in the world existed but the two of them and the shadow of their pain and the warmth that eased it.

Finally Henry murmured, "Are you ready?"

Vincent nodded. He clung awkwardly to Henry's broad shoulders as he hoisted him up into his arms for the second time. Dimly he realized how not so long ago he would have died rather than allow himself to be carried like this. Now, mortifying as it was...he couldn't bear the thought of dying without ever having known what it felt like.

The drive from Alderwood to Newport was just long enough to give Vincent a couple good hours' worth of sleep. Henry had returned the amulet to Sierra so Ava could direct her as she drove, which helped too. By the time Vincent woke, the worst of the heaviness in his heart and body had faded. Now only the residue of his near-death remained.

For a while he watched with eyes half-lidded as the darkening pines flickered past the backseat window, his forehead pressed against the cold glass. It was nearly sunset now, judging by the light—although it was difficult. The sky was just as perpetually overcast here as it was in Alderwood thanks to the broken portal, although that vague miasma of darkness seemed lighter here somehow. It was far easier to ignore those spectral ripples drifting between the trees.

Finally they turned off the main road, down a long dirt driveway that meandered through forest so dense that the shadows within made it feel like night had already fallen. The tires crunched and rumbled until they reached a clearing, where a little wood cabin hunkered beneath a smoking chimney, its windows glowing like amber eyes watching their approach.

The four of them—Vincent, Henry, Casey, and Sierra, having convinced Roman to stay behind and guard their possessed packmates—hopped out of Sierra's Jeep and started warily up to the house. This time Vincent could carry himself, albeit with a heavy limp. Then, when they were only halfway across the clearing, the front door swung open.

Golden light spilled over them in a bright rectangle, broken only by the silhouette at its center. They froze in place.

"Welcome." A woman's voice drifted from the doorway, husky with age but almost musical, colored by the amusement of someone who saw more than they were telling. "Friends of my granddaughter, I believe?"

"How did you know that?" Henry asked, bewildered.

"I don't get many visitors all the way out here," said Magdalena, the smile obvious in her tone despite the shadow obscuring her features. "Especially teenagers. Why don't you come inside?"

"I'm twenty-one..." Casey muttered.

They crept up to the porch, Henry taking the lead. Magdalena moved aside to hold the door open for them, her details finally emerging from the dark. She watched them with glittering eyes, her pale face etched with wrinkles that seemed to accentuate that knowing smile she wore. Very little of her resembled Ava—unless Vincent simply hadn't seen her in too long to recall, which he thought with a stab of guilt. He avoided meeting the old woman's eyes as he passed, but he felt them following him like claws in his back.

The interior of the little cabin was simple, but cozy. The centerpiece was the large fireplace with its crackling fire, around which cushions and armchairs were arranged as if waiting to be filled. They seemed pleased somehow as Magdalena invited her guests to do so, the heat from the fire lapping over their tired bodies.

As their host fetched ginger tea and shortbread, Vincent's attention moved over the countless shelves of books swallowing every wall, all of their covers embedded with dust too stubborn to be swept away. Then his gaze fell upon a deck of tarot cards spread over a purple cloth on a writing desk. Something rose thick in his throat. They looked identical to Ava's.

"You all look like you haven't had a decent meal in days." Magdalena's rasp jolted Vincent out of his thoughts. She had appeared behind him like a cat, unnoticed until the last moment. His skin prickled. "Any vegetarians? Mushroom-haters? I have chicken stew if it suits your fancy."

Vincent could almost hear Casey's sarcastic reply involving how many carnivores the old woman was currently entertaining, but she kept quiet.

"We'd love some," said Henry, as brightly as he could muster. "Thank you *so* much. It's been a while since I've had a home-cooked meal. Don't know about you guys."

The rest of them murmured and nodded, unable to resist the idea of it despite their discomfort.

Magdalena seemed all too happy to oblige, and soon returned from the kitchen with a little cart on wheels, piled high with bowls and a burgeoning dutch oven shaped like a pumpkin.

"That's a lot of food," said Henry as she began ladling out heaping spoonfuls of a pale broth laden with vegetables and whole chicken legs. "You weren't gonna eat all this by yourself, were you?"

Magdalena's infamous smile deepened, her wrinkles following suit. She didn't reply. She only spoke again when all the refreshments had been passed around, and everyone sat warily with steaming bowls in their laps, none of them quite sure what to do.

"Well, it's not poison," she croaked, nearly grinning. Vincent got the distinct impression she was enjoying the effect of her own mystique on her guests. That was the first thing that truly reminded him of Ava. It was also what convinced him to take his first bite of chicken—he wasn't going to let her get away with it.

The first bite barely got room to breathe. Before he knew it he had scarfed half his bowl, his senses filled to the brim with warmth and meat. The old woman was clearly right—he hadn't had enough to eat in some time. It was only too easy to forget, given the circumstances. But once the heat and weight of it began to fill his yearning stomach, he could almost feel his strength trickling back in.

"That's better," Magdalena lilted as the clink of utensils filled the little room. "Now, you must be calling on me for something important. Given the state of things lately...coming all this way isn't for the faint of heart."

Everyone's enthusiasm for the food stalled. The air in the room suddenly felt much heavier, bringing an uncomfortable silence with it. Nobody wanted to take on the burden of what had to come next.

So, of course, Henry tried. "We're all sorry to come here like this, out of nowhere, but...but you need to know. You deserve to know..."

"You must be wondering why your granddaughter isn't with us, if we're her friends," Vincent broke in. He was tired of leaving things for Henry to solve. The guilt wriggled in his gut–but he deserved to have to do this, for so many reasons.

He took in a deep breath. Then:

"The truth is, she's dead. We didn't mean for it to happen, but it did, because we didn't keep her safe. And we're so sorry. More than we could ever atone for."

Those uncanny eyes did not change, to his great surprise. They seared into him, through him, unmoving and unreadable, dark in the firelight. They unnerved him so much he couldn't hold that terrible silence between them, and so he kept talking.

"But the thing is, Ava's not gone. Not yet. She's stuck in the mortal world, in that amulet." He pointed to the turquoise gleaming on its silver chain around Sierra's neck. She froze, as if doing so would make her invisible. "She wants to move on, and we want to help her. We owe her that much, if nothing else. We just don't know how to do it. We were hoping you would."

That was it. That was all. There was nothing else to say, no matter how much Vincent wanted to fill the silence. It lingered, prowling around them, mocking their misery.

Then, at last, Magdalena spoke, without a single twitch in her expression: "Thank you for telling me this. But I already saw it long ago."

CHAPTER 22

MORTAL WOUNDS

Magdalena returned to her bowl, spooning stew to her lips. The act was so outrageously nonchalant that it again screamed of Ava, which was somehow worse in this moment.

Everyone stared at her. Sierra found her voice first.

"What do you mean, you *saw it*? Did someone already tell you what happened?"

"No. I knew long before it had come to pass."

"She has the Sight," Henry breathed.

The old woman nodded, a bland smile creasing her face. "I know you. You're Nathan's boy. You look just like him."

Not just, Vincent thought stubbornly, hating the memory of those familiar, unfamiliar eyes boring into him.

"So you must know what I can do," she continued. "Yes. I predicted my own granddaughter's death."

"And–and what, you didn't tell her?" Casey demanded. Vincent could see her hackles rising, but he couldn't blame her.

"Oh, I did tell her. She's known for years."

The ground lurched beneath Vincent. He stared at Magdalena, but didn't see her. All the pieces were clicking into place.

"That's why…" Henry murmured.

"She didn't want to get involved in anything," Vincent finished. The guilt was rising again like bile in his throat.

"Telling her was my greatest regret," said Magdalena, her grief sharpening her rasp. "I poisoned her. I saw the light leave her eyes, and it never came back after that moment. She was so afraid of dying that she stopped living."

"But she helped us anyway…with the seance…" Vincent mumbled.

"She must have truly believed that wasn't the danger," said Henry, subdued.

Magdalena nodded slowly. "She always found comfort in the occult. It came naturally to her, where other things didn't."

"Why didn't she tell any of us?" said Sierra, her eyes shining with unfallen tears.

"She didn't really want to be friends," Henry replied quietly.

"Would you have believed her?" asked Magdalena. It was more a statement than a question.

"I would've," Henry said instantly. "Especially knowing who you are."

"Ah, she revealed my secrets, then." Magdalena smiled sadly into her stew. "She was such a proud girl."

"If we'd known, we could've stopped it," Casey insisted. She glared at Magdalena. "*You* knew. Why didn't *you* stop it?"

The old seer regarded her for a long, thoughtful moment, leaden with her sorrow. "Prophecies are not a manual. Details are not so easily read. And even if they were...you see what happens when one tries to meddle with fate. Somehow, the knots work themselves out anyway, no matter how tightly you wind the thread."

"That's bullshit," Casey growled. "You let your own goddamn granddaughter waltz right into her death."

"It sounds like we all did."

Casey flinched. But that only made her angrier. "We didn't know she was gonna die! We thought she was safe!"

"What would you have me do? Lock her in a padded room for the rest of her life?" Magdalena shook her head. "She practically did that on her own. No, such is the seer's burden. We see, but we cannot act. If we do, as I did...often it only makes everything worse."

"So what?" Vincent broke in, his own temper beginning to heat his chest. "Are you saying fate is inevitable? There's some grand plan for all of us, and there's no changing it?"

"Perhaps." Magdalena shrugged. "I am only a seer, not a god. I hold very few answers, in the grand scheme of things."

"That's not an answer," Vincent argued. "You can't tell me there's no point trying to make things better. That everything just...is the way it is, forever."

It couldn't be. If it was...if everything he had ever done was all for nothing, after all...

To his surprise, the old woman softened. "Oh, I don't think that's it. Maybe fate alone knows how things will change, and who will change them, and when...but it's our job as mere mortals to act as we will, and hope fate has taken our desires into account."

Vincent searched her face for answers, a betrayal of any great truth she might be hiding. But he found only sincerity and a profound sympathy. He felt his rage waning.

"I'm not mortal," he admitted, a final and meager attempt to argue. "I'm a hellhound."

"But you *are* mortal. We all are, even in so many different ways. Didn't you know?"

Again the room swayed around him as the idea struck, piercing straight through him. *Mortal?* It wasn't possible. Since he was only a pup, he knew he was immortal. He would live until he was killed, somehow, in the line of duty. He served his masters, and that was all, and that was why he wasn't fickle or fallible or headstrong like mortals were.

...But he *was*. Wasn't that why he felt like such a failure? He had made a mistake, and dozens more after that, and he wanted things and resented other things and felt so much...

All things he wasn't meant to do, or be, according to his father. But he did, and he was. And now he was here, living his own mortal life like he realized he wanted, and suddenly this old woman was telling him it was because he was mortal all along.

Did that mean it wasn't wrong, after all, to want it?

He realized his gaze had drifted towards Henry, the way the firelight played over his beautiful features, those bright eyes that believed everything good of the world. For once he let himself linger there until he was ready to look away.

Magdalena went on: "All this to say...whatever you're planning, do it. Don't let the what-ifs hold you back."

Vincent shifted his attention back to her in surprise. "What do you mean?"

"I've seen your intentions. You've made great waves in the state of the world already. I cannot see the outcome, exactly...but I know you will make even greater ones, should you proceed." Any trace of light in her face suddenly extinguished. "But should you follow my granddaughter's path...I fear you will end as she did."

Vincent found himself looking at Casey, and she looked back at him. At once he knew they were thinking the same thing, and Casey hated him for it—but she knew he was right all along.

We were never going to be happy hiding together in California. We can't hide from who we are, or what that means.

"Thank you," Henry murmured. But the shadow of his thoughts had fallen over his face, more troubled than grateful. "We...actually have another question for you. Something related to that. But you know that already, don't you?"

"Now you're catching on. Yes. I sensed it. I can't promise you specifics, but...I will do my best."

Henry glanced at Vincent. He nodded back at him. Henry sucked in a breath, then:

"We need to find a portal to Heaven. Or...make one."

Magdalena blinked at him in surprise. "Well, that's a new one. But...it does illuminate things for me in its own right."

"Does it?" asked Henry.

Magdalena didn't reply. Instead her gaze slid to the empty corner of the ceiling. She was silent—unnervingly so.

"We were hoping you would know how," Vincent pressed. "Since you have so much experience…"

The old woman's attention snapped back to him. His heart jumped. "Not with that, unfortunately. But I have seen something…"

"What?" Casey urged.

"You must find help from an unexpected source. It may not be the help you want…but if you do not seek it, you will find yourselves outmatched."

"What kind of source?" Sierra asked, exchanging a bewildered glance with the others.

"I feel like a lot of our help is unexpected…" Casey grumbled.

"That, I don't know," said Magdalena. "But I can sense the power of the forces you contend with. You are already outmatched, but…if you cannot even the odds enough to get close to the heart of this power, you will undoubtedly fail."

"And we're still gonna let Ava go?" said Casey. "Those magical surges she can do have been our ace in the hole! What if she's the unexpected source?"

"We're not holding her hostage," Vincent shot back. "She's already had enough of that."

Casey growled out a sigh. "No, you're right. I didn't mean it. I just…I don't know how we're gonna do this."

The uncertainty in her voice struck Vincent at a new angle. Was she…afraid?

Well, of course she was. It was stupid not to be—impossible, even. But he still wasn't used to her showing it, even after everything.

He reached over to lay a gentle hand on her forearm. "It'll be okay, Casey. We'll figure it out. We always do."

She didn't answer, but she didn't pull away.

"And we know more now," Sierra added, her tone soft. Her hand found Casey's shoulder. "We have a direction. Thank you, Magdalena."

The old witch nodded, a sad, knowing smile creasing her lips.

"It's time, then," said Henry, quietly. "You can help Ava move on, can't you?"

"Not me. But you can, if she is truly ready."

"What do we need to do?"

Magdalena took in a great breath and then exhaled, as if weighing the enormity of the task inside her chest. "'Moving on,' as you put it, is a tricky business. She must find closure, regarding what happened during her life–and her death. Only then will she be able to release her grip on this world."

Everyone glanced at each other, uncertainty scrawled across their faces.

"How do we know if she's ready?" Sierra asked.

"She's been very insistent..." Henry pointed out.

"Either way, we have to try," said Vincent. "What's the process? Is it a ritual?"

"Oh, always." Magdalena rose from her armchair and fetched a tall black candle from her desk, lighting it with shaky fingers. She set it down on the rug in the center of their little circle. It felt both tiny and ominous in the face of the robust glow of the fireplace.

"Someone will need to lend her their energy." Her gaze moved across each of them.

Henry opened his mouth instantly, but Vincent beat him to it. "I'll–"

"*No*, Vincent. God," Casey snapped. "Remember how well that went last time?"

"I owe it to her. I was the one who–"

"No one cares. You're too weak right now, and you know it." She squared her shoulders, meeting Magdalena's eyes. "Ava died because she let a ghost possess her, and he got her involved in things. He didn't keep her safe, and neither did we. We were all stupid, but I was the one who saw the whole thing for what it was. I didn't try hard enough to help her. I should be the one to do it now."

"But Casey...you *hate* this." Sierra grasped her arm pleadingly. "You got so mad at me when I let her possess me. You can't–"

"Yeah, 'cause she took you over. You let her stay." Casey's eyes were little patches of void as she met Sierra's. "I won't let that happen to me."

Sierra slowly released her. "You'd better not," she whispered.

"I promise."

Casey caught Vincent's eye. He nodded, once.

You're strong enough. I believe in you.

She seemed to understand, and the smallest twitch of a smile tugged at the corner of her mouth. Then she held out a hand towards Sierra. Reluctantly she lifted the amulet's chain over her head and placed it in Casey's palm, not once breaking her gaze. They were saying something to each other, too, without a word. Vincent could only marvel at it—when had they gotten so close?

Casey slipped the amulet around her neck, clutching the stone to her chest. She sucked in a deep breath, then turned to Magdalena. "What now?"

"Now you let her in."

Casey grimaced. She sat stone-still as the seconds ticked by.

Finally Sierra moved closer, resting a gentle hand on her arm again. Casey startled, looking up at her.

"If you wanna do this...you have to give yourself up, Casey. You have to let her become you and you her. You can't have secrets anymore."

Casey growled something too quietly for Vincent to hear. Immediately Sierra's hand moved to hers, grasping it fervently.

"You won't lose yourself. You're not like me."

Something creased Casey's brow—something sad.

Her eyelids slid shut.

Almost instantly her body gave a great shudder. The candle flickered.

Suddenly the shadows from the fireplace leaped even higher, as if in excitement. And then they felt darker, deeper...

Casey's eyes shot open. Her gaze crawled across their little circle, one by one; then it stuck on Magdalena.

Tears welled in her dark eyes, gleaming in the firelight. "Grandma?"

Magdalena burst into a smile, and in a blink the two women were embracing tightly, as if they would never get the chance again. Magdalena cradled Casey's head like a child's, her many rings glittering in Casey's jet-black hair.

Finally they broke apart, and Magdalena held Casey's face in both hands as if searching for Ava deep in her eyes. She beamed so hard her wrinkles turned to canyons–she had found her there.

"Ava, my dearest...I'm so sorry. For everything. I–"

"I heard," Ava said, brushing away her tears with Casey's fist. "I've been here the whole time. I never thought I'd get to see you again..." She broke off, shaking her head fiercely. "Don't you dare blame yourself for this. You did everything you could. I was being stupid. I really was."

Vincent's heart gripped in surprise, and then sorrow. He had never heard Ava apologize before. But it was too late.

"That doesn't matter," said Magdalena, her own eyes glistening. "I wish things could have been different for you. For all of us."

"But they're not. They couldn't have been. Just like you always said." She heaved a deep, shaky sigh. "I was always going to die young."

"I wish you hadn't done that stupid seance," Vincent broke in, unable to help it any longer. Ava turned to him as if only just realizing he was there. He was stunned by the remorse in her eyes.

"Vincent..."

"I'm sorry," he said, before she could get another word in. "If this is your time for closure...know that. I should have done more for you. I shouldn't have asked so much of you. This wasn't your fight–it was mine. It was all my fault people were dying, and that we needed help in the first place. If I hadn't let Benjamin go...you wouldn't have died."

"Yes, I would have."

Vincent's heart missed a beat. She looked so sad...but not for herself. For him.

"I would've died some other way, if it wasn't while helping you. Helping Percy. If I was going to die anyway...I might as well have done it doing something good."

"You shouldn't have had to be anything for anyone," Henry put in, his voice breaking. He was close to tears, too. "A shield or a medium for us, a conduit for Percy...nobody had the right to take any of that from you. I'm sorry I didn't see it–didn't stop it. That's not the person I want to be."

Ava turned that expression towards him, too, and it looked just the same. "I forgive you, Henry. It sucked, but...you needed me, or other people were gonna die. Sometimes that's just how it is."

"What?" Henry shook his head helplessly. "How could you say that? After everything that happened to you...being used over and over..."

"I wasn't helpless, Henry." An edge returned to her voice. It sounded almost like Casey again. "You saw the kind of power I have. If I really wanted to, I could've kept myself out of everything, peer pressure or not. Percy or not. But...I don't know. Maybe something in me knew this was gonna be the way I went out."

"That doesn't sound like the Ava I know." Vincent didn't mean for it to sound so churlish, but he didn't know how else to say it.

Finally Ava broke his gaze. "Well...I guess I realized some things."

"Some things?" Henry pressed.

She was quiet for a moment. "I've been dead for a while now. I know how it feels to be a ghost, like all these others. Some of them because I didn't help. I could've stopped it. It's so lonely...so horribly lonely. Even more than it was being alive." She breathed a mirthless laugh. "I get how Percy felt, now. I wish he hadn't held onto me the way he did, but...he was kind to me. I could feel the care he had for me. For a second there, neither of us felt as alone as we were before. It was kind of a relief, actually. Staring death in the face for once, instead of constantly trying to avert my eyes. Pretending it wasn't coming for me."

"You...let him stay," said Sierra softly.

Ava's eyes met hers, and there was something much gentler between the two of them.

"I could've pushed him out, if I really tried. But...I didn't know what would happen to him if I did. And...I think I felt it. Death circling me. I needed to be where I was. It was...nice, for a little while, to finally have someone there who understood what it all meant for me. How it felt."

Sierra nodded. "I felt it, too. When you and I were together."

Ava's expression melted into something darker, sadder. "I'm...I'm sorry, Sierra. For keeping you. I'm...no better than Percy, am I? Not really. I let it all take over just the same as he did. Being dead. It felt like being warm again, after starving in the snow for so long...I just couldn't let you go. Even now, here with Casey, it feels so *good,* so *right*...I feel real again."

Sierra grasped her hands, holding them tight as if to remind her of that warmth. "Don't be so hard on yourself, please...I can't even imagine what it must be like to...to be dead. Alone forever with your own fears..." She shook her head as if dislodging her own from her mind. "That little taste I got from you was more than I could take. God, we need to help these people...these ghosts..." She threw a miserable glance at Vincent, at Henry.

"We will," Henry insisted. "We'll find a way."

"That's why we're here," Vincent added. "Ava is going to be the first. She deserves to be."

Ava looked thunderstruck. "You...forgive me?"

Vincent shrugged. "That's up to Sierra. It's her body–"

"No–not just that. For not helping. For being selfish. For *everything.* Especially for what I put you through, Vincent, down in the Shadowhand base. I...I almost got you *killed.* And still you guys have been helping me, all this time...trying to make things right. I never once gave you any good reason to care about me, but..."

"But we do," Sierra finished, squeezing her hands. "Even if they don't understand you like I do, being in your mind like I was...we all know what it's like. Feeling like you're not good enough. Like you're in this by yourself, at the end of the day. Like nobody really cares about you, and it's worse to give it your all and be disappointed than to just...take care of yourself, on your own. Save yourself the indignity and the heartache."

She spoke to Ava, but those soft brown eyes had settled on Henry and Vincent, almost pleading. She didn't need to–Vincent understood. Even if Ava had always seemed standoffish, unreasonably proud, haughty even...she was always alone. He had seen that. Why hadn't he recognized it?

She's just like me.

Maybe that was why he resented her so much. The thought weighed heavy on his heart.

"They understand that," Sierra insisted again, when neither of them responded.

"No," said Vincent. "We didn't. We didn't know any of that, before now. Because you never said anything."

"But you helped us anyway, in spite of all that," Henry put in. "Even after everything we couldn't do for you...you lent us your powers. You saved our lives, twice. We're so grateful for that. You've more than made up for whatever you didn't do before."

"But you helped me before I did any of that," Ava protested. "Even when I was just berating you and demanding things of you, you still took me with you, and you were sorry I died, and you wanted to help me move on–"

"Yeah–because you're a *person*, Ava," Vincent growled. "The things you do or don't do don't change that. You deserve a peaceful ending, because it's the end. Nothing else matters after that. No amount of punishment or purgatory would change you, when your life is over. And I don't like seeing people suffer."

His words seemed to resonate through the little cabin. He could feel Henry's gaze on him, warming him.

Then Henry said, "That's just what we've been trying to show you, Ava. It's why we did all of this–trying to help everyone, trying to stop the murders, even if it put us in danger. Because we don't want to see anyone suffer. Because we know what it feels like. And no one stopped it for us. You shouldn't have to earn relief."

Ava stared at them for so long, it seemed like the night would pass before she broke. Then she finally spoke, her voice softer than Vincent had ever heard it: "You're all so much better than I am."

"No, we're not–" Henry began.

"If we are, it's because we chose it," Vincent interrupted fiercely. "I was born to make people suffer. But I decided to leave that behind–and now, I'm going to stop it from happening altogether. I'm tired of all of us sitting around suffering together and making each other suffer so we feel less alone in it. And you could choose that too, Ava, if you wanted to."

Ava's borrowed eyes flickered over his face, searching out every scrap of intention and willpower etched into it. In hers he saw hope glimmer, but only briefly.

"But...I have to go now, Vincent. I can feel it. I don't belong here anymore," she murmured. "It's just like you said...this is my ending. I can't change anything anymore. My life is over."

Vincent nodded, closing his eyes. "You're right. You deserve your peace." But that wasn't the end of it. It couldn't be. Because... "...Even if your life is over, you aren't, though. Not really. Like it or not, you've changed all of us. All the people who knew you. And talking with you now, even as a ghost...I realize a lot more than I did before this. That's thanks to you. So...thank you, Ava."

He mustered a smile—a real one, from somewhere deep and tender inside himself. She deserved that much. Even now, as every moment of her waning existence ticked closer to its end, the thoughts she had planted in him were settling into place. Even she, who had tried so hard to not become a part of his story.

For a moment he wondered how many small things he himself had changed in other people. The idea came with a little burst of unexpected pleasure.

But then something else arrived too—a familiar voice puncturing his mind.

"*I-I'm gonna miss you, Ava. I...I know I have no right to...but I need you to know. You made me feel the most alive I've ever felt since I died.*"

Ava turned Casey's head around the room, unsure where to look. Finally she settled her gaze on the candle, its little flame still burning steady. "Percy...you're coming with me."

Percy snorted, a petulant sound that could only be made deliberately, given his lack of lungs. It was so unlike him Vincent wondered for a brief moment if Benjamin had interjected–but he hadn't. "*You think I'm allowed where you're going?*"

Something flickered in Ava's eyes that surprised Vincent. It almost looked like pain. "You didn't do anything wrong when you were alive. Surely they'll–"

"*God is not forgiving,*" Percy hissed. "*And death isn't the end. You should know that more than anyone. You earned the right to move on–I've done nothing but hurt people since the moment I died.*"

"You're still on this?" Ava demanded. "I thought after everything, you'd be done with the self-pity–"

"*It's not self-pity!*" Percy's spectral voice pierced everyone's skulls, making them flinch with very real pain. Even he seemed to realize his transgression, and grew quiet. But his presence lingered behind each of their eyes like a shadow.

"...I...I think I forgive you, Percy."

"*You...what?*"

"No...I do. I forgive you. It's...it's so small, now, in the grand scheme of things. Like we bumped into each other in the dark, for just a moment."

"*No...it can't be. It's not. I kidnapped you, I made you die, all because I couldn't stand being alone and cold–*"

"And it's over now. Whatever it was, whatever happened...it doesn't matter anymore. You fucked up, and I fucked up, and we know better now, and now it's over."

"*But I–*"

"If you knew I would die, would you have done it?"

"*No–of course not, I–*"

"And would you do it again, now, if you got the chance?"

"*Never!*"

"Then what does it matter, Percy? Now that both our lives are over? I forgive you–not because it wasn't wrong, but because you're different now, and because it doesn't do anyone any good for you to keep suffering for it. I'm going away now, and I don't care anymore. So stop using me as an excuse to wallow. Move *on*, damn it—move on with me. We can go together, like we did before."

Percy sputtered nonsense, as if he just couldn't get a handle on his own words. He finally choked out: "*I can't. Even if I took all that, even if I forgave myself...I'd be going to Hell now. I'm sure of it.*"

Ava gritted Casey's teeth. "And what if you're not? Are you just gonna stay here forever, believing you're evil and going to Hell if you let yourself move on? Didn't you hear what I—"

"*Vincent is right,*" Percy broke in. Interrupting was something new from him too, which caught Vincent's curiosity. "*Even if I'm dead now, I can still help stop all the suffering. For me...and anyone else who would go to Hell. So I'm...I'm gonna stay.*"

"How are you even gonna help?" Ava said roughly. That sounded a lot more like her old self. "You don't have my magic."

"*I...I don't know. But I have to. I'll find a way.*"

At first she remained defiant. Then, slowly, it faded to something...sadder.

"...Okay. If I can't stop you...take care of them, Percy. They still have their whole lives ahead of them. Make sure none of it goes to waste."

"*I will. I swear it.*" He spoke without a tremor. Without a shred of doubt. It hardly sounded like him anymore, for better or worse. Vincent wasn't sure which it was, yet—if Percy's guilt would galvanize his confidence, or something more worrisome.

Casey's head nodded. Then Ava turned towards her grandmother, solemn, resolute. Tired.

"I'm ready, grandma."

Magdalena's tears had dried, but the grief was carved into every crease in her face. She went to her bookshelf, returning with a matchbox and a bundle of herbs that were tied into a stick with twine. Quietly she lit the match and pressed it to the leaves, which began smoking at once. A pleasant, heady scent wafted from them. Vincent's heart jolted as he realized—it smelled almost exactly like the incense filling the palace in Tartarus. It couldn't be a coincidence.

The old woman left the herbs on a little plate at the mantle, letting the haze slowly fill the room. She crossed to her granddaughter's side and cradled her head one last time, pressing a kiss to her crown, taking in the final remnants of her spirit lingering in Casey's black eyes.

"Be good, my Ava," she murmured. "Let yourself fade. Be at peace."

Everyone stood silent, subdued. Ava closed Casey's eyes.

For all the trappings of death Vincent had seen over the years–souls in the Underworld, ghosts, and corpses even more recently...he realized he had never witnessed the moment a soul left its body behind. Not up close. Even the old werewolf's death had been little more than a silhouette in the night. Now, as he watched, it perturbed him more than anything he had yet seen. Because, even staring it in the face, he couldn't tell when it happened. The moment everything that was Ava disappeared from the world forever. It was different when she left Sierra's body, because she was still *there*...just, elsewhere. But this was the last time. If she truly reached Heaven...he may never speak to her again. It was the end. A true end.

Suddenly, he realized just why humans feared death so deeply. Never before had he considered what it meant to never be able to see someone again. He had never had to. They would always be in Hell.

When the moment happened, it happened softly. Vincent searched Casey's face fervently, his throat tightening as he tried to catch any glimpse of Ava. But he just couldn't. He searched and searched, and she was still and silent. Before he knew it, her eyes were open again, looking around dazedly.

"Ava...is she...?"

"She's gone," said Magdalena, her voice breaking.

A hole opened in Vincent's heart. Something had left the world, and it would never be the same.

Suddenly, he couldn't bear the smell of that smoke for another moment. He made for the door, bursting out into the cool night air. He let the darkness welcome him, striding out across the clearing until he stopped in its center.

He tipped his head back, yearning for the glimmer of stars in the indigo sky, a desperate reminder of something bright beyond the gloom.

But there were no stars. The sky was dark. Everything was dark, because of him.

The swish of grass sounded behind him. He didn't move. A hand, warm and tender, slipped into his. In spite of himself, in spite of everything, it sent a flutter through his core.

Henry didn't speak. Together they stood, gazing out at the black treeline. It was quiet. So quiet.

Then, a sound.

At first, Vincent didn't believe it. He held his breath, and so did Henry.

It came again. A little trill, echoing from the trees. Pure, musical. Bright.

"A mockingbird," breathed Henry.

The black silhouette of the trees blurred. Vincent blinked it away, fighting back the burning behind his eyes.

"But...the birds are gone," he murmured. "The portal..."

Henry's hand squeezed his. "Vincent—look up."

He did. Through the haze that had covered the sky for so long now, a single star shone.

No...two. More. Slowly, the clouds were drifting, fading. There was a hole there now, like a mirror to Vincent's heart. Except this one gleamed with stars—countless, brighter than he had ever seen before, flickering as if they were alive. The more he looked, the more seemed to appear, stretching on forever into the darkness beyond the sky.

"They...they must have fixed the portal," Vincent whispered. That's all it was. And it was a bad thing, he knew that, but...it was more than that. It felt like more. His heart trembled.

They stood there for some time, watching as the stars twinkled back to life. He thought about everything that had happened, everything from his first step into the sunlight so long ago to the frigid darkness that almost claimed his life deep below the earth. The people that had saved him, time and again—Henry, Percy, Roman, Sierra, Casey, Dex, Ava. All of them had, he realized with a start. Even Benjamin, in his own strange way. If he had never appeared in Hell, never convinced Vincent to come with him, to care for him...he would still be guarding tortured souls in the Underworld.

Instead, he was here. And he wouldn't be, if those damned souls frozen in the Cocytus River hadn't chosen to save him, too. Even for all their own reasons, the worst of them had chosen to save him.

"We have to fix this," he said, his own voice sounding far away. "We have to save *everyone*. Every soul, for all eternity..."

It was an enormous task. Impossible. But he had to try. *They* had to try. It was the closest anything had felt to *right* so far.

Then, Henry's hand tightened over his. "We will. I know it. I swear it. With you leading the charge..." Vincent felt his gaze falling on his face in the dark, the warmth in it. "If anyone can do it, I know it's you. It's always been you."

Vincent's heart skipped. How long had it been since Henry looked at him like that? It almost felt like a dream—like the dream that kept coming back to him, haunting his nights. Except here, that sunlit forest was only a vision. Here, in the real world, it was dark.

Not for long, he thought, with a strange determination. Never before had he felt so...hopeful. Maybe what rose before them *was* insurmountable, impossible...the idea of thwarting the very order of Heaven and Hell. But if he could make Henry look at him like that, after everything...maybe there was a chance. For a lot of impossible things.

"I can't do this alone." Vincent leaned closer to him, hardly daring to breathe. "I never could, from the very start..."

Henry didn't move away. "I couldn't, either. If I had to...I would've been dead long ago."

"At least you didn't start off with Benjamin as your company."

A soft laugh escaped Henry's throat. "Tough act to follow." He was close now, so close...

Vincent stopped. He wanted so badly to close the gap, to *finally* leave those dreams behind. But...

"Do we really deserve each other, Henry? After all this?"

Henry stopped, too. His breath was warm. The scent of clove and jasmine, enveloping Vincent's senses. Every part of him ached with it.

"I won't kiss you this time," Henry whispered. "I can't. Not unless you want it. Not until you believe it, too."

Vincent's heart nearly cracked in two. It hurt, god, it hurt–whatever they were or weren't, it *needed* this, it needed *him*–

He surged forward, their mouths crashing together. They were all hunger, all lightning, a storm between them that had been building and building, dark and heavy with promise. It could have been a flood, a cyclone, devastation in their wake. Even now, it nearly was. But instead, after the first flash, it broke into gentle rain. Henry softened first, his lips warm and questing. Vincent's followed, receding into a tender yearning. They drank each other in as if their thirst could never be sated, and nothing else existed in the whole world–not the darkness, not the stars.

"Make me deserve it," Vincent gasped as their kiss finally broke, his arms tight around Henry's neck, his chest crushed against him. He could feel every curve of his body, that thudding heart strong beneath. He was so *real*, so very real.

Henry's eyes gleamed in the shadows, in the starlight. "Make *me* deserve it!" he laughed. God, what a sound. But then it faded, and something more solemn crept in. "You did. We both did. Just...stay this time, Vincent. Please." His arms pressed around Vincent's ribcage, keeping him close. As if he was afraid what would happen if he let go. "Don't leave me alone."

Vincent's heart clenched. He sounded so small. So young, so afraid. Something he never imagined he would think of Henry Wellfellow, before all of this. Before they rescued him from the Shadowhand. Before he went to Hell and back. He had always felt larger than life, even in his worst moments, even when he was only a human standing weaponless against a hellhound. But now...something had changed.

And that was okay. Every moment of weakness, every moment of desperation Vincent had witnessed in their college days had crystallized into this–something real, something with cracks like his, something that was small enough to hold and be held.

And as he held him, he wondered what Henry was so afraid of. Whether he was thinking of the night they first kissed, Vincent leaving him to torture Jake in the shed behind the gym. Losing Vincent to the monster that would do *anything* to protect him. Or whether he was thinking of that frozen river deep beneath the earth, Vincent's life ebbing away with the wind...

He stretched up to press his forehead against Henry's. An echo from long ago, that very same night their lips first met. The act that had finally allowed Vincent to shift from a hellhound into a human without trying to hide from him. He was sure Henry knew it, too.

"I'm not going anywhere, Henry. We fight together, until the end."

Something warm and damp brushed his cheek, dripped down. A shudder of a sigh passed through Henry's body.

"Good...good. I just...can't do this on my own. Any of it. I'm...not strong enough." The last of it was barely a whisper, as if Henry himself was afraid of hearing the words. They sent a thrill through Vincent's core–Henry, not strong enough?

"Bullshit," he growled. "You're the strongest person I know. You're–"

"I'm only human," Henry insisted, finally drawing his face away from Vincent's. Those vibrant eyes shone with tears. "All this time, you've shielded me. I would have been dead long ago, without you. Or...or I wouldn't be myself anymore," he added, his voice breaking. "And when you weren't there...when I thought I lost you...*everything* went dark."

Seeing him standing there, overflowing with the fear and the heartache, quieted something inside Vincent. He had hardly known it was there before now. Some of his hunger eased with it, and he was surprised by the shape of the space it left behind.

Henry wasn't perfect anymore. He never was. He needed Vincent as much as Vincent needed him. And he finally understood that. He...*wanted* that. Suddenly, Vincent wasn't just standing in his shadow–they were side-by-side, the light in their faces, the darkness at their backs.

So Vincent lifted his hands to Henry's face, and swept away those shining tears. "And my strength doesn't matter without you. You've given me something to fight for. Something *good*. Without you...I'd be nothing but a demon."

Something cracked in Henry's expression, and more tears flooded to replace the ones Vincent took away. They flowed over his fingers; they belonged to him. Those eyes were like an open wound, so raw that another Vincent from another time wouldn't have been able to stand it. But this one did. This one finally could. He didn't look away for a single moment.

"This strength is for both of us," he said. "We can only wield it together."

Finally, finally, Henry broke. The tears coursed on, but they caught on his dimples. That brilliant smile returned—softer now, timid, but true. No longer the smile of a hero carved into marble.

He nodded into Vincent's hands, sniffling. "O-okay. I'll believe you, Vinny. I'll trust you."

Vincent smiled back, his heart blazing in the hearth of his ribcage. If this was his only shot to set things right, to forge a world where everyone could have a second chance—where he and Henry could be happy—he would do anything to make it real.

Thank you so much for reading!
If you liked this story, please rate and review on Amazon/Goodreads!
It helps other readers find my work, so I can keep making more.

COMING SOON

Find out what happens next in

BOOK 3: SHADOWS WE CAST

Getting the band back together to take on the forces of Heaven and Hell...

ACKNOWLEDGEMENTS

Second books are especially daunting. How do you live up to your debut? Well, hopefully, you don't...you make it ten times better. I'm not sure if I hit that exact number, but here's to hoping. And it wouldn't be possible without the help of all my cheerleaders/(loving) critics. So the biggest thank-you goes to Darla, Sketch, and Sarah for your unwavering diligence and wisdom. Thanks for sticking with me through Hell and back.

The next accolades, of course, go to my family. Pierce, Darla, our fur babies, Mom and Dad: you keep me smiling no matter the challenges life brings. I love you all. Without you, I'd be holed up in a dark corner somewhere writing about the wallpaper.

And finally, thank you to all the incredible fans and fellow authors who have come out of the woodwork to support my writing. I'm completely astounded by your passion and kindness. I genuinely never thought anyone would read and connect with my work as quickly and ardently as you have. I owe everything to you, without whom I would be yelling into the void. You're the reason I write—to connect with other people who feel and love a little like I do.

If you like my stories, please share with someone you think would like them too! Making a living as an author has been my dream since I was a little bullied middle-schooler drowning my loneliness in books, and readers like you make that dream real. So thank you, from the depths of my weird little heart.

ABOUT THE AUTHOR

James Chance has always been haunted by monsters. Everyone has some kind of creature inside them. Everyone is a little dark and strange. His stories explore how our monsters make us human–and what we should do about it. Drawing from a background in nonprofit finance and sociology, he strives to forge understanding between people in an increasingly weird world. He lives in Southern California with his family of rescues (animals included).

Find me on social media! 

Instagram:	instagram.com/aferalchance
Threads:	threads.net/@aferalchance
Bluesky:	aferalchance.bsky.social
TikTok:	tiktok.com/@author.james.chance
YouTube:	youtube.com/@feralchance
Tumblr:	a-feral-chance.tumblr.com
Ko-Fi:	ko-fi.com/jameschance

**Sign up for my newsletter and receive
a free short story prequel to *Our Dark Mirror*!**

 **aferalchance.com**

www.ingramcontent.com/pod-product-compliance
Lightning Source LLC
Chambersburg PA
CBHW030342120726
47901CB00007B/1876